AF234821

Blue Lights
Hot Work in the Soudan

By

R. M. Ballantyne

Blue Lights
Hot Work in the Soudan
by R. M. Ballantyne

Copyright © 2024

All Rights reserved.
No part of this publication may be reproduced,
stored in a retrieval system, or transmitted in any
form or by any means, electronic, mechanical,
photocopying or Otherwise, without the written
permission of the publisher.

The author/editor asserts the moral right to
be identified as the author/editor of this work.

ISBN: 978-93-59395-97-5

Published by

DOUBLE 9 BOOKS
2/13-B, Ansari Road, Daryaganj
New Delhi – 110002
info@double9books.com
www.double9books.com
Tel. 011-40042856

This book is under public domain

ABOUT THE AUTHOR

R. M. Ballantyne was a Scottish writer of young adult literature who produced more than a hundred books between 24 April 1825 and 8 February 1894. He was also a skilled artist; some of his watercolors were on display at the Royal Scottish Academy. The ninth of ten children and youngest son of Alexander Thomson Ballantyne (1776-1847) and his wife Anne, Ballantyne was born in Edinburgh on April 24, 1825. (1786-1855). Robert's uncle James Ballantyne (1772-1833) was Sir Walter Scott's printer, and Alexander worked as a newspaper editor and printer in the family business "Ballantyne & Co" based at Paul's Works on the Canongate. The family is documented to have resided at 20 Fettes Row in Edinburgh's northern New Town in 1832-1833. The Ballantyne printing company collapsed the next year with debts of £130,000 as a result of a UK-wide banking crisis, which caused a decrease in the family's finances. Ballantyne moved to Canada at the age of 16 and worked for the Hudson's Bay Company for five years. He traveled by canoe and sleigh to the regions that are now the provinces of Manitoba, Ontario, and Quebec to trade with the local First Nations and Native Americans for furs; these experiences served as the inspiration for his book The Young Fur Traders.

CONTENTS

Chapter One-Hot Work in the Soudan

The False Step

There is a dividing ridge in the great northern wilderness of America, whereon lies a lakelet of not more than twenty yards in diameter. It is of crystal clearness and profound depth, and on the still evenings of the Indian summer its surface forms a perfect mirror, which might serve as a toilet-glass for a Redskin princess.

We have stood by the side of that lakelet and failed to note the slightest symptom of motion in it, yet somewhere in its centre there was going on a constant and mysterious division of watery particles, and those of them which glided imperceptibly to the right flowed southward to the Atlantic, while those that trembled to the left found a resting-place by the frozen shores of Hudson's Bay.

As it is with the flow and final exit of those waters, so is it, sometimes, if not always, with the spirit and destiny of man.

Miles Milton, our hero, at the age of nineteen, stood at the dividing ridge of his life. If the oscillating spirit, trembling between right and wrong, had decided to lean to the right, what might have been his fate no one can tell. He paused on the balance a short time, then he leaned over to the left, and what his fate was it is the purpose of this volume to disclose. At the outset, we may remark that it was not unmixed good. Neither was it unmitigated evil.

Miles had a strong body, a strong will, and a somewhat passionate temper: a compound which is closely allied to dynamite!

His father, unfortunately, was composed of much the same materials. The consequences were sometimes explosive. It might have profited the son much had he studied the Scripture lesson, "Children, obey your parents in the Lord." Not less might it have benefited the father to have pondered the words, "Fathers, provoke not your children to wrath."

Young Milton had set his heart on going into the army. Old Milton had resolved to thwart the desire of his son. The mother Milton, a meek and loving soul, experienced some hard times between the two. Both loved *her* intensely, and each loved himself, not better perhaps, but too much!

It is a sad task to have to recount the disputes between a father and a son. We shrink from it and turn away. Suffice it to say that one day Miles and his father had a Vesuvian meeting on the subject of the army. The son became petulant and unreasonable; the father fierce and tyrannical. The end was that they parted in anger.

"Go, sir," cried the father sternly; "when you are in a better frame of mind you may return."

"Yes, father, I will go," cried the son, starting up, "and I will *never* return."

Poor youth! He was both right and wrong in this prophetic speech. He did return home, but he did not return to his father.

With fevered pulse and throbbing heart he rushed into a plantation that lay at the back of his father's house. He had no definite intention save to relieve his feelings by violent action. Running at full speed, he came suddenly to a disused quarry that was full of water. It had long been a familiar haunt as a bathing-pool. Many a time in years past had he leaped off its precipitous margin into the deep water, and wantoned there in all the abandonment of exuberant youth. The leap was about thirty feet, the depth of water probably greater. Constant practice had rendered Miles so expert at diving and swimming that he had come to feel as much at home in the water as a New-Zealander.

Casting off his garments, he took the accustomed plunge by way of cooling his heart and brain. He came up from the depths refreshed, but not restored to equanimity. While dressing, the sense of injustice returned as strongly as before, and, with it, the hot indignation, so that on afterwards reaching the highway he paused only for a few moments. This was the critical point. Slowly but decidedly he leaned to the left. He turned his back on his father's house, and caused the stones to spurt from under his heels as he walked rapidly away.

If Miles Milton had thought of his mother at that time he might have escaped many a day of bitter repentance, for she was as gentle as her husband was harsh; but the angry youth either forgot her at the moment, or, more probably, thrust the thought of her away.

Poor mother! if she had only known what a conflict between good and evil was going on in the breast of her boy, how she would have agonised in prayer for him! But she did not know. There was, however, One who did know, who loved him better even than his mother, and who watched and guarded him throughout all his chequered career.

It is not improbable that in spite of his resolves Miles would have relented before night and returned home had not a very singular incident intervened and closed the door behind him.

That day a notorious swindler had been tracked by a red-haired detective to the manufacturing city to which Miles first directed his steps. The bills describing the swindler set forth that he was quite young, tall, handsome, broad-shouldered, with black curling hair, and a budding moustache; that he was dressed in grey tweeds, and had a prepossessing manner. Now this chanced to be in some respects an exact description of Miles Milton!

The budding moustache, to be sure, was barely discernible, still it was sufficiently so for a detective to found on. His dress, too, was brown tweed, not grey; but of course dresses can be changed; and as to his manner, there could not be two opinions about that.

Now it chanced to be past one o'clock when Miles entered the town and felt himself impelled by familiar sensations to pause in front of an eating-house. It was a poor eating-house in a low district, but Miles was not particular; still further, it was a temperance coffee-house, but Miles cared nothing for strong drink. Strong health and spirits had served his purpose admirably up to that date.

Inside the eating-house there sat several men of the artisan class, and a few of the nondescript variety. Among the latter was the red-haired detective. He was engaged with a solid beef-steak.

"Oho!" escaped softly from his lips, when his sharp eyes caught sight of our hero. So softly did he utter the exclamation that it might have been a mere remark of appreciation addressed to the steak, from which he did not again raise his eyes for a considerable time.

The place was very full of people — so full that there seemed scarcely room for another guest; but by some almost imperceptible motion the red-haired man made a little space close to himself. The man next to him, with a hook-nose, widened the space by similar action, and Miles, perceiving that there was room, sat down.

"Bread and cheese," he said to the waiter.

"Bread an' cheese, sir? Yessir."

Miles was soon actively engaged in mechanically feeding, while his mind was busy as to future plans.

Presently he became aware that the men on either side of him were scanning his features and person with peculiar attention.

"Coldish weather," remarked the red-haired man, looking at him in a friendly way.

"It is," replied Miles, civilly enough.

"Rather cold for bathin', ain't it, sir?" continued the detective carelessly, picking his teeth with a quill.

"How did you know that I've been bathing?" demanded Miles in surprise.

"I didn't know it."

"How did you guess it then?"

"Vell, it ain't difficult to guess that a young feller 'as bin 'avin' a swim w'en you see the 'air of 'is 'ead hall vet, an' 'is pocket-'ankercher lookin' as if it 'ad done dooty for a towel, not to mention 'is veskit 'avin' bin putt on in a 'urry, so as the buttons ain't got into the right 'oles, you see!"

Miles laughed, and resumed his bread and cheese.

"You are observant, I perceive," he said.

"Not wery partiklarly so," returned Redhair; "but I do observe that your boots tell of country roads. Was it a long way hout of town as you was bathin' this forenoon, now?"

There was a free and easy familiarity about the man's tone which Miles resented, but, not wishing to run the risk of a disagreement in such company, he answered quietly — "Yes, a considerable distance; it was in an old quarry where I often bathe, close to my father's house."

"Ha! jest so, about 'alf-way to the willage of Ramplin', w'ere you slep' last night, if report speaks true, an' w'ere you left the *grey tweeds*, unless, p'r'aps, you sunk 'em in the old quarry."

"Why, what on earth do you mean?" asked Miles, with a look of such genuine surprise that Redhair was puzzled, and the man with the hooked nose, who had been listening attentively, looked slightly confused.

"Read that, sir," said the detective, extracting a newspaper cutting from his pocket and laying it on the table before Miles.

While he read, the two men watched him with interest, so did some of those who sat near, for they began to perceive that something was "in the wind."

The tell-tale blood sprang to the youth's brow as he read and perceived the meaning of the man's remarks. At this Redhair and Hook-nose nodded to each other significantly.

"You don't mean to say," exclaimed Miles, in a tone of grand indignation which confirmed the men in their suspicion, "that you think this description applies to *me*?"

"I wouldn't insinivate too much, sir, though I have got my suspicions," said Redhair blandly; "but of course that's easy settled, for if your father's 'ouse is anyw'ere hereabouts, your father won't object to identify his son."

"Ridiculous!" exclaimed Miles, rising angrily at this interruption to his plans. The two men rose promptly at the same moment. "Of course my father will prove that you have made a mistake, but—"

He hesitated in some confusion, for the idea of re-appearing before his father so soon, and in such company, after so stoutly asserting that he would *never* more return, was humiliating. The detective observed the hesitation and became jocose.

"If you'd rather not trouble your parent," said Redhair, "you've got no call to do it. The station ain't far off, and the sooner we get there the better for all parties."

A slight clink of metal at this point made Miles aware of the fact that Hook-nose was drawing a pair of handcuffs from one of his pockets.

The full significance of his position suddenly burst upon him. The thought of being led home a prisoner, or conveyed to the police-station handcuffed, maddened him; and the idea of being thus unjustly checked at the very outset of his independent career made him furious. For a few moments he stood so perfectly still and quiet that the detectives were thrown slightly off their guard. Then there was an explosion of some sort within the breast of Miles Milton. It expended itself in a sudden impulse, which sent Redhead flat on the table among the crockery, and drove Hook-nose into the fireplace among the fire-irons. A fat little man chanced to be standing in the door-way. The same impulse, modified, shot that little man into the street like a cork out of a bottle, and next moment Miles was flying along the pavement at racing speed, horrified at what he had done, but utterly reckless as to what might follow!

Hearing the shouts of pursuers behind him, and being incommoded by passers-by in the crowded thoroughfare, Miles turned sharply into a by-street, and would have easily made his escape—being uncommonly swift of foot—had he not been observed by an active little man of supple frame and presumptuous tendencies. Unlike the mass of mankind around him—who stared and wondered—the active little man took in the situation at a glance, joined in the pursuit, kept well up, thus forming a sort of connecting-link between the fugitive and pursuers, and even took upon himself to shout

"Stop thief!" as he ran. Miles endeavoured to throw him off by putting on, as schoolboys have it, "a spurt." But the active little man also spurted and did not fall far behind. Then Miles tried a second double, and got into a narrow street, which a single glance showed him was a blind alley! Disappointment and anger hereupon took possession of him, and he turned at bay with the tiger-like resolve to run a-muck!

Fortunately for himself he observed a pot of whitewash standing near a half-whitened wall, with a dirty canvas frock and a soiled billycock lying beside it. The owner of the property had left it inopportunely, for, quick as thought, Miles wriggled into the frock, flung on the billycock, seized the pot, and walked in a leisurely way to the head of the alley. He reached it just as the active little man turned into it, at the rate of ten miles an hour. A yell of "Stop thief!" issued from the man's presumptuous lips at the moment.

His injunction was obeyed to the letter, for the would-be thief of an honest man's character on insufficient evidence was stopped by Miles's bulky person so violently that the whitewash was scattered all about, and part of it went into the active man's eyes.

To squash the large brush into the little man's face, and thus effectually complete what his own recklessness had begun, was the work of an instant. As he did it, Miles assumed the rôle of the injured party, suiting his language to his condition.

"What d'ee mean by that, you houtrageous willain?" he cried savagely, to the great amusement of the bystanders, who instantly formed a crowd round them. "Look wot a mess you've bin an' made o' my clean frock! Don't you see?"

The poor little man could not see. He could only cough and gasp and wipe his face with his coat-tails.

"I'd give you in charge o' the pleece, I would, if it wasn't that you've pretty well punished yourself a'ready," continued Miles. "Take 'im to a pump some o' you, 'cause I ain't got time. Good-day, spider-legs, an' don't go for to run into a hartist again, with a paint-pot in 'is 'and."

So saying, Miles pushed through the laughing crowd and sauntered away. He turned into the first street he came to, and then went forward as fast as was consistent with the idea of an artisan in a hurry. Being utterly ignorant of the particular locality into which he had penetrated — though well enough acquainted with the main thoroughfares of the city — his only care was to put as many intricate streets and lanes as possible between himself and the detectives. This was soon done, and thereafter, turning into à darkish passage, he got rid of the paint-pot and borrowed costume.

Fortunately he had thrust his own soft helmet-shaped cap into his breast at the time he put on the billycock, and was thus enabled to issue from the dark passage very much like his former self, with the exception of a few spots of whitewash, which were soon removed.

Feeling now pretty safe, our hero walked a considerable distance through the unknown parts of the city before he ventured to inquire the way to thoroughfares with which he was familiar. Once in these, he proceeded at a smart pace to one of the railway stations, intending to leave town, though as yet he had formed no definite plan of action. In truth, his mind was much troubled and confused by the action of his conscience, for when the thought of leaving home and entering the army as a private soldier, against his father's wishes, crossed his mind, Conscience faithfully shook his head; and when softer feelings prevailed, and the question arose irresistibly, "Shall I return home?" the same faithful friend whispered, "Yes."

In a state of indecision, Miles found himself borne along by a human stream to the booking-office. Immediately in front of him were two soldiers, — one a sergeant, and the other a private of the line.

Both were tall handsome men, straight as arrows, and with that air of self-sufficient power which is as far removed from arrogance as it is from cowardice, and is by no means an uncommon feature in men of the British army.

Miles felt a strong, unaccountable attraction towards the young private. He had not yet heard his voice nor encountered his eye; indeed, being behind him, he had only seen his side-face, and as the expression on it was that of stern gravity, the attractive power could not have lain in that. It might have lain in the youthful look of the lad, for albeit a goodly man in person, he was almost a boy in countenance, being apparently not yet twenty years of age.

Miles was at last roused to the necessity for prompt and decisive action by the voice of the sergeant saying in tones of authority —

"Portsmouth — third — two — single."

"That's the way to go it, lobster!" remarked a shabby man, next in the line behind Miles.

The grave sergeant paid no more regard to this remark than if it had been the squeak of a mouse.

"Now, then, sir, your carridge stops the way. 'Eave a'ead. Shall I 'elp you?" said the shabby man.

Thus admonished, Miles, scarce knowing what he said, repeated the sergeant's words —

"Portsmouth — third — two — single."

"Vy, you ain't agoin' to pay for *me*, are you?" exclaimed the shabby man in smiling surprise.

"Oh! beg pardon. I mean *one*," said Miles to the clerk, quickly.

The clerk retracted the second ticket with stolid indifference, and Miles, hastening to the platform, sat down on a seat, deeply and uncomfortably impressed with the fact that he possessed little or no money! This unsatisfactory state of things had suddenly burst upon him while in the act of paying for his ticket. He now made a careful examination of his purse, and found its contents to be exactly seven shillings and sixpence, besides a few coppers in his trousers-pocket.

Again indecision assailed him. Should he return? It was not too late. "Yes," said Conscience, with emphasis. "No," said Shame. False pride echoed the word, and Self-will re-echoed it. Still our hero hesitated, and there is no saying what the upshot might have been if the bell had not rung at the moment, and, "Now, then, take your seats!" put an end to the controversy.

Another minute, and Miles Milton was seated opposite the two soldiers, rushing towards our great southern seaport at the rate of forty miles an hour.

Chapter Two-Shows some of the Consequences of the False Step, and introduces the Reader to Peculiar Company

Our hero soon discovered that the sergeant was an old campaigner, having been out in Egypt at the beginning of the war, and fought at the famous battle of Tel-el-Kebir.

In his grave and undemonstrative way and quiet voice, this man related some of his experiences, so as not only to gain the attention of his companion in arms, but to fascinate all who chanced to be within earshot of him—not the least interested among whom, of course, was our friend Miles.

As the sergeant continued to expatiate on those incidents of the war which had come under his own observation, three points impressed themselves on our hero: first, that the sergeant was evidently a man of serious, if not religious, spirit; second, that while he gave all due credit to his comrades for their bravery in action, he dwelt chiefly on those incidents which brought out the higher qualities of the men, such as uncomplaining endurance, forbearance, etcetera, and he never boasted of having given "a thorough licking" to the Egyptians, nor spoke disparagingly of the native troops; lastly, that he seemed to lay himself out with a special view to the unflagging entertainment of his young comrade.

The reason for this last purpose he learned during a short halt at one of the stations. Seeing the sergeant standing alone there, Miles, after accosting him with the inevitable references to the state of the weather, remarked that his comrade seemed to be almost too young for the rough work of soldiering.

"Yes, he is young enough, but older than he looks," answered the sergeant. "Poor lad! I'm sorry for him."

"Indeed! He does not seem to me a fit subject for pity. Young, strong, handsome, intelligent, he seems pretty well furnished to begin the battle of life—especially in the army."

"'Things are not what they seem,'" returned the soldier, regarding his young questioner with something between a compassionate and an amused look. "'All is not gold that glitters.' Soldiering is not made up of brass bands, swords, and red coats!"

"Having read a good deal of history I am well aware of that," retorted Miles, who was somewhat offended by the implication contained in the sergeant's remarks.

"Well, then, you see," continued the sergeant, "all the advantages that you have mentioned, and which my comrade certainly possesses, weigh nothing with him at all just now, because this sudden call to the wars separates him from his poor young wife."

"Wife!" exclaimed Miles; "why, he seems to me little more than a boy — except in size, and perhaps in gravity."

"He is over twenty, and, as to gravity — well, most young fellows would be grave enough if they had to leave a pretty young wife after six months of wedded life. You see, he married without leave, and so, even if it were a time of peace, his wife would not be recognised by the service. In wartime he must of course leave her behind him. It has been a hard job to prevent him from deserting, and now it's all I can do to divert his attention from his sorrow by stirring him up with tales of the recent wars."

At this point the inexorable bell rang, doors were banged, whistles sounded, and the journey was resumed.

Arrived at Portsmouth, Miles was quickly involved in the bustle of the platform. He had made up his mind to have some private conversation with the sergeant as to the possibility of entering her Majesty's service as a private soldier, and was on the point of accompanying his military travelling companions into the comparative quiet of the street when a porter touched his cap —

"Any luggage, sir?"

"Luggage? — a — no — no luggage!"

It was the first moment since leaving home that the thought of luggage had entered into his brain! That thought naturally aroused other thoughts, such as lodgings, food, friends, funds, and the like. On turning to the spot where his military companions had stood, he discovered that they were gone. Running to the nearest door-way he found it to be the wrong one, and before he found the right one and reached the street the two soldiers had vanished from the scene.

"You seem to be a stranger here, sir. Can I direct you?" said an insinuating voice at his elbow.

The speaker was an elderly man of shabby-genteel appearance and polite address. Miles did not quite like the look of him. In the circumstances, however, and with a strangely desolate feeling of loneliness creeping over him, he did not see his way to reject a civil offer.

"Thank you. I am indeed a stranger, and happen to have neither friend nor acquaintance in the town, so if you can put me in the way of finding a respectable lodging—a—a *cheap* one, you will greatly oblige me."

"With pleasure," said the man, "if you will accompany—"

"Stay, don't trouble yourself to show me the way," interrupted Miles; "just name a house and the street, that will—"

"No trouble at all, sir," said the man. "I happen to be going in the direction of the docks, and know of excellent as well as cheap lodgings there."

Making no further objection, Miles followed his new friend into the street. For some time, the crowd being considerable and noisy, they walked in silence.

At the time we write of, Portsmouth was ringing with martial music and preparations for war.

At all times the red-coats and the blue-jackets are prominent in the streets of that seaport; for almost the whole of our army passes through it at one period or another, either in going to or returning from "foreign parts." But at this time there was the additional bustle resulting from the Egyptian war. Exceptional activity prevailed in its yards, and hurry in its streets. Recruits, recently enlisted, flocked into it from all quarters, while on its jetties were frequently landed the sad fruits of war in the form of wounded men.

"Have you ever been in Portsmouth before?" asked the shabby-genteel man, on reaching a part of the town which was more open and less crowded.

"Never. I had no idea it was so large and bustling," said Miles.

"The crowding and bustling is largely increased just now, of course, in consequence of the war in Egypt," returned the man. "Troops are constantly embarking, and others returning. It is a noble service! Men start in thousands from this port young, hearty, healthy, and full of spirit; they return—those of them who return at all—sickly, broken-down, and with no spirit at all except what they soon get poured into them by the publicans. Yes; commend me to the service of my Queen and country!"

There was a sneering tone in the man's voice which fired his companion's easily roused indignation.

"Mind what you say about our Queen while in *my* company," said Miles sternly, stopping short and looking the man full in the face. "I am a loyal subject, and will listen to nothing said in disparagement of the Queen or of her Majesty's forces."

"Bless you, sir," said the man quickly, "I'm a loyal subject myself, and wouldn't for the world say a word against her Majesty. No more would I disparage her troops; but, after all, the army ain't perfect, you know. Even *you* must admit that, sir. With all its noble qualities there's room for improvement."

There was such an air of sincerity — or at least of assumed humility — in the man's tone and manner that Miles felt it unjustifiable to retain his indignation. At the same time, he could not all at once repress it, and was hesitating whether to fling off from the man or to forgive him, when the sound of many voices, and of feet tramping in regular time, struck his ear and diverted his attention. Next moment the head of a regiment, accompanied by a crowd of juvenile admirers, swept round the corner of the street. At the same instant a forest of bayonets gleamed upon the youth's vision, and a brass band burst with crashing grandeur upon his ear, sending a quiver of enthusiasm into the deepest recesses of his soul, and stirring the very marrow in his bones!

Miles stood entranced until the regiment had passed, and the martial strains were softened by distance; then he looked up and perceived that his shabby companion was regarding him with a peculiar smile.

"I think you've a notion of being a soldier," he said, with a smile.

"Where is that regiment going?" asked Miles, instead of answering the question.

"To barracks at present; to Egypt in a few days. There'll be more followin' it before long."

It was a distracting as well as an exciting walk that Miles had through the town, for at every turn he passed couples or groups of soldiers, or sailors, or marines, and innumerable questions sprang into and jostled each other in his mind, while, at the same moment, his thoughts and feelings were busy with his present circumstances and future prospects. The distraction was increased by the remarks and comments of his guide, and he would fain have got rid of him; but good-feeling, as well as common-sense, forbade his casting him off without sufficient reason.

Presently he stopped, without very well knowing why, in front of a large imposing edifice. Looking up, he observed the words *Soldiers' Institute* in large letters on the front of it.

"What sort of an Institute is that?" he asked.

"Oh! it's a miserable affair, where soldiers are taken in cheap, as they say, an' done for," returned the shabby man hurriedly, as if the subject were distasteful to him. "Come along with me and I'll show you places where soldiers – ay, and civilians too – can enjoy themselves like gentlemen, an' get value for their money."

As he spoke, two fine-looking men issued from a small street close to them, and crossed the road – one a soldier of the line, the other a marine.

"Here it is, Jack," exclaimed the soldier to his friend; "Miss Sarah Robinson's Institoot, that you've heard so much about. Come an' I'll show you where you can write your letter in peace – "

Thus much was overheard by Miles as they turned into a side-street, and entered what was obviously one of the poorer districts of the town.

"Evidently that soldier's opinion does not agree with yours," remarked Miles, as they walked along.

"More's the pity!" returned the shabby man, whose name he had informed his companion was Sloper. "Now we are getting among places, you see, where there's a good deal of drinking going on."

"I scarcely require to be told that," returned Miles, curtly; for he was beginning to feel his original dislike to Mister Sloper intensified.

It did not indeed require any better instructor than eyes and ears to inform our hero that the grog-shops around him were full, and that a large proportion of the shouting and swearing revellers inside were soldiers and seamen.

By this time it was growing dark, and most of the gin-palaces were beginning to send forth that glare of intense and warm light with which they so knowingly attract the human moths that constitute their prey.

"Here we are," said Sloper, stopping in front of a public-house in a narrow street. "This is one o' the *respectable* lodgin's. Most o' the others are disreputable. It's not much of a neighbourhood, I admit."

"It certainly is not very attractive," said Miles, hesitating.

"You said you wanted a cheap one," returned Sloper, "and you can't expect to have it cheap and fashionable, you know. You've no occasion to be afraid. Come in."

The arguments of Mr Sloper might have failed to move Miles, but the idea of his being *afraid* to go anywhere was too much for him.

"Go in, then," he said, firmly, and followed.

The room into which he was ushered was a moderately large public-house, with a bar and a number of tables round the room, at which many men and a few women were seated; some gambling, others singing or disputing, and all drinking and smoking. It is only right to say that Miles was shocked. Hitherto he had lived a quiet and comparatively innocent country life. He knew of such places chiefly from books or hearsay, or had gathered merely the superficial knowledge that comes through the opening of a swing-door. For the first time in his life he stood inside a low drinking-shop, breathing its polluted atmosphere and listening to its foul language. His first impulse was to retreat, but false shame, the knowledge that he had no friend in Portsmouth, or place to go to, that the state of his purse forbade his indulging in more suitable accommodation, and a certain pride of character which made him always determine to carry out what he had resolved to do—all these considerations and facts combined to prevent his acting on the better impulse. He doggedly followed his guide to a small round table and sat down.

Prudence, however, began to operate within him. He felt that he had done wrong; but it was too late now, he thought, to retrace his steps. He would, however, be on his guard; would not encourage the slightest familiarity on the part of any one, and would keep his eyes open. For a youth who had seen nothing of the world this was a highly commendable resolve.

"What'll you drink?" asked Mr Sloper.

Miles was on the point of saying "Coffee," but, reflecting that the beverage might not be readily obtainable in such a place, he substituted "Beer."

Instead of calling the waiter, Mr Sloper went himself to the bar to fetch the liquor. While he was thus engaged, Miles glanced round the room, and was particularly struck with the appearance of a large, fine-looking sailor who sat at the small table next to him, with hands thrust deep into his trousers-pockets, his chin resting on his broad chest, and a solemn, owlish stare in his semi-drunken yet manly countenance. He sat alone, and was obviously in a very sulky frame of mind—a condition which he occasionally indicated through a growl of dissatisfaction.

As Miles sat wondering what could have upset the temper of a tar whose visage was marked by the unmistakable lines and dimples of good-humour, he overheard part of the conversation that passed between the barman and Mr Sloper.

"What! have they got hold o' Rattling Bill?" asked the former, as he drew the beer.

"Ay, worse luck," returned Sloper. "I saw the sergeant as I came along lead him over to Miss Robinson's trap—confound her!"

"Don't you go fur to say anything agin Miss Robinson, old man," suddenly growled the big sailor, in a voice so deep and strong that it silenced for a moment the rest of the company. "Leastways, you may if you like, but if you do, I'll knock in your daylights, an' polish up your figur'-head so as your own mother would mistake you fur a battered saucepan!"

The seaman did not move from his semi-recumbent position as he uttered this alarming threat, but he accompanied it with a portentous frown and an owlish wink of both eyes.

"What! have *you* joined the Blue Lights?" asked Sloper, with a smile, referring to the name by which the religious and temperance men of the army were known.

"No, I ha'n't. Better for me, p'r'aps, if I had. Here, waiter, fetch me another gin-an'-warer. An' more o' the gin than the warer, mind. Heave ahead or I'll sink you!"

Having been supplied with a fresh dose of gin and water, the seaman appeared to go to sleep, and Miles, for want of anything better to do, accepted Sloper's invitation to play a game of dominoes.

"Are the beds here pretty good?" he asked, as they were about to begin.

"Yes, first-rate—for the money," answered Sloper.

"That's a lie!" growled the big sailor. "They're bad at any price— stuffed wi' cocoa-nuts and marline-spikes."

Mr Sloper received this observation with the smiling urbanity of a man who eschews war at all costs.

"You don't drink," he said after a time, referring to Miles's pot of beer, which he had not yet touched.

Miles made no reply, but by way of answer took up the pot and put it to his lips.

He had not drunk much of it when the big seaman rose hurriedly and staggered between the two tables. In doing so, he accidentally knocked the pot out of the youth's hand, and sent the contents into Mr Sloper's face and down into his bosom, to the immense amusement of the company.

That man of peace accepted the baptism meekly, but Miles sprang up in sudden anger.

The seaman turned to him, however, with a benignantly apologetic smile.

"Hallo! messmate. I ax your parding. They don't leave room even for a scarecrow to go about in this here cabin. I'll stand you another glass. Give us your flipper!"

There was no resisting this, it was said so heartily. Miles grasped the huge hand that was extended and shook it warmly.

"All right," he said, laughing. "I don't mind the beer, and there's plenty more where that came from, but I fear you have done some damage to my fr—"

"Your *friend*. Out with it, sir. Never be ashamed to acknowledge your friends," exclaimed the shabby man, as he wiped his face. "Hold on a bit," he added, rising; "I'll have to change my shirt. Won't keep you waitin' long."

"Another pot o' beer for this 'ere gen'lem'n," said the sailor to the barman as Sloper left the room.

Paying for the drink, he returned and put the pot on the table. Then, turning to Miles, he said in a low voice and with an intelligent look—

"Come outside for a bit, messmate. I wants to speak to 'ee."

Miles rose and followed the man in much surprise.

"You'll excuse me, sir," he said, when a few yards away from the door; "but I see that you're green, an' don't know what a rascally place you've got into. I've been fleeced there myself, and yet I'm fool enough to go back! Most o' the parties there—except the sailors an' sodgers—are thieves an' blackguards. They've drugged your beer, I know; that's why I capsized it for you, and the feller that has got hold o' you is a well-known decoy-duck. I don't know how much of the ready you may have about you, but this I does know, whether it be much or little, you wouldn't have a rap of it in the mornin' if you stayed the night in this here house."

"Are you sure of this, friend?" asked Miles, eyeing his companion doubtfully.

"Ay, as sure as I am that my name's Jack Molloy."

"But you've been shamming drunk all this time. How am I to know that you are not shamming friendship now?"

"No, young man," returned the seaman with blinking solemnity. "I'm not shammin' drunk. I on'y wish I was, for I'm three sheets in the wind at this minute, an' I've a splittin' headache due i' the mornin'. The way as you've got to find out whether I'm fair an' above-board is to look me straight in the face an' don't wink. If that don't settle the question, p'r'aps it'll convince you w'en I tells you that I don't care a rap whether you go back to that there grog-shop or not. Only I'll clear my conscience—leastways, wot's left of it—by tellin' ye that if you do—you—you'll wish as how you hadn't—supposin' they leave you the power to wish anything at all."

"Well, I believe you are a true man, Mister Molloy—"

"Don't Mister me, mate," interrupted the seaman.

"My name's Jack Molloy, at your service, an' that name don't require no handle—either Mister or Esquire—to prop it up."

The way in which the sailor squared his broad shoulders when he said this rendered it necessary to prop himself up. Seeing which, Miles afforded the needful aid by taking his arm in a friendly way.

"But come, let us go back," he said. "I must pay for my beer, you know."

"Your beer is paid for, young man," said Molloy, stopping and refusing to move. "*I* paid for it, so you've on'y got to settle with *me*. Besides, if you go back you're done for. And you've no call to go back to say farewell to your dear friend Sloper, for he'll on'y grieve over the loss of your tin. As to the unpurliteness o' the partin'—he won't break his heart over that. No—you'll come wi' me down to the *Sailors' Welcome* near the dock-gates, where you can get a good bed for sixpence a night, a heavy blow-out for tenpence, with a splendid readin'-room, full o' rockin' chairs, an' all the rest of it for nothin'. An there's a lavatory—that's the name that they give to a place for cleanin' of yourself up—a lavatory—where you can wash yourself, if you like, till your skin comes off! W'en I first putt up at the *Welcome*, the messmate as took me there said to me, says he, 'Jack,' says he, 'you was always fond o' water.' 'Right you are,' says I. 'Well,' says he, 'there's a place in the *Sailors' Welcome* where you can wash yourself all day, if you like, for nothing!'

"I do b'lieve it was that as indooced me to give in. I went an' saw this lavatory, an' I was so took up with it that I washed my hands in every bason in the place—one arter the other—an' used up ever so much soap, an'—would you believe it?—my hands wasn't clean after all! Yes, it's one the wery best things in Portsm'uth, is Miss Robinson's Welcome—"

"Miss Robinson again!" exclaimed Miles.

"Ay—wot have you got to find fault wi' Miss Robinson?" demanded the sailor sternly.

"No fault to find at all," replied Miles, suffering himself to be hurried away by his new friend; "but wherever I have gone since arriving in Portsmouth her name has cropped up!"

"In Portsmouth!" echoed the sailor. "Let me tell you, young man, that wherever you go all over the world, if there's a British soldier there, Miss Sarah Robinson's name will be sure to crop up. Why, don't you know that she's 'The Soldiers' Friend'?"

"I'm afraid I must confess to ignorance on the point—yet, stay, now you couple her name with 'The Soldier's Friend,' I have got a faint remembrance of having heard it before. Have I not heard of a Miss Weston, too, in connection with a work of some sort among sailors?"

"Ay, no doubt ye have. She has a grand Institoot in Portsm'uth too, but she goes in for sailors *only*—all over the kingdom—w'ereas Miss Robinson goes in for soldiers an' sailors both, though mainly for the soldiers. She set agoin' the *Sailors' Welcome* before Miss Weston began in Portsm'uth, an' so she keeps it up, but there ain't no opposition or rivalry. Their aims is pretty much alike, an' so they keep stroke together wi' the oars. But I'll tell you more about that when you get inside. Here we are! There's the dockgates, you see, and that's Queen Street, an' the *Welcome's* close at hand. It's a teetotal house, you know. All Miss Robinson's Institoots is that."

"Indeed! How comes it, then, that a man—excuse me—'three sheets in the wind,' can gain admittance?"

"Oh! as to that, any sailor or soldier may get admittance, even if he's as drunk as a fiddler, if he on'y behaves his-self. But they won't supply drink on the premises, or allow it to be brought in—'cept inside o' you, of coorse. Cause why? you can't help that—leastwise not without the help of a stomach-pump. Plenty o' men who ain't abstainers go to sleep every night at the *Welcome*, 'cause they find the beds and other things so comfortable. In fact, some hard topers have been indooced to take the pledge in consekince o' what they've heard an' seen in this *Welcome*, though they came at first only for the readin'-room an' beds. Here, let me look at you under this here lamp. Yes. You'll do. You're something like a sea-dog already. You won't object to change hats wi' me?"

"Why?" asked Miles, somewhat amused.

"Never you mind that, mate. You just putt yourself under my orders if you'd sail comfortably before the wind. I'll arrange matters, an' you can square up in the morning."

As Miles saw no particular reason for objecting to this fancy of his eccentric friend, he exchanged his soft cap for the sailor's straw hat, and they entered the *Welcome* together.

Chapter Three-The "Sailors' Welcome"— Miles has a Night of it and Enlists—His Friend Armstrong has an Agreeable Surprise at the Soldiers' Institute

It was not long before our hero discovered the reason of Jack Molloy's solicitude about his appearance. It was that he, Miles, should pass for a sailor, and thus be in a position to claim the hospitality of the *Sailors' Welcome*,—to the inner life of which civilians were not admitted, though they were privileged, with the public in general, to the use of the outer refreshment-room.

"Come here, Jack Molloy," he said, leading his friend aside, when he made this discovery. "You pride yourself on being a true-blue British tar, don't you?"

"I does," said Jack, with a profound solemnity of decision that comported well with his character and condition.

"And you would scorn to serve under the French flag, or the Turkish flag, or the Black flag, or any flag but the Union Jack, wouldn't you?"

"Right you are, mate; them's my sentiments to a tee!"

"Well, then, you can't expect *me* to sail under false colours any more than yourself," continued Miles. "I scorn to sail into this port under your straw hat, so I'll strike these colours, bid you good-bye, and make sail for another port where a civilian will be welcome."

Molloy frowned at the floor for some moments in stern perplexity.

"You've took the wind out o' my sails entirely, you have," he replied at last; "an' you're right, young man, but I'm troubled about you. If you don't run into this here port you'll have to beat about in the offing all night, or cast anchor in the streets, for I don't know of another lodgin' in Portsm'uth w'ere you could hang out except them disrepitible grog-shops. In coorse, there's the big hotels; but I heerd you say to Sloper that you was bound to do things cheap, bein' hard up."

"Never mind, my friend," said Miles quickly. "I will manage somehow; so good-night, and many thanks to you for the interest you have taken in—"

"Avast, mate! there's no call to go into action in sitch a hurry. This here *Sailors' Welcome* opens the doors of its bar an' refreshment-room, an' spreads its purvisions before all an' sundry as can afford to pay its moderate demands. It's on'y the after-cabin you're not free to. So you'll have a bit supper wi' me before you set sail on your night cruise."

Being by that time rather hungry as well as fatigued, Miles agreed to remain for supper. While they were engaged with it, he was greatly impressed with the number of sailors and marines who passed into the reading-room beyond the bar, or who sat down at the numerous tables around to have a hearty supper, which they washed down with tea and coffee instead of beer or gin—apparently with tremendous appetite and much satisfaction.

"Look ye here," said Jack Molloy, rising when their "feed" was about concluded, "I've no doubt they won't object to your taking a squint at the readin'-room, though they won't let you use it." Following his companion, Miles passed by a glass double door into an enormous well-lighted, warm room, seventy feet long, and of proportionate width and height, in which a goodly number of men of the sea were busy as bees—some of them reading books or turning over illustrated papers and magazines, others smoking their pipes, and enjoying themselves in rocking-chairs in front of the glowing fire, chatting, laughing, and yarning as free-and-easily as if in their native fo'c's'ls, while a few were examining the pictures on the walls, or the large models of ships which stood at one side of the room. At the upper end a full-sized billiard-table afforded amusement to several players, and profound interest to a number of spectators, who passed their comments on the play with that off-hand freedom which seems to be a product of fresh gales and salt-water. A door standing partly open at the upper end of this apartment revealed a large hall, from which issued faintly the sound of soft music.

"Ain't it snug? and there's no gamblin' agoin' on there," remarked Molloy, as they returned to their table; "that's not allowed—nor drinkin', nor card-playin', but that's all they putt a stop to. She's a wise woman is Miss Robinson. She don't hamper us wi' no rules. Why, bless you, Jack ashore would never submit to rules! He gits more than enough o' them afloat. No; it's liberty hall here. We may come an' go as we like, at all hours o' the day and night, an' do exactly as we please, so long as we don't smash up the furnitur', or feed without payin', or make ourselves a gineral noosance. They don't even forbid swearin'. They say they leave the matter o' lingo to our own good taste and good sense. An' d'you know, it's wonderful what an' amount o' both we've got w'en we ain't worried about it! You'll scarce hear an oath in this house from mornin' to evenin', though you'll hear a deal o' snorin' doorin' the night! That's how the place takes so well, d'ee see?"

"Then the *Welcome* is well patronised, I suppose?"

"Patronised!" exclaimed the seaman; "that's so, an' no mistake. Why, mate—But what's your name? I've forgot to ax you that all this time!"

"Call me Miles," said our hero, with some hesitation.

"*Call* you Miles! *Ain't* you Miles?"

"Well, yes, I am; only there's more of my name than that, but that's enough for your purpose, I daresay."

"All right. Well, Miles, you was askin' how the house is patronised. I'll tell 'ee. They make up about two hundred an' twenty beds in it altogether, an' these are chock-full a'most every night. One way or another they had forty-four thousand men, more or less, as slep' under this roof last year—so I've bin told. That's patronisin', ain't it? To say nothin' o' the fellers as comes for—grub, which, as you've found, is good for the money, and the attendants is civil. You see, they're always kind an' attentive here, 'cause they professes to think more of our souls than our bodies—which we've no objection to, d'ee see, for the lookin' arter our souls includes the lookin' arter our bodies! An' they don't bother us in no way to attend their Bible-readin's an' sitchlike. There they are in separate rooms; if you want 'em you may go; if you don't, you can let 'em alone. No compulsion, which comes quite handy to some on us, for I don't myself care much about sitchlike things. So long's my body's all right, I leaves my soul to look arter itself."

As the seaman said this with a good-natured smile of indifference, there sprang to the mind of his young companion words that had often been impressed on him by his mother: "What shall it profit a man if he should gain the whole world, and lose his own soul?" but he made no reference to this at the time.

"Hows'ever," continued Molloy, "as they don't worrit us about religion, except to give us a good word an' a blessin' now an' again, and may-hap a little book to read, we all patronises the house; an it's my opinion if it was twice as big as it is we'd fill it chock-full. I would board as well as sleep in it myself—for it's full o' conveniences, sitch as lockers to putt our things in, an' baths, and what not, besides all the other things I've mentioned—but the want o' drink staggers me. I can't git along without a drop o' drink."

Miles thought that his nautical friend appeared to be unable to get along without a good many drops of drink, but he was too polite to say so.

"Man alive!" continued Jack Molloy, striking his huge fist on his thigh with emphasis; "it's a wonderful place is this *Welcome*! An' it's a lively place too. Why, a fellow hanged his-self in one o' the bunks overhead not long ago."

"You don't mean that?" exclaimed Miles, rather shocked.

"In course I does. But they heard 'im gaspin', an cut him down in time to save him. It was drink they say as made him do it, and they got him to sign the pledge arterwards. I believe he's kep' it too. Leastwise I know many a hard drinker as have bin indooced to give it up and stuck to it—all through comin' here to have a snooze in a comfortable hunk. They give the bunks names—cubicles they calls 'em in the lump. Separately, there's the 'Commodore Goodenough Cot,' an' the 'Little Nellie Cot,' an' the 'Sunshine Cot'—so called 'cause it hain't got a port-hole to let in the daylight at all; and the 'Billy Rough 'un'—"

"The what?"

"'The Billy Rough 'un'—arter the ship o' that name, you know—"

"Oh! you mean the *Bellerophon*."

"Well, young man, an' didn't I *say* the 'Billy Rough 'un'? Then there's the— But what's your hurry?" said the seaman, as Miles rose.

"It's getting late now, friend. If I'm to find another lodging I must be off. Doubtless, I'll find some respectable house to take me in for the night." Miles suppressed a yawn as he put on his cap.

"I don't believe you will," returned Molloy, also rising, and giving full vent to a sympathetic and vociferous yawn. "Hows'ever, w'en a young feller insists on havin' his way, it's best to give him plenty of cable and let him swing. He's sure to find out his mistake by experience. But look ye here, Miles, I've took a fancy to you, an' I'd be sorry to think you was in difficulties. If," he continued, thrusting a hand into his breeches-pocket, and bringing up therefrom a mass of mixed gold, silver, and copper—"if you don't objec' to accep' of a loan of—"

"Thank you—no, my friend. It is very kind of you," said Miles quickly; "but I have quite enough for present necessities. So good-night."

"All right," returned the sailor, thrusting the money back into his pocket. "But if you should ever want a jaw with Jack Molloy while you're in this here port you've only got to hail him at the *Sailors' Welcome,* an' if he should happen to be out, they always can tell you where he's cruisin'. Good-night, an' luck go wi' ye!"

Another tremendous yawn finished the speech, and next moment Miles found himself in the street, oppressed with a strange and miserable sensation which he had never before experienced. Indeed, he had to lean against the house for a few minutes after coming out into the fresh air, and felt as if the power of connected thought was leaving him.

He was aroused from this condition by the flashing of a light in his eyes. Opening them wide, he beheld a policeman looking at him earnestly.

"Now, then, young fellow," said the guardian of the night; "d'you think you can take care of yourself?"

"Oh! yes, quite well. It's only a giddy feeling that came over me. I'm all right," said Miles, rousing himself and passing on.

He staggered slightly, however, and a short "Humph!" from the policeman showed that he believed the youth to be something more than giddy.

Ashamed to be even unjustly supposed to be intoxicated, Miles hurried away, wondering very much what could be the matter with him, for he had not tasted a drop of strong drink, except the half-glass of beer he had swallowed before Molloy chanced to knock it out of his hand. Suddenly he remembered that the sailor had said the beer was drugged. If he could have asked the barman who had served him, that worthy could have told him that this was true; that the whole glassful, if swallowed, would, ere long, have rendered him insensible, and that what he had already taken was enough to do him considerable damage.

As he walked onward, he became rapidly worse; the people and the streets seemed to swim before him; an intense desire to sleep overpowered every other feeling, and at last, turning into a dark entry, he lay down and pillowed his head on a door-step. Here he was found by a policeman; a stretcher was fetched, and he was conveyed to the station as "drunk and incapable!"

When brought before the Inspector the following morning, shame and reckless despair were the tenants of his breast. Those tenants were not expelled, but rather confirmed in possession, when the Inspector — after numerous questions, to which Miles returned vague unsatisfactory replies — adopted the rôle of the faithful friend, and gave him a great deal of paternal advice, especially with reference to the avoidance of strong drink and bad companions.

Miles had the wisdom, however, to conceal his feelings, and to take the reproof and advice in good part. Afterwards, on being set free, he met a recruiting sergeant, who, regarding him as a suitable subject for the service of her Majesty, immediately laid siege to him. In his then state of mind the siege was an easy one. In short, he capitulated at once and entered the Queen's service, under the name of John Miles.

We need scarcely say that his heart misgave him, that his conscience condemned him, and that, do what he would, he could not shut out the fact that his taking so hasty and irrevocable a step was a poor return for all the care and anxiety of his parents in years gone by. But, as we have said, or hinted, Miles was one of those youths who, when they have once made up their minds to a certain course of action, fancy that they are bound to pursue it to the end. Hence it was that he gave his name as John Miles instead of Miles Milton, so that he might baffle any inquiries as to what had become of him.

Once enlisted, he soon began to realise the fact that he was no longer a free agent — at least not in the sense in which he had been so up to that period of his life. Constant drill was the order of the day for some weeks; for there was a demand for more troops for Egypt at the time, and regiments were being made up to their full strength as fast as possible.

During this period Miles saw little of his companions in arms personally, save that group of recruits who were being "licked into shape" along with him. At first he was disappointed with these, for most of them were shy, unlettered men; some, raw lads from the country; and others, men who seemed to have been loafers before joining, and were by no means attractive.

The drill-sergeant, however, was a good, though stern man, and soon recognised the differences in character, aptitude, and willingness among his raw recruits. This man, whose name was Hardy, made a powerful impression on our hero from the first; there was something so quiet and even gentle about him, in spite of his firm and inflexible demands in regard to the matters of drill and duty. To please this man, Miles gave himself heart and soul to his work, and was soon so efficient as to be allowed to join the regiment.

And here he found, to his surprise and satisfaction, that the sergeant and young .soldier with whom he had travelled to Portsmouth were members of the company to which he was attached. As we have said, Miles had taken a great fancy at first sight to the young private, whose name was William Armstrong. Our hero was of an affectionate disposition, and would have allowed his warm feelings to expend themselves on a dog rather than have denied them free play. No wonder, then, that he was attracted by the handsome manly countenance and deferential manner of Armstrong, who, although an uneducated youth, and reared in the lower ranks of life, was gifted with those qualities of the true gentleman which mere social position can neither bestow nor take away. His intellect also was of that active and vigorous fibre which cannot be entirely repressed by the want of scholastic training.

The affection was mutual, for the contrasts and similarities of the two men were alike calculated to draw them together. Both were tall, broad, square-shouldered, erect, and soldierly, yet, withal, modest as well in demeanour as in feeling, and so exactly like to each other in size and figure, and in the quiet gravity of their expressions, that they might well have been taken for twin brothers. When, in uniform, the two strode along the streets of Portsmouth, people were apt to turn and look at them, and think, no doubt, that with many such men in the British army it would go hard with the foes of Old England!

The bond of union was still further strengthened by the fact that while the comparatively learned Miles was enthusiastic and communicative, the unlettered Armstrong was inquisitive and receptive, fond of prying into the nature of things, and always ready as well as competent to discuss — not merely to *argue*. Observe the distinction, good reader. Discussion means the shaking of any subject into its component parts with a desire to understand it. Argument has come very much to signify the enravelment of any subject with a view to the confusion and conquest of an opponent. Both young men abhorred the latter and liked the former. Hence much of their harmony and friendship.

"Will you come with me up town?" said Armstrong to Miles one day, as he was about to quit the barrack-room. "I'm going to see if there's any news of my Emmy."

"I did not know you expected her," said Miles. "Come along, I'm ready."

"I don't expect her yet," returned Armstrong, as they left the barracks; "I only look for a letter, because it was on Wednesday that I wrote telling her of my going to Egypt, and she can scarce have had time to get ready to come down, poor girl! In fact I am going to engage a room for her. By the way, I heard this morning that there's to be another draft for Egypt, so you'll have a chance to go."

"I'm rejoiced to hear it," returned Miles; "for, to say the truth, I had been growing envious of your good fortune in being ordered on active service."

"Hooroo, Armstrong, where away now?" cried an unmistakably Irish voice, as a smart little soldier crossed the street to them, and was introduced to Miles as Corporal Flynn, belonging to another company in his own regiment.

"My blissin' on ye, Miles. John, is it?"

"Yes, John," replied our hero, much amused at the free-and-easy address of the little corporal.

"Well, John Miles," he said, "I don't know whether ye'll laugh or cry whin I tell ye that you'll likely be warned this evenin' for the draft that's goin' to Aigypt."

"I certainly won't cry," returned Miles, with a laugh. Yet the news brought a sudden feeling into his breast which was strongly allied to the opposite of laughter, for the thought of parting from father and mother without bidding them farewell fell upon his spirit with crushing weight; but, like too many men who know they are about to do wrong, Miles hardened his heart with the delusive argument that, having fairly taken the step, it was impossible for him now to retrace it. He knew—at least he thought— that there was still the possibility of being bought off, and that his stern father would only be too glad to help him. He also knew that at least he had time to write and let them know his circumstances, so that they might run down to Portsmouth and bid him good-bye; but he had taken the bit in his teeth, and now he resolved to abide the consequences.

Turning from his companions while they conversed, he looked into a shop-window.

"Your chum's in the blues," said the lively corporal, in a lower voice.

"Young fellows are often in that state after joining, ain't they?" returned Armstrong.

"True for ye—an' more shame to them, whin they ought to be as proud as paycocks at wearin' her gracious Majesty's uniform. But good luck to 'ee! I must be off, for I'm bound for Aigypt mesilf."

"I am glad that I shall have the chance of seeing your wife, for I've been much interested in her since your friend Sergeant Gilroy told me about her," said Miles, as they resumed their walk. "Surely it is hard of them to refuse to let her go with the regiment."

"Well, it *is* hard," returned the young soldier; "but after all I cannot find fault with the powers that be, for I married with my eyes open. I knew the rule that those who marry without leave must leave their wives at home, for only a certain number of families can go abroad with a regiment—and that only in peace-time."

"It might have been well," continued Armstrong, slowly, while a sad expression clouded his face for a few moments, "if I had waited, and many a time has my conscience smitten me for my haste. But what could I do? Emmy most unaccountably fell in love wi' me — *thank God*! for I do think that the greatest earthly blessing that can be given to mortal man is the love of a gentle, true-hearted girl. The wealth of the Indies cannot purchase that, and nothing else in life can supply the want of it. Can you wonder that I grasped the treasure when within my reach?"

"I certainly cannot; and as certainly I do not blame you," returned the sympathetic Miles.

"Of course I fell in love with Emmy," continued the soldier, with a slightly confused look. "I could no more help that than I could help growing up. Could I?"

"Certainly not," said Miles.

"Well, you see," continued his friend, "as the affair was arranged in heaven, according to general belief, what was I that I should resist? You see, Emmy's father, who's a well-to-do farmer, was willing, and we never gave a thought to Egypt or the war at the time. She will be well looked after while I'm away, and I'll send her every penny of my pay that I can spare, but — "

He stopped abruptly, and Miles, respecting his feelings, remarked, by way of changing the subject, that the pay of a private soldier being so small very little could be saved out of that.

"Not much," assented his comrade; "but, little as it is, we can increase it in various ways. For one thing, I have given up smoking. That will save a little; though, to say truth, I have never expended much on baccy. Then I have joined Miss Robinson's Temperance Band — "

"Strange how often that lady's name has been in my ears since I came to Portsmouth!" said Miles.

"Not so strange after all," returned Armstrong, "when one reflects that she has been the means of almost changing the character of the town within the last few years — as far at least as concerns the condition of soldiers, as well as many of the poorer classes among its inhabitants — so Sergeant Gilroy tells me."

As some of the information given by Sergeant Gilroy to the young soldier may be interesting to many readers, we quote a few of his own words.

"Why, some years ago," he said, "the soldiers' wives, mothers, and sisters who came down here to see the poor fellows set sail for foreign parts found it almost impossible to obtain lodgings, except in drinking-houses which no respectable woman could enter. Some poor women even preferred to spend a winter night under railway arches, or some such shelter, rather than enter these places. And soldiers out of barracks had nowhere else to go to for amusement, while sailors on leave had to spend their nights in them or walk the streets. Now all that is changed. The Soldiers' Institute supplies 140 beds, and furnishes board and lodging to our sisters and wives at the lowest possible rates, besides reception-rooms where we can meet our friends; a splendid reading-room, where we find newspapers and magazines, and can write our letters, if we like, in peace and quiet; a bar where tea and coffee, bread and butter, buns, etcetera, can be had at all reasonable hours for a mere trifle; a coffee and smoking room, opening out of which are two billiard-rooms, and beyond these a garden, where we can get on the flat roof of a house and watch the arrival and departure of shipping. There is a small charge to billiard-players, which pays all expenses of the tables, so that not a penny of the Institute funds is spent on the games. Of course no gambling is allowed in any of Miss Robinson's Institutes. Then there are Bible-class rooms, and women's work-rooms, and a lending library, and bathrooms, and a great hall, big enough to hold a thousand people, where there are held temperance meetings, lectures with dissolving views, entertainments, and 'tea-fights,' and Sunday services. No wonder that, with such an agency at work for the glory of God and the good of men, Portsmouth is almost a new place. Indeed, although Miss Robinson met with powerful opposition at first from the powers that be, her Institute is now heartily recognised and encouraged in every way at the Horse Guards. Indeed, it has recently been visited by the Prince of Wales and the Duke of Cambridge, and highly approved of by these and other grandees."

While the two soldiers were chatting about the past and present of the Institute they arrived at its door.

"Here we are. Come into the reception-room, Miles, while I make inquiry about my letters."

They entered the house as he spoke. The reception-room is on the right of the passage. Armstrong opened the door and looked in, but, instead of advancing, he stood transfixed, gazing before him open-mouthed as though he had seen a spectre, for there, in front of the fire, sat a beautiful, refined-looking girl, with golden hair and blue eyes, gazing pensively at the flickering flames.

Miles was not kept long in suspense as to who she was.

"Emmy!"

"Oh, Willie!"

These were exclamations which would have revealed all in a moment, even though Emmy had not sprung up and rushed into Willie's open arms. How she ever emerged from the embrace of those arms with unbroken bones is a mystery which cannot be solved, but she did emerge in safety, and with some confusion on observing that Miles had witnessed the incident with admiring gaze!

"Never mind him, Emmy," said the young soldier, laughing; "he's a good friend, a comrade. Shake hands with him."

The action, and the ease of manner with which Emmy obeyed, proved that grace and small hands are not altogether dependent on rank or station.

"Excuse me," said Miles, after a few words of salutation; "I'll go and have a look at the library."

So saying he quitted the room, leaving the young couple alone; for there chanced to be no other visitors to the reception-room at the time. In the lobby he found several soldiers and a couple of sailors enjoying coffee at the bar, and was about to join them when a man came forward whose dress was that of a civilian, though his bearing proclaimed him a soldier.

"Hallo, Brown," exclaimed one of the soldiers, "d'ye know that a troop-ship has just come in!"

"Know it? of course I do; you may trust the people of this house to be first in hearing such news."

"Mr Tufnell told me of it. I'm just going down to the jetty to boil the kettle for them."

As he spoke, two ladies of the Institute descended the broad staircase, each with a basket on her arm.

They entered into conversation for a few minutes with the soldiers at the bar, and it was abundantly evident to Miles, from the kindly tone of the former and the respectful air of the latter, that they were familiar acquaintances, and on the best of terms.

"Are you all ready, Brown?" asked one of the ladies of the soldier-like civilian, whom we have already mentioned.

"All ready, Miss; a man has already gone to order the bread and butter and light the fire. I hear the vessel is crowded, so we may expect a full house to-night."

Miles pricked up his ears on hearing this, and when Brown went out, leaving the two ladies to finish their conversation with the soldiers, he followed him.

"Pardon me," he said, on overtaking the man. "Did I understand correctly that a troop-ship has just arrived?"

"Right," said Brown. "I am just going down to the embarkation jetty to get coffee ready for the men. You seem to have joined but a short time, apparently, for though I am familiar with your uniform I have not seen yourself before."

"True, it is not long since I joined, and this is my first visit to the Institute."

"I hope it won't be the last, friend," returned Brown heartily. "Every soldier is welcome there, and, for the matter of that, so is every sailor and marine."

"I have heard as much. May I accompany you to this jetty to see the troops arrive, and this coffee business that you speak of?"

"You may, and welcome," said Brown, leading his companion through the town in the direction of the docks, and chatting, as they walked along, about the army and navy; about his own experiences in the former; and about the condition of soldiers at the present time as contrasted with that of the days gone by.

Chapter Four-The Embarkation Jetty—And Nipped in the Bud

Bronzed faces under white helmets crowded the ports and bulwarks of the great white leviathan of the deep—the troop-ship *Orontes*—as she steamed slowly and cautiously up to the embarkation jetty in Portsmouth harbour.

On the jetty itself a few anxious wives, mothers, and sisters stood eagerly scanning the sea of faces in the almost hopeless endeavour to distinguish those for which they sought. Yet ever and anon an exclamation on the jetty, and an answering wave of an arm on the troop-ship, told that some at least of the anxious ones had been successful in the search.

"Don't they look weather-beaten?" remarked Miles to his companion.

"Sure it's more like sun-dried they are," answered a voice at his side. Brown had gone to the shed to prepare his coffee and bread against the landing of the troops, and a stout Irishwoman had taken his place. Close to her stood the two ladies from the Institute with baskets on their arms.

"You are right," returned Miles, with a smile; "they look like men who have seen service. Is your husband among them?"

"Faix, I'd be sorprised if he *was*," returned the woman; "for I left him in owld Ireland, in the only landed property he iver held in this world—six futt by two, an' five deep. He's been in possession six years now, an' it wouldn't be aisy to drive him out o' that, anyhow. No, it's my son Terence I've come to look afther. Och! there he is! Look, look, that's him close by the funnel! Don't ye see 'im? Blissins on his good-lookin' face! Hooroo! Terence—Terence Flynn, don't ye recognise yer owld mother? Sure an' he does, though we haven't met for tin year. My! hasn't he got the hair on his lips too—an' his cheeks are like shoe-leather—my darlint!"

As the enthusiastic mother spoke in the tones of a public orator, there was a general laugh among those who were nearest to her; but she was forgotten immediately, for all were too deeply intent on their own interests to pay much regard to each other just then.

The great vessel was slow in getting alongside and making fast to the jetty—slow at least in the estimation of the impatient—for although she might leap and career grandly in wanton playfulness while on her native billows, in port a careless touch from her ponderous sides would have crushed part of the jetty into fragments. Miles therefore had ample time to look about him at the various groups around.

One young woman specially attracted his attention, for she stood apart from every one, and seemed scarcely able to stand because of weakness. She was young and good-looking. Her face, which was deadly pale, contrasted strongly with her glossy raven-black hair, and the character of her dress denoted extreme poverty.

The ladies from the Institute had also observed this poor girl, and one of them, going to her side, quietly addressed her. Miles, from the position in which he stood, could not avoid overhearing what was said.

"Yes, Miss, I expect my husband," said the woman in answer to a question. "He's coming home on sick-leave. I had a letter from him a good while ago saying he was coming home in the *Orontes*."

"I hope you will find that the sea air has done him good," said the lady, in that tone of unobtrusive sympathy which is so powerfully attractive,—especially to those who are in trouble. "A sea voyage frequently has a wonderful effect in restoring invalids. What is his name?"

"Martin—Fred Martin. He's a corporal now."

"You have not recognised him yet, I suppose?"

"Not yet, Miss," answered Mrs Martin, with an anxious look, and shivering slightly as she drew a thin worn shawl of many patches closer round her shoulders. "But he wouldn't expect me to meet him, you see, knowing that I'm so poor, and live far from Portsmouth. But I was so anxious, you see, Miss, that our kind Vicar gave me enough money to come down."

"Where did you spend the night?" asked the lady, quickly.

The poor woman hesitated, and at last said she had spent the night walking about the streets.

"You see, Miss," she explained apologetically, "I didn't know a soul in the town, and I couldn't a-bear to go into any o' the public-houses; besides, I had no money, for the journey down took nearly all of it."

"Oh, I am so sorry that you didn't know of our Institute," said the lady, with much sympathy in voice and look; "for we provide accommodation for soldiers' wives who come, like you, to meet their husbands returning from abroad, and we charge little, or even nothing, if they are too poor to pay."

"Indeed, Miss! I wish I had known of it. But in the morning I had the luck to meet a policeman who directed me to a coffee-tavern in a place called Nobbs Lane—you'll not know it, Miss, for it's in a very poor part o' the town—where I got a breakfast of as much hot pea-soup and bread as I could eat for three-ha'pence, an' had a good rest beside the fire too. They told me it was kept by a Miss Robinson. God bless her whoever she is! for I do believe I should have been dead by now if I hadn't got the rest and the breakfast."

The woman shivered again as she spoke, and drew the thin shawl still closer, for a sharp east wind was blowing over the jetty at the time.

"Come with me; you are cold. I know Nobbs Lane well. We have a shed and fire here on the jetty to shelter people while waiting. There, you need not fear to miss your husband, for the men won't land for a long time yet."

"May I follow you, madam?" said Miles, stepping forward and touching his cap in what he supposed to be the deferential manner of a private soldier. "I am interested in your work, and would like to see the shed you speak of."

The lady looked up quickly at the tall young soldier who thus addressed her.

"I saw you in the lobby of the Institute this morning, did I not?"

"You did, madam. I was waiting for a friend who is a frequenter of the Institute. One of your own people brought me down here to see the arrival of the *Orontes*, and the coffee-shed; but I have lost him in the crowd, and know not where the shed is."

"Here it is," returned the lady, pointing to an iron structure just behind them. "You will find Mr Brown there busy with the coffee, and that small shed beside it is the shelter-room. You are welcome to inspect all our buildings at any time."

So saying, the lady led Mrs Martin into the shed last referred to, and Miles followed her.

There was a small stove, in the solitary iron room of which the shed consisted, which diffused a genial warmth around. Several soldiers' wives and female relatives were seated beside it, engaged in quieting refractory infants, or fitting a few woollen garments on children of various ages. These garments had been brought from the Institute, chiefly for the purpose of supplying the wives and children returning from warmer climes to England;

and one of them, a thick knitted shawl, was immediately presented to Mrs Martin as a gift, and placed round her shoulders by the lady's own hands.

"You are *very* kind, Miss," she said, an unbidden tear rolling down her cheek as she surveyed the garment and folded it over her breast.

"Have you any children?" asked the lady.

"None. We had one—a dear baby boy," answered the young wife sadly, "born after his father left England. God took him home when he was two years old. His father never saw him; but we shall all meet again," she added, brightly, "in the better land."

"Ah! it makes me glad to hear you say that God took him *home*. Only the spirit of Jesus could make you regard heaven as the home where you are all to meet again. Now I would advise you to sit here and keep warm till I go and make inquiry about your husband. It is quite possible, you know, that he may be in the sick bay, and they won't let any one on board till the vessel is made fast. You are quite sure, I suppose, that it was the *Orontes* in which your husband said he was coming?"

"Yes, quite sure."

The lady had asked the question because a vague fear possessed her regarding the cause of the soldier's not having been seen looking eagerly over the side like the other men.

Hurrying from the shed, with her basket on her arm, she made for the gangway, which had just been placed in position. She was accompanied by her companion, also carrying her basket. Miles took the liberty of following them closely, but not obviously, for he formed only one of a stream of men and women who pushed on board the instant that permission was given.

While one of the ladies went in search of one of the chief officers, the other quietly and unobtrusively advanced among the returning warriors, and, opening her basket, drew therefrom and offered to each soldier an envelope containing one or two booklets and texts, and a hearty invitation to make free use of the Soldiers' Institute during their stay in Portsmouth.

A most bewildering scene was presented on the deck of that great white vessel. There were hundreds of soldiers in her, returning home after longer or shorter absences in China, India, the Cape, and other far-away parts of the earth. Some were stalwart and bronzed by the southern sun; others were gaunt, weak, and cadaverous, from the effect of sickness, exposure, or wounds; but all were more or less excited at having once again set eyes on Old England, and at the near prospect of once more embracing wives, mothers, and sweethearts, and meeting with old friends. The continual noise of manly voices hailing, exclaiming, chaffing, or conversing, and the general babel of sounds is indescribable. To Miles Milton, who had never before even imagined anything of the sort, it seemed more like a vivid dream than a reality. He became so bewildered with trying to attend to everything at once that he lost sight of the shorter of the ladies, whom he was following, but, pushing ahead, soon found her again in the midst of a group of old friends—though still young soldiers—who had known the Institute before leaving for foreign service, and were eagerly inquiring after the health of Miss Robinson, and Tufnell the manager, and others.

During his progress through this bustling scene, Miles observed that the soldiers invariably received the gifts from the lady with respect, and, many of them, with hearty expressions of thanks, while a few stopped her to speak about the contents of the envelopes. So numerous were the men that the work had to be done with business-like celerity, but the visitor was experienced. While wasting no time in useless delay, she never hurried her movements, or refused to stop and speak, or forced her way through the moving throng. Almost unobserved, save by the men who chanced to be next to her, she glided in and out amongst them like a spirit of light—which, in the highest sense, she was—intent on her beneficent mission. Her sole aim was to save the men from the tremendous dangers that awaited them on landing in Portsmouth, and bring them under Christian influence.

Those dangers may be imagined when it is told that soldiers returning from abroad are often in possession of large sums of money, and that harpies of all kinds are eagerly waiting to plunder them on their arrival. On one occasion a regiment came home, and in a few days squandered three thousand pounds in Portsmouth. Much more might be said on this point, but enough has been indicated to move thoughtful minds—and our story waits.

Suddenly the attention of Miles, and every one near him, was attracted by the loud Hibernian yell of a female voice exclaiming—

"Oh, Terence, me darlin' son, here ye are; an' is it yersilf lookin' purtier a long way than the day ye left me; an' niver so much as a scratch on yer face for all the wars ye've bin in—bad luck to thim!"

Need we say that this was Mrs Flynn? In her anxiety to meet her son she had run against innumerable men and women, who remonstrated with her variously, according to temperament, without, however, the slightest effect. Her wild career was not checked until she had flung herself into the arms of a tall, stalwart trooper with drooping moustache, who would have done credit to any nationality under the sun, and whose enthusiasm at the happy meeting with his mother was almost as demonstrative as her own, but more dignified.

Others there were, however, whose case was very different. One who came there to meet the strong healthy man to whom she had said good-bye at the same spot several years before, received him back a worn and wasted invalid, upright still with the martial air of discipline, but feeble, and with something like the stamp of death upon his brow. Another woman found her son, strong indeed and healthy, as of yore, but with an empty sleeve where his right arm should have been—his days of warfare over before his earthly sun had reached the zenith!

Whilst Miles was taking note of these things, and moralising in spite of his distaste just then to that phase of mental occupation, the other lady of the Institute appeared and spoke hurriedly to her companion.

"Go," she said, "tell Mrs Martin that her husband is *not* on board the *Orontes*. Let Tufnell, if he is at the shed, or our missionary, take her up to the Institute without delay. Let them take this note to Miss Robinson at the same time."

The younger lady looked inquiringly at her companion, but the latter pushed on hurriedly and was soon lost in the crowd, so she went at once on shore to obey her instructions.

Being thus left to look after himself, Miles went about gazing at the varied, interesting, and curious scenes that the vessel presented. No one took any notice of him, for he was only one soldier among hundreds, and so many people from the shore had been admitted by that time that strange faces attracted no attention.

We have referred chiefly to soldiers' friends, but these, after all, formed a small minority of the visitors, many of whom were tradesmen of the town—tailors, shoemakers, and vendors of fancy articles—who had come down with their wares to tempt the returning voyagers to part with their superfluous cash. Even in the midst of all the pushing and confusion, one man was seen trying on a pair of boots; near to him was a sailor, carefully inspecting a tailor's book of patterns with a view to shore-going clothes; while another, more prompt in action, was already being measured for a suit of the same.

Descending to the 'tween-decks, our hero found that the confusion and noise there were naturally greater, the space being more limited and the noise confined. There was the addition of bad air and disagreeable smells here; and Miles could not help reflecting on the prospect before him of long voyages under cramped circumstances, in the midst of similar surroundings. But, being young and enthusiastic, he whispered to himself that he was not particular, and was ready to "rough it" in his country's cause!

In a remarkably dark region to which he penetrated, he found himself in the women's quarters, the disagreeables of which were increased by the cries of discontented children, and the yells of inconsolable infants — some of whom had first seen the light of this world in the sad twilight of 'tween-decks! Shrinking from that locality, Miles pursued his investigations, and gradually became aware that sundry parrots and other pets which the soldiers and sailors had brought home were adding their notes of discord to the chorus of sounds.

While he was looking at, and attempting to pat, a small monkey, which received his advances with looks of astonished indignation, he became conscious of the fact that a number of eyes were looking down on him through a crevice at the top of a partition close to his side.

"Who are these?" he asked of a sailor, who stood near him.

"Why, them are the long-term men."

"I suppose you mean prisoners?"

"Yes; that's about it," replied the tar. "Soldiers as has committed murder — or suthin' o' that sort — an' got twenty year or more for all I knows. The other fellers further on there, in chains, is short-term men. Bin an' done suthin' or other not quite so bad, I suppose."

Miles advanced "further on," and found eight men seated on the deck and leaning against the bulkhead. If his attention had not been drawn to them, he might have supposed they were merely resting, but a closer glance showed that they were all chained to an iron bar. They did not seem very different from the other men around them, save that they were, most of them, stern and silent.

A powerful feeling of compassion rose in our hero's breast as he looked at these moral wrecks of humanity; for their characters and prospects were ruined, though their physique was not much impaired. It seemed to him such an awful home-coming, after, perhaps, long years of absence, thus, in the midst of all the bustle and joy of meetings and of pleasant anticipations, to be waiting there for the arrival of the prison-van, and looking forward to years of imprisonment instead of reunion with friends and kindred.

At sight of them a thought sprang irresistibly into our hero's mind, "This is the result of wrong-doing!"

His conscience was uncomfortably active and faithful that morning. Somehow it pointed out to him that wrong-doing was a long ladder; that the chained criminals before him had reached the foot; and that he stood on the topmost rung. That was all the difference between them and himself—a difference of degree, not of principle.

Pushing his way a little closer to these men, he found that his was not the only heart that pitied them. His friend, the younger lady, was there speaking to them. He could not hear what she said, for the noise drowned her voice; but her earnest, eager look and her gesticulations told well enough that she was pointing them to the Saviour of sinners—with what effect, of course, he could not tell, but it was evident that the prisoners at least gave her their attention.

Leaving her thus engaged, Miles continued for a considerable time his progress through the ship. Afterwards he observed, by a movement among the men, that a detachment was about to land. Indeed he found that some of the soldiers had already landed, and were making their way to the coffee-shed.

Following these quickly to the same place, he found that innumerable cups of hot coffee and solid slices of bread and butter were being served out as fast as they could be filled and cut. A large hole or window opened in the side of the shed, the shutter of which was hinged at the bottom, and when let down formed a convenient counter.

Behind this counter stood the two ubiquitous ladies of the Institute acting the part of barmaids, as if to the manner born, and with the same business-like, active, yet modest, ready-for-anything air which marked all their proceedings.

And truly their post was no sinecure. To supply the demands of hundreds of hungry and thirsty warriors was not child's-play. Inside the shed, Miles found his friend Brown busy with a mighty caldron of hot water, numerous packets of coffee, and immense quantities of sugar and preserved milk. Brown was the fountain-head. The ladies were the distributing pipes— if we may say so; and although the fountain produced can after can of the coveted liquid with amazing rapidity, and with a prodigality of material that would have made the hair of a private housewife stand on end, it was barely possible to keep pace with the demand.

At a large table one of the missionaries of the Institute cut up and buttered loaves at a rate which gave the impression that he was a conjurer engaged in a species of sleight-of-hand. The butter, however, troubled him, for, the weather being cold, it was hard, and would not spread easily. To overcome this he put a pound or so of it on a plate beside the boiler-fire to soften. Unfortunately, he temporarily forgot it, and on afterwards going for it, found that it had been reduced to a yellow liquid. However, hungry soldiers, rejoicing in the fact of having at last reached home, are not particular. Some of them, unaccustomed, no doubt, to be served by ladies, asked for their supply deferentially, accepted it politely, and drank it with additional appreciation.

"We want more, Brown," said one of the ladies, glancing back over her shoulder as she poured out the last drop from her large jug; "and more buns and bread, please."

"Here you are, Miss," cried Brown, who was warm by that time in spite of the weather, as he bore his brimming and steaming pitcher to the window — or hole in the wall — and replenished the jugs. "The buns are all done, an' the bread won't hold out long, but I've sent for more; it won't be long. I see we shall need several more brews," he added, as he turned again towards the inexhaustible boiler.

"Shall I assist you?" said Miles, stepping into the shed and seizing a loaf and a knife.

"Thank you. Go ahead," said Brown.

"Put another lump of butter near the fire," said the missionary to our hero; "not too close. I melted the last lump altogether."

"A cup o' coffee for my Terence, an' wan for mesilf, my dear," exclaimed a loud voice outside.

There was no mistaking the speaker. Some of the men who crowded round the counter laughed, others partially choked, when the strapping Terence said in a hoarse whisper, "Whist, mother, be civil; don't ye see that it's ladies, no less, is sarvin' of us?"

"Please, ma'am, can I 'ave some coffee?" asked a modest soldier's wife, who looked pale and weary after the long voyage, with three children to look after.

A cup was promptly supplied, and three of the newly-arrived buns stopped the mouths of her clamorous offspring.

"Can ye give me a cup o' tea?" demanded another soldier's wife, who was neither so polite nor so young as the previous applicant.

It is probable that the ladies did not observe the nature of her demand, else they would doubtless have explained that they had no tea, but a cup of coffee was silently handed to her.

"Ah! this is *real* home-tea, this is," she said, smacking her lips after the first sip. "A mighty difference 'tween this an' what we've bin used to in the ship."

"Yes, indeed," assented her companion. Whether it was tea she had been accustomed to drink on board the troop-ship we cannot tell, but probably she was correct as to the "mighty difference." It may be that the beverages supplied in foreign lands had somewhat damaged the power of discrimination as to matters of taste in these soldiers' wives. At all events an incident which occurred about the same time justifies this belief.

"Mr Miles," said the missionary, pausing a moment to wipe his brow in the midst of his labours, "will you fetch the butter now?"

Miles turned to obey with alacrity—with too much alacrity, indeed, for in his haste he knocked the plate over, and sent the lump of butter into the last prepared "brew" of coffee!

"Hallo! I say!" exclaimed Brown, in consternation. "More coffee, Brown," demanded the ladies simultaneously, at that inauspicious moment.

"Yes, Miss, I—I'm coming—directly," cried Brown.

"Do be quick, please!"

"What's to be done?" said Brown, making futile endeavours to fish out the slippery mass with the stirring-stick.

"Shove it down and stir it well about," suggested Miles.

Whether conscience was inoperative at that moment we know not, but Brown acted on the suggestion, and briskly amalgamated the butter with the coffee, while the crowd at the port-hole politely but continuously demanded more.

"Don't be in a 'urry, Tom," cried a corporal, removing his pith helmet in order to run his fingers through his hair; "it's a 'eavenly state o' things now to what it was a few years ago, w'en we an' our poor wives 'ad to sit 'ere for hours in the heat or cold, wet or dry, without shelter, or a morsel to eat, or a drop to drink, till we got away up town to the grog-shops."

"Well, this *is* civilisation at last!" remarked a handsome and hearty young fellow, who had apparently been ignorant of the treat in store for him, and who sauntered up to the shed just as the butter-brew was beginning to be served out.

"Why, I declare, it's chocolate!" exclaimed one of the women, who had been already served with a cup, and had resolved to "go in," as she said, for another pennyworth.

"So it is. My! ain't it nice?" said her companion, smacking her lips.

Whether the soldiers fell into the same mistake, or were too polite to take notice of it, we cannot tell, for they drank it without comment, and with evident satisfaction, like men of simple tastes and uncritical minds.

We turn now to a very different scene.

In one of the private sitting-rooms of the Institute sat poor young Mrs Martin, the very embodiment of blank despair. The terrible truth that her husband had died, and been buried at sea, had been gently and tenderly broken to her by Miss Robinson.

At first the poor girl could not—would not—believe it. Then, as the truth gradually forced itself into her brain, she subsided into a tearless, expressionless, state of quiescence that seemed to indicate a mind unhinged. In this state she remained for some time, apparently unconscious of the kind words of Christian love that were addressed to her.

At last she seemed to rouse herself and gazed wildly round the room.

"Let me go," she said. "I will find him somewhere. Don't hinder me, please."

"But you cannot go anywhere till you have had food and rest, dear child," said her sympathetic comforter, laying her hand gently on the girl's arm. "Come with me."

She sought to lead her away, but the girl shook her off.

"No," she exclaimed, starting up hastily, so that the mass of her dark hair fell loose upon her shoulders, contrasting forcibly with the dead whiteness of her face and lips. "No. I cannot go with you. Fred will be getting impatient. D'you think I'll ever believe it? Dead and buried in the sea? Never!"

Even while she spoke, the gasp in her voice, and the pressure of both hands on her poor heart, told very plainly that the young widow did indeed believe it.

"Oh! may God Himself comfort you, dear child," said the lady, taking her softly by the hand. "Come—come with me."

Mrs Martin no longer refused. Her spirit, which had flashed up for a moment, seemed to collapse, and without another word of remonstrance she meekly suffered herself to be guided to a private room, where she was put to bed.

She never rose from that bed. Friendless, and without means, she would probably have perished in the streets, or in one of the dens of Portsmouth, had she not been led to this refuge. As it was, they nursed her there, and did all that human skill and Christian love could devise; but her heart was broken. Towards the end she told them, in a faint voice, that her Fred had been stationed at Alexandria, and that while there he had been led to put his trust in the Saviour. She knew nothing of the details. All these, and much more, she had expected to hear from his own lips.

"But he will tell me all about it soon, thank God!" were the last words she uttered as she turned her eyes gratefully on the loving strangers who had found and cared for her in the dark day of her calamity.

Chapter Five-Difficulties met and overcome

Miles and his friend Brown, after their work at the jetty, had chanced to return to the Institute at the moment referred to in the last chapter, when the poor young widow, having become resigned, had been led through the passage to her bedroom. Our hero happened to catch sight of her face, and it made a very powerful impression on him—an impression which was greatly deepened afterwards on hearing of her death.

In the reception-room he found Armstrong still in earnest conversation with his wife.

"Hallo, Armstrong! still here? Have you been sitting there since I left you?" he asked, with a smile and look of surprise.

"Oh no!" answered his friend; "not all the time. We have been out walking about town, and we have had dinner here—an excellent feed, let me tell you, and cheap too. But where did you run off to?"

"Sit down and I'll tell you," said Miles.

Thereupon he related all about his day's experiences. When he had finished, Armstrong told him that his own prospect of testing the merits of a troop-ship were pretty fair, as he was ordered for inspection on the following day.

"So you see," continued the young soldier, "if you are accepted—as you are sure to be—you and I will go out together in the same vessel."

"I'm glad to hear that, anyhow," returned Miles.

"And *I* am very glad too," said little Emily, with a beaming smile, "for Willie has told me about you, Mr Miles; and how you first met and took a fancy to each other; and it *will* be so nice to think that there's somebody to care about my Willie when he is far away from me."

The little woman blushed and half-laughed, and nearly cried as she said this, for she felt that it was rather a bold thing to say to a stranger, and yet she had such a strong desire to mitigate her husband's desolation when absent from her that she forcibly overcame her modesty. "And I want you to do me a favour, Mr Miles," she added.

"I'll do it with pleasure," returned our gallant hero.

"I want you to call him Willie," said the little woman, blushing and looking down.

"Certainly I will—if your husband permits me."

"You see," she continued, "I want him to keep familiar with the name I've been used to call him—for comrades will call him Armstrong, I suppose, and—"

"Oh! Emmy," interrupted the soldier reproachfully, "do you think I require to be *kept in remembrance* of that name? Won't your voice, repeating it, haunt me day and night till the happy day when I meet you again on the Portsmouth jetty, or may-hap in this very room?"

Miles thought, when he heard this speech, of the hoped-for meeting between poor Mrs Martin and her Fred; and a feeling of profound sadness crept over him as he reflected how many chances there were against their ever again meeting in this world. Naturally these thoughts turned his mind to his own case. His sinful haste in quitting home, and the agony of his mother on finding that he was really gone, were more than ever impressed on him, but again the fatal idea that what was done could not be undone, coupled with pride and false shame, kept him firm to his purpose.

That evening, in barracks, Miles was told by his company sergeant to hold himself in readiness to appear before the doctor next morning for inspection as to his physical fitness for active service in Egypt.

Our hero was by this time beginning to find out that the life of a private soldier, into which he had rushed, was a very different thing indeed from that of an officer—to which he had aspired. Here again pride came to his aid—in a certain sense,—for if it could not reconcile him to his position, it at all events closed his mouth, and made him resolve to bear the consequences of his act like a man.

In the morning he had to turn out before daylight, and with a small band of men similarly situated, to muster in the drill-shed a little after eight. Thence they marched to the doctor's quarters.

It was an anxious ordeal for all of them; for, like most young soldiers, they were enthusiastically anxious to go on active service, and there was, of course, some uncertainty as to their passing the examination.

The first man called came out of the inspection room with a beaming countenance, saying that he was "all right," which raised the hopes and spirits of the rest; but the second appeared after inspection with a woe-begone countenance which required no interpretation. No reason was given for his rejection; he was simply told that it would be better for him not to go.

Miles was the third called.

As he presented himself, the doctor yawned vociferously, as if he felt that the hour for such work was unreasonably early. Then he looked at his subject with the critical air of a farmer inspecting a prize ox.

"How old are you?" he asked.

"Nineteen, sir."

"Are you married?"

Miles smiled.

"Did you hear me?" asked the doctor sharply. "You don't need to smile. Many a boy as long-legged and as young as you is fool enough to marry. Are you married?"

Miles flushed, looked suddenly stern, squared his shoulders, drew himself up with an air that implied, "You won't catch *me* tripping again;" and said firmly, yet quite respectfully —

"No, sir."

The doctor here took another good look at his subject, with a meaning twinkle in his eye, as if he felt that he had touched a tender point. Then he felt his victim's pulse, sounded his chest, and ordered him to strip. Being apparently satisfied with the result of his examination, he asked him if he "felt all right."

Reflecting that his mother had often told him he was made up of body, soul, and spirit, and that in regard to the latter two he was rather hazy, Miles felt strongly inclined for a moment to say, "Certainly not," but, thinking better of it, he answered, "Yes, sir," with decision.

"Have you anything to complain of?" asked the doctor.

The mind of our hero was what we may style rapidly reflective. In regard to the decrees of Fate, things in general, and his father's conduct in particular, he had a decided wish to complain, but again he laid restraint on himself and said, "No, sir."

"And do you wish to go to Egypt?"

"Yes, sir!" was answered with prompt decision.

"Then you may go," said the doctor, turning away with an air of a man who dismisses a subject from his mind.

When all the men had thus passed the medical examination, those of them who were accepted mustered their bags and kits before Captain

Lacey, commander of the company to which they were attached, and those who wanted anything were allowed to draw it from the stores.

Captain Lacey was a fine specimen of a British soldier—grave, but kind in expression and in heart; tall, handsome, powerful, about thirty years of age, with that urbanity of manner which wins affection at first sight, and that cool, quiet decision of character which inspires unlimited confidence.

As the troop-ship which was to convey them to Egypt was to start sooner than had been intended, there was little time for thought during the few hours in England that remained to the regiment. The men had to draw their pith helmets, and fit the ornaments thereon; then go the quartermaster's stores to be fitted with white clothing, after which they had to parade before the Colonel, fully arrayed in the martial habiliments which were needful in tropical climes. Besides these matters there were friends to be seen, in some cases relatives to be parted from, and letters innumerable to be written. Miles Milton was among those who, on the last day in Portsmouth, attempted to write home. He had been taken by Sergeant Gilroy the previous night to one of the Institute entertainments in the great hall. The Sergeant had tried to induce him to go to the Bible-class with him, but Miles was in no mood for that at the time, and he was greatly relieved to find that neither the Sergeant nor any of the people of the Institute annoyed him by thrusting religious matters on his attention. Food, lodging, games, library, baths, Bible-classes, prayer-meetings, entertainments were all there to be used or let alone as he chose; perfect freedom of action being one of the methods by which it was sought to render the place attractive to the soldiers.

But although Miles at once refused to go to the class, he had no objection to go to the entertainment.

It was a curious mixture of song, recitation, addresses, and readings, in which many noble sentiments were uttered, and not a few humorous anecdotes and incidents related. It was presided over by Tufnell, the manager, a soldierly-looking man, who had himself originally been in the army, and who had, for many years, been Miss Robinson's right-hand man. There could not have been fewer than a thousand people in the hall, a large proportion of whom were red-coats and blue-jackets, the rest being civilians; and the way in which these applauded the sentiments, laughed at the humour, and rejoiced in the music, showed that the provision for their amusement was thoroughly appreciated.

Whether it was the feeling of good-fellowship and sympathy that pervaded the meeting, or some word that was dropped at a venture and found root in his heart, Miles could not tell, but certain it is that at that entertainment he formed the resolution to write home before leaving. Not that he had yet repented of the step he had taken, but he was sorry for the manner in which he had done so, and for allowing so much time to elapse that now the opportunity of seeing his parents before starting was lost.

As it was impossible for him to write his letter in the noise of the barrack-room, he went off next day to the reading-room of the Institute, and there, with no other sounds to disturb him than the deep breathing of some studious red-coats, and the chirping pen of a comrade engaged like himself, he began to write.

But his thoughts somehow would not work. His pen would not write. He even fancied that it had a sort of objection to spell. So it had, when not properly guided by his hesitating hand. The first part went swimmingly enough:—

"Dearest mother,
I'm so sorry—"

But here he stopped, for the memory of his father's severity re-aroused his indignation, and he felt some doubt as to whether he really was sorry. Then, under the impulse of this doubt, he wrote a long letter, in imagination, in which he defended his conduct pretty warmly, on the ground that he had been driven to it.

"Driven to what?" asked Something within him. "To the course which I have taken and am now defending," replied Something-else within him hotly.

"Then the course was a wrong one, else you wouldn't have to defend it!" rejoined the first Something.

"Well—yes—n–no, it wasn't," returned the second Something doggedly.

Before this internal dispute could be carried further, Miles was aroused by a sudden burst of noisy voices, as if a lunatic asylum had been let loose into the hall below. Rising quickly, he hurried down with his studious comrades to see what it could be all about.

"It's only another troop-ship come in, and they've all come up here without giving us warning to get ready," said Tufnell, as he bustled about, endeavouring to introduce order into what appeared to Miles to be the reproduction of Babel, *minus* the bricks.

The fact was that a troop-ship having arrived rather suddenly, a sergeant had driven up in hot haste from the docks to make arrangements for the reception of the soldiers' wives and children!

"Look sharp!" he cried, on entering the hall abruptly; "sixteen families are on their way to you."

"All right; we can take 'em in," was the prompt reply; and orders were given to set the food-producing machinery of the establishment instantly in motion. But almost before the preparation had fairly begun, the advance-guard of the army, largely composed of infantry, burst upon them like a thunder-clap, and continued to pour in like a torrent. There were men shouting, women chattering, tired children whining, and excited children laughing; babies yelling or crowing miscellaneously; parrots screaming; people running up and down stairs in search of dormitories; plates and cups clattering at the bar, as the overwhelmed barmaids did their best to appease the impatient and supply the hungry; while the rumbling of control-wagons bringing up the baggage formed a sort of bass accompaniment to the concert.

"You see, it varies with us a good deal," remarked Brown to Miles, during a lucid interval, "Sometimes we are almost empty, a few hours later we are overflowing. It comes hard on the housekeeper, of course. But we lay our account wi' that, and, do you know, it is wonderful what can be done in trying circumstances, when we lay our account wi' them! — Yes, Miss, it's all ready!" shouted the speaker, in reply to a soft female voice that came down the wide staircase, as it were, over the heads of the turbulent crowd.

In a moment he disappeared, and Tufnell stood, as if by magic, in his place.

"Yes," said the manager, taking up his discourse where the other had left off; "and in a few minutes you'll see that most of these wives and children of the soldiers will be distributed through the house in their bed-rooms, when our ladies will set to work to make acquaintance with them; and then we'll open our stores of warm clothing, of which the poor things, coming as they do from warm climates, are often nearly or quite destitute."

"But where do you get these supplies from?" asked Miles.

"From kind-hearted Christians throughout the country, who send us gifts of old and new garments, boots and shoes, shawls and socks, etcetera, which we have always in readiness to meet sudden demands; and I may add that the demands are pretty constant. Brown told you just now that we have varied experience. I remember once we got a message from the Assistant Quartermaster-General's office to ask how many women and children we could accommodate, as a shipful was expected. We replied that we could take 140, and set to work with preparations. After all, only one woman came! To-day we expected nobody, and—you see what we have got!"

The genial countenance of the manager beamed with satisfaction. It was evident that "what he had got" did not at all discompose him, as he hurried away to look after his flock, while the originator—the heart and soul of all this—although confined to her room at that time with spine complaint, and unable to take part in the active work, as she had been wont to do in years gone by, heard in her chamber the softened sound of the human storm, and was able to thank God that her Soldiers' Institute was fulfilling its destiny.

"Hallo! Miles!" exclaimed Armstrong, over the heads of the crowd; "I've been looking for you everywhere. D'you know we run a chance of being late? Come along, quick!"

Our hero, who, in his interest in the scene, had forgotten the flight of time, hurried out after his comrade as the band struck up "Home, sweet Home," and returned to barracks, utterly oblivious of the fact that he had left the unfinished letter to his mother on the table in the reading-room.

Chapter Six-The Unfinished Letter—Too Late!

Next morning young Milton—or, as he was called by his comrades, John Miles—rose with the depressing thought that it was to be his last day in England. As he was dressing, it flashed across him that he had left his unfinished letter on the reading-room table, and, concluding that it would be swept away in the rush of people there—at all events that, not having been folded or addressed, it could not be posted—his depression was deepened.

The first thing that roused him to a better frame of mind was the smell of tea!

Most people are more or less familiar with teapots; with the few teaspoonfuls of the precious leaf which thrifty housekeepers put into these pots, and the fragrant liquid that results. But who among civilians, (save the informed), can imagine a barrack-room teapot?

Open your ears, O ye thrifty ones! while we state a few facts, and there will be no need to tell you to open your eyes.

Into the teapot which supplied Miles with his morning cup there was put, for *one* making, eight pounds of tea!—not ounces, observe, but pounds,—twenty-nine pounds of sugar, and six gallons—an absolute cowful—of milk! The pot itself consisted of eight enormous coppers, which were filled with boiling water to the brim.

"Yes, sir," remarked the military cook, who concocted the beverage, to a speechless visitor one day; "it *is* a pretty extensive brew; but then, you see, we have a large family!"

A considerable portion of this large family was soon actively engaged in preparation for immediate embarkation for Egypt. Then the General made the men a farewell speech. It was a peculiar speech—not altogether suited to cheer timid hearts, had any such been there, but admirably adapted to British soldiers.

"Men," said he, "I am very glad to see you parade looking so well and clean and comfortable and ready for active service. You will be dirty enough, sometimes, where you are going, for the country is hot and unhealthy, and not over clean. You will have hardships, hard times, and plenty of hard work, as well as hard beds now and then, and very likely the most of you will never come back again; but you would be unworthy of the name of British soldiers if you allowed such thoughts to trouble your minds. I sincerely express the hope, however, that you will all come home again safe and sound. I have not the slightest doubt that every man of you will do his duty in the field faithfully and well; but I'm not so sure of your wisdom in camp and barracks, so I will give you a word of advice. There is far more danger in getting drunk in hot countries than in England. Let me advise you, then, not to get drunk; and I would warn you particularly against the vile stuff they will offer for sale in Egypt. It is rank poison. If you had stomachs lined with brass you might perhaps stand it—not otherwise. Then I would warn you against the sun. In Egypt the sun is sometimes like a fiery furnace. Never expose yourself when you can avoid doing so, and, above all, never go outside your tents without your helmets on. If you do, you'll repent it, and repentance will probably come too late. I wish you all a prosperous voyage, and may God keep you all!"

Delivered in a sharp, stern, unsentimental tone, this brief speech had probably a much more powerful effect on the men than a more elaborate exhortation would have had. The impression was deepened by the remarks of an old officer, who made a very brief, soldierly speech after the General, winding up with the information that he had himself been in Egypt, and assuring them that if they did not take care of themselves there was little chance of a man of them returning alive!

"May you have a pleasant passage out," he said, in conclusion; "and, in the name of the Portsmouth Division, I wish you victory in all your battles, and a hearty good-bye."

The men who were not going away were then called on to give their departing friends three cheers, which they did with right good-will. Captain Lacey, who was in charge of the detachment, stepped to the front, drew his sword, gave the order to shoulder arms, form fours, right turn, quick march, and away they went with the united bands of two regiments playing "The girl I left behind me!"

The girls they were about to leave behind them were awaiting them at the barrack-gates, with a considerable sprinkling of somewhat older girls to keep them company. Many of the poor creatures were in tears for the men whom they might never see again, and lumps in several manly throats rather interfered with the parting cheer delivered by the detachment at the gate. Most of them accompanied the soldiers as far as the Dockyard gates. Emily Armstrong was not among them. She had parted the previous night from her husband at his earnest request, and returned by rail to her father's house, there to await, as patiently as she might, the return of her "Willie."

"Noble defenders of our country!" observed an enthusiastic citizen, as they passed through the gates.

"Food for powder," remarked a sarcastic publican, as he turned away to resume his special work of robbing powder of its food and his country of its defenders.

Proceeding to the Embarkation Jetty, the detachment was marched on board the troop-ship, where the men were at once told off to their respective messes, and proceeded without delay to make themselves at home by taking possession of their allotted portion of the huge white-painted fabric that was to bear them over the waves to distant lands.

Taking off their belts and stowing them overhead, they got hold of their bags, exchanged their smart uniforms for old suits of clothes, and otherwise prepared themselves for the endurance of life on board a transport.

To his great satisfaction, Miles found that several of the comrades for whom he had by that time acquired a special liking were appointed to the same mess with himself. Among these were his friend Willie Armstrong, Sergeants Gilroy and Hardy, Corporal Flynn, a private named Gaspard Redgrave, who was a capital musician, and had a magnificent tenor voice, Robert Macleod, a big-boned Scotsman, and Moses Pyne, a long-legged, cadaverous nondescript, who was generally credited with being half-mad, though with a good deal of method in his madness, and who was possessed of gentleness of spirit, and a cheerful readiness to oblige, which seemed a flat contradiction of his personal appearance, and rendered him a general favourite.

While these were busy arranging their quarters a soldier passed with several books in his hand, which he had just received from one of the ladies from the Institute.

"Hallo, Jack!" cried Moses Pyne; "have the ladies been aboard?"

"Of course they have. They've been all over the ship already distributin' books an' good-byes. If you want to see 'em you'll have to look sharp, Moses, for they're just goin' on shore."

"See 'em!" echoed Moses; "of course I wants to see 'em. But for them, I'd be—"

The rest of the sentence was lost in the clatter of Moses' feet as he stumbled up the ladder-way. Remembering his letter at that moment, Miles followed him, and reached the gangway just as the visitors were leaving.

"Excuse me," he said to one of them, stopping her.

"Oh! I'm so glad to have found you," she said.

"I have been looking for you everywhere. Miss Robinson sent you this little parcel of books, with her best wishes, and hopes that you will read them."

"Thanks, very much. I will, with pleasure. And will you do me a favour? I left a letter on the reading-room table—"

A sudden and peremptory order of some sort caused a rush which separated Miles from the visitor and cut short the sentence, and the necessity for the immediate departure of all visitors rendered its being finished impossible.

But Miss Robinson's representative did not require to be told that a forgotten letter could only want posting. On returning, therefore, to the Institute, she went at once to the reading-room, where she found no letter! Making inquiry, she learned from one of the maids that a sheet of paper had been found with nothing on it but the words, "Dearest mother, I'm so sorry"; and that the same had been duly conveyed to Miss Robinson's room. Hasting to the apartment of her friend, she knocked, and was bidden enter.

"You have got an unfinished letter, it seems?" she began.

"Yes; here it is," interrupted Miss Robinson, handing the sheet to her assistant. "What a pity that it gives no clew to the writer—no address!"

"I am pretty sure as to the writer," returned the other. "It must have been that fine-looking young soldier, John Miles, of whom we have seen a little and heard so much from Sergeant Gilroy."

Hereupon an account was given of the hurried and interrupted meeting on board the troop-ship; and the two ladies came to the conclusion that as nothing was known about the parents or former residence of John Miles no steps of any kind were possible. The letter was therefore carefully put by.

That same evening there alighted at the railway station in Portsmouth an elderly lady with an expression of great anxiety on her countenance, and much perturbation in her manner.

"Any luggage, ma'am?" asked a sympathetic porter—for railway porters are sometimes more sympathetic than might be expected of men so much accustomed to witness abrupt and tender partings.

"No; no luggage. Yes—a small valise—in the carriage. That's it."

"Four-wheeler, ma'am?"

"Eh! no—yes—yes."

"Where to, ma'am?" asked the sympathetic porter, after the lady was seated in the cab.

"Where to?" echoed Mrs Milton, (for it was she), in great distress. "Oh! where — where shall I drive to?"

"Really, ma'am, I couldn't say," answered the porter, with a modest look.

"I've — I — my son! My dear boy! Where shall I go to inquire? Oh! what *shall* I do?"

These would have been perplexing utterances even to an unsympathetic man.

Turning away from the window, and looking up at the driver, the porter said solemnly —

"To the best 'otel you know of, cabby, that's not too dear. An' if you've bin gifted with compassion, cabby, don't overcharge your fare."

Accepting the direction, and exercising his discretion as well as his compassion, that intelligent cabby drove, strange to say, straight to an hotel styled the "Officers' House," which is an offshoot of Miss Robinson's Institute, and stands close beside it!

"A hofficer's lady," said the inventive cabby to the boy who opened the door. "Wants to putt up in this 'ere 'ouse."

When poor Mrs Milton had calmed her feelings sufficiently to admit of her talking with some degree of coherence, she rang the bell and sent for the landlord.

Mr Tufnell, who was landlord of the Officers' House, as well as manager of the Institute, soon presented himself, and to him the poor lady confided her sorrows.

"You see, landlord," she said, whimpering, "I don't know a soul in Portsmouth; and — and — in fact I don't even know how I came to your hotel, for I never heard of it before; but I think I must have been sent here, for I see from your looks that you will help me."

"You may depend on my helping you to the best of my power, madam. May I ask what you would have me do?"

With much earnestness, and not a few tears, poor Mrs Milton related as much of her son's story as she thought necessary.

"Well, you could not have come to a better place," said Tufnell, "for Miss Robinson and all her helpers sympathise deeply with soldiers. If any one can find out about your son, *they* can. How were you led to suspect that he had come to Portsmouth?"

"A friend suggested that he might possibly have done so. Indeed, it seems natural, considering my dear boy's desire to enter the army, and the number of soldiers, who are always passing through this town."

"Well, I will go at once and make inquiry. The name Milton is not familiar to me, but so many come and go that we sometimes forget names."

When poor Mrs Milton was afterwards introduced to Miss Robinson, she found her both sympathetic and anxious to do her utmost to gain information about her missing son, but the mother's graphic descriptions of him did not avail much. The fact that he was young, tall, handsome, curly-haired, etcetera, applied to so many of the defenders of the country as to be scarcely distinctive enough; but when she spoke of "My dear Miles," a new light was thrown on the matter. She was told that a young soldier answering to the description of her son had been there recently, but that his surname — not his Christian name — was Miles. Would she recognise his handwriting?

"Recognise it?" exclaimed Mrs Milton, in a blaze of sudden hope. "Ay, that I would; didn't I teach him every letter myself? Didn't he insist on making his down-strokes crooked? and wasn't my heart almost broken over his square O's?"

While the poor mother was speaking, the unfinished letter was laid before her, and the handwriting at once recognised.

"That's his! Bless him! And he's sorry. Didn't I say he would be sorry? Didn't I tell his father so? Darling Miles, I — "

Here the poor creature broke down, and wept at the thought of her repentant son. It was well, perhaps, that the blow was thus softened, for she almost fell on the floor when her new friend told her, in the gentlest possible manner, that Miles had that very day set sail for Egypt.

They kept her at the Institute that night, however, and consoled her much, as well as aroused her gratitude, by telling of the good men who formed part of her son's regiment; and of the books and kind words that had been bestowed on him at parting; and by making the most they could of the good hope that the fighting in Egypt would soon be over, and that her son would ere long return to her, God willing, sound and well.

Chapter Seven-Miles begins to discover himself—Has a few Rough Experiences—And falls into Pea-Soup, Salt-Water, and Love

While his mother was hunting for him in Portsmouth, Miles Milton was cleaving his way through the watery highway of the world, at the rate of fifteen knots.

He was at the time in that lowest condition of misery, mental and physical, which is not unfrequently the result of "a chopping sea in the Channel." It seemed to him, just then, an unbelievable mystery how he could, at any time, have experienced pleasure at the contemplation of food! The heaving of the great white ship was nothing to the heaving—well, it may perhaps be wiser to refrain from particulars; but he felt that the beating of the two thousand horse-power engines—more or less—was child's-play to the throbbing of his brain!

"And this," he thought, in the bitterness of his soul, "this is what I have sacrificed home, friends, position, prospects in life for! This is—soldiering!"

The merest shadow of the power to reason—if such a shadow had been left—might have convinced him that that was *not* soldiering; that, as far as it went, it was not even sailoring!

"You're very bad, I fear," remarked a gentle voice at the side of his hammock.

Miles looked round. It was good-natured, lanky, cadaverous Moses Pyne.

"Who told you I was bad?" asked Miles savagely, putting a wrong— but too true—interpretation on the word.

"The colour of your cheeks tells me, poor fellow!"

"Bah!" exclaimed Miles. He was too sick to say more. He might have said less with advantage.

"Shall I fetch you some soup?" asked Moses, in the kindness of his heart. Moses, you see, was one of those lucky individuals who are born with an incapacity to be sick at sea, and was utterly ignorant of the cruelty he perpetrated. "Or some lobscouse?" he added.

"Go away!" gasped Miles.

"A basin of—"

Miles exploded, literally as well as metaphorically, and Moses retired.

"Strange," thought that healthy soldier, as he stalked away on further errands of mercy, stooping as he went to avoid beams—"strange that Miles is so changeable in character. I had come to think him a steady, reliable sort of chap."

Puzzling over this difficulty, he advanced to the side of another hammock, from which heavy groans were issuing.

"Are you very bad, corporal?" he asked in his usual tone of sympathy.

"Bad is it?" said Flynn. "Och! it's worse nor bad I am! Couldn't ye ax the captin to heave-to for a—"

The suggestive influence of heaving-to was too much for Flynn. He pulled up dead. After a few moments he groaned—

"Arrah! be off, Moses, av ye don't want my fist on yer nose."

"Extraordinary!" murmured the kindly man, as he removed to another hammock, the occupant of which was differently constituted.

"Moses," he said, as the visitant approached.

"Yes, Gaspard," was the eager reply, "can I do anything for you?"

"Yes; if you'd go on deck, refresh yourself with a walk, and leave us all alone, you'll con—fer—on—"

Gaspard ceased to speak; he had already spoken too much; and Moses Pyne, still wondering, quietly took his advice.

But if the Channel was bad, the Bay of Biscay was, according to Flynn, "far badder."

Before reaching that celebrated bay, however, most of the men had recovered, and, with more or less lugubrious aspects and yellow-green complexions, were staggering about, attending to their various duties. No doubt their movements about the vessel were for some time characterised by that disagreement between action and will which is sometimes observed in feeble chickens during a high wind, but, on the whole, activity and cheerfulness soon began to re-animate the frames and spirits of Britain's warriors.

And now Miles Milton began to find out, as well as to fix, in some degree, his natural character. Up to this period in his life, a mild existence in a quiet home, under a fairly good though irascible father and a loving

Christian mother, had not afforded him much opportunity of discovering what he was made of. Recent events had taught him pretty sharply that there was much room for improvement. He also discovered that he possessed a very determined will in the carrying out of his intentions, especially when those intentions were based upon his desires. Whether he would be equally resolute in carrying out intentions that did *not* harmonise with his desires remained to be seen.

His mother, among her other teachings, had often tried to impress on his young mind the difference between obstinacy and firmness.

"My boy," she was wont to say, while smoothing his curly head, "don't mistake obstinacy for firmness. A man who says 'I *will* do this or that in spite of all the world,' against advice, and simply because he *wants* to do it, is obstinate. A man who says, 'I *will* do this or that in spite of all the world,' against advice, against his own desires, and simply because it is the right thing to do, is firm."

Remembering this, and repenting bitterly his having so cruelly forsaken his mother, our hero cast about in his mind how best he could put some of her precepts into practice, as being the only consolation that was now possible to him. You see, the good seed sown in those early days was beginning to spring up in unlikely circumstances. Of course the habit of prayer, and reading a few verses from the Bible night and morning, recurred to him. This had been given up since he left home. He now resumed it, though, for convenience, he prayed while stretched in his hammock!

But this did not satisfy him. He must needs undertake some disagreeable work, and carry it out with that degree of obstinacy which would amount to firmness. After mature consideration, he sought and obtained permission to become one of the two cooks to his mess. Moses Pyne was the other.

Nothing, he felt, could be more alien to his nature, more disgusting in every way to his feelings — and he was right. His dislike to the duties seemed rather to increase than to diminish day by day. Bitterly did he repent of having undertaken the duty, and earnestly did he consider whether there might not be some possible and honourable way of drawing back, but he discovered none; and soon he proved — to himself as well as to others — that he did indeed possess, at least in some degree, firmness of character.

The duties that devolved on him were trying. He had to scrub and keep the mess clean and tidy; to draw all the provisions and prepare them for cooking; then, to take them to the galley, and fetch them when cooked. That this last was no simple matter, such as any shore-going tail-coated waiter might undertake, was brought forcibly out one day during what seamen style dirty weather.

It was raining at the time. The sea was grey, the sky was greyer, and as the steamer itself was whitey-grey, it was a grave business altogether.

"Is the soup ready, Moses?" asked Miles, as he ascended towards the deck and met his *confrère* coming down.

"I don't know. Shall I go an' see?"

"No; you can go and look after the table. I will fetch the soup."

"A nasty sea on," remarked a voice, which sounded familiar in Miles's ears as he stepped on deck.

"Hallo! Jack Molloy!" he exclaimed, catching hold of a stanchion to steady himself, as a tremendous roll of the vessel caused a sea to flash over the side and send a shower-bath in his face. "What part of the sky did you drop from? I thought I had left you snug in the *Sailors' Welcome*."

"Werry likely you did, John Miles," answered the tar, balancing himself with perfect ease, and caring no more for spray than if he had been a dolphin; "but I'm here for all that—one o' the crew o' this here transport, though I means to wolunteer for active sarvice when I gets out. An' no wonder we didn't come across each other sooner! In sitch a enormous tubful o' lobsters, etceterer, it's a wonder we've met at all. An' p'r'aps you've bin a good deal under hatches since you come a-boord?"

Molloy said this with a knowing look and a grin. Miles met the remark in a similar spirit.

"Yes, Jack, I've been paying tribute to Neptune lately."

"You looks like it, Miles, judgin' by the colour o' your jib. Where away now?"

"Going for our soup."

"What! made you cook o' the mess?"

"Ay; don't you wish you were me?"

Another roll and flash of spray ended the conversation and separated the friends.

The pea-soup was ready when our hero reached the galley. Having filled the mess-tureen with the appetising mixture, he commenced the return journey with great care, for he was now dependent entirely on his legs, both hands being engaged. Miles was handy, if we may say so, with his legs. Once or twice he had to rush and thrust a shoulder against the bulwarks, and a dash of spray served for salt to the soup; but he was progressing favourably and had traversed full three-quarters of the distance to the hatch when a loud "Hooroo!" caused him to look round smartly.

He had just time to see Corporal Flynn, who had slipped and fallen, come rolling towards him like a sack of flour. Next moment he was swept off his legs, and went into the lee scuppers with his comrade in a bath of pea-soup and salt-water!

Fortunately, the obliging wave which came in-board at the same moment mingled with the soup, and saved both men from a scalding.

Such mishaps, however, were rare, and they served rather to enliven the voyage than otherwise.

Besides the duties already mentioned, our hero had to wash up all the dishes and other things at meal-hours; to polish up the mess-kettles and tin dishes; and, generally, to put things away in their places, and keep things in apple-pie order. Recollecting another of his mother's teachings—"Whatever is worth doing at all is worth doing well"—he tried his best, and was so ably seconded by the amiable Moses, that the Miles-Moses mess came to be at last regarded as the best-kept one on board.

One morning, after clearing up the dishes and putting things in order, Miles went on deck for a little fresh air. On the way up he met an elderly gentleman whose dress proclaimed him a clergyman.

He looked earnestly at our hero, and, nodding kindly, spoke a few words to him in passing. Miles had been aware that there was a clergyman on board going out to Egypt with his family—whether in connection with the troops or for health he did not know. He was much impressed with the looks and expression of this man. It seemed to him as if there were some sort of attractive power about him which was unaccountably strong, and he felt quite interested in the prospect of hearing him preach on the following Sunday.

While on deck the previous day, he had seen the figures of two ladies, whom he rightly judged to be the family above referred to, but as there was nearly the whole distance of the ship's length between them, he could not distinguish their faces.

On taking his place when Sunday came, he observed that the family were present, seated, however, in such a position that he could only see their backs. Speculating in a listless way as to what sort of faces they had, he whiled away the few minutes before the service began.

He was recalled from this condition by the tones of the clergyman's voice, which seemed to have the same effect on him as his look and manner had the day they first met. During the sermon Miles's attention was riveted, insomuch that he almost forgot where he was. The text was a familiar one—"God is Love,"—but the treatment of it seemed entirely new: the boundless nature of that love; its incomprehensible and almighty force; its enduring certainty and its overwhelming immensity, embracing, as it did, the whole universe in Christ, were themes on which the preacher expatiated in a way that Miles had never before dreamed of.

"All subordinate love," said the preacher, in concluding, "has its source in this. No wonder, then, that it is spoken of in Scripture as a love 'which passeth knowledge.'"

When the men rose to leave, it could be easily seen that they were deeply impressed. As they went out slowly, Miles passed close to the place where the ladies sat. The slighter of the two was talking in a low tone to her companion, and the young soldier was struck with the wonderful resemblance in her tone to that of the preacher. He wondered if her face also resembled his in any degree, and glanced back, but the head was turned away.

"I like that parson. He has got *brains*," remarked Sergeant Hardy, as he walked along the deck with Sergeant Gilroy and Corporal Flynn.

"Sur' an' I like him too," said the corporal, "for he's got *heart*!"

"Heart and brains," returned Gilroy: "a grand combination! What more could we want?"

"Don't you think that *tongue* is also essential?" asked Miles. "But for the preacher's eloquence his heart and brain would have worked in vain."

"Come now, John Miles, don't you be risin' up into poethry. It's not yer natur—though ye think it is. Besides, av a man's heart an' brains is all right, he can make good use of 'em widout much tongue. Me own notion is that it's thim as hasn't got much to spake of, aither of heart or brain, as is over-fond o' waggin' the tongue."

"That's so, Flynn. You're a living example of the truth of your own opinion," retorted Miles.

"Och! is it angered ye are at gittin' the worst o' the argiment?" rejoined the corporal. "Niver mind, boy, you'll do better by and by—"

As Flynn descended the ladder while he spoke, the sense of what he said was lost, but the truth of his opinion still continued to receive illustration from the rumbling of his voice, until it was swallowed up in the depths of the vessel.

Next day our hero received a shock from which he never finally recovered!

Be not alarmed, reader; it was not paralytic in its nature. It happened on this wise:

Miles had occasion to go to the fore part of the ship on some culinary business, without his coat, and with his sleeves rolled up above his elbows.

Arrived there, he found that the captain was taking the ladies round the ship to point out some of its interesting details. As Miles came up, the younger lady turned round so as to present her full face to him. It was then that poor Miles received the shock above referred to. At that moment a little boy with wings and a bow stepped right in front of the young lady and shot straight at Miles Milton! The arrow entered his heart, and he—no, he did not fall; true men in such circumstances never fall! They stand transfixed, sometimes, or stupefied. Thus stood Miles and stared. Yes, though naturally modest and polite, he stood and stared!

And small blame to him, as Flynn might have said, for before him stood his ideal of a fairy, an angel, a sylph—or anything beautiful that best suits your fancy, reader! Sunny hair, sunny eyes—earnest and inquiring eyes—sunny smiles, and eyebrows to match. Yes, she had eyebrows distinctly darker than her hair, and well-defined over a pair of large brown eyes.

Poor Miles was stricken, as we have said; but—would you believe it?—there were men there looking at that girl at that time who, to use their own phraseology, would not have accepted a dozen of her for the girls they had left behind them! One young fellow in particular murmured to himself as follows—"Yes, very well in her way, no doubt, but she couldn't hold a candle to my Emmy!" Perhaps the most cutting remark of all—made mentally, of course—was that of Sergeant Grady, who, for reasons best known to himself, had left a wife, describable as a stout well-favoured girl of forty, behind him.

"In twenty years or so," he thought, "she may perhaps be near as good-lookin' as my Susy, but she'll never come quite up to her—never!"

"Come this way, Mrs Drew," said the captain. "I will show you the men's quarters. Out of the way, my man!"

Flushing to the roots of his hair, Miles stepped hastily aside.

As he did so there was heard an awful rend of a sort that tests the temper of women! It was followed by a musical scream. The girl's dress had caught on a block tackle.

Miles leaped forward and unhooked it. He was rewarded with a smiling "Thank you," which was followed by a blush of confusion as Miss Drew's mother exclaimed, "Oh! Marion—how *could* you?" by way of making things easier for her, no doubt!

"You did that, young man, about as smart as I could a' done it myself," growled a voice behind him.

The speaker was Jack Molloy, and a general titter followed Miles as he hurried away.

As we have said, the weather became much worse when the troop-ship drew near to the Bay of Biscay; and it soon became evident that they were not to cross that famous portion of the Atlantic without experiencing some of the violent action for which it is famed. But by that time most of the soldiers, according to Molloy, had got their sea-legs on, and rather enjoyed the tossing than otherwise.

"I do like this sort o' thing," said a beardless young fellow, as a number of the men sat on camp-stools, or stood on the weather-side of the deck, chatting together about past times and future prospects.

"Ha!" exclaimed a seaman, who stood near them coiling up a rope; "hold on till you've got a taste o' the Bay. This is a mill-pond to that. And you'll have the chance to-night. If you don't, I'm a Dutchman."

"If I do, you'll have a taste of it too, old salt-water, for we're in the same boat," retorted the young red-coat.

"True, but we ain't in the same body;" returned the sailor. "I should just like to see your four-futt legs wobblin' about in a nor'-west gale. You'd sing another song."

"Come, Macleod," cried Moses Pyne, "tip us a Gaelic song."

"Hoots, man, wull ye be wantin' to be made sea-seek? — for that's what'll do it," said the big Scotsman. "Na, na, let Gaspard sing us 'The Bay o' Biscay O!' That'll be mair appropriate."

There was a general chorus of assent to this; and as Gaspard Redgrave was an obliging man, untroubled by false modesty, he cleared his throat and began. His voice, being a really splendid one, attracted all the men who chanced to be within range of it: among others, Miles, who was passing at the moment with a bag of biscuits in one hand and a meat-can in the other. He leaned up against one of those funnels which send fresh air down to the stokers of steam-ships. He had listened only a few moments when Marion Drew glided amongst the men, and seemed to stand as if entranced with delight in front of him, steadying herself by a rope, for the vessel was pitching a good deal as well as rolling considerably.

At the first chorus the crowd burst forth with wild enthusiasm —

"As we lay, on that day,
In the Bay of Biscay O!"

Dwelling with unnecessary length and emphasis on the "O!"

At the close of the second verse the men were preparing to burst forth again when Miles observed an approaching billow which caused him to start in alarm. Although unused to the aspect of waves, he had an instinctive feeling that there was danger approaching. Voices of warning were promptly raised from different parts of the vessel, but already the loud chorus had begun and drowned every other sound. Miles dropped his biscuits and sprang towards Marion, who, with flashing eyes and parted lips, was gazing at Gaspard. He just reached her when the wave burst over the side, and, catching most of the men quite unprepared, swept them with terrible violence towards the lee-side of the deck.

Marion was standing directly in the line of this human cataract, but Miles swung her deftly round into the lee of the funnel, a handle of which she happily caught, and clung to it like a limpet.

Her preserver was not so fortunate. The edge of the cataract struck him, swept him off his legs, and hurled him with many comrades against the lee bulwarks, where he lay stunned and helpless in the swishing water.

Of course soldiers and sailors ran from all parts of the vessel to the rescue, and soon the injured men were carried below and attended to by the doctors; and, considering the nature of the accident, it was matter for surprise that the result was no worse than some pretty severe contusions and a few broken ribs.

When Miles recovered consciousness, he found himself in his hammock, with considerable pain in various parts of his body, and the Reverend James Drew bending over him.

"You're all right now, my fine fellow," he said, in a low comforting voice. "No bones broken, so the doctors say. Only a little bruised."

"Tell me, sir," said Miles, rousing himself, "is—is your daughter safe?"

"Yes, thanks be to God, and to your prompt assistance, she is none the worse—save the fright and a wetting."

Miles sank back on his pillows with a feeling of profound satisfaction.

"Now, you must try to sleep if you can," said the clergyman; "it will do you good."

But Miles did not want anything to do him good. He was quite content to lie still and enjoy the simple fact that he had rescued Marion, perhaps from death—at all events from serious injury! As for pain—what was that to him? was he not a soldier—one whose profession requires him to suffer *anything* cheerfully in the discharge of duty! And was not love the highest duty?

On the strength of some such thoughts he forgot his pain and calmly went to sleep.

Chapter Eight-Has Reference to many Things connected with Mind, Matter, and Affections

The wave which had burst with such disastrous effect on the deck of the troop-ship was but the herald of one of those short, wild storms which occasionally sweep with desolating violence over the Atlantic Ocean, and too frequently strew with wreck the western shores of Europe.

In the Bay of Biscay, as usual, the power of the gale was felt more severely than elsewhere.

"There's some sort o' mystery about the matter," said Jack Molloy to William Armstrong, as they cowered together under the shelter of the bridge. "Why the Atlantic should tumble into this 'ere bay with greater wiolence than elsewhere is beyond my comprehension. But any man wi' half an eye can see that it *do* do it! Jist look at that!"

There was something indeed to look at, for, even while he spoke, a mighty wave tumbled on board of the vessel, rushed over the fore deck like Niagara rapids in miniature, and slushed wildly about for a considerable time before it found its way through the scuppers into the grey wilderness of heaving billows from which it sprang.

The great ship quivered, and seemed for a moment to stagger under the blow, while the wind shrieked through the rigging as if laughing at the success of its efforts, but the whitey-grey hull rose heavily, yet steadily, out of the churning foam, rode triumphant over the broad-backed billow that had struck her, and dived ponderously into the valley of waters beyond.

"Don't you think," said the young soldier, whose general knowledge was a little more extensive than that of the seaman, "that the Gulf Stream may have something to do with it?"

Molloy looked at the deck with philosophically solemn countenance. Deriving no apparent inspiration from that quarter, he gazed on the tumultuous chaos of salt-water with a perplexed expression. Finally and gravely he shook his weather-beaten head —

"Can't see that nohow," he said. "In course I knows that the Gulf Stream comes out the Gulf o' Mexico, cuts across the Atlantic in a nor'-

easterly direction, goes slap agin the west of England, Ireland, and Scotland, and then scurries away up the coast o' Norway—though *why* it should do so is best known to itself; p'r'aps it's arter the fashion of an angry woman, accordin' to its own sweet will; but what has that got for to do wi' the Bay of Biscay O? That's wot I wants to know."

"More to do with it than you think, Jack," answered the soldier. "In the first place, you're not quite, though partly, correct about the Gulf Stream—"

"Well, I ain't zactly a sciencrific stoodent, you know. Don't purfess to be."

"Just so, Jack. Neither am I, but I have inquired into this matter in a general way, an' here's *my* notions about it."

"Draw it fine, Willum; don't be flowery," said the sailor, renewing his quid. "Moreover, if you'll take the advice of an old salt you'll keep a tighter grip o' that belayin'-pin you've got hold of, unless you wants to be washed overboard. Now then, fire away! I'm all attention, as the cat said at the mouth o' the mouse-hole."

"Well, then," began Armstrong, with the slightly conscious air of superior knowledge, "the Gulf Stream does *not* rise in the Gulf of Mexico—"

"Did I say that it did, Willum?"

"Well, you said that it *came out of* the Gulf of Mexico—and, no doubt, so far you are right, but what I mean is that it does not originate there."

"W'y don't you say what you mean, then, Willum, instead o' pitchin' into a poor chap as makes no pretence to be a purfessor? Heave ahead!"

"Well, Jack," continued the soldier, with more care as to his statements, "I believe, on the best authority, that the Gulf Stream is only part of a great ocean current which originates at the equator, and a small bit of which flows north into the Atlantic, where it drives into the Gulf of Mexico. Finding no outlet there it rushes violently round the gulf—"

"Gits angry, no doubt, an' that's what makes it hot?" suggested the sailor.

"Perhaps! Anyhow, it then flows, as you say, in a nor'-easterly direction to the coasts of Great Britain and Ireland. But it does more than that. It spreads as it goes, and also rushes straight at the coasts of France and Spain. Here, however, it meets a strong counter current running south along these same coasts of France an' Spain. That is difficulty number one. It has to do battle wi' that current, and you know, Jack, wherever there's a battle there's apt to be convulsions of some sort. Well, then, a nor'-westerly gale comes on and rolls the whole o' the North Atlantic Ocean against these coasts. So here you have this part of the Gulf Stream caught in another direction — on the port quarter, as you sailors might call it — "

"Never mind wot us sailors might call it, Willum. Wotever you say on that pint you're sure to be wrong. Heave ahead!"

"Well, then," continued Armstrong, with a laugh, "that's trouble number two; and these troubles, you'll observe, apply to the whole west coast of both countries; but in the Bay of Biscay there is still another difficulty, for when these rushing and tormented waters try to escape, they are met fair in the face by the whole north coast of Spain, and thus — "

"I sees it!" exclaimed Molloy, with a sudden beam of intelligence, "you've hit the nail on the head, Willum. Gulf Stream flies at France in a hot rage, finds a cool current, or customer, flowin' down south that shouts 'Belay there!' At it they go, tooth an' nail, when down comes a nor'-wester like a wolf on the fold, takes the Stream on the port quarter, as you say, an' drives both it an' the cool customer into the bay, where the north o' Spain cries 'Avast heavin', both o' you!' an' drives 'em back to where the nor'-wester's drivin' 'em on! No wonder there's a mortal hullaballoo in the Bay o' Biscay! Why, mate, where got ye all that larnin'?"

Before his friend could reply, a terrific plunge of the vessel, a vicious shriek of the wind, and the entrance of another tremendous sea, suggested that the elements were roused to unusual fury at having the secrets of their operations thus ruthlessly revealed, and also suggested the propriety of the two friends seeking better shelter down below.

While this storm was raging, Miles lay in his hammock, subjected to storms of the bosom with occasional calms between. He was enjoying one of the calms when Armstrong passed his hammock and asked how he was getting on.

"Very well, Willie. Soon be all right, I think," he replied, with a contented smile.

For at that moment he had been dwelling on the agreeable fact that he had really rescued Marion Drew from probable death, and that her parents gratefully recognised the service — as he learned from the clergyman himself, who expressed his gratitude in the form of frequent visits to and pleasant chats with the invalid.

The interest and sympathy which Miles had felt on first seeing this man naturally increased, and at last he ventured to confide to him the story of his departure from home, but said nothing about the changed name. It is needless to relate all that was said on the occasion. One can easily imagine the bearing of a good deal of it. The result on Miles was not very obvious at the time, but it bore fruit after many days.

The calm in our hero's breast was not, however, of long duration. The thought that, as a private in a marching regiment, he had not the means to maintain Marion in the social position to which she had been accustomed, was a very bitter thought, and ruffled the sea of his feelings with a stiff breeze. This freshened to something like a gale of rebellion when he reflected that his case was all but hopeless; for, whatever might have been the truth of the statement regarding the French army under Napoleon, that "every soldier carried a marshal's baton in his knapsack," it did not follow that soldiers in the British army of the present day carried commissions in *their* knapsacks. Indeed, he knew it was by no means a common thing for men to rise from the ranks, and he was well aware that those who did so were elevated in virtue of qualities which he did not possess.

He was in the midst of one of his bosom storms when Sergeant Hardy came to inquire how he did.

Somehow the quiet, grave, manly nature of that sergeant had a powerful effect, not only on Miles but on every one with whom he came in contact. It was not so much his words as his manner that commended him. He was curiously contradictory, so to speak, in character and appearance. The stern gravity of his countenance suggested a hard nature, but lines of good-humour lurking about the eyes and mouth put to flight the suggestion, and acts of womanly tenderness on many occasions turned the scale the other way. A strong, tall, stiffly upright and slow-moving frame, led one to look only for elephantine force, but when circumstances required prompt action our sergeant displayed powers of cat-like activity, which were all the more tremendous that they seemed incongruous and were unexpected. From his lips you looked for a voice of thunder—and at drill you were not disappointed—but on ordinary occasions his speech was soft and low; bass indeed as to its quality, but never harsh or loud.

"A gale is brewing up from the nor'-west, so Jack Molloy says," remarked Hardy, as he was about to pass on.

"Why, I thought it was blowing a gale *now*!" returned Miles. "At least it seems so, if we may judge from the pitching and plunging."

"Ah, lad, you are judging from the landlubber's view-point," returned the sergeant. "Wait a bit, and you will understand better what Molloy means when he calls this only a 'capful of wind.'"

Miles had not to wait long. The gale when fully "brewed up" proved to be no mean descendant of the family of storms which have tormented the celebrated bay since the present economy of nature began; and many of those who were on board of the troop-ship at that time had their eyes opened and their minds enlarged as to the nature of a thorough gale; when hatches have to be battened down, and the dead-lights closed; when steersmen have to be fastened in their places, and the maddened sea seems to roar defiance to the howling blast, and all things movable on deck are swept away as if they were straws, and many things not meant to be movable are wrenched from their fastenings with a violence that nothing formed by man can resist, and timbers creak and groan, and loose furniture gyrates about until smashed to pieces, and well-guarded glass and crockery leap out of bounds to irrecoverable ruin, and even the seamen plunge about and stagger, and landsmen hold on to ring-bolts and belaying-pins, or cling to bulkheads for dear life, while mighty billows, thundering in-board, hiss along the decks, and everything, above, below, and around, seems being swept into eternity by the besom of destruction!

But the troop-ship weathered the storm nobly; and the good Lord sent fine weather and moderate winds thereafter; and ere long the soldiers were enjoying the sunshine, the sparkling waters, and the sight of the lovely shores of the blue Mediterranean.

Soon after that broken bones began to mend, and bruises to disappear; and our hero, thoroughly recovered from his accident, as well as greatly improved in general health, returned to his duties.

But Miles was not a happy man, for day by day he felt more and more severely that he had put himself in a false position. Besides the ever-increasing regret for having hastily forsaken home, he had now the bitter reflection that he had voluntarily thrown away the right to address Marion Drew as an equal.

During the whole voyage he had scarcely an opportunity of speaking a word to her. Of course the warm-hearted girl did not forget the important service that had been rendered to her by the young soldier, and she took more than one occasion to visit the fore part of the vessel for the purpose of expressing her gratitude and asking about his health, after he was able to come on deck; but as her father accompanied her on these occasions, the conversation was conducted chiefly between him and the reverend gentleman. Still, it was some comfort to hear her voice and see her eyes beaming kindly on him.

Once the youth inadvertently expressed his feelings in his look, so that Marion's eye-lids dropped, and a blush suffused her face, to hide which she instantly became unreasonably interested in the steam-winch beside which they were standing, and wanted to understand principles of engineering which had never troubled her before!

"What *is* the use of that curious machine?" she asked, turning towards it quickly.

"W'y, Miss," answered Jack Molloy, who chanced to be sitting on a spare yard close at hand working a Turk's head on a manrope, "that's the steam-winch, that is the thing wot we uses w'en we wants to hoist things out o' the hold, or lower 'em into it."

"Come, Marion, we must not keep our friend from his duties," said Mr Drew, nodding pleasantly to Miles as he turned away.

The remark was called forth by the fact that Miles had been arrested while on his way to the galley with a dish of salt pork, and with his shirt-sleeves, as usual, tucked up!

Only once during the voyage did our hero get the chance of talking with Marion alone. The opportunity, like most pieces of good fortune, came unexpectedly. It was on a magnificent night, just after the troop-ship had left Malta. The sea was perfectly calm, yet affected by that oily motion which has the effect of breaking a reflected moon into a million fragments. All nature appeared to be hushed, and the stars were resplendent. It was enough, as Jack Molloy said, to make even a bad man feel good!

"Do 'ee speak from personal experience, Jack?" asked a comrade on that occasion.

"I might, Jim, if *you* wasn't here," retorted Molloy; "but it's not easy to feel bad alongside o' *you*."

"That's like a double-edged sword, Jack—cuts two ways. W'ich way d'ee mean it?"

"'W'ichever way you please,' as the man said w'en the alligator axed 'im w'ether he'd prefer to be chawed up or bolted whole."

Concluding that, on the whole, the conversation of his friends did not tend to edification, Miles left them and went to one of the starboard gangways, from which he could take a contemplative view of Nature in her beautiful robe of night. Curiously enough, Marion chanced to saunter towards the same gangway, and unexpectedly found him there.

"A lovely night, Mr Miles," she remarked.

Miles started, and turned with slight confusion in his face, which, happily, the imperfect light concealed.

"Beautiful indeed!" he exclaimed, thinking of the face before him—not of the night!

"A cool, beautiful night like this," continued the girl—who was of the romantic age of sixteen—"will remain long, I should think, in your memory, and perhaps mitigate, in some degree, the hardships that are before you on the burning sand of Egypt."

"The memory of this night," returned Miles, with fervour, "will remain with me *for ever*! It will not only mitigate what you are pleased to call hardships, but will cause me to forget them altogether—forget *everything*!"

"Nay, that were impossible," rejoined Marion, with a slight laugh; "for a true soldier cannot forget Duty!"

"True, true," said Miles dubiously; "at least it ought to be true; and I have no doubt is so in many cases, but—"

What more he might have said cannot now be told, for they were interrupted at the moment by Captain Lacey, who, happening to walk in that direction, stopped and directed Miss Drew's attention to a picturesque craft, with high lateen sails, which had just entered into the silver pathway of the moon on the water.

Miles felt that it would be inappropriate in him to remain or to join in the conversation. With a heart full of disappointment and indignation he retired, and sought refuge in the darkest recesses of the pantry, to which he was welcome at all times, being a great favourite with the steward.

Whether it was the smell of the cheese or the ketchup we know not, but here better thoughts came over our hero. Insignificant causes often produce tremendous effects. The touching of a trigger is but a small matter; the effects of such a touch are sometimes deadly as well as touching. Possibly the sugar, if not the cinnamon, may have been an element in his change of mind. At all events it is safe to say that the general smell of groceries was associated with it.

Under the benign influence of this change he betook himself to the berth of the chief ship's-carpenter, with whom also he was a favourite.

Finding the berth empty, and a light burning in it, he sat down to wait for his friend. The place was comparatively quiet and retired. Bethinking himself of the little packet which he had received at Portsmouth, and which still lay unopened in the breast-pocket of his shell-jacket, he pulled it out. Besides a Testament, it contained sundry prettily covered booklets written by Miss Robinson and others to interest the public in our soldiers, as well as to amuse the soldiers themselves. In glancing through "Our Soldiers and Sailors," "Institute Memories," "Our Warfare," "The Victory," "Heaven's Light our Guide," "Good-bye," and similar works, two facts were suddenly impressed upon his mind, and strongly illuminated—namely, that there is such a thing as living for the good of others, and that up to that time he had lived simply and solely for himself!

The last sentence that had fallen from the lips of Marion that night was also strongly impressed upon him:— "a true soldier cannot forget Duty!" and he resolved that "Duty" should be his life's watchword thenceforward. Such is the influence that a noble-minded woman may unconsciously have over even an unsteady man!

Soon after this the troop-ship reached the end of her voyage, and cast anchor off the coast of Egypt, near the far-famed city of Alexandria.

Chapter Nine-Our Hero meets a Friend unexpectedly in Peculiar Circumstances, and has a very Strange Encounter

Miles Milton's first experience in Alexandria was rather curious, and, like most surprising things, quite unlooked for.

The troops were not permitted to land immediately on arrival, but of course no such prohibition lay on the passengers, who went off immediately. In the hurry of doing so, the clergyman and his family missed saying good-bye to Miles, who happened to be on duty in some remote part of the vessel at the time, and the shore-boat could not be delayed. This caused Mr and Mrs Drew much regret, but we cannot add that it caused the same to Miss Drew, because that young lady possessed considerable command of feature, and revealed no feeling at all on the occasion.

Miles was greatly disappointed when he found that they had gone, but consoled himself with the hope that he could make use of his first day's leave to find them out in the town and say good-bye.

"But why encourage hope?" thought Miles to himself, with bitterness in his heart; "I'm only a private. Marion will never condescend to think of *me*. What have I to offer her except my worthless self?" (you see Miles was beginning to see through himself faintly.) "Even if my father were a rich man, able to buy me out of the army and leave me a fortune—which he is not—what right have I to expect that a girl like Marion would risk her happiness with a fellow who has no profession, no means of subsistence, and who has left home without money and without leave? Bah! Miles, you are about the greatest goose that ever put on a red coat!"

He was getting on, you see! If he had put "sinner" for "goose," his shot would have been nearer the mark; as it was, all things considered, it was not a miss. He smarted considerably under the self-condemnation. If a comrade had said as much he would have resented it hotly, but a man is wonderfully lenient to himself!

Under the impulse of these feelings he sought and obtained leave to go into the town. He wished to see how the new Soldiers' Institute being set up there was getting along. He had promised Miss Robinson to pay it a visit. That was his plea. He did not feel called upon to inform his officer of his intention to visit the Drews! That was quite a private matter—yet it was the main matter; for, on landing, instead of inquiring for the spot where the new Institute was being erected, he began a search among the various hotels where English visitors were wont to put up. The search was successful. He found the hotel, but the family had gone out, he was told, and were not expected back till evening.

Disappointment, of course, was the result; but he would wait. It is amazing what an amount of patience even impatient men will exercise when under the influence of hope! There was plenty of time to run down and see the Institute, but he might miss his friends if they should chance to come in and go out again during his absence. What should he do?

"Bother the Institute!" he muttered to himself. "It's only bricks an' mortar after all, and I don't know a soul there."

He was wrong on both of these points, as we shall see.

"What's the use of my going?" he murmured, after a reflective pause.

"You promised the ladies of the Portsmouth Institute that you'd go to see it, and report progress," said that extraordinary Something inside of him, which had a most uncomfortable way of starting up and whispering when least expected to do so.

"And," added Something, "every gentleman should keep his word."

"True," replied Miles, almost angrily, though inaudibly; "but I'm *not* a gentleman, I'm only a private!"

"Goose!" retorted that pertinacious Something; "is not every private a gentleman who acts like one? And is not every gentleman a blackguard who behaves as such?"

Miles was silenced. He gave in, and went off at once to visit the Institute.

As he walked down the long straight street leading to the Grand Square, which had been almost destroyed by the bombardment, he passed numerous dirty drinking-shops, and wondered that English soldiers would condescend to enter such disgusting places. He was but a young soldier, and had yet to learn that, to men who have been fairly overcome by the power of the fiend Strong Drink, no place is too disgusting, and no action too mean, so that it but leads to the gratification of their intolerable craving. It is said that in two streets only there were 500 of these disreputable drinking-shops.

All sorts and conditions of men passed him as he went along: Turks, Greeks, Arabs, Negroes, Frenchmen, Italians, and Englishmen, the gay colours of whose picturesque costumes lent additional brilliancy to the sunny scene. The sight of the dark-skinned men and veiled women of the Arab quarter did more, however, than anything else to convince our hero that he had at last really reached the "East" — the land of the ancient Pharaohs, the Pyramids, the Arabian Nights' Entertainments, and of modern contention!

Presently he came upon the piece of waste ground which had been chosen as the site of the new Institute. It was covered with the ruins — shattered cement, glass, tiles, and general wreckage — of the buildings that had stood there before the bombardment, and on three sides it was surrounded by heaps of stones, shattered walls, and rubbish, some acres in extent. But the place had the great advantage of being close to the old harbour, not far from the spot where ancient Alexandria stood, and was open to the fresh, cooling breezes that came in from the sea.

Arab workmen were busily employed at the time on the foundations of the building, under the superintendence of an unmistakable and soldierly-looking Englishman, whose broad back was presented to Miles as he approached. Turning suddenly round, Mr Tufnell, the manager of the Portsmouth Institute, confronted the visitor with a stern but perspiring visage, which instantly became illuminated with a beaming smile.

"What! Tufnell!" exclaimed our hero, in amazement.

"Ay, Miles; as large as life."

"Larger than life, if anything," said Miles, grasping the proffered hand, and shaking it warmly. "Why, man, the air of Egypt seems to magnify you."

"More likely that the heat of Egypt is making me grow. What are you rubbing your eyes for?"

"To make sure that they do not deceive," answered Miles. "Did I not leave you behind me at Portsmouth?"

"So you did, friend; but the voyage in a troop-ship is not the fastest method of reaching Egypt. As you see, I've overshot you in the race. I have come to put up the new building. But come to my palace here and have a talk and a cup of coffee. Glad to see that the voyage has agreed with you."

They reached the palace to which the manager referred, and found it to be a cottage of corrugated iron amidst the rubbish.

"Here," said Tufnell, offering his friend a chair, "I spend all my time and reign supreme — monarch of all I survey. These are my subjects," he added, pointing to the Arab workmen; "that wilderness of rubbish is my kingdom; and yon heap of iron and stone is the material out of which we mean to construct our Alexandria Institute. To save time, (the most valuable article in the world, if you'll believe me), Miss Robinson, as, perhaps, you may have heard, bought an old iron edifice in London, known as the Brompton Oratory, and sent it out here — like a convict — at Government expense. You see, not only the public, but Government, have now come to recognise the value of her work for soldiers."

"And your subjects, the Arabs — are they obedient and loyal?" asked Miles.

"Pretty well; but they give me some trouble now and then. The other day, for instance, we had a sad accident, which at one time I feared would land us in serious difficulties. It is necessary, you must know, in laying foundations here, to dig through the sand some twelve to fifteen feet till water is reached, and then we lay a solid stone foundation about nine feet wide. Well, while digging this foundation, the sand fell in on one of the workmen. I off coat at once and set to work with a shovel, shouting to the fellows to help me. Instead of helping, they rushed at me in a body to prevent my interfering in the matter. Then they quarrelled among themselves as to the best way of getting the man out, and the result was that the poor fellow was suffocated, though he might easily have been rescued by prompt action. But that was not the end of it! The relations and friends of the man came down, made Eastern howling and lamentation over him, and laid his corpse at the door of my cottage, holding me responsible for his life, and demanding compensation! And it was not till I had paid a few francs to every brother and cousin and relative belonging to him that their grief was appeased and the dead body carried away.

"Still the matter did not end here, for next day the workmen said the accident was owing to the omission of a sacrifice at the commencement of the work, and they must have a lamb to kill on the ground, or more lives would certainly be lost. So I bought them a lamb, which they duly killed, cooked, and ate, after sprinkling its blood on the four corners of the foundation and on the walls. I had the skin of this lamb dressed and sent home as a curiosity." See note 1.

"You appear to have pretty rough times of it then, on the whole," said Miles.

"I never counted on smooth times," returned Tufnell; "besides, being used to roughing it, I am always glad to do so in a good cause. My palace, as you see, is not a bad one, though small. It is pretty hot too, as you seem to feel; and they tell me there will be some interesting variety in my experiences when the rainy season sets in! I wouldn't mind it so much if I could only be left to sleep in peace at nights. I stay here, you see, night and day, and what wi' the Arabs prowling around, whispering and trying to get in, and the wild dogs makin' the neighbourhood a place o' public meeting—barking, howling, and quarrelling over their sorrows like human bein's, they don't give me much rest."

"I have read of these dogs before," said Miles. "Are they really as wild and dangerous as they get credit for?"

"If you'd seen the fight I had wi' them the other night you'd have no doubt on that point. Why, a gang of 'em made a regular attack on me, and if it hadn't been that I was pretty active with my sword-stick, they'd have torn me in bits. Let me advise you never to go out after nightfall without one. Is that one in your hand?"

"No, it is merely a cane."

"Well, exchange with me. There's no saying when you may want it."

Tufnell took a light sword-stick which lay on the table and handed it to Miles, who accepted it laughingly, and without the slightest belief that he should ever have occasion to use it.

In chatting about the plans of the building and the prospects of success, our hero became at last so deeply interested—partly, no doubt, because of his friend's enthusiasm—that he forgot the flight of time, and the evening was advancing before he rose to leave.

"Now, Tufnell," he said suddenly, "I must be off, I have another call of importance to make."

"What! won't you stop and have a cup of coffee with me?"

"Impossible. My business is urgent. I want to see friends whom I may not have the chance of seeing again. Good-night."

"Good-night, then, and have a care of the dogs, specially after nightfall."

On returning to the hotel shortly after sunset, Miles came to the conclusion that his love must certainly be "true," for its course was not running "smooth." His friends had not yet returned. Mrs Drew had indeed come back, alone in a cab, but she had "von headik an' vas go to the bed."

Waiting about in front of the hotel for an hoar or two proved to be too much for our hero's nerves; he therefore made up his mind to exhaust his nervous system by means of a smart walk. Soon he found himself in a lonely place, half-way between the Grand Square and the Ramleh Gate, with a deliciously cool breeze playing on his brow, and a full moon sailing overhead.

No one was moving about on the road along which he walked. He had it all to himself at first, and the evening would have been quiet as well as beautiful but for the yelping dogs which had, by that time, come out of their day-dens to search and fight for food and hold their nightly revels.

All round him were the heaps of rubbish caused by bombardment, and the ruined houses which war had rendered tenantless, though here and there the uprising of new buildings proved that the indomitable energy of man was not to be quelled by war or anything else. A flickering oil-lamp placed here and there at intervals threw a sickly yellow light into dark recesses which the moonbeams failed to reach. Intermingled with these were a few date-palms and bananas. After a time he observed a couple of figures in advance of him — a man and woman — walking slowly in the same direction.

Not wishing to have his thoughts disturbed, he pushed on, intending to pass the wayfarers. He had got to within a hundred paces of them when he became aware of a violent pattering sound behind him. Stopping and looking back he saw a pack of eight or nine of the wild, half-famished dogs of the place coming along the road at full gallop. He was quite aware that they were the savage, masterless creatures which keep close in hiding during the day, and come out at night to search for something to devour, but he could not bring himself to believe that any sort of dog was a dangerous animal. He therefore merely looked at them with interest as being natives of the place!

They passed without taking notice of him — as ugly and wolfish a pack as one could wish to see — led by a big fellow like a ragged disreputable collie. They also passed, with apparent indifference, the wayfarers in advance, who had stopped to look at them.

Suddenly, and without a note of warning, the whole pack turned and rushed back, yelling fiercely, towards the man and woman. The latter clung to the left arm of the former, who raised his stick, and brought it down with such good-will on the skull of the foremost dog that it reeled back with an angry howl. It was not cowed, however, for it came on again, but the man, instead of striking it, thrust the end of his stick down its throat and checked it a second time. Still unsubdued, the fierce animal flew at him once more, and would certainly have overcome him if Miles had not run to the rescue at the first sign of attack. Coming up quickly, he brought his cane down on the dog's head with all his might, having quite forgotten the sword in the excitement of the moment! The blow did nothing to the dog, but it shattered the cane, leaving the sword exposed! This was fortunate. A quick thrust sent the dog flying away with yells of pain and fear, followed by all his companions, who seemed to take their cue entirely from their leader.

Turning to congratulate the wayfarers on their escape, Miles confronted Mr Drew and his daughter Marion!

If he had encountered the glare of the great sea-serpent he could scarcely have been taken more completely aback.

"My dear young friend," said the clergyman, recovering himself and grasping the passive hand of the young soldier with enthusiasm, though he could not help smiling at his obvious embarrassment, "you seem to have been raised up to be our rescuer!"

"I hope I have been raised up for something even more satisfactory than that," thought Miles, but he did not say so! What he did say—in a stammering fashion—was to the effect that he hoped he might be called on to—to—render many more such trifling services—no—he did not quite mean that, but *if* they should ever again be in danger, he hoped they would call on him to—to—that is—

"But I hope sincerely," he added, changing the subject abruptly, "that you are not hurt, Miss Drew?"

"Oh dear no; only a little frightened. But, father, are you sure that *you* are not hurt?"

"Quite sure; only a little sprain, I think, or twist in my right ankle. The attack was so sudden, you see, that in the hurry to meet it my foot turned over. Give me your arm, my young friend. There; it will be all right in a few minutes. How you tremble, Marion! Your nerves have received a greater shock than you imagine, and a lame man is but a poor support. Give her your other arm, Mr Miles. You are stout enough to support us both."

Stout enough to support them both! Ay, at that moment Miles felt stout enough to support the entire world, like Atlas, on his own broad shoulders! With a blush, that the moon generously refused to reveal, Marion laid her hand lightly on the soldier's arm. It was much too light a touch, and did not distribute with fairness the weight of his burden, for the old gentleman hung heavily on the other arm. Mr Drew walked very slowly, and with evident pain, for the twist of the ankle had been much more severe than he at first imagined.

"You will come in and sup with us," said Mr Drew, on at last reaching the hotel door.

"Impossible. I am exceedingly sorry, but my time has almost expired. Indeed, I fear it has expired already, and duty comes before everything else. Your daughter taught me that lesson, sir, on board ship!"

"Oh you hypocrite!" remarked his familiar and plain-spoken internal friend; "where was this grand sense of duty when you left home in a rage without 'by your leave' to father or mother?" Miles could make no reply. He had a tendency to silence when this friend spoke, and returned to barracks in a pensive mood, just in time, as Armstrong said, to save his bacon.

Note 1. This fleece is now, among other curiosities, at the Portsmouth Institute.

Chapter Ten-Off to the Wars

The troops sent out to Egypt at that time were much wanted to reinforce the southern frontier and defend it from the attacks of Osman Digna, who, with a large host of the dusky warriors of the Soudan, was giving the defenders much trouble, and keeping them incessantly on the *qui vive*.

Miles Milton had no time while in Alexandria for anything but duty. He saw Marion only once again before leaving, but did not find an opportunity to converse with her alone. To do him justice, he had not the most distant intention of declaring the state of his feelings, even if the opportunity had been given. He merely desired to be in her company for a little on any terms whatever!

On that occasion, however, he contrived to scorch his heart with a double dose of jealousy, for he found two young men visiting the clergyman, each of whom seemed to be a friend of the family. One was a spendthrift named Rentworth—a young traveller of that loose, easy-going type which is occasionally met with in foreign parts, squandering the money of a rich father. He was a decidedly handsome young fellow, but with the stamp of dissipation already on his countenance. The other was a telegraph engineer, with honesty and good-nature in every line of his plain countenance.

Both of these youths paid marked attention to Marion—at least Miles thought so—and he hated them both accordingly; all the more that he *felt* their eyes to be fixed upon him while he was bidding her "farewell." He did not say "Good-bye." That was too commonplace—in the circumstances almost childish.

There was one gleam of comfort in the fact, however, that Marion echoed the word, and that he thought—indeed he was sure—her hand trembled slightly as she returned, or rather received, his squeeze. Miles was very stern of countenance and remarkably upright in figure while these adieux were being said—for the glare of his rivals, he thought, was upon him.

How the poor fellow got through the preparations and packing and parades that were necessary when the order came abruptly for the regiment to start for Suez we cannot tell. He went about everything mechanically, or like a man in a dream. And it was not till they had fairly started in the railway train that he became alive to the serious fact that he was actually off to the wars!

The accommodation for passengers in that train was not good. Distinctly bad, indeed, would be the proper term to apply to the kind of cattle-truck in which Miles found himself with a detachment of the gallant 310th Infantry; and soon the blinding dust of Egypt reminded our young soldier that the real battle of life had fairly begun.

"You'll get over it in time, my poor fellow," said his friend Armstrong, who sat beside him.

"You need the same consolation yourself, friend Willie," retorted Miles, wiping the dust out of the corners of his eyes.

"I didn't mean *that*," returned his friend. "*You* know what I mean! But cheer up; absence makes the heart grow fonder — at the same time it makes a fellow fit for duty. I have gone through it myself, and know all about it."

Miles flushed and felt inclined at first to resent this allusion to the state of his affections, but he was fortunately saved from taking any notice of it by a sudden burst of laughter among the men at a remark from Corporal Flynn, who, although this was his first visit to Egypt, had undertaken to point out to his comrades the various localities which he chose to assume were more or less connected with Scripture history!

The first part of the journey was not particularly interesting, and what with the fine sand and the great heat the men began to experience the discomforts of an Eastern climate, and to make frequent application to their water-bottles. It would have been well if they had contented themselves with water, and with the cold tea which some of them had been provident enough to save up at breakfast; but when they reached the first station where there was a five minutes' halt, some of them managed to smuggle strong drink into the train. One immediate result was that the men became more noisy.

"Come, give us a song, Gaspard," cried several voices, apparently inspired at the same moment with the same idea and desire.

"Wan wid a rousin' chorus, boy," cried Flynn.

Gaspard complied, being ever ready to oblige, but whether it was the heat, or the dust, or the "rousin'" chorus, or the drink, the song was a partial failure. Perhaps it was the excess of *tremulo* induced by the motion of the train! At all events it fell flat, and, when finished, a hilarious loud-voiced man named Simkin, or Rattling Bill, struck up "Rule Britannia," which more than made amends for the other, and was sung with intense vigour till the next station was reached.

Here more drink was smuggled on board the train, and, as a natural consequence, men became troublesome. A morose man named Sutherland, who was apt to grow argumentative and quarrelsome in his cups, made an assertion in reference to something terrestrial, which had no particular interest for any mortal man. Simkin contradicted it. Sutherland repeated it. Simkin knocked Sutherland's helmet overboard. Sutherland returned the compliment in kind, and their comrades had to quell an intestine war, while the lost head-pieces were left on the arid plain, where they were last seen surrounded by wonder-stricken and long-legged natives of the Flamingo tribe.

This loss was a serious one, for exposure of the head to the sun in such a climate is exceedingly dangerous, and the old hands had great difficulty in impressing the fact on Rattling Bill and Sutherland, who, with the obstinacy of "greenhorns," made light of the danger, and expressed disbelief in sunstroke.

Of course considerable interest was manifested when the station of Tel-el-Kebir was reached.

"It's two mile from this, I've bin towld," said Flynn, "where the great battle was fowt."

"How d'ee know that, Flynn?" asked one.

"How do I know anything I'm towld but by belaivin' it?" returned the corporal.

"It's my opeenion," said the big Scotsman Macleod, "that if there had been ony better troops than Egeeptians to fecht wi', oor men an' my Lord Wolseley wadna hae fund it sic an easy job."

"But it is said that the Egyptians were brave enough, and fought and died like men till they were fairly overpowered," said Moses Pyne, who, being young and ardent, besides just, felt bound to stand up for dead foes.

"I'm no objeckin' to their bravery," returned the Scot. "They did the best they could; but what was to be expeckit o' a wheen men that was dragged to the field against their wull, an' made to fecht afore they weel kent hoo to use their airms?"

"Anyhow they gave us a chance to show what British soldiers can do," said Rattling Bill.

"An' sure there's plenty more where they came from to give us another chance," said Flynn.

"That's true, boys. Three cheers for the heroes of Tel-el-Kebir, dead and livin'!" cried Armstrong, setting the example.

The response was prompt and hearty, and for a few moments a forest of white helmets waved in the air.

The enthusiasm was not allowed to cool, for the next station was Kassassin, where the Life Guards and our cavalry made their midnight charges; and where there occurred, perhaps, one of the longest day's fighting in the war of 1882. Here, also, they saw the graves of the poor fellows who fell at that time, but the sight did not depress the men much. The somewhat lugubrious Sutherland alone seemed to take a serious view of such matters.

"It's a' vera weel for licht-hearted lads like you to laugh an' cheer," he said, "but there's naething mair certain than that some o' you that's laughin' an' cheerin' yenoo, an' boastin' o' lickin' the Soudan neegers, 'll fill sandy graves afore lang."

"You don't know that, Scotty. Pr'a'ps we'll *all* escape and return to old England together," said one of his comrades.

"Arrah! if I *did* git into wan o' the sandy graves ye spake of," remarked Flynn, "I do belaive I'd rise out of it just for the pleasure o' contradictin' you, Sutherland."

"H'm! nae doot. Contradictiousness whiles maks fowk lively that wad be dull an' deed eneuch withoot it. But did onybody iver hear o' a reg'ment gaun' oot to the wars an' comin' back jist as it went? That's the question—"

"As Hamlet's ghost said when he was takin' a night-walk to cool his-self," interposed Simkin.

"It wasna his ghost; it was his faither's ghost," cried Sutherland; "an' I'm no' sure that—"

"Howld yer tongues, both o' ye!" cried Flynn; "sure the loss o' yer helmets is beginning to tell on yer heads already. What can the line be I see in the distance over there? I do belaive it's another o' thim broad rivers that seem to cut up this land all into stripes."

"Why, it's the canal, man," cried Moses Pyne, who was more or less enthusiastic about all the sights and scenes they were passing. "Don't ye see the ships?"

"Sure enough, you're right, Moses, as ye ginerally are whin you're not wrong. There's some ships comin' wan way, an' some goin' the other. Och! but he *is* a great jainius that Frenchman as tied the two says togither — Lips—Lisps—what is it they calls him? I've clane forgot."

"Lesseps," said Miles, as he gazed with unusual interest on this wonderful highway of nations.

The troops reached Suez after a ten hours' journey, the distance being about 230 miles. Our hero made the acquaintance here of a private of marines named Stevenson, with whom he afterwards served in the Soudan, and with whom he became very friendly, not only because their spirits were sympathetic, but because, having been brought up in the same part of England, they had similar memories and associations in regard to "home." Only those who have wandered long and far from their native land can understand the attractive influence that arises between men who meet abroad, and find that they can chat about the same places and persons in the "old country."

It was Saturday when the troops arrived at Suez, and the heavy dew that fell rendered the night bitterly cold, and felt to be so all the more because of the intense heat of the day. Sunday began with "rousing out" at six, breakfast at seven, parade at eight, and "divine service" thereafter. As there was no clergyman at the place at the time, the duty was performed by one of the officers. Doubtless among the officers there are men who not only can "read prayers" well, but who have the spirit of prayer in them. That such, however, is not always the case may be gathered from the remark of one of the men upon this occasion.

"W'y, you know, Tom," said this rather severe critic to his comrade confidentially, "there's one advantage in fast readin', that it gets the business soon over, which is some sort o' comfort to fellows that has got to attend whether they like it or not, hot or cold, fresh or tired, unless dooty prevents. But the hofficer that did dooty to-day seemed to me to 'ave made a wager to read the prayers against time, an' that can do no good at all to any one, you know. Far better, in my opinion, to 'ave no service at all. No wonder men won't listen. Why, it's a mockery—that's what it is."

A walk round Suez with Armstrong and Stevenson till tattoo at 9:30 finished the day, and convinced Miles and his friends that the sooner they bade adieu to that place the better for all of them.

Their wishes were gratified almost sooner than they wished!

Chapter Eleven-New and Sad mingled with Curious Experiences

At Suez Miles Milton first made acquaintance with the shady side of war.

Before the commanding officer, after parade next morning, they received marching orders, and kit-muster followed. In the afternoon the *Loch-Ard* steamer came in from Suakim, with sick, wounded, and invalids, and a large party was told off to assist in landing them and their baggage. Miles was one of the party. The dock where the vessel lay was three miles off, and the greater part of this distance the invalids were brought by train; but the latter part of the journey had to be done on foot by those who could walk, and on stretchers by those who could not.

Oh! it was pitiful to see those battered, sunburnt, bloodless young men, with deep lines of suffering on their faces, aged before their time, and the mere wrecks of what they once were. Men who had gone to that region strong, active, ruddy, enthusiastic, and who, after a few months, returned thus feeble and shattered—some irreparably so; others with perhaps years of joyless life before them; a few with the unmistakable stamp of death already on their brows.

There were about forty altogether. Some, as we have said, were carried from the vessel, and not one of the forlorn band could get on without the assistance of their fresh comrades from England.

One tall, deep-chested young soldier, who must have been a splendid specimen of manhood when he landed in Egypt, was supported on one side by Miles, and on the other by Stevenson.

"Halt a moment," said the invalid, in a weak voice and with an apologetic smile. "I—I can't get along quite as fast as I used to."

His trembling legs and bowed back did not require the tongue or the large sunken eyes to confirm that obvious truth.

"Poor fellow!" said Miles—with difficulty, owing to the lump in his throat—"you ought to have had a stretcher. Here, sit down a bit on this stone. Have you been wounded?"

"Ay," returned the man with a look of quiet resignation that seemed to have become habitual to him, "I have been wounded, but not by spear or bullet. It's the climate that has done for me. I used to think that nothing under the sun could quell me, but the Lord has seen fit to bring down my pride in that matter. At the same time, it's only fair to say that He has also raised me up, and given me greater blessings than He has taken away. They told me in Portsmouth that He would, and it has come true."

"At the Institute?" asked Stevenson, eagerly.

"Ay—the Soldiers' Institute," answered the invalid.

"God bless you!" returned the marine, grasping his hand. "It was there I was brought to God myself. Cheer up, brother! You'll soon be in hospital, where good food an' physic an' nursing will bring you round, may-hap, an' make you as ship-shape as ever."

"It may be so, if He wills it so," returned the trooper softly; "but I have a little book called 'Our Warfare,' and a letter from the 'Soldier's Friend' in my pocket, which has done me more good than all the hospitals and physic in Egypt can do. Come, let us go on. I'm better now."

Rising and putting a long arm round the shoulders of each of his new friends, the trooper slowly brought up the rear of the touching procession which had already passed them on its way to Suez.

In the vessel which had brought those unfortunate men from Suakim, Miles and his comrades soon found themselves advancing down that region of sweltering heat called the Red Sea. The sight of the disabled men had naturally, at first, a depressing effect on the men; but the influence of robust health, youth, strong hope, and that light-hearted courage which makes the British soldier so formidable to his foes, soon restored to most of them their wonted free-and-easy enjoyment of the present and disregard for the future. Even the serving out of cholera-belts and pocket-filters failed to allay their exuberant spirits.

The *Loch-Ard*, although doubtless a good ship for carrying coals, was very ill-suited to convey troops. But in times of war, and in distant lands, soldiers lay their account with roughing it.

They soon found that a little of the physic which is supposed to be "rough on rats" would have been of advantage; for the very first night many of the men were awakened by those creatures nibbling at their toes! Everything on board was dirty: the tin pannikins were rusty, the biscuit was mouldy and full of creatures that the captain called weevils and Macleod styled wee-deevils. Some of the biscuit was so bad that it had to be thrown away, and the remainder eaten, as Moses said, with closed eyes!

"It's an ill wind that blaws naebody guid," said Macleod to Moses Pyne, as he came on deck to enjoy a pipe after their first dinner on board. "What d'ee think that queer cratur Flynn is doin' doon below?"

"Nothing very useful, I daresay," said Moses.

"Ye're wrang for ance. He's lyin' in ambush there, makin' war on the rats—ay, an' he's killed twa or three a'ready!"

"You don't say so! I'll go and see the fun."

So saying Moses went below, but had just reached the foot of the ladder when a boot caught him violently on the shins.

"Hi! hallo! ho!" shouted Moses.

"Och! git out o' the line o' fire wid ye! There's another!" growled Flynn, as he fired a second boot, which whizzed past the intruder, and a sharp squeak told that it had not been fired in vain!

Moses beat a hasty retreat, and the Irishman continued the fight with that indomitable perseverance for which his countrymen are famous. There is no saying how long the action would have lasted, but in his energy he knocked away the support of a shelf behind him and a small cask of large nails, taking him in rear, sent him sprawling on the deck and routed him.

This misadventure did not, however, terminate the war. On the contrary, rat-hunting became a favourite pastime during the voyage down the Red Sea. Our hero, of course, took his turn at the fighting, but we believe that he never received a medal for his share in that war.

They spent one Sunday on the deep, but the only record made of it in the journal of the soldier from which most of our facts are gathered is that they "had prayers in racing style—against time!"

As if to cleanse themselves from the impropriety of this act the soldiers had a grand washing of clothes on the following day, and the day after that they arrived at Suakim.

"It is what I call a dreary, dismal-looking town," said Miles to Armstrong, as they approached.

"Might be worse," replied his friend.

"Ye aye tak a cheery view o' things, Airmstrong."

"An' what for no?" asked Sutherland.

"You may well ask why not," said Sergeant Hardy. "I think it wisest to look always on the bright side of things."

"Whether it's dreary or pleasant we'll have to make the best we can of it, boys," said Stevenson; "for this is to be our home for some time to come."

"Horrible!" growled Simkin, whose spirit was essentially rebellious.

"Ochone!" sighed Flynn, who, we need scarcely say, was essentially jolly.

Further remark was cut short by the voice of Captain Lacey ordering the men to fall in, as the colonel in command was coming on board to inspect them.

The night of the arrival of the 310th was dreadfully hot, insomuch that many of the men found it impossible to sleep. But in the silence of that night food for reflection was supplied to the wakeful, in the form of sounds that were new to many, but soon became familiar to all—namely, the boom of big guns and the rattle of musketry. Osman Digna was making one of his customary attacks on the town, and the defenders were repelling him. Of course the sanguine among the new arrivals were much excited, and eager to join in the fray; but their services were not required that night. Osman and his dusky hordes were being repulsed as usual, and the reinforcements were obliged to content themselves with merely listening to the sounds of war.

Chapter Twelve-In Action at last

No time was lost in sending the newly-arrived troops to their sphere of duty.

There was something appropriate in their landing on that day of gunpowdery memories, the 5th of November. It was four o'clock when they disembarked. By four-thirty they were drawn up and inspected by the General, and immediately thereafter marched off in detachments to their respective stations—to Sphinx Redoubt, Fort Commodore, Bulimba, and other points of defence.

The detachment in which Miles Milton found himself was led by Captain Lacey to Sphinx Redoubt, where he was greatly pleased to find that his new friend, private Stevenson of the marines, was also stationed with some of his comrades.

There are probably times in the experiences of most of us when we seem to awake out of a long dream and begin to appreciate fully that the circumstances in which we are placed are stern realities after all. Such a time of awakening came to our hero when he and his comrades each received fifty rounds of ball-cartridge, and stood ready to repel assault on the defences of Suakim.

Hitherto drill and reviews had seemed to him a good deal like playing at soldiers. Even when the distant sound of the big guns and the rattle of small arms touched his ear, the slumber of unbelief was only broken—not quite dispelled. But now, weighted with the deadly missiles, with rifle in hand, with ears alert to every sound, and eyes open to every object that might present itself on the sandy waste beyond the redoubt, and a general feeling of expectancy pervading his thoughts and feelings, he became clearly convinced that the recent past was no flight of the imagination—that he was in very truth a soldier, and that his fighting career had in reality begun!

Now, it may not be out of place here to state that our hero was not by nature a combative man. We think it necessary to point this out, because the somewhat pugnacious introduction of Miles into our story may have misled the reader on this point. His desire for a soldier's life was founded on a notion that it would prove to be a roving, jovial, hilarious sort of life, with plenty of sport and adventure in foreign lands. Of course he knew that it implied fighting also, and he was quite ready for that when it should be required of him; but it did not occur to him to reflect very profoundly that soldiering also meant, in some instances, exposure to withering heat during the day and stifling heat during the night; to thirst that seems unquenchable, and fatigue from prolonged duty that seems irreparable; to fits of sickness that appear to eliminate from stalwart frames all the strength they had ever possessed; and fits of the "blues" that render the termination of life a subject of rather pleasant contemplation than otherwise. But all these things he found out at Suakim!

Moreover, it had not occurred to him to think deeply on the fact that fighting meant rushing at a fellow-man whose acquaintance he had not made before; against whom he had not the slightest feeling of ill-will, and skewering him with a bayonet, or sending a bullet into him which would terminate his career in mid-life, and leave a wife and children — perhaps a mother also — disconsolate. But he also found that out at Suakim!

We repeat that Miles had no desire to fight, though, of course, he had no objection. When the officer in command sent him and his comrades to their station — after the ball-cartridge supply just referred to — and told them to keep a sharp look-out, for Osman Digna was giving them a great deal of trouble at the time, and pointed out where they were to go if attacked, and warned them to be ready to turn out on the instant that the bugle should sound the alarm, Miles was as full of energy and determination to fight and die for his country as the best of his comrades, though he did not express so strong a wish for a "brush with the enemy," as some of them did, or sympathise much with Corporal Flynn when he said —

"It's wishin' I am that Osman an' his dirty naygurs would come down on us this night, for we're fresh an' hearty, just off the say, burnin' for fame an' glory, ivery mother's son of us, an' fit to cut the black bastes up into mince-meat. Och! but it's thirsty I am!"

"If ye spoke less an' thocht mair ye wadna be sae dry, maybe," remarked Saunders, in a cynical tone.

"Hoots, man, let the cratur alane," said Macleod, as he busied himself polishing up some dim parts of his rifle. "It's no muckle pleesure we're like to hae in this het place. Let the puir thing enjoy his boastin' while he may."

"Sure an' we're not widout consolation anyhow," retorted the corporal; "for as long as we've got you, Mac, and your countryman, to cheer us wid your wise an' lively talk we'll niver die o' the blues."

As he spoke a tremendous explosion not far off caused the redoubt to tremble to its foundations. At the same moment the alarm sounded, the men sprang up, seized their arms, and stood ready for an attack; but to their surprise no attack was made.

"Surely it must have been one of the mines you were telling me about," said Miles, in a low voice to Sergeant Gilroy, who stood near to him.

"It was one of them unquestionably, for a corporal of the Berkshire regiment told me Lieutenant Young placed the mine there yesterday."

While Gilroy was speaking, Lieutenant Young himself came along, engaged in earnest conversation with Captain Lacey, and stood still close beside Miles.

"What puzzles me, is that they have not followed it up with a few volleys, according to their usual custom," said the former, in a low voice. "Luckily they seldom do any harm, for they are uncommonly bad shots, but they generally try their best to do us mischief, and always make a good deal of noise about it."

"Perhaps," suggested Captain Lacey, "your mine has done so much execution this time, and killed so many men, that they've got a fright and run away."

"It may be so, but I think not. The Soudanese are not easily frightened, as we have some cause to know."

"Have you many mines about?" asked the captain.

"Yes, we have a good many. And they form a most important part of our defence, for we are not very well supplied with men, and the Egyptian troops are not to be depended on unless backed up by ours. These mines require to be carefully handled, however, for our shepherds take the cattle out to graze every day, so that if I were to fail to disconnect any of them in the mornings, we should have some of our cattle blown up; and if I failed to connect them again at night, the enemy would attack us more vigorously. As it is, they are very nervous about the mines. They have pluck to face any foe that they can see, but the idea of an unseen foe, who lurks underground anywhere, and may suddenly send them into the sky like rockets, daunts them a bit."

"And little wonder!" returned the captain. "From what you say I judge that you have the management of most of the mines."

"Of all of them," answered the lieutenant, with a modest look.

There was more than modesty in this young officer of Engineers; there was heroism also. He might have added, (though he did not), that this duty of connecting and disconnecting the mines each night and morning was such a dangerous service that he declined to take men out with him, and invariably did the work personally and alone.

The mystery of the explosion on the night we write of was explained next morning when a party sallied forth to see what damage had been done. They found, instead of dismembered men, the remnants of a poor little hare which had strayed across the fatal line of danger and been blown to atoms. Thus do the lives of the innocent too often fall a sacrifice to the misdeeds of the guilty!

Next night, however, the defenders were roused by a real attack.

The day had been one of the most trying that the new arrivals had yet experienced. The seasoned men, who had been formed by Nature, apparently, of indestructible material, said it was awful. The thermometer stood at above 110 degrees in the shade; there was not a breath of air moving; the men were panting, almost choking. Even the negroes groaned, and, drawing brackish water from a well in the fort, poured it over their heads and bodies—but with little benefit, for the water itself was between 95 and 100 degrees!

"It'll try some o' the new-comers to-night, if I'm not mistaken," remarked one of the indestructible men above referred to, as he rose from dinner and proceeded to fill his pipe.

"Why d'you think so?" asked Sergeant Hardy, whose name was appropriate, for he continued for a long time to be one of the indestructibles.

"'Cause it's always like this when we're goin' to have a horrible night."

"Do the nights vary much?" asked Armstrong, who was still busy with his knife and fork.

"Of course they do," returned the man. "Sometimes you have it quite chilly after a hot day. Other times you have it suffocatin'—like the Black Hole of Calcutta—as it'll be to-night."

"What sort o' hole was that?" asked Simkin, whose knowledge of history was not extensive.

"It was a small room or prison into which they stuffed a lot of our men once, in India, in awful hot weather, an' kep' them there waitin' till the Great Mogul, or some chap o' that sort, should say what was to be done wi' them. But his Majesty was asleep at the time, an' it was as much as their lives was worth to waken him. So they had to wait, an' afore he awakened out o' that sleep most o' the men was dead—suffocated for want o' fresh air."

"I say, Mac, pass the water," said Moses Pyne. "It makes a feller feel quite gaspy to think of."

The weather-prophet proved to be right. That night no one could sleep a wink, except the big Scotsman Macleod. To make matters worse, the insects of the place were unusually active. One of them especially, not much bigger than a pin-point, was irritating out of all proportion to its size, and it kept up, during the night, the warfare which the innumerable flies had waged during the day.

"It's no use trying to sleep, Willie," said Miles to Armstrong, who was next to him, as they lay on the flat roof of the redoubt, with their rifles resting on the sandbags which formed a slight protection from the enemy's fire when one of the frequent attacks was made on the town.

"So I find," returned his friend. "I have tried everything. Counting up to hundreds of thousands has made me rather more wakeful. I find that thinking of Emmy does me most good, but even that won't produce sleep."

"Strange!" remarked Miles. "I have been trying the same sort of thing — without success. And I've had an unusually hard day of it, so that I ought to be ready for sleep. You were in luck, being on police-duty."

"H'm! I don't think much of my luck. But let's hear what you have been up to all day."

"Well, first, I began by turning out at 5:30 a.m.," said Miles, rolling with a sigh on his other side, for a uniform, cross-belts, boots, ammunition, etcetera, don't, after all, form an easy night-dress. "After a cup of coffee I fell in with a lot of our fellows, and was told off for fatigue-duty. Worked away till 7:30. Then breakfast. After that I had to clear up the mess; then got ready for inspection parade at 9:30, after which I had to scrub belts, and clean up generally. Dinner over, I was warned to go on night-guard; but, for some reason which was not stated to me, that was changed, and I'm not sorry for it, because the heat has taken a good deal out of me, and I prefer lying here beside you, Willie, to standing sentry, blinking at the desert, and fancying every bush and stone to be a dusky skirmisher of Osman Digna. By the way, if that mountain range where the enemy lies is twelve or fourteen miles distant from the town, they have a long way to come when they take a fancy to attack us — which is pretty often too. They say he has got two hundred thousand men with him. D'you think that can be true?"

A gentle trumpet-note from his friend's nose told Miles that he had brought about what thoughts of Emmy had failed to accomplish!

Thoughts of Marion had very nearly brought himself to a similar condition, when a trumpet-blast, the reverse of gentle, roused the whole line of defence, and, immediately after, sharp firing was heard in the direction of the right Water fort, which was manned by marines with two Krupp guns and a Gardner. A few rounds from the big guns drove the enemy back in that direction.

Miles and those around him, however, had not to turn out. Owing to their position on the roof of the Sphinx Redoubt, they had only to roll on their fronts, rest their rifles on the sandbags, and they were at once ready for action.

Round the various forts and redoubts deep and broad trenches had been dug, and they were rendered otherwise as strong as possible. The right and left Water forts formed the first line of defence. The latter fort, being manned by Egyptian troops, was more frequently favoured with the attentions of Osman than the others, for the marines were splendid men, and the native chief was well aware of that. All the places around, which offered the slightest shelter to the enemy, had been carefully measured as to distance, so that the exact range could be fixed at a moment's notice. Then the war-vessels and one of the forts were furnished with electric lights, so that by bringing these to bear on the foe, as well as the big and little guns—not to mention mines and rifles—the attacking host had always a warm reception when they paid a visit to the town, and never stayed long!

The defenders required all these aids, however; for, besides a regiment of Egyptian infantry, a company of Royal Engineers, and about 500 marines, there was only one small battalion of British troops and a regiment of Egyptian cavalry. These last were extremely useful. Every day they went out scouting and clearing around Suakim, and had frequent skirmishes with the enemy, in all of which they were said to have behaved very well indeed.

Our party on the redoubt had not lain there long when a sheet of flame seemed to flash out of the darkness in front of them. It was followed by the rattle of small arms. Instantly the redoubt replied; bullets whizzed overhead, and our hero received what has of late been called a "baptism of fire."

But he was so busy plying his own weapon that he scarcely realised the fact that death was ever and anon within a few inches of him, until a bullet ripped the sandbag on which his rifle rested and drove the sand into his face. He became a wiser man from that hour, and soon acquired the art of performing his duty with the least possible exposure of his person, and that for the briefest possible space of time!

Like a first-rate detective, the electric light sought out and exposed their foes; then withering volleys sent them scurrying across the country back to their native hills.

"Sure it's wid wan eye open we've got to slape whin the murtherin' rascals come down on us like that," observed Corporal Flynn, when the firing had slackened to a few dropping shots on both sides.

"Av they'd only stand fornint us in the open, it's short work we'd make o' them. There's no more pluck in them than in my smallest finger."

It seemed as if righteous retribution were being meted out that night, for a spent ball entered the fort at that moment and, strange to say, hit the extreme tip of the corporal's little finger!

A howl, as much of surprise as pain, apprised his comrades of the fact, and a hearty laugh followed when the trifling extent of the injury was ascertained.

"Serves you right, Flynn, for boasting," said Armstrong, with a grim smile, as he stretched himself out and rested his head on a sandbag. "Moreover, you are unjust, for these black fellows are as brave a lot o' men as British troops have ever had to face. Good-night, boys, I'm off to the land of Nod!"

Chapter Thirteen-Tells of some of the Trials, Uncertainties, Dangers, and Disasters of War

Uncertain moonlight, with a multitude of cloudlets drifting slowly across the sky so as to reveal, veil, partially obscure, or sometimes totally blot out the orb of night, may be a somewhat romantic, but is not a desirable, state of things in an enemy's country, especially when that enemy is prowling among the bushes.

But such was the state of things one very sultry night when our hero found himself standing in the open alone, and with thoughts of a varied and not wholly agreeable nature for his companions.

He was on sentry duty.

It was intensely dark when the clouds partially veiled the moon, for she was juvenile at the time—in her first quarter; and when the veil was partially removed, the desert, for it was little better, assumed an indistinct and ghostly-grey appearance.

Sombre thoughts naturally filled the mind of our young soldier as he stood there, alert, watchful, with weapons ready, ears open to the slightest sound, and eyes glancing sharply at the perplexing shadows that chased each other over the ground like wanton Soudanese at play. His faculties were intensely strung at what may well be styled "attention," and riveted on that desert land to which Fate—as he called his own conduct—had driven him. Yet, strange to say, his mysterious spirit found leisure to fly back to old England and revisit the scenes of childhood. But he had robbed himself of pleasure in that usually pleasant retrospect. He could see only the mild, sorrowful, slightly reproachful, yet always loving face of his mother when in imagination he returned home. It was more than he could bear. He turned to pleasanter memories. He was back again at Portsmouth, in the reading-room of the Soldiers' Institute, with red-coated comrades around him, busy with newspaper and illustrated magazine, while the sweet sound of familiar music came from the adjoining rooms, where a number of Blue Lights, or rather red-coats, who were not ashamed to own and serve their Maker, were engaged with songs of praise.

Suddenly he was back in Egypt with his heart thumping at his ribs. An object seemed to move on the plain in front of him. The ready bayonet was lowered, the trigger was touched. Only for a moment, however. The shadow of a cloud had passed from behind a bush—that was all; yet it was strange how very like to a real object it seemed to his highly-strung vision. A bright moonbeam next moment showed him that nothing to cause alarm was visible.

Mind is not so easily controlled as matter. Like a statue he stood there in body, but in mind he had again deserted his post. Yet not to so great a distance as before. He only went the length of Alexandria, and thought of Marion! The thought produced a glow, not of physical heat—that was impossible to one whose temperature had already risen to the utmost attainable height—but a glow of soul. He became heroic! He remembered Marion's burning words, and resolved that Duty should henceforth be his guiding-star!

Duty! His heart sank as he thought of the word, for the Something within him became suddenly active, and whispered, "How about your duty to parents? You left them in a rage. You spent some time in Portsmouth, surrounded by good influences, and might have written home, but you didn't. You made some feeble attempts, indeed, but failed. You might have done it several times since you landed in this country, but you haven't. You know quite well that you have not fully repented even yet!"

While the whispering was going on, the active fancy of the youth saw the lovely face of Marion looking at him with mournful interest, as it had been the face of an angel, and then there came to his memory words which had been spoken to him that very day by his earnest friend Stevenson the marine: "No man can fully do his duty to his fellows until he has begun to do his duty to God."

The words had not been used in reference to himself but in connection with a discussion as to the motives generally which influence men. But the words were made use of by the Spirit as arrows to pierce the youth's heart.

"Guilty!" he exclaimed aloud, and almost involuntary followed, "God forgive me!"

Again the watchful ear distinguished unwonted sounds, and the sharp eye—wonderfully sharpened by frequent danger—perceived objects in motion on the plain. This time the objects were real. They approached. It was "the rounds" who visited the sentries six times during each night.

In another part of the ground, at a considerable distance from the spot where our hero mounted guard, stood a youthful soldier, also on guard, and thinking, no doubt, of home. He was much too young for service in such a climate—almost a boy. He was a ruddy, healthy lad, with plenty of courage and high spirit, who was willing to encounter anything cheerfully, so long as, in so doing, he could serve his Queen and country. But he was careless of his own comfort and safety. Several times he had been found fault with for going out in the sun without his white helmet. Miles had taken a fancy to the lad, and had spoken seriously but very kindly to him that very day about the folly of exposing himself in a way that had already cost so many men their lives.

But young Lewis laughed good-naturedly, and said that he was too tough to be killed by the sun.

The suffocating heat of that night told upon him, however, severely—tough though he was or supposed himself to be—while he kept his lonely watch on the sandy plain.

Presently a dark figure was seen approaching. The sentinel at once challenged, and brought his rifle to the "ready." The man, who was a native, gave the password all right, and made some apparently commonplace remark as he passed, which, coupled with his easy manner and the correct countersign, threw the young soldier off his guard. Suddenly a long sharp knife gleamed in the faint light and was drawn across the body of Lewis before he could raise a hand to defend himself. He fell instantly, mortally wounded, with his entrails cut open. At the same moment the tramp of the rounds was heard, and the native glided back into the darkness from which he had so recently emerged.

When the soldiers came to the post they found the poor young soldier dying. He was able to tell what had occurred while they were making preparations to carry him away, but when they reached the fort they found that his brief career had ended.

A damp was cast on the spirits of the men of his company when they learned next day what had occurred, for the lad had been a great favourite; but soldiers in time of war are too much accustomed to look upon death in every form to be deeply or for long affected by incidents of the kind. Only the comrades who had become unusually attached to this poor youth mourned his death as if he had been a brother in the flesh as well as in the ranks.

"He was a good lad," said Sergeant Gilroy, as they kept watch on the roof of the fort that night. "Since we came here he has never missed writing to his mother a single mail. It is true, being an amiable lad, and easily led through his affections, he had given way to drink to some extent, but no later than yesterday I prevailed upon him to join our temperance band—"

"What? become a Blue Light!" exclaimed Sutherland, with something of a sneer in his tone.

"Ah, comrade; and I hope to live to see you join our band also, and become one of the bluest lights among us," returned the sergeant good-humouredly.

"Never!" replied Sutherland, with emphasis; "you'll never live to see that."

"Perhaps not, but if I don't live to see it some one else will," rejoined the sergeant, laying his hand gently on the man's shoulder.

"Is that you again? It's wishin' I am that I had you in ould Ireland," growled Corporal Flynn, referring to Osman Digna, whose men had opened fire on the neighbouring fort, and again roused the whole garrison. "Slape is out o' the question wi' such a muskitos buzzin' about. Bad luck to 'ee!"

"What good would it do to send him to Ireland?" asked Simkin, as he yawned, rolled over, and, like the rest of his comrades, loaded his rifle.

"Why, man, don't ye see, av he was in ould Ireland he couldn't be disturbin' our night's rest here. Moreover, they'd make a dacent man of 'im there in no time. It's always the way; if an English blackguard goes over to Ireland he's almost sure to return home more or less of a gintleman. That's why I've always advised you to go over, boy. An' maybe if Osman wint he'd— Hallo!"

A flash of light and whistling of bullets overhead effectually stopped the Irishman's discourse. Not that he was at all alarmed by the familiar incident, but being a change of subject it became more absorbingly interesting than the conversation, besides necessitating some active precautions.

The firing seemed to indicate an attack in several places along the line of defence. At one of the posts called the New House the attack was very sharp. The enemy could not have been much, if at all, over three hundred yards distant in the shelter of three large pits. Of course the fire was vigorously returned. A colonel and major were there on the redoubt, with powerful field-glasses, and directed the men where to fire until the General himself appeared on the scene and took command. On the left, from Quarantine Island, the Royal Engineers kept up a heavy cross-fire, and on the right they were helped by a fort which was manned by Egyptian troops. From these three points a heavy fire was kept up, and continued till six o'clock in the morning.

By that time, the enemy having been finally driven out of the pits, a party was sent across to see what execution had been done. It was wonderfully little, considering the amount of ammunition and energy expended. In the first pit one man was found dead; a bullet had entered his forehead and come out at the back of his head. Moving him a little on one side they found another man under him, shot in the same way. All round the pit inside were large pools of blood, but no bodies, for the natives invariably dragged or carried away their dead when that was possible. In the other two pits large pools of blood were also found, but no bodies. Beyond them, however, one man was discovered shot through the heart. He had evidently been dragged along the sand, but the tremendous fire of the defenders had compelled the enemy to drop him. Still further on they found twelve more corpses which had been dragged a short way and then left.

Close to these they observed that the sand had been disturbed, and on turning it up found that a dozen of bodies had been hastily buried there. Altogether they calculated that at least fifty of the enemy had been killed on that occasion—a calculation which was curiously verified by the friendly tribes asking permission to bury the dead according to the Soudanese custom. This was granted, of course, and thus the exact number killed was ascertained, but how many had been wounded no one could tell.

"Fifty desolated homes!" remarked one of the men, when the number of killed was announced at mess that day. He was a cynical, sour-visaged man, who had just come out of hospital after a pretty severe illness. "Fifty widows, may-hap," he continued, "to say nothin' o' child'n—that are just as fond o' husbands an' fathers as *ours* are!"

"Why, Jack Hall, if these are your sentiments you should never have enlisted," cried Simkin, with a laugh.

"I 'listed when I was drunk," returned Hall savagely.

"Och, then, it sarves ye right!" said Flynn. "Even a pig would be ashamed to do anythin' whin it was in liquor."

The corporal's remark prevented the conversation taking a lugubrious turn, to the satisfaction of a few of the men who could not endure to look at anything from a serious point of view.

"What's the use," one of them asked, "of pullin' a long face over what you can't change? Here we are, boys, to kill or be killed. My creed is, 'Take things as they come, and be jolly!' It won't mend matters to think about wives and child'n."

"Won't it?" cried Armstrong, looking up with a bright expression from a sheet of paper on which he had just been writing. "Here am I writin' home to *my* wife—in a hurry too, for I've only just heard that word has been passed, the mail for England goes to-day. I'm warned for guard to-night, too; an' if the night takes after the day we're in for a chance o' suffocation, to say nothing o' insects—as you all know. Now, won't it mend matters that I've got a dear girl over the sea to think about, and to say 'God bless her, body and soul?'"

"No doubt," retorted the take-things-as-they-come-and-be-jolly man, "but—but—"

"But," cried Hall, coming promptly to his rescue, "have not the Soudanese got wives an' children as well as us?"

"I daresay they have—some of 'em."

"Well, does the thought of your respective wives an' children prevent your shooting or sticking each other when you get the chance?"

"Of course it don't!" returned Armstrong, with a laugh as he resumed his pencil. "What would be the use o' comin' here if we didn't do that? But I haven't time to argue with you just now, Hall. All I know is that it's my duty to write to my wife, an' I won't let the chance slip when I've got it."

"Bah!" exclaimed the cynic, relighting his pipe, which in the heat of debate he had allowed to go out.

Several of the other men, having been reminded of the mail by the conversation, also betook themselves to pen and pencil, though their hands were more familiar with rifle and bayonet. Among these was Miles Milton. Mindful of his recent thoughts, and re-impressed with the word *Duty*, which his friend had just emphasised, he sat down and wrote a distinctly self-condemnatory letter home. There was not a word of excuse, explanation, or palliation in it from beginning to end. In short, it expressed one idea throughout, and that was—Guilty! and of course this was followed by his asking forgiveness. He had forgiveness—though he knew it not—long before he asked it. His broken-hearted father and his ever-hopeful mother had forgiven him in their hearts long before—even before they received that treasured fragment from Portsmouth, which began and ended with:

"Dearest Mother, I am sorry—"

After finishing and despatching the letter, Miles went out with a feeling of lightness about his heart that he had not felt since that wretched day when he forsook his father's house.

As it was still early in the afternoon he resolved to take a ramble in the town, but, seeing Sergeant Gilroy and another man busy with the Gardner gun on the roof of the redoubt, he turned aside to ask the sergeant to accompany him; for Gilroy was a very genial Christian, and Miles had lately begun to relish his earnest, intelligent talk, dashed as it was with many a touch of humour.

The gun they were working with at the time had been used the day before in ascertaining the exact range of several objects on the ground in front.

"I'll be happy to go with you, Miles, after I've given this gun a clean-out," said Gilroy. "Turn the handle, Sutherland."

"I'll turn the handle if it's a' richt," said the cautious Scot, with some hesitation.

"It is all right," returned the sergeant. "We ran the feeder out last night, you know, and I want to have the barrels cleaned. Turn away."

Thus ordered a second time, Sutherland obeyed and turned the handle. The gun went off, and its contents passed through the sergeant's groin, making a hole through which a man could have passed his arm.

He dropped at once, and while some ran for the doctor, and some for water, others brought a stretcher to carry the poor fellow to hospital. Meanwhile Miles, going down on his knees beside him, raised his head and moistened his pale lips with water. He could hardly speak, but a smile passed over his face as he said faintly, "She'll get my presents by this mail. Write, Miles—break it to her—we'll meet again—by the side of Jesus—God be praised!"

He ceased, and never spoke again.

Gilroy was a married man, with five children. Just before the accident he had written to his wife enclosing gifts for his little ones, and telling, in a thankful spirit, of continued health and safety. Before the mail-steamer with his letter on board was out of sight he was dead!

Chapter Fourteen-Describes some of Osman Digna's Eccentricities and Other Matters

One day Miles and his friend Armstrong went to have a ramble in the town of Suakim, and were proceeding through the bazaar when they encountered Simkin hurrying towards them with a much too serious expression on his face!

"Have you heard the n–news?" he asked, on coming up.

"No; what's up?"

"The old shep–shepherd's bin killed; all the c–cattle c–captured, an' the Egyptian c–cavalry's bin sent out after them."

"Nonsense! You're dreaming, or you've bin drinking," said Miles.

"Neither dreamin' nor drinkin'," returned Simkin, with indignation, as he suddenly delivered a blow at our hero's face. Miles stopped it, however, gave him a playful punch in the chest, and passed on.

At first Simkin seemed inclined to resent this, but, while he swayed about in frowning indecision, his comrades left him; shaking his head, therefore, with intense gravity, he walked away muttering, "Not a bad fellow Miles, after all, if he w–wasn't so fond o' the b–bottle!"

Miles was at the same moment making the same remark to his friend in reference to Simkin, and with greater truth.

"But I don't wonder that the men who drink go in for it harder than ever here," continued Miles. "There is such hard work, and constant exposure, and so little recreation of any sort. Yet it is a pity that men should give way to it, for too many of our comrades are on the sick-list because of it, and some under the sod."

"It is far more than a pity," returned Armstrong, with unwonted energy. "Drink with its attendant evils is one of the great curses of the army. I have been told, and I can well believe it, that drink causes more loss to an army than war, the dangers of foreign service, and unhealthy climates, all put together."

"That's a strong statement, Willie, and would need to be founded on good authority. Who told you?"

"Our new parson told me, and he is in my opinion a good authority, because he is a Christian, if ever a man was; and he is an elderly man, besides being uncommonly clever and well informed. He told us a great many strong facts at the temperance meeting we held last night. I wish you had been there, Miles. It would have warmed your heart, I think."

"Have you joined them, Willie?"

"Yes, I have; and, God helping me, I mean to stick by them!"

"I would have gone to the meeting myself," said Miles thoughtfully, "if I had been asked."

"Strange," returned Armstrong, "that Sergeant Hardy said to me he thought of asking you to accompany us, but had an idea that you wouldn't care to go. Now, just look at that lot there beside the grog-shop door. What a commentary on the evils of drink!"

The lot to which he referred consisted of a group of miserable loungers in filthy garments and fez-caps, who, in monkey-like excitement, or solemn stupidity, stood squabbling in front of one of the many Greek drinking-shops with which the town was cursed.

Passing by at the moment, with the stately contempt engendered by a splendid physique and a red coat, strode a trooper—one of the defenders of the town. His gait was steady enough, but there was that unmistakable something in the expression of his face which told that he was in the grip of the same fiend that had captured the men round the grog-shop door. He was well-known to both Armstrong and Miles.

"Hallo! Johnson," cried the latter. "Is there any truth in the—"

He stopped, and looked steadily in the trooper's eyes without speaking.

"Oh yes, I know what you mean," said Johnson, with a reckless air. "I know that I'm drunk."

"I wouldn't say exactly that of you," returned Miles; "but—"

"Well, well, I say it of myself," continued the trooper. "It's no use humbuggin' about it. I'm swimmin' wi' the current. Goin' to the dogs like a runaway locomotive. Of course I see well enough that men like Sergeant Hardy, an' Stevenson of the Marines, who have been temperance men all their lives, enjoy good health—would to God I was like 'em! And I know that drinkers are dyin' off like sheep, but that makes it all the worse for me, for, to tell you the honest truth, boys—an' I don't care who knows it—I *can't* leave off drinkin'. It's killin' me by inches. I know, likewise, that all the old hard drinkers here are soon sent home ruined for life—such of 'em at least as don't leave their miserable bones in the sand, and I know that I'm on the road to destruction, but I can't—I *won't* give it up!"

"Ha! Johnson," said Armstrong, "these are the very words quoted by the new parson at the temperance meetin' last night—an' he's a splendid fellow with his tongue. 'Hard drinker,' says he, 'you are humbuggin' yourself. You say you *can't* give up the drink. The real truth is, my man, that you *won't* give it up. If only I could persuade you, in God's strength, to say "I *will*," you'd soon come all right.' Now, Johnson, if you'll come with me to the next meetin'—"

"What! *me* go to a temperance meetin'?" cried the trooper with something of scorn in his laugh. "You might as well ask the devil to go to church! No, no, Armstrong, I'm past prayin' for—thank you all the same for invitin' me. But what was you askin' about news bein' true? What news?"

"Why, that the old shepherd has been killed, and all our cattle are captured, and the Egyptian cavalry sent after them."

"You don't say so!" cried the trooper, with the air of a man who suddenly shakes off a heavy burden. "If that's so, they'll be wantin' us also, no doubt."

Without another word he turned and strode away as fast as his long legs could carry him.

Although there might possibly be a call for infantry to follow, Miles and his friend did not see that it was needful to make for their fort at more than their ordinary pace.

It was a curious and crowded scene they had to traverse. Besides the grog-shops already mentioned there were numerous coffee-houses, where, from diminutive cups, natives of temperate habits slaked their thirst and discussed the news—of which, by the way, there was no lack at the time; for, besides the activity of Osman Digna and his hordes, there were frequent arrivals of mails, and sometimes of reinforcements, from Lower Egypt. In the side-streets were many smithies, where lance-heads and knives were being forged by men who had not the most distant belief that such weapons would ever be turned into pruning-hooks. There were also workers in leather, who sewed up passages of the Koran in leathern cases and sold them as amulets to be worn on necks and arms. Elsewhere, hairdressers were busy greasing and powdering with the dust of red-wood the bushy locks of Hadendoa dandies. In short, all the activities of Eastern city life were being carried on as energetically as if the place were in perfect security, though the only bulwark that preserved it, hour by hour, from being swept by the innumerable hordes of Soudan savagery, consisted of a few hundreds of British and Egyptian soldiers!

Arrived at the Sphinx Fort, the friends found that the news was only too true.

The stolen cattle belonged to the people of Suakim. Every morning at six o'clock it was the custom of the shepherds to go out with their herds and flocks to graze, there being no forage in or near the town. All had to be back by sunset, when the gates were locked, and no one was allowed out or in till six the next morning. The women, who carried all the water used in the waterless town, had of course to conform to the same rule. Like most men who are constantly exposed to danger, the shepherds became careless or foolhardy, and wandered rather far with their herds. Osman was too astute to neglect his opportunities. On this occasion an old shepherd, who was well-known at Sphinx Redoubt, had strayed too far. The Soudanese swept down, cut off his retreat, killed him, and, as we have said, carried off his cattle.

It was to retrieve, if possible, or avenge this disaster that the Egyptian cavalry sallied forth. They were seen galloping after the foe when Miles reached the roof of the redoubt, where some of his comrades were on duty, while Captain Lacey and several officers were looking on with field-glasses.

"They are too late, I fear, to do much good," remarked one of the officers.

"Don't I wish I was goin' wid them!" whispered Corporal Flynn to a comrade.

"Ye wad be a queer objec' on the ootside o' a horse," remarked Macleod cynically.

"Why, Mac, ye wouldn't have me go *inside* of a horse, would ye?"

"It wad be much the same which way ye went," returned the Scot.

"Ah, thin, the horse wouldn't think so, unless he was a donkey!"

"Well done!" exclaimed Captain Lacey at that moment, as the cavalry cut off and succeeded in recapturing a few of the cattle, and gave the enemy several volleys, which caused them to beat a hasty retreat. This, however, turned out to be a *ruse* on the part of Osman, who had his men concealed in strong force there. He tried to draw the cavalry away from Suakim, and was very nearly successful. In the ardour of pursuit the Egyptians failed to observe that the Soudanese were creeping round their rear to cut off retreat. On discovering their mistake, and finding that their small force of two hundred men was being surrounded by thousands of Arab warriors, it was almost too late. Turning at once, they galloped back, and could be seen, through the field-glasses, turning now and then gallantly to engage the pursuing foe.

No help could be rendered them at first, as they were beyond the range of all the forts; nevertheless, they got in safely, with little injury to man or beast, and driving before them the animals that had been recovered.

Next day the body of the poor old shepherd was brought in and buried, without a coffin, by his relations.

Miles, being off duty at the time, went to see the funeral, and found that Eastern and Western ideas on this point, as on many others, are wide as the poles asunder. No doubt the grief of the near relations was as real as it was demonstrative, but it required more credulity than he possessed to enable him to believe that the howling, shouting, and singing of many mourners was indicative of genuine feeling. The creation of noise, indeed, seemed to be their chief method of paying respect to the dead.

As deaths in Suakim were very numerous at this time, owing to much sickness among natives as well as troops, the sounds of mourning, whether by volley or voice, became so frequent that orders were at last given to cease firing over the soldiers' graves when they were buried.

Just ahead of the shepherd's body came some poor women, who were weeping, falling down at intervals, and kissing the ground. On reaching the wall round the land side of the town these women stopped, formed a circle, and kneeled on the sand while the body was passing them, then they leaned forward and kissed the ground, continuing in that position till all the procession had passed. There the women remained, not being allowed to go to the grave, and the singing and shouting were continued by boys, who kept running round the bier as it was borne along. On reaching the grave the body was put in with the face toward the east, and covered up with stones and mortar. Then the grave was filled up with sand, a brief prayer was offered — the mourners kneeling — after which the people went home.

Sad thoughts filled the mind of our young soldier as he returned to the fort, but the sadness was soon turned to indignation when he got there.

For some time past a Soudanese youth of about seventeen or eighteen years of age had been coming about the Sphinx Redoubt and ingratiating himself with the men, who took a great fancy to him, because he was amiable in disposition, somewhat humorous as well as lively, and handsome, though black! They used to give him something to eat every time he came, and made quite a pet of him. One day while he was out in the open country, Osman's men captured this youth and took him at once before their leader, who, probably regarding him as a deserter, ordered both his hands to be cut off close to the wrists. The cruel deed was done, and the poor lad was sent back to Suakim. It was this that roused the wrath of Miles as well as that of his comrades. When they saw the raw stumps and the haggard look of the poor fellow, who had suffered much from loss of blood, they got into a state of mind that would have made them ready to sally forth, if so required, and assault the entire Soudan in arms!

"Och! av I only had 'im here," said Flynn, clenching his teeth and fists at the same time. "It's—it's—it's—"

"Mince-meat you'd make of him," said Moses.

"No—it's *cat's* mate—the baste!"

The others were equally angry, though not quite so emphatic, but they did not waste their time in useless regrets. They hurried the young Soudanese to the doctor, who carefully dressed his wounds, and every care was thereafter taken of him by the men, until completely restored to health.

It may interest the reader to know that this poor fellow was afterwards well looked after. Some sort of employment in the garrison was obtained for him, and he was found to be a useful and willing servant, despite the absence of his hands.

That night a furious sand-storm burst upon the town, accompanied by oppressive heat.

"It always seems to me," said Miles to Gaspard Redgrave, who lay next him, "that mosquitoes and sand-flies, cats and dogs, and in fact the whole brute creation, becomes more lively when the weather is unusually hot. Just listen to these cats!"

"Like a colony of small children being murdered," said Gaspard.

"It's awfu'," observed Saunders, in a kind of solemn astonishment as a frightful caterwaul burst upon their ears. "I wadna like to hear teegers in the same state o' mind."

"Or elephants," murmured Moses Pyne, who was more than half asleep.

The cats were indeed a great nuisance, for, not satisfied with getting on the flat roofs of the houses at nights, and keeping up a species of war-dance there, they invaded the soldiers' quarters, upsetting things in the dark—thus demonstrating the absurdity of the proverb that cats see best in the dark—stealing whatever they could lay hold of, and inducing half-slumbering men to fling boots and shoes, or whatever came most handy, at them.

Rats also were innumerable, and, to the great surprise—not to say indignation—of the men, neither dogs nor cats paid the least attention to the rats!

After a time the storm, both of animate and inanimate nature, began to abate, and the weary overworked soldiers were dropping off to sleep when a tremendous explosion effectually roused them.

"There goes another mine!" cried Armstrong, starting up.

"It don't require a prophet to tell us that," growled Gaspard, as he yawned and slowly picked up his rifle.

Explosions were of quite common occurrence at that time, but had to be attended to nevertheless.

That Osman had taken advantage of the very dark night to make an earlier attack than usual was evident, for shots were fired immediately after the explosion occurred, as usual. These were replied to, but the effect of the explosion, it was supposed, must have been unusually severe, for the enemy withdrew after exchanging only a few shots.

This surmise was afterwards proved to be correct. On going to the spot the following morning, they found that at least a dozen of their foes must have been blown up, for legs and arms and other human remains were picked up in all directions. These the soldiers gathered, with the aid of the friendly natives, and burned.

No attack was made for four days after that, but then the untiring enemy became as troublesome as ever.

Spies afterwards said that when Osman heard of this incident, and of the number of men killed, he said, "it served them right. They had no business to go touching things that did not belong to them!"

Chapter Fifteen-Athletics—A New Acquaintance turns up—An Expedition undertaken, followed by a Race for Life

Energetic and exhilarating exercise has sometimes the effect of driving away sickness which doctors' stuff and treatment fail to cope with successfully. In saying this we intend no slight either to doctors' stuff or treatment!

After the troops had been some time at Suakim the effect of the climate began to tell on them so severely that a very large proportion of Europeans were in hospital, and many who strove hard to brave it out were scarcely fit for duty.

Great heat did not, however, interfere with Miles Milton's health. He was one of those fortunates who seem to have been made of tougher clay than the average of humanity. But his friend Armstrong was laid up for a considerable time. Even Robert Macleod was knocked over for a brief period, and the lively Corporal Flynn succumbed at last. Moses Pyne, however, stood the test of hard work and bad climate well, and so, for a time, did Sergeant Hardy. It was found generally that the abstainers from strong drink suffered less from bad health and unwholesome surroundings than their fellows, and as there were a good many in the regiment, who were constantly endeavouring to convince their comrades of the advantages of total-abstinence, things were not so bad as they might have been.

It was about this time that one of the generals who visited Suakim instituted athletic games, thereby vastly improving the health and spirits of the men. And now Miles Milton learned, for the first time, what an immense power there lies in "scientific training!"

One evening, when out walking with Stevenson, he took it into his head to race with him, and, having been a crack runner at school, he beat him easily.

"Why, Miles," said his friend, when the short race was over, "I had no idea you could run so well. If you choose I will put you in training for the coming sports. You must know that I have run and walked and competed in the track many a time at home, and have trained and brought out runners who had no notion of what was in them till I proved it to them by training. Will you go in for it, and promise to do as I bid you?"

"I have no objection," replied Miles, with a light laugh.

If he had known what his friend intended to do he might not have agreed so readily, for, from that hour till the day of the sports, Stevenson made him go through an amount of running—even after being made stiff by previous runs—that he would never have agreed to undertake unless forced to do so. We say *forced*, because our hero regarded a promise once given as sacred. His was a curiously compound nature, so that while in some points of conduct he was lax—as we have seen—in others he was very strict. He was peculiarly so in regard to promises. His comrades soon came to know this, and ultimately came to consider him a very reliable man.

Having, then, promised his friend to keep sternly to his work, he did so, with the result that his strength increased wonderfully. Another result was that he carried off the first prize in all the races.

In order to make the most of time and avoid the evils of noonday heat, it was arranged that the races, etcetera, for the Egyptian soldiers and natives in Government employ should come off in the morning, and that the British troops should run in the later and cooler parts of the day. With the temperature at 120 degrees in the shade it would have been dangerous for Europeans to compete. The sports, including our familiar cricket, were greatly enjoyed, and the result was a decided improvement in the health of the whole force.

Boat-races were also included in these sports. At the conclusion of one of these, Miles, to his great surprise, encountered his old acquaintance of the *Sailors' Welcome*, big Jack Molloy.

"Why, Jack!" exclaimed Miles, as the hearty tar wrung his hand, "who'd have expected to see *you* here?"

"Ah, who indeed? an' I may say ditto."

"I'm *very* glad to see you, Molloy, for, to say truth, I thought I had seen the last of you when we parted in the troop-ship. I've often thought of you since, and of our first evening together in the—the—what was its name?"

"The *Sailors' Welcome*—man alive! I wonder you've forgot it. Blessin's on it! *I* ain't likely to forget it. Why, it was there, (did I ever tell you?) the wery night arter I met you, that a messmate took me to the big hall, back o' the readin'-room. It's no use me tryin' fur to tell you all I heard in that there big hall, but when I come out—blow'd if I didn't sign the pledge right away, an' I ain't took a drop o' grog since!"

"Glad to hear it, Jack, for, to say truth, I never saw the evil of grog so clearly as I have since coming out here and seeing strong stout men cast down by it in dozens,—many of them kind-hearted, right-thinking men, whom I would have thought safe from such a thing. Indeed I have more than half a mind to join the Good Templars myself."

"Young man," said Molloy, sternly, "if it takes the death of dozens o' stout kind-hearted men to force you to make up half your mind, how many d'ee want to die before you make up the whole of it?"

"But I said that my mind was *more* than half made up," returned Miles, with a smile.

"Now lookee here," rejoined the sailor earnestly, "it's all wery well for milksops an' nincompoops and landlubbers to go in for half-an'-half work like that, but you're not the man I takes you for if you ain't game for more than that, so I ax you to promise me that you'll sign the pledge right off, as I did, first time you gits the chance."

"But you forget I'm only a landlubber who, according to you, is fit for only half-an-half measures," said Miles, who, not being addicted to much wine, felt disinclined to bind himself.

"No matter," returned the sailor, with deepening earnestness, "if you go in fur it you'll *never* repent it! Take my word for that. Now, I ax ye to promise."

"Well, I *do* promise—the very first time I get the chance; and that will be to-morrow night, for our new parson has started temperance meetings, and he is a great teetotaller."

"An' you promise to stick to it?" added Molloy.

"When I give a promise I *always* stick to it!" returned Miles gravely.

"Right you are, lad. Give us your flipper!"

The foregoing conversation took place at the harbour, a little apart from the noisy group of soldiers and sailors who were discussing the circumstances of the recent boat-race.

Immediately after it Molloy returned to his ship in the harbour, and our hero to his post in the line of defence.

One of those who had been conspicuous that day in arranging and starting the races, acting as umpire at the cricket, and, generally, putting heart and spirit into everything by his quiet good-nature and self-denying activity, was the young officer of Engineers, who has been already mentioned as the manager of the mines that were laid around Suakim. Poor fellow! little did he imagine that that was to be his last day on earth!

Every morning, as before mentioned, this young officer went out alone to perform the dangerous work of disconnecting the mines, so that the inhabitants of the town might go out and in and move about during the day-time in safety. Again, a little before sunset every evening, he went out and reconnected them, so that the enemy could not approach the place without the risk of being blown to pieces. At the same time the gates were closed, and no one was allowed to leave or enter the town.

On this particular evening the lieutenant went out as usual on his dangerous mission just after six o'clock. He had not been long gone when a loud explosion was heard, and a cloud of smoke was seen where one of the mines had been laid down. A party at once sallied out, and found, as they had feared, that the brave young fellow had perished. He had been literally blown to pieces, his head being found in one place, while other portions of his body were scattered around.

This melancholy incident cast a gloom over the whole place. The remains of the heroic young engineer were buried next day with military honours. The garrison was not, however, left long in peace to think over his sad fate, for the very next night a determined attack was made all along the line. The annoying persistency of these attacks seemed to have stirred the indignation of the general in command, for he ordered out a small force of cavalry to carry the war into the enemy's country.

Critics say that this act was ill advised, and that the cavalry should not have been despatched without the support of infantry. Critics are not always or necessarily right. Indeed, we may venture to say that they are often wrong! We do not pretend to judge, but, be this as it may, the cavalry was ordered to destroy the village of Handoub about fifteen miles inland on the caravan route to Berber, and to blow up the enemy's magazine there.

The force consisted of a troop of the 19th Hussars, and another of Egyptian cavalry—about fifty men all told—under command of Captain Apthorp. Our intemperate friend Johnson was one of the little band. He was sober then, however, as he sat bolt upright on his powerful steed, with a very stern and grave visage, for he had a strong impression that the duty before them was no child's-play.

A four hours' ride brought them to the village. The few Arabs who dwelt in it fled at once on their approach, and in a very short time the place was effectually destroyed, along with a large quantity of ammunition.

But no sooner had the soldiers finished the work, and begun to prepare for their return, than they discovered that a large force of the enemy was assembling to cut off their retreat.

No time for thought after that! At least six thousand of the foe, having heard of the expedition, had crept down through the thick bush from the direction of Hasheen, thirsting for vengeance. Two miles on the Suakim side of Handoub they formed a line and opened fire on the leading cavalry scouts.

Seeing that the Arabs were in such force, Captain Apthorp at once made for their flank, in the direction of the sea-coast. At full speed, with horses fatigued by a fifteen miles' journey, they had to ride for life. It was neck or nothing now! The Egyptian cavalry, under Captain Gregorie, and accompanied by Captain Stopford of the Grenadier Guards and other officers, followed closely.

As they went along at racing speed, with more than a dozen miles of wilderness to traverse, and death behind them, Private King of the Hussars fell from his horse wounded. Captain Gregorie came up with him, stopped, and took the wounded man up behind him. It was a generous but desperate act, for what could be expected of a double-weighted horse in such a region and with such a race before it?

For about half a mile he carried the wounded trooper, who then swooned and fell off, dragging the captain along with him, the freed horse rejoining its troop, while the Arabs came yelling on not a hundred and fifty yards behind.

There would have been but little chance for Captain Gregorie at that terrible crisis if self-denying courage equal to his own had not dwelt in the breast of Private Baker of the Hussars. Seeing what had occurred, this hero coolly rode back, took the captain up behind him, (see frontispiece,) and, regaining his troop, enabled the latter to capture and remount his own steed. Of course poor King — whether dead or alive they could not tell — had to be left to his fate.

Heroism would seem to feed upon itself and multiply, for this same Private Baker, soon afterwards, saw two more troopers, and shouted to a comrade to turn back with him to their rescue. The comrade, however, did not see his way to do so. Perchance he did not hear! Anyhow he galloped on, but Captain Gregorie hearing the summons, at once answered it, turned, and galloped back with Baker.

They were only just in time to take up and rescue the two men. At the same time Captain Stopford performed a similar gallant act in rescuing a dismounted trooper.

It is deeds of self-sacrifice and heroism such as these — not the storming of a breach, or the fighting against overwhelming odds — that bring out the noblest qualities of our soldiers, and arouse the admiration of mankind!

The race for life was so close run that when the force at last reached the sea-shore it was little more than sixty yards in advance of the foe, and so exhausted were the horses that eight of them fell, and their riders were captured—four being Englishmen and four Egyptians. It is right to add that one of the Egyptians also displayed conspicuous courage in rescuing a comrade.

While these stirring incidents were taking place on the plain, Miles and some of his comrades were seated on the roof of the redoubt, looking out anxiously for the return of the cavalry. At last, in the afternoon, a cloud of dust was seen on the horizon, and the officers who had glasses could soon make out that the men appeared to be racing towards the town at full speed, while the enemy, on camels and horses, and on foot, were racing down to the sea to cut off their retreat. No sooner was this understood than our men rose with an uncontrollable burst, seized their rifles, flung on ammunition-belts, and rushed out to the rescue, regardless for the moment of the officers shouting to them to come back. The news spread like wildfire, and the men ran out just as they were—some in white jackets, some in red, others in blue; many in their shirts, with their sleeves rolled up; cavalry, artillery, marines, infantry—all going helter-skelter towards the enemy. Fortunately they saw from the ships what was going on, and quickly got their guns to bear, so that the moment our men had escaped clear of the enemy they opened fire. But for this more men would certainly have been lost, for the overtaxed horses were beginning to give in and lose ground. Had they been a few minutes later in reaching the sea, it is probable that not a man of that force would have returned to Suakim.

As it was, the men came in pale and terribly fatigued. The horses could scarcely walk, and two of them died on the following day.

Note.—Since the foregoing was written, we have learned, with profound regret, that the gallant Captain Gregorie was killed by his horse falling with him in 1886.

Chapter Sixteen-Letters from Home— Flynn is Exalted and brought Low— Rumours of War in the Air

Events in life sometimes ripple along like the waters of a little stream in summer. At other times they rush with the wild impetuosity of a hill-torrent in winter.

For some time after the incidents just narrated the life of our hero rippled—but of course it must be clearly understood that a Suakim ripple bore some resemblance to a respectable freshet elsewhere! Osman Digna either waited for reinforcements before delivering a grand assault, or found sufficient entertainment to his mind, and satisfaction to his ambition, in acting the part of a mosquito, by almost nightly harassment of the garrison, which was thus kept continually on the alert.

But there came a time at length when a change occurred in the soldier-life at Suakim. Events began to evolve themselves in rapid succession, as well as in magnified intensity, until, on one particular day, there came— metaphorically speaking—what is known among the Scottish hills as a spate.

It began with the arrival of a mail from England. This was not indeed a matter of rare occurrence, but it was one of those incidents of the campaign which never lost its freshness, and always sent a thrill of pleasure to the hearts of the men—powerfully in the case of those who received letters and packets; sympathetically in those who got none.

"At long last!" exclaimed Corporal Flynn, who was observed by his comrades, after the delivery of the mail, to be tenderly struggling with the complicated folds of a remarkable letter—remarkable for its crookedness, size, dirt, and hieroglyphic superscription.

"What is it, Flynn?" asked Moses—one of the unfortunates who had received no letter by that mail.

"A letter, sure. Haven't ye got eyes, Moses?"

"From your wife, corporal?"

"Wife!" exclaimed Flynn, with scorn; "no! It's mesilf wouldn't take the gift of a wife gratis. The letter is from me owld grandmother, an' she's better to me than a dozen wives rowled into wan. It's hard work the writin' of it cost her too—poor owld sowl! But she'd tear her eyes out to plaze me, she would. 'Corporal, darlint,'—that's always the way she begins her letters now; she's that proud o' me since I got the stripes. I thowt me mother or brother would have writ me too, but they're not half as proud of me as my—"

"Shut up, Flynn!" cried one of the men, who was trying to decipher a letter, the penmanship of which was obviously the work of an unaccustomed hand.

"Howld it upside down; sometimes they're easier to read that way—more sinsible-like," retorted the corporal.

"Blessin's on your sweet face!" exclaimed Armstrong, looking at a photograph which he had just extracted from his letter.

"Hallo, Bill! that your sweetheart?" asked Sergeant Hardy, who was busy untying a parcel.

"Ay, sweetheart an' wife too," answered the young soldier, with animation.

"Let me see it, Willie," said Miles, who was also one of the disconsolate non-receivers, disconsolate because he had fully expected a reply to the penitent letter which he had written to his mother.

"First-rate, that's Emmy to a tee. A splendid likeness!" exclaimed Miles, holding the photograph to the light.

"Arrah! then, it's dead he must be!"

The extreme perplexity displayed in Flynn's face as he said this and scratched his head produced a hearty laugh.

"It's no laughin' matter, boys," cried the corporal, looking up with an expression so solemn that his comrades almost believed it to be genuine. "There's my owld uncle Macgrath gone to his long home, an' he was the support o' me grandmother. Och! what'll she do now wid him gone an' me away at the wars?"

"Won't some other relation look after her, Flynn?" suggested Moses.

"Other relation!" exclaimed the corporal; "I've got no other relations, an' them that I have are as poor as rats. No, uncle Macgrath was the only wan wid a kind heart an' a big purse. You see, boys, he was rich—for an Irishman. He had a grand farm, an' a beautiful bit o' bog. Och! it'll go hard wid—"

"Read on, Flynn, and hold your tongue," cried one of his comrades; "p-r-aps he's left the old woman a legacy."

The corporal did read on, and during the perusal of the letter the change in his visage was marvellous, exhibiting as it did an almost magical transition from profound woe, through abrupt gradations of surprise, to intense joy.

"Hooray!" he shouted, leaping up and bestowing a vigorous slap on his thigh. "He's gone an' left the whole farm an' the beautiful bog to *me*!"

"What hae ye got there, sergeant?" asked Saunders, refolding the letter he had been quietly perusing without paying any regard to the Irishman's good news.

"A parcel of booklets from the Institute," answered Hardy, turning over the leaves of one of the pamphlets. "Ain't it good of 'em?"

"Right you are, Hardy! The ladies there never forget us," said Moses Pyne. "Hand 'em round, sergeant. It does a fellow's heart good to get a bit o' readin' in an out-o'-the-way place like this."

"Comes like light in a dark place, don't it, comrade?" said Stevenson, the marine, who paid them a visit at that moment, bringing a letter which had been carried to the wrong quarter by mistake. It was for Miles Milton. "I know'd you expected it, an' would be awfully disappointed at finding nothing, so I brought it over at once."

"*You* come like a gleam of sunshine in a dark place. Thanks, Stevenson, many thanks," said Miles, springing up and opening the letter eagerly.

The first words sent a chill to his heart, for it told of his father having been very ill, but words of comfort immediately followed — he was getting slowly but surely better, and his own letter had done the old man more good in a few days than all the doctor's physic had done in many weeks. Forgiveness was freely granted, and unalterable love breathed in every line. With a relieved and thankful heart he went on reading, when he was arrested by a sudden summons of his company to fall in. Grasping his rifle he ran out with the rest.

"What is it?" he whispered to a sergeant, as he took his place in the ranks. "Osman again?"

"No, he's too sly a fox to show face in the day-time. It's a steamer coming with troops aboard. We're goin' down to receive them, I believe."

Soon after, the overworked garrison had the immense satisfaction and excitement of bidding welcome to reinforcements with a stirring British cheer.

These formed only the advance-guard. For some time after that troops were landed at Suakim every day. Among them the 15th Sikhs, a splendid body of men, with grand physique and fierce aspect, like men who "meant business." Then came the Coldstream Guards, the Scots and the Grenadier Guards, closely followed by the Engineers and Hospital and Transport Corps, the Shropshire Regiment, and many others. The desire of these fresh troops to meet the enemy was naturally strong, and the earnest hope of every one was that they would soon sally forth and "have a go," as Corporal Flynn expressed it, "at Osman Digna on his own ground."

Poor Corporal Flynn! His days of soldiering were nearly over!

Whether it was the excess of strong feeling raised in the poor fellow's breast by the news of the grand and unexpected legacy, or the excitement caused by the arrival of so many splendid troops and the prospect of immediate action—or all put together—we cannot say, but certain it is that the corporal fell sick, and when the doctors examined the men with a view to decide who should march to the front, and who should remain to guard the town, he was pronounced unfit for active service. Worse than that, he was reported to have entered upon that journey from which no traveller returns.

But poor Flynn would not admit it, though he grew weaker from day to day. At last it was reported that he was dying, and Sergeant Hardy got leave to go off to the hospital ship to see him, and convey to him many a kind message from his sorrowful comrades, who felt that the regiment could ill spare his lively, humorous spirit.

The sergeant found him the picture of death, and almost too weak to speak.

"My dear fellow," said Hardy, sitting down by his cot and gently taking his hand, "I'm sorry to see you like this. I'm afraid you are goin' to leave us."

The corporal made a slight motion with his head, as if of dissent, and his lips moved.

Hardy bent his ear over them.

"Niver a bit, owld man," whispered Flynn.

"Shall I read the Bible to you, lad?" inquired the sergeant.

The corporal smiled faintly, and nodded.

After reading a few verses Hardy began to talk kindly and earnestly to the dying man, who lay with his eyes closed.

When he was about to leave, Flynn looked up, and, giving his comrade's hand a gentle squeeze, said, in a stronger whisper than before—

"Thankee, sergeant. It's kind o' ye to be so consarned about my sowl, and I agrees wid ivery word ye say; but I'm not goin' away yit, av ye plaze."

He ceased to speak, and again closed his eyes. The doctor and the chaplain chanced to enter the hospital together as Hardy retired. The result of their visit was that they said the corporal was dead, and orders were given to make his coffin. A firing party was also told off to bury him the next morning with military honours. Early next morning, accordingly, the firing party started for the hospital ship with the coffin, but, before getting half-way to it, they were signalled to go back, for the man was not yet dead!

In short, Corporal Flynn had begun to talk in a wild way about his estate in Ireland, and his owld grandmother; and either the influence of these thoughts, or Hardy's visit, had given him such a fillip that from that day he began to revive. Nevertheless he had received a very severe shake, and, not very long after, was invalided home. Meanwhile, as we have said, busy preparations were being made by General Graham—who had arrived and taken command of the forces—to offer battle to Osman's troops.

In the midst of all the excitement and turmoil, however, the new chaplain, who turned out to be "a trump," managed to hold a temperance meeting; and the men who desired to serve God as well as their Queen and country became more energetic than ever in trying to influence their fellows and save themselves from the curse of strong drink, which had already played such havoc among the troops at Suakim.

Miles attended the meeting, and, according to promise, signed the total-abstinence pledge. Owing to the postponement of meetings and the press of duty he had not been able to do it sooner.

Shortly after that he was passed by the doctors as fit for duty in the field. So were Armstrong, Moses Pyne, and most of those strong and healthy men whose fortunes we have followed thus far.

Then came the bustle and excitement of preparation to go out and attack the enemy, and in the midst of it all the air was full of conflicting rumours—to the effect that Osman Digna was about to surrender unconditionally; that he would attack the town in force; that he was dead; or that he had been summoned to a conference by the Mahdi!

"You may rest assured," said Sergeant Hardy one day to his comrades, as they were smoking their pipes after dinner, "that nobody knows anything at all for certain about the rebel chief."

"I heard that a spy has just come in with the information that he has determined not to wait for our attack, if we go out, but to attack us in our zereba," said Miles. "He is evidently resolved not to commit the same mistake he made last year of letting us attack *him*."

"He has pluck for anything," remarked Moses.

Osman proved, that same evening, that he had at least pluck enough to send a pithy defiance to his foes, for an insulting letter was received by General Graham, in which Osman, recounting the victories he had gained over Hicks and Baker Pasha, boasted of his having destroyed their armies, and dared the general to come out and fight him. To this the British General replied, reminding Osman of our victories of El-Teb and Tamai, and advising him to surrender unless he wanted a worse beating than he had got before!

Mutual defiance having been thus comfortably hurled, the troops were at once detailed for service in the field, and the very next day set forth. As our hero did not, however, accompany that expedition, and as it returned to Suakim without doing anything remarkable — except some energetic and even heroic fighting, which is by no means remarkable in British troops, — we will pass on to the expedition which was sent out immediately after it, and in which Miles Milton not only took an active part, but distinguished himself. With several of his comrades he also entered on a new and somewhat unusual phase of a soldier's career.

Chapter Seventeen-The Expedition—
Enemy reported—Miles in a Dilemma

Every one has heard of the expedition, sent out under Sir John McNeill, in which that gallant general and his brave troops fought with indomitable heroism, not only against courageous foes, but against errors which, as a civilian, we will not presume to criticise, and against local difficulties which were said to be absolutely insurmountable.

Blame was due somewhere in connection with that expedition. Wherever it lay, we have a strong conviction—founded on the opinion of one who was present—that it did not rest with the commander of the force. It is not, however, our part to comment, but to describe those events which bore upon the fortunes of our hero and his immediate friends and comrades.

It was about four o'clock on an uncommonly hot morning that the bugle sounded in Suakim, and soon the place was alive with men of all arms, devouring a hasty breakfast and mustering eagerly, for they were elated at the near prospect of having "another slap at Osman!"

Strange, the unaccountably exultant joy which so many men experience at the prospect of killing each other! No doubt the Briton maintains that it is all in defence of Queen and country, hearth and home. An excellent reason, of course! But may not the Soudanese claim that the defence of chief and country, tent and home, is an equally good reason—especially when he rises to defend himself from the exactions and cruelty of those superlative tyrants, the Turks, or rather, the Turkish Pashas?—for we verily believe that the rank and file of all civilised nations would gladly live at peace if their rulers would deal in arbitration instead of war! We almost feel that an apology is due for introducing such a remark in a book about soldiers, for their duty is clear as well as hard, and bravely is it done too. Moreover, they are in no way responsible for the deeds of those:

> "Fine old English gentlemen
>   Who sit at home at ease,
> And send them forth to fight and die
>   Beyond the stormy seas!"

The troops composing this expedition consisted of one squadron of the 5th Lancers, one battalion Berkshire Regiment, one battalion of Marines, one Field Company Royal Engineers, a detachment of the Royal Navy in charge of four Gardner guns, a regiment of Sikhs, Bengal Native Infantry, Bombay Native Infantry, and a body of Madras Sappers. Along with these was sent an immense convoy of 1500 camels, besides a large number of mules with carts bearing iron water-tanks.

The orders for the expedition were that they should proceed eight miles into the bush, and there make three zerebas, or defensive enclosures of bushes, capable of sheltering the entire force.

The march was begun by McNeill moving off with his European troops in square formation. The Indian contingent, under General Hudson, followed, also in square, and in charge of the transport.

"A goodly force!" remarked Armstrong, in a low tone to Miles, as they stepped off, shoulder to shoulder, for, being both about the same size, and unusually tall, they marched together on the right flank of their company.

"Don't speak in the ranks, Willie," returned Miles, with a slight smile, for he could not shut his eyes to the fact that this strict regard for orders was due more to Marion Drew's remarks about a soldier's *duty* than to principle.

"H'm!" grunted Robert Macleod, who marched next to them, and had no conscientious scruples about talking, "we may mairch oot smert eneugh, but some o' us'll no' come back sae hearty."

"Some of us will never come back at all," replied Armstrong, gravely.

By six o'clock the rear-guard had left Suakim, and the whole of the force moved across the plain, in parts of which the men and carts sank deep in the soft sand, while in other parts the formations were partly broken by thick bush, in which the force became somewhat entangled. The cavalry went in advance as scouts. The guns, water-carts, and ammunition-wagons were in the centre, and the Indian Brigade came last, surrounding the unwieldy mass of baggage-animals. Last of all came the telegraph detachment, unrolling as they went the wire that kept open communication with head-quarters.

That a mistake had been made somewhere was obvious; but as the soul of military discipline is obedience without question, the gallant leader pressed forward, silently and steadily, whatever he may have thought.

Soon the force became so hopelessly entangled in the difficulties of the way, that the rate of advance dwindled down to little more than one mile an hour.

Not long after starting a trooper was seen galloping back, and Miles, who marched at the right corner of his square, observed that it was his friend Johnson, looking very stern indeed. Their eyes met.

"Not half enough of cavalry," he growled, as he flew past to report, "The enemy in sight—retiring in small parties in the direction of Tamai."

In returning, Johnson again rode close past the same corner of the square, and, bending low in his saddle for a moment, said to Miles, "I have signed the pledge, my boy."

A slight laugh from several of those who heard him greeted the information, but he probably did not hear it, for next moment his charger cleared a low bush in a magnificent stride, and in a few seconds man and horse were lost to sight in the bush.

"More need to sign his will," remarked Simkin, in a somewhat cynical tone.

"He has done that too," said Armstrong. "I heard him say so before we started."

The troops were halted to enable the two generals to consult at this point.

While the men stood at ease, enjoying the brief rest from severe toil under such a burning sun, our hero heard a low voice at his elbow say—

"Have *you* signed your will, John Miles?" It was a startling, as well as a sudden, question!

Miles turned quickly and found that it was Captain Lacey who had put it.

The feeling of dislike with which our young soldier had regarded the captain ever since his interruption of the conversation between himself and Marion, on board ship, had abated, but had not by any means disappeared. He had too much sense, however, to allow the state of his feelings to influence his looks or bearing.

"Yes, sir," he replied; "I made it out last night, as you advised me, in the service form. It was witnessed by our colonel and Captain Smart and the doctor. To say truth, I thought it absurd for a man who has nothing to leave to make his will, but as you said, sir, I should like my dear mother to get my kit and any arrears of pay that may be due to me after I'm gone."

"I did not mean you to take such a gloomy view of your prospects," said Captain Lacey, with a laugh. "But you know in our profession we always carry our lives in our hands, and it would be foolish not to take ordinary precautions—"

The order to resume the march here cut short the conversation, and the force continued its slow and all but impossible advance. Indeed it was soon seen that to reach the distance of eight miles out, in the circumstances, was quite beyond the power of the troops, willing, anxious, and vigorous though they were, for the bush became closer and higher as they advanced, so that a mounted man could not see over it, and so dense that the squares, though only a short distance apart, could not see each other. This state of things rendered the management of the baggage-animals extremely difficult, for mules are proverbially intractable, and camels—so meek in pictures!— are perhaps the most snarling, biting, kicking, ill-tempered animals in the world.

The day was advancing and the heat increasing, while the dust raised by the passage of such a host caused so much distress to man and beast that the general began to fear that, if an attack should be made by the enemy at that time, the greater part of the transport would have to be sacrificed. The force was therefore halted a second time, and the generals again met to consult.

They were very unwilling to give in. Another effort to advance was made, but things grew worse and worse. The day, as Moses remarked, was boiling red-hot! The carts with the heavy water-tanks sank deep in the soft sand; many of the camels' loads fell off, and these had to be replaced. Replacing a camel's load implies prevailing on a hideously tall and horribly stubborn creature to kneel, and this in the centre of a square which was already blocked up with carts and animals, as well as shouting, angry, and exhausted drivers!

At last it became evident that further progress that day was out of the question. The rear face of Hudson's square was obliterated by the straggling and struggling multitude; camels and loads were down in all directions, and despair of maintaining their formation was settling down on all ranks.

In these circumstances it became absolutely necessary to halt and form their zerebas where they stood — and that without delay. The best place they could find was selected. The European square formed a guard, while the rest threw off jackets, and, with axes and choppers, went to work with a will. Some cut down bushes, some filled sandbags to form a breastwork for guns and ammunition, and others erected the bushy walls of their woodland fortification. The Lancers covered about three miles of country as scouts. Hudson — who had to return to Suakim that night before dark — was ordered, with three regiments in line and advanced files, to cover McNeill and the working-party, while the commander himself went about encouraging the tired men, and urging them to increased exertion.

While the soldiers of all arms were thus busily engaged, a body of sailors was ordered to run one of their Gardner guns up to the corner of the square where Miles and Armstrong stood. They halted close to them, and then Miles became aware that one of the nautical gunners was no other than Jack Molloy.

"Hallo, Jack! Why, you've got a knack of turning up unexpectedly everywhere!" he exclaimed, when his friend was at leisure.

"That's wery much your own case," retorted the seaman heartily. "What brought *you* here?"

Miles slapped one of his legs by way of indicating the mode of conveyance.

"Ay, lad, and they'd need to be stout timbers too, to make headway through such a sea of sand," returned Molloy, feeling his own limbs with tenderness. "D'ee think we're in for a brush to-night, lad?"

Before the latter could reply, an aide-de-camp ran up and spoke a few hurried words to Captain Lacey, who turned to his company and called them to attention.

"Fours, right — quick march!" he said, and away they went, past the flank of Hudson's men, to guard a hollow which left that part of the square somewhat exposed. When halted and drawn up in line several files were thrown out in advance. Miles and Sutherland formed the flanking file on the right, the latter being rear-rank man to the former.

"It's a grand hiding-hole," observed Sutherland, as he peered cautiously over the edge of a low bank into a hollow where rocks and undergrowth were thickly intermingled.

"Keep a sharp look-out on your left, Sutherland," said Miles, "I will guard the right—"

He stopped abruptly and threw forward his rifle, for at that moment he observed a swarthy, black-bearded Arab, of large proportions and muscular frame, creeping forward a short distance below him. Evidently he had not heard or seen the approach of the two soldiers, for he was gazing in a different direction from them.

Miles raised his rifle and took aim at the man, but he felt an unconquerable repugnance to shoot. He had never yet met the enemy hand-to-hand. His experience heretofore had been confined to long-range firing at men who were firing at himself and his comrades, and in which, of course, he could not be sure that his bullets took effect. But now he was within fifty yards of a splendid-looking man who did not see him, who was, at the moment, innocent of any intention of injuring him, and whose expressive side-face he could clearly distinguish as he crept along with great caution towards a rock which hid the zereba of the Europeans from his view.

Miles was a good rifle-shot. A touch of the trigger he knew would be certain death to the Arab.

"I *cannot* do it!" he muttered, as he lowered his weapon and looked back over his shoulder at his comrade. The Scot, who was something of a naturalist, was engrossed at the moment in the contemplation of a little bird which was twittering on a twig in quite an opposite direction.

Miles glanced again at the Arab in a flutter of agitation as to what was his duty. The man *might* be one of the friendly natives! He could not tell.

At that moment another man appeared on the scene. He was a thin but powerful native, and armed with a short spear, such as is used when fighting at close quarters. He obviously was not troubled with scruples about committing murder, and Miles soon became aware that the thin man was "stalking" the big Arab—with what intent, of course, our soldier could only guess, but the malignant expression of the savage's countenance left little doubt on that point.

Here was a complication! Our hero was on the point of calling Sutherland from the contemplation of his little bird when he saw the thin native pounce on the Arab, who was still creeping on hands and knees. He turned just in time to divert the first spear-thrust, but not in time to draw his own long knife from its sheath as he fell. The thin savage holding him down, and having him at terrible disadvantage on his back, raised his spear, and was about to repeat the deadly thrust when Miles fired and shot him in the head.

The Arab rose, shook himself clear of the dying man, and, with astounding coolness, walked calmly towards a large rock, though Miles was reloading in haste, and Sutherland was taking steady aim at him. He looked at the soldiers and held up his hand with something like a smile of remonstrance, as Sutherland pulled the trigger. At the same moment Miles struck up the muzzle, and the ball whizzed over the Arab's head as he passed behind the rock and disappeared.

"What for did ye that?" demanded the Scot fiercely.

"Would you kill a man that was smiling at you?" retorted Miles.

The two men ran back to report to their company what they had seen. At the same moment, the company, being recalled, doubled back to its position in the square.

Here they found the defence work so far advanced that the generals were beginning to feel some confidence in their being able to repel any attack. At the same time the men were working with tremendous energy, for news had just come in that the enemy was advancing in strong force.

Chapter Eighteen-Wherein are described an Assault, a Furious Fight, and some Strange Personal Encounters

It was nearly two o'clock in the afternoon when Captain Lacey and his company resumed their place in the square.

About that time an officer of the Berkshire Regiment represented the condition of his men as requiring attention. They certainly did require it, for they had been without food since four o'clock that morning, and were consequently in urgent need of provender as well as rest and water—the last having been all consumed.

As it was imperative that the work should go on, it was found necessary to serve out food by wings.

Accordingly, the men of one half-battalion received rations and water, and were then sent to their zereba with the Gardner guns, while the other half, still lying in reserve by their piled arms, received their rations.

The marines also sat down for brief rest and refreshment. Among them was our sedate friend Stevenson, who invariably carried his small Bible with him in all his campaigns. After quickly consuming his allowance, and while waiting for water, he sat down to read a few verses of the 23rd Psalm,—for Stevenson was one of those quiet, fearless men who cannot be laughed out of doing right, and who have no fear of the face of man, whether scowling in anger or sneering in contempt.

"Hallo, Tom!" said a light-hearted comrade near him, "this is a queer time to be readin' your Bible. We'll be havin' you sayin' your prayers next!"

"I've said *them* already, Fred," replied the marine, replacing the book in his pouch. "As you say, it *is* a queer time to be readin' the Word, but not an unsuitable time, for this may be the last chance that you and I will ever have of readin' it. Our next orders may be to meet God face to face."

Stevenson was yet speaking when a Lancer was seen approaching at a wild gallop. He dashed up to the generals and informed them that the enemy was gathering in front.

The message was barely delivered when another Lancer rode up and reported the enemy close at hand.

The order, "Stand to your arms!" was promptly given and as promptly obeyed, without flurry or disorder.

Next minute a wild uproar was heard, and the Lancers were seen galloping towards the square with thousands of the swarthy warriors of the desert at their heels — nay, even mixed up with them!

On they came, a dark, frantic, yelling host, with irresistible fury, and, perchance, patriotism! Shall we deny to those men what we claim for ourselves — love of hearth and home, of country, of freedom? Can we not sympathise with men who groaned under an insolent and tyrannical yoke, and who, failing to understand or appreciate the purity of the motives by which we British were actuated, could see nothing in us except the supporters of their enemies?

They hurled themselves on that part of the large zereba which was defended by the Bengal Native Infantry. These fired a volley, but failed to check the impetuous rush. Everything went down before the savages, and the Native Infantry broke and fled, throwing into dire confusion the transport animals which stood in their immediate rear.

General McNeill himself dashed in among the panic-stricken men and sought to arrest them. He succeeded for a time in rallying some of them in Number 1 zereba, but another rush of the Arabs sent them flying a second time, and some of the enemy got into the square, it is said, to the number of 112. The Berkshire men, however, stood fast, and not a soul who got into that square ever got out of it alive. In this wretched affair the 17th Bengal Native Infantry lost their brave commander. He was killed while trying to rally them.

The confusion was now increased by the enemy driving the baggage-animals hither and thither, especially on to another half-battalion square of the Berkshire Regiment. Here, however, they were effectually checked. As the Atlantic billows burst in impotent turmoil on the cliffs of Cornwall, so the enemy fell upon and were hurled back by the steadfast Berkshire Regiment, which scarcely lost a man, while over two hundred of their opponents lay dead around them.

The Bombay Regiment also stood fast, and redeemed, to some extent, the credit of their country; while the Sikhs, as might have been expected of them, never flinched for a moment, but strewed the plain around them with dead and dying men.

There was horrible carnage for some time — unflinching valour being opposed to desperate courage; and while a burning sense of injury, with a resolve to conquer or die, was the motive power, no doubt, on one side, on the other there was the high sense of duty to Queen and country, and the pride of historical renown.

Owing to the suddenness of the attack, and the occupation of the troops at the moment, there was some mixing up of men of different regiments. One company of Sikhs, who were helping to unload the camels when the fight began, having been prevented from joining their own regiment, cast in their lot with the marines. The better to help their European comrades these vigorous fellows leaped outside the zereba and lay down in front of it, and the two bodies together gave the charging foe such a warm reception that they never got within twenty yards of them.

But there was a fearful scene of butchery among the baggage-animals, and many unequal hand-to-hand conflicts. There was terrible slaughter also among the working parties that had gone out to cut bushes with which to finish the zerebas, with coats off and away from their arms. Some individuals of the marines, who, as a body, suffered severely, were surrounded by a dozen Arabs, and their bodies were afterwards found covered with spear-wounds. This was the case with a sergeant named Mitchel, who had charge of a wood-cutting party and had been quietly chatting with our friend Stevenson just before the attack. Another case was that of Private Stanton, who had been through the Egyptian campaign of 1882, had fought at Kassassin, Tel-el-Kebir, El-Teb, and Tamai. When this expedition of which we write was arranged, he was one of the first to volunteer. He chanced to be outside the zereba when the attack was made, and failed to appear at muster. Next day he was found dead, with many spear-wounds, at some distance from the force. Poor fellow! he had not been killed outright, and had attempted to crawl towards the zerebas, but in his confusion had crept away in the wrong direction, and had slowly bled to death on the sands of the desert.

During the rapid progress of this terrible scene of bloodshed, Miles and his friend Armstrong stood and fought shoulder to shoulder in the front rank at their allotted corner of the square—chiefly with bullet, but also, on several occasions, with bayonet, when the rush of the enemy threatened to break through all barriers, and drive in the line of defenders. They would certainly have succeeded, had these defenders been less powerful and resolute.

"Well done!" exclaimed a deep bass voice, in evident enthusiasm, close to Miles.

The latter glanced round. It was the voice of his friend Jack Molloy, who helped to work the Gardner gun, and who was at the moment admiring the daring act of an officer of Sikhs.

Two men of the Berkshire Regiment, who had been employed outside the zereba, were pursued by several Arabs, and it was evident that their death was almost certain, when the Sikh officer referred to rushed out to the rescue, sprang between the men and their pursuers, killed three of the latter in succession with three rapid sword-cuts, and enabled the soldiers to escape, besides which, he checked the rush at that part of the square, and returned to his post in safety.

The cheer of the Berkshire men and others who witnessed this feat was heard to rise above even the yells of combatants, the shrieks of the wounded, the rattle and crash of fire-arms, and the general turmoil and din of war.

In one of the working parties that were out when the assault began was our friend Moses Pyne and his comrade Rattling Bill Simkin. These had been separated from the rest of their party when the first wild rush was made by the foe. The formation of the ground favoured their dropping into a place of concealment, thus for the moment saving them from the fate of being surrounded and cut to pieces, like too many of their straggling comrades. For a few seconds they lay close while the enemy rushed past like a torrent, to the assault just described.

Then Moses uprose, with an expression of stern resolve on his usually meek countenance.

"Simkin," he said, as his comrade also got up, "I'm not goin' to lie hidin' here while our boys are engaged wi' the savages."

"No more am I, Moses," returned Rattling Bill, with something of the jovially reckless air still lingering on his solemnised visage. "But we've not much chance of getting back to the zerebas without arms."

"What d'ee call *that*?" asked Moses, holding out his chopper.

"A very good weapon to fight the bush with," answered Simkin, "but not worth much against Arab spears. However, comrade, choppers are all we have got, so we must make the most of 'em. They say a good workman can work with any tools. What d'ee propose to try? I'll put myself under your orders, Moses; for, although you are a meekish sort of a fellow, I really believe you have a better headpiece than most of us."

"I propose that we simply go at 'em," said Moses. "Take 'em in rear, cut our way through, and get into the zereba — that's all. It don't take much of a headpiece to think that out."

"Go ahead, then! I'll back you," said Rattling Bill, without the least touch of bravado, as he bared his right arm to the shoulder. Both men were in shirts and trousers, with sleeves tucked up and their brawny arms exposed — Arabesquely brown up to the elbow, and infantinely white above that!

The intended rush might have been successful, but for a change in the tactics of the enemy. Seeing that they were severely repulsed at the corner of the square, where Molloy and his tars worked the Gardner gun, while Miles and his comrades plied bullet and bayonet, the Arab chief sent a body of his followers to reinforce this point. It was just at the moment that Moses and Simkin made the dash from their place of concealment, so that they actually leaped, without having intended it, into the very midst of the reinforcements!

Two of the Arabs went down before the choppers instantly, and the others — almost panic-stricken by the suddenness and severity of the assault — turned to fly, supposing, no doubt, that an ambush had caught them. But seeing only two men they ran back, and would certainly have made short work of them if rescuers had not come up.

And at this point in the fight there was exhibited a curious instance of the power of friendship to render steady men reckless. The incident we have just described was witnessed by the troops, for, the moment the two soldiers left their place of concealment they were in full view of the large zereba.

"That's Moses!" exclaimed Armstrong excitedly.

Without a moment's hesitation he sprang over the defence-works and ran to the rescue, clubbing his rifle as he went and felling two Arabs therewith.

"You shan't die alone, Willie!" muttered our hero, as he also leaped the fence and followed his friend, just in time to save him from three Arabs who made at him simultaneously. Two of these Miles knocked down; his comrade felled the other. Then they turned back to back; Moses and Simkin did the same, and thus formed a little *impromptu* rallying square. This delayed the catastrophe, which seemed, however, inevitable. The brave little quartette, being surrounded by foes, could do nothing but parry with almost lightning speed the spear-thrusts that were made at them continually.

Seeing this, the heart of Jack Molloy bounded within him, and friendship for the moment overcame the sense of duty.

"You can only die once, Jack!" he exclaimed, drew his cutlass, leaped out of the zereba, and went at the foe with a thunderous roar, which, for a moment, actually made them quail.

Infected with a similar spirit, Stevenson, the marine, also lost his head, if we may say so. Resolving to run a-muck for friendship's sake, he followed the sailor, and increased the rallying square to five, while Molloy skirmished round it, parrying spear-thrusts, at once with left arm and cutlass, in quite a miraculous manner, roaring all the time like an infuriated lion, and causing the enemy to give back in horror wherever he made a rush.

A root, however, tripped him up at last, and he fell forward headlong to the ground. A dozen spears were pointed at his broad back, when a tall majestic Arab sprang forward and held up one hand, while with the other he waved a sword.

At that moment a strong force of the enemy came down with an impetuous rush on that corner of the zereba, and, coming between it and the little knot of combatants, hid them from view.

The attack at this point was very determined, and for a few moments the issue seemed doubtful, for although the enemy fell in heaps they came on in such numbers that the defenders were almost overwhelmed. Steadiness, however, combined with indomitable courage, prevailed. Everywhere they were repulsed with tremendous loss. Many instances of personal bravery occurred, of course, besides those we have described, but we may not pause to enumerate these. Tenacity of life, also, was curiously exhibited in the case of some of the desperately wounded.

One man in charge of two mules outside the zereba was trying to bring them in when he was attacked, and received three terrible spear-wounds in the back and one in the arm, which cut all the muscles and sinews. Yet this man ultimately recovered, though, of course, with the loss of his arm.

Another man lost a leg and an arm, and was badly wounded in the other leg and in the hand, and, lastly, he was shot in the jaw. After being operated on, and having his wounds dressed, the doctor asked him how he felt.

"All right, sir," he answered. "They've crippled me in arms and legs, and they've broke my jaw, but, thank God, they have not broke my heart yet!"

It was eight minutes to three when the Arabs made their first rush, and it was just ten minutes past three when the enemy was finally repelled and the bugle sounded "Cease firing." Yet into these pregnant eighteen minutes all that we have described, and a vast deal more, was crowded. Nearly four hundred of our men were killed and wounded, while the enemy, it is believed, lost over two thousand.

It is said by those who were present at the engagement that the officers of the 17th Bengal Infantry were heard to say that if their men had not given way, there would have been no "disaster" at all, and General McNeill instead of being accused of permitting himself to be surprised, would have got credit for a heroic defence against overwhelming odds. If he had carried out his instructions, and pressed on to the end of eight miles, instead of prudently halting when he did, there can be no doubt that the force would have been surprised and absolutely cut to pieces.

Chapter Nineteen-Refers to Sergeant Hardy, Amytoor-Lawyer Sutherland, and other Matters

Among the wounded in the great fight which we have just described was Hardy the sergeant.

His position at the time the Arabs broke into the square was close to the right flank of the Indian Native Regiment, which gave way, so that it was he and a number of the flank men of his company who had to do most of the hand-to-hand fighting necessary to repair the disaster and drive back the enemy. Of course every soldier engaged in that part of the fight was, for a time, almost overwhelmed in the confusion, and many of them were surrounded and severely wounded.

When the Native Infantry broke, Hardy's captain sprang to the front, sword in hand, and cut down two of the foe. As he did so, he was, for a moment, separated from his company and surrounded. A powerful Arab was on the point of thrusting his spear into the captain's back when Hardy observed his danger, bayoneted the Arab, and saved the officer. But it was almost at the cost of his own life, for another Arab, with whom he had been fighting at the moment, took advantage of the opportunity to thrust his spear into the chest of the sergeant, who fell, as was thought, mortally wounded.

This, however, was not the case, for when the fight was over, his wound, although dangerous, was not supposed to be fatal, and he went into hospital on returning to Suakim. He was a Blue Light, and his temperance habits told in his favour. So did his religion, for the calm equanimity with which he submitted to the will of God, and bore his sufferings, went far to assist the doctor in grappling with his wound. But his religion did more than that, for when he thought of the heaven that awaited him, if he should die, and of being "for ever with the Lord," his heart was filled with joy; and joy not only "does not kill,"—it is absolutely a source of life. In the sergeant's case it formed an important factor in restoring him to partial health.

One evening, some time after the battle of McNeill's zereba, Sutherland and Gaspard Redgrave were seated beside the sergeant's bed—cheering him up a bit, as they said—and chatting about the details of the recent fight. Once or twice the sergeant had tried to lead the conversation to religious subjects, but without success, for neither Sutherland nor Gaspard were seriously disposed, and both fought shy of such matters.

"Well, it's very kind of you to come an' cheer me up, lads," said Hardy at last; "and I hope I may live to do the same for you, if either of you ever gets knocked over. Now, I want each of you to do me a favour. Will you promise?"

"Of course we will," said Gaspard quickly.

"If we can," said the more cautious Scot.

"Well, then, Gaspard, will you sing me a song? I think it would do me good."

"With the greatest pleasure," answered the soldier; "but," he added, looking round doubtfully, "I don't know how they might like it here."

"They'll not object; besides, you can sing low. You've got the knack of singin' soft—better than any man I ever heard."

"Well, what shall it be?" returned the gratified Gaspard.

"One of Sankey's hymns," said the sergeant, with the remotest semblance of a twinkle in his eye, as he took a small hymn-book from under his pillow and gave it to his friend.

Gaspard did not seem to relish the idea of singing hymns, but he had often heard the Blue Lights sing them, and could not plead ignorance of the tunes; besides, being a man of his word, he would not refuse to fulfil his promise.

"Sing Number 68, 'Shall we gather at the river?' I'm very fond of that hymn."

In a sweet, soft, mellow voice, that charmed all who were within hearing, Gaspard began the hymn, and when he had finished there was heard more than one "Amen" and "Thank God" from the neighbouring beds.

"Yes, comrades, we shall gather there," said the sergeant, after a brief pause, "for the same Almighty Saviour who saved *me* died for *you* as well. I ain't used to wettin' my cheeks, as *you* know, lads, but I s'pose my wound has weakened me a bit! Now Sutherland, the favour I have to ask of—"

"If ye're thinkin' o' askin' me to pray," broke in the alarmed Scotsman, "ye may save your breath. When I promised, I said, 'if I *can*.' Noo, I can *not* pray, an' it's nae use askin' me to try. Whatever I may come to in this warld, I'll no be a heepycrit for ony leevin' man."

"Quite right, Sutherland—quite right. I had no intention of asking you to pray," replied Hardy, with a faint smile. "What I want you to do is to draw out my will for me."

"Oh! I'm quite willin' to do that," returned the relieved Scot.

"You see," continued the sergeant, "one never knows what may be the result of a bad wound in a climate like this, and if it pleases my Father in heaven to call me home, I should like the few trifles I possess to go in the right direction."

"That's a wise-like sentiment," returned his friend, with an approving nod and thoughtful frown.

"Now, as you write a capital hand, and know how to express yourself on paper," continued Hardy, "it strikes me that you will do the job better than any one else; and, being a friend, I feel that I can talk freely to you on my private affairs. So you'll help me?"

"I'm wullin' to try, serjint, and ac' the legal adviser—amytoor-like, ye ken."

"Thank you. Can you come to-morrow morning?"

"No, serjint, I canna, because I've to start airly the morn's mornin' wi' a pairty to meet the Scots Gairds comin' back frae Tamai, but the moment I come back I'll come to ye."

"That will do—thank you. And now, Gaspard, what's the news from England? I hear that a mail has just come in."

"News that will make your blood boil," said Gaspard sternly.

"It would take a good deal of powerful news to boil the little blood that is left in me," said Hardy, languidly.

"Well, I don't know. Anyhow it makes mine boil. What d'you think of McNeill's brave defence being represented in the papers as a disaster?"

"You don't mean that!"

"Indeed I do. They say that it was a disaster! whereas it was a splendid defence under singularly adverse circumstances! They say that General McNeill permitted himself to be surprised! If he had tried to carry out his instructions to the full extent, it would indeed have been such a surprise that the surprising thing would have been if a single man of us had returned alive to tell the tale—as you and I know full well. The truth is, it was the fault of the Intelligence Department that nearly wrecked us, and it was

McNeill's prudence and our pluck that saved us, and yet these quill-drivers at home—bah!"

The soldier rose in hot indignation and strode from the room.

"He's a wee thing roosed!" remarked Sutherland, with a good-humoured yet slightly cynical grin. "But guid-nicht to ye, ma man. Keep up hert an' I'll come an' draft yer wull i' the mornin'."

So saying the "amytoor" lawyer took his departure, and was soon tramping over the desert sands with a band of his comrades.

They were not, however, permitted to tramp in peace, for their indefatigable foe hung on their skirts and annoyed them the greater part of the way. Toward evening they met the Guards, and as it was too late to return to Suakim the force bivouacked in McNeill's deserted zereba, surrounded by graves and scarcely buried corpses.

Only those who were there can fully understand what that meant. All round the zereba, and for three miles on the Suakim side of it, the ground was strewn thickly with the graves of Europeans, Indians, and Arabs, and so shallow were these that from each of them there oozed a dark, dreadful stain. To add to the horrors of the scene, portions of mangled and putrefying corpses protruded from many of them—ghastly skulls, from the sockets of which the eyes had been picked by vultures and other obscene birds. Limbs of brave men upon which the hyena had already begun his dreadful work, and half-skeleton hands, with fingers spread and bent as if still clutching the foe in death-agony, protruded above the surface; mixed with these, and unburied, were the putrefying carcases of camels and mules—the whole filling the air with a horrible stench, and the soul with a fearful loathing, which ordinary language is powerless to describe, and the inexperienced imagination cannot conceive.

Oh! it is terrible to think that from the Fall till now man has gone on continually producing and reproducing scenes like this—sometimes, no doubt, unavoidably; but often, too often, because of some trifling error, or insult, on the part of statesmen, or some paltry dispute about a boundary, or, not infrequently, on grounds so shadowy and complex that succeeding historians have found it almost impossible to convey the meaning thereof to the intellects of average men!

Amid these dreadful memorials of the recent fight the party bivouacked!

Next day the troops returned to Suakim, and Sutherland, after breakfast, and what he called a wash-up, went to see his friend Sergeant Hardy, with pen, ink, and paper.

"Weel, serjint, hoo are ye the day?"

"Pretty well, thank you—pretty well. Ah! Sutherland, I have been thinking what an important thing it is for men to come to Jesus for salvation while in their health and strength; for now, instead of being anxious about my soul, as so many are when the end approaches, I am rejoicing in the thought of soon meeting God—my Father! Sutherland, my good fellow, it is foolish as well as wrong to think only of this life. Of all men in the world we soldiers ought to know this."

The sergeant spoke so earnestly, and his eyes withal looked so solemnly from their sunken sockets, that his friend could not help being impressed.

"I believe ye're no' far wrang, serjint, an' I tak' shame to mysel' that I've been sic a harum-scarum sinner up to this time."

Sutherland said this with a look so honest that Hardy was moved to put out his large wasted hand and grasp that of his friend.

"Comrade," he said, "God is waiting to be gracious. Jesus is ever ready and willing to save."

Sutherland returned the pressure but made no reply; and Hardy, praying for a blessing on the little that had been said, changed the subject by saying—

"You have brought paper and ink, I see."

"Ay, but, man, ye mauna be speakin' o' takin' yer depairture yet. This draftin' o' yer wull is only a precaution."

"Quite right, lad. I mean it only as a precaution," returned Hardy, in a cheerful tone. "But you seem to have caught a cold—eh? What makes you cough and clear your throat so?"

"A cauld! I wush it was only a cauld! Man, it's the stink o' thae corps that I canna get oot o' my nose an' thrapple."

Hereupon Sutherland, by way of entertaining his invalid friend, launched out into a graphic account of the scene he had so recently witnessed at McNeill's zereba. When that subject was exhausted, he arranged his writing materials and began with all the solemnity of a lawyer.

"Noo, serjeant, what div ye want me to pit doon?"

"Well, I must explain first that I have very little to leave, and no one to leave it to."

"What! Nae frien's ava?"

"Not one. I have neither wife nor child, brother nor sister. I have indeed one old cousin, but he is rich, and would not be benefited by my poor little possessions; besides, he's a cross-grained old fellow, and does not deserve anything, even though I had something worth leaving. However, I bear him no ill-will, poor man, only I don't want what I do leave to go to him, which it would if I were to die without a will; because, of course, he is my natural heir, and—"

"Haud ye there, man," said the Scot abruptly but slowly. "If he's your nait'ral heir, ye're *his* nait'ral heir tae, ye ken."

"Of course, I am aware of that," returned the sergeant with an amused look; "but the old man is eccentric, and has always boasted that he means to leave his wealth to some charity. Indeed, I know that he has already made his will, leaving his money to build an hospital—for incurables of some sort, I believe."

"Ma certy! If I was his lawyer," said Sutherland, with ineffable scorn, "I wad advise him to erec' an hospital in his lifetime for incurable eediots, an' to gang in himsel' as the first patient. But, come awa wi' yer wull, serjint."

"Get ready, then, my lawyer, and see that you put it down all ship-shape, as poor Molloy would have said."

"Oh, ye needna fear," said the Scot, "I'm no' sic an ass as to trust to my ain legal knowledge. But jist you say what ye want an' I'll pit it doon, and then write it into a form in the reg'lar way."

After mentioning a few trifling legacies to various comrades, Hardy said that he had managed to save a hundred pounds during his career, which he wished to divide between his two comrades, John Miles and Willie Armstrong, for whom he expressed strong regard.

Sutherland, instead of noting this down, looked at his friend in sad surprise, thinking that weakness had caused his mind to wander.

"Ye forget, serjint," he said softly, "that Miles an' Airmstrang are baith deed."

"No, lad; no one can say they are certainly dead."

"Aweel—we canna exactly say it, but when ye consider o' the born deevils that have gotten haud o' them, we are entitled to *think* them deed ony way."

"They are reported as 'missing,' that is all, and that is enough for me. You write down what I tell you, lad. Now, have you got it down?"

"Ay, fifty to each."

"There may be some interest due on the account," said the sergeant thoughtfully; "besides, there may be a few things in my kit that I have forgotten—and it's not worth while dividing such trifles between them."

"Weel, weel, ye've only to mak yin o' them yer residooary legitee, an' that'll pit it a' richt."

"True, my lawyer. Let it be so," said Hardy, with a short laugh at the thought of making so much ado about nothing. "Make Miles my residuary legatee. And now, be off, draw it out fair, an' leave me to rest, for I'm a trifle tired after all this legal work."

The will thus carefully considered was duly made out, signed, and witnessed, after which Sergeant Hardy awaited with cheerful resignation whatever fate should be appointed to him.

His strong frame and constitution, undamaged by youthful excess, fought a vigorous battle for life, and he began slowly to mend; but the climate of Suakim was so bad for him that he was finally sent down to the hospital at Alexandria, where, under much more favourable circumstances, he began to recover rapidly.

One of the nurses there was very kind to him. Finding that the sergeant was an earnest Christian, she had many interesting talks with him on the subject nearest his heart.

One day she said to him with unusual animation:

"The doctor says you may go down to the Soldiers' Institute that has recently been set up here, and stay for some time to recruit. It is not intended for invalids, you know, but the ladies in charge are intimate friends of mine, and have agreed to let you have a room. The Institute stands on a very pleasant part of the shore, exposed to the fresh sea-breezes; and there are lots of books and newspapers and games, as well as lectures, concerts, prayer-meetings, Bible-readings, and—"

"Ay, just like Miss Robinson's Institute at Portsmouth," interrupted Hardy. "I know the sort o' thing well."

"The Alexandrian Soldiers' Institute is *also* Miss Robinson's," returned the nurse, with a pleased look; "so if you know the one at Portsmouth, there is no need for my describing the other to you. The change will do you more good in a week than months at this place. And I'll come to see you frequently. There is a widow lady staying there just now to whom I will introduce you. She has been helping us to nurse here, for she has great regard for soldiers; but her health having broken-down somewhat, she has transferred her services to the Institute for a time. She is the widow of a clergyman who came out here not long ago and died suddenly. You will find her a very sympathetic soul."

Chapter Twenty-Old Friends in New Aspects

On the evening of the third day after the conversation narrated in the last chapter, Sergeant Hardy sat in an easy-chair on the verandah of the Soldiers' Institute at Alexandria, in the enjoyment of a refreshing breeze, which, after ruffling the blue waters of the Mediterranean, came like a cool hand on a hot brow, to bless for a short time the land of Egypt.

Like one of Aladdin's palaces the Institute had sprung up — not exactly in a night, but in a marvellously short space of time. There was more of interest about it, too, than about the Aladdin buildings; for whereas the latter were evolved magically out of that mysterious and undefinable region termed Nowhere, the Miss Robinson edifice came direct from smoky, romantic London, without the advantage of supernatural assistance.

When Miss Robinson's soldier friends were leaving for the seat of war in Egypt, some of them had said to her, "Three thousand miles from home are three thousand good reasons why you should think of us!" The "Soldiers' Friend" took these words to heart — also to God. She did think of them, and she persuaded other friends to think of them, to such good purpose that she soon found herself in possession of funds sufficient to begin the work.

As we have seen, her energetic servant and fellow-worker, Mr Thomas Tufnell, was sent out to Egypt to select a site for the building. The old iron and wood Oratory at Brompton was bought, and sent out at Government expense — a fact which speaks volumes for the Government opinion of the value of Miss Robinson's work among soldiers.

In putting up the old Oratory, Tufnell had transformed it to an extent that might almost have made Aladdin's Slave of the Lamp jealous. Certainly, those who were wont to "orate" in the building when it stood in Brompton would have failed to recognise the edifice as it arose in Egypt on the Boulevard Ramleh, between the Grand Square of Alexandria and the sea.

The nave of the old Oratory had been converted into a room, ninety-nine feet long, with couches and tables running down both sides, a billiard-table in the centre, writing materials in abundance, and pictures on the walls. At one end of the room stood a pianoforte, couches, and easy-chairs, and a door opened into a garden facing the sea. Over the door were arranged several flags, and above these, in large letters, the appropriate words, "In the name of the Lord will we set up our banners." At the other end was a temperance refreshment bar. On a verandah facing the sea men could repose on easy-chairs and smoke their pipes or cigars, while contemplating the peculiarities of an Eastern climate.

It was here that our friend Sergeant Hardy was enjoying that blessed state of convalescence which may be described as gazing straight forward and thinking of nothing!

Of course there were all the other appliances of a well-equipped Institute—such as sleeping-cabins, manager's room, Bible-class room, lavatory, and all the rest of it, while a handsome new stone building close beside it contained sitting-rooms, bed-rooms, club-room for officers, kitchens, and, by no means least, though last, a large lecture-hall.

But to these and many other things we must not devote too much space, for old friends in new aspects claim our attention. Only, in passing from such details, it may not be out of place to say that it has been remarked that the sight of Miss Robinson's buildings, steadily rising from the midst of acres of ruins, while men's minds were agitated by the bombardment and its results, produced a sense of security which had a most beneficial and quietening effect on the town! Indeed, one officer of high rank went so far as to say that the Institute scheme had given the inhabitants more confidence in the intentions of England than anything yet done or promised by Government!

In a rocking-chair beside the sergeant reclined a shadow in loose— remarkably loose—fitting soldier's costume.

"What a blessed place to sit in and rest after the toils and sufferings of war," said Hardy, to the shadow, "and how thankful I am to God for bringing me here!"

"It's a hivenly place intirely," responded the shadow, "an' 'tis mesilf as is thankful too—what's left o' me anyhow, an' that's not much. Sure I've had some quare thoughts in me mind since I come here. Wan o' them was— what is the smallest amount o' skin an' bone that's capable of howldin' a thankful spirit?"

"I never studied algebra, Flynn, so it's of no use puttin' the question to me," said Hardy; "besides, I'm not well enough yet to tackle difficult questions, but I'm real glad to see you, my boy, though there *is* so little of you to see."

"That's it, sarjint; that's just where it lies," returned Flynn, in a slow, weak voice. "I've bin occupied wi' that question too—namely, how thin may a man git widout losin' the power to howld up his clo'es?"

"You needn't be uneasy on that score," said Hardy, casting an amused glance at his companion, "for there's plenty o' flesh left yet to keep ye goin' till you get to old Ireland. It rejoices my heart to see you beside me, thin though you are, for the report up country was that you had died on the way to Suez."

"Bad luck to their reports! That's always the way of it. I do think the best way to take reports is to belaive the exact opposite o' what's towld ye, an' so ye'll come nearest the truth. It's thrue I had a close shave. Wan day I felt a sort o' light-hiddedness—as if I was a kind o' livin' balloon—and was floatin' away, whin the doctor came an' looked at me.

"'He's gone,' says he.

"'That's a lie!' says I, with more truth than purliteness, maybe.

"An' would ye belave it?—I began to mind from that hour! It was the doctor saved me widout intindin' to—good luck to him! Anyhow he kep' me from slippin' my cable that time, but it was the good nursin' as brought me back—my blissin' on the dear ladies as give their hearts to this work all for love! By the way," continued Flynn, coughing and looking very stern, for he was ashamed of a tear or two which *would* rise and almost overflow in spite of his efforts to restrain them—but then, you see, he was very weak! "By the way," he said, "you'll niver guess who wan o' the nurses is. Who d'ee think?—guess!"

"I never *could* guess right, Flynn."

"Try."

"Well, little Mrs Armstrong."

"Nonsense, man! Why, she's nursin' her old father in England, I s'pose."

"Miss Robinson, then?"

"H'm! You might as well say the Prime Minister. How d'ee s'pose the Portsmuth Institute could git along widout *her*? No, it's our friend Mrs Drew!"

"What! The wife o' the reverend gentleman as came out with us in the troop-ship?"

"That same—though she's no longer the wife of the riverend gintleman, for he's dead—good man," said Flynn, in a sad voice.

"I'm grieved to hear that, for he *was* a good man. And the pretty daughter, what of her?"

"That's more nor I can tell ye, boy. Sometimes her mother brings her to the hospital to let her see how they manage, but I fancy she thinks her too young yet to go in for sitch work by hersilf. Anyhow I've seen her only now an' then; but the poor widdy comes rig'lar—though I do belave she does it widout pay. The husband died of a flyer caught in the hospital a good while since. They say that lots o' young fellows are afther the daughter, for though the Drews are as poor as church rats, she's got such a swate purty face, and such innocent ways wid her, that I'd try for her mesilf av it wasn't that I've swore niver to forsake me owld grandmother."

Chatting thus about times past and present, while they watched the soldiers and seamen who passed continuously in and out of the Institute—intent on a game, or some non-intoxicant refreshment, or a lounge, a look at the papers, a confab with a comrade, or a bit of reading—the two invalids enjoyed their rest to the full, and frequently blessed the lady who provided such a retreat, as well as her warm-hearted assistants, who, for the love of Christ and human souls, had devoted themselves to carry on the work in that far-off land.

"I often think—" said Hardy.

But what he thought was never revealed; for at that moment two ladies in deep mourning approached, whom the sergeant recognised at a glance as Mrs Drew and her daughter Marion. The faces of both were pale and sorrowful; but the beauty of the younger was rather enhanced than otherwise by this, and by contrast with her sombre garments.

They both recognised the sergeant at once, and, hastening forward, so as to prevent his rising, greeted him with the kindly warmth of old friends.

"It seems such a long time since we met," said the elder lady, "but we have never forgotten you or the comrades with whom we used to have such pleasant talks in the troop-ship."

"Sure am I, madam," said the sergeant, "that they have never forgotten *you* and your kind—kind—"

"Yes, my husband was *very* kind to you all," said the widow, observing the delicacy of feeling which stopped the soldier's utterance; "he was kind to every one. But we have heard some rumours that have made me and my daughter very sad. Is it true that a great many men of your regiment were killed and wounded at the battle fought by General McNeill?"

"Quite true, madam," answered the sergeant, glancing at the daughter with some surprise; for Marion was gazing at him with an intensely anxious look and parted lips. "But, thank God, many were spared!"

"And — and — how are the two fine-looking young men that were so fond of each other — like twins almost — "

"Sure, didn't I tell ye, misthress, that they was both ki — "

"Hold your tongue, Flynn," interrupted the widow, with a forced smile. "You are one of my most talkative patients! I want to hear the truth of this matter from a man who has come more recently from the scene of action than yourself. What do you think, Mr Hardy?"

"You refer to John Miles and William Armstrong, no doubt, madam," said the sergeant, in a somewhat encouraging tone. "Well, if Flynn says they were killed he has no ground whatever for saying so. They are only reported missing. Of course that is bad enough, but as long as a man is only missing there is plenty of room for hope. You see, they may have managed to hide, or been carried off as prisoners into the interior; and you may be sure the Arabs would not be such fools as to kill two men like Miles and Armstrong; they'd rather make slaves of 'em, in which case there will be a chance of their escaping, or, if we should become friendly again wi' these fellows, they'd be set free."

"I'm so glad to hear you say so, and I felt sure that my desponding patient here was taking too gloomy a view of the matter," said Mrs Drew, with a significant glance at Marion, who seemed to breathe more freely and to lose some of her anxious expression after the sergeant's remarks.

Perhaps at this point a little conversation that took place between Mrs Drew and her daughter that same evening may not be out of place.

"Dear May," said the former, "did I not tell you that Flynn took too gloomy a view of the case of these young soldiers, in whom your dear father was so much interested? But, darling, is it not foolish in you to think so much about Miles?"

"It may be foolish, mother, but I cannot help it," said Marion, blushing deeply; for she was very modest as well as simple.

"May, dear, I wonder that you can make such an admission!" said the mother remonstratively.

"Is it wrong to make such an admission to one's own mother, when it is true?" asked Marion, still blushing, but looking straight in her mother's eyes; for she was very straightforward as well as modest and simple!

"Of course not, dear, but — but — in short, Miles is only a — a — soldier, you know, and — "

"*Only* a soldier!" interrupted Marion, with a flash from her soft brown eyes; for she was an enthusiast as well as straightforward, modest, and simple! "I suppose you mean that he is only a private, but what then? May not the poorest private in the army rise, if he be but noble-minded and worthy and capable, to the rank of a general, or higher — if there is anything higher? Possibly the Commander-in-Chief-ship may be open to him!"

"True, my love, but in the meantime his social position is — "

"Is quite as good as our own," interrupted Marion; for she was a desperate little radical as well as an enthusiast, straightforward, modest, and simple!

"You know he let out something about his parents and position, and *of course* he told the truth. Besides, I repeat that I cannot *help* loving him, and surely we are not responsible for our affections. We cannot love and hate to order. I might fall in love with — with — well, it's no good talking; but, anyhow, I could not help it. I could be silent if you like, but I could not help myself."

Mrs Drew seemed a little puzzled how to deal with her impetuous daughter, and had begun to reply, when May interrupted her. Flushing deeply, for she was very sensitive, and with a feeling that amounted almost to indignation, she continued —

"I wonder at you, mother — it's so unlike you; as if those unworthy considerations of difference of rank and station could influence, or ought to influence, one in such a question as this!"

Mrs Drew paused for a moment. She knew that her daughter gave expression to the views that had marked the dealings of the husband and father, so lately lost to them, in every action of his life. Marion's happiness, too, during the remainder of her days, might be involved in the result of the present conversation, and she was moved to say —

"My dear, has John Miles ever spoken to you?"

"Oh! mother, how can you ask me? If he had done so, would I have delayed one minute in letting you know?"

"Forgive me, dearest. I did you wrong in admitting the thought even for a moment. But you spoke so earnestly — as if you might have some reason for thinking that he cared for you."

"Don't you know," answered Marion, looking down, and a little confused, "that men can speak with their eyes as well as their lips? I not only feel sure that he cares for me, but I feel sure, from the sentiments he expressed to me on the voyage, that *nothing* would induce him to talk to me of love while in his present position."

"How does all this consist, my love," asked Mrs Drew, "with your knowledge of the fact that he left home in anger, and would not be persuaded, even by your dear father, to write home a penitent letter?"

Marion was silent. This had not occurred to her before. But love is not to be turned from its object by trifles. She was all that we have more than once described her to be; but she was not a meta-physician or a philosopher, capable of comprehending and explaining occult mysteries. Enough for her if she loved Miles and Miles loved her, and then, even if he did not deserve her love, she would remain true—secretly but unalterably true—to him as the needle is to the pole!

"Has it not occurred to you, dear," said her mother, pursuing her advantage in a meditative tone, "that if Miles has been so plain-spoken and eloquent with his blue eye, that your pretty brown ones may have said something to *him*?"

"Never!" exclaimed the girl, with an indignant flash. "Oh! mother, can you believe me capable of—of—no, I never looked at him except with the air of a perfect stranger—at least of a—a—but why should I try to deny what could not possibly be true?"

Mrs Drew felt that nothing was to be gained from pursuing the subject—or one aspect of it—further.

"At any rate," she said, "I am glad, for his own sake, poor young fellow, that Sergeant Hardy spoke so hopefully."

"And for his comrades' sakes as well," said Marion. "You know, mother, that his friend Armstrong is also reported as missing, and Stevenson the marine, as well as that dear big bluff sailor, Jack Molloy. By the way, do you feel well enough to go to the lecture to-night? It is to be a very interesting one, I am told, with magic-lantern illustrations, and I don't like to go alone."

"I am going to-night, so you may make your mind easy," said her mother. "I would not miss this lecturer, because I am told that he is a remarkably good one, and the hall is likely to be quite full."

In regard to this lecture and some other things connected with the Alexandrian Institute, our friend Sergeant Hardy learned a good deal from the lady at the head of it, not long after the time that Mrs Drew had the foregoing conversation with Marion.

It is scarcely needful to say that the Lady-Superintendent was a capable Christian as well as an enthusiast in her work.

"Come to my room, Sergeant Hardy, and I'll tell you all about it," she said, leading the way to her apartment, where the sergeant placed himself upon a chair, bolt upright, as if he were going to have a tooth drawn, or were about to illustrate some new species of sitting-drill.

Chapter Twenty One-Shows how the Lady of the Institute discourses to the Sergeant, how Jack-Tars go out on the Spree, and how Music Conquers Warriors

"It seems wonderful to me, madam," said Sergeant Hardy, looking round the lady's room with an admiring gaze, "how quickly you have got things into working order here. When I remember that last year this place was a heap of rubbish, it seems like magic."

"Ah! the work of God on earth seems magical the more we reflect on it," returned the lady. "The fact that our Institute was conceived, planned, and carried into successful operation by an invalid lady, in spite of discouragement, and, at first, with inadequate means, is itself little short of miraculous, but what is even more surprising is the fact that the Government, which began by throwing cold water on her Portsmouth work, has ended by recognising it and by affording us every facility here in Alexandria."

"Well, you see, madam, I suppose it's because they see that we soldiers and sailors likes it, an' it does a power o' good — don't you think?"

"No doubt, but whatever may be the reason, Sergeant, we are very thankful for the encouragement. I suppose you have heard what a grand occasion our opening day was?"

"No, madam, I haven't. You see, away at Suakim we was so constantly taken up with the attentions of Osman Digna that we had little time for anything but eatin' and sleepin' when we wasn't on sentry an' fightin', so that we often missed bits of news. Was there a great turn-out o' men?"

"Indeed there was," returned the lady, with animation; "and not only of men, but of all the Alexandrian notables. It was on the 23rd of February last (1885) that our Institute was opened by Major-General Lennox, V.C., C.B., who was in command of the garrison. This was not the first time by any means that the soldiers had paid us a visit. A number of men, who, like yourself, Sergeant Hardy, sympathise with our work in its spiritual aspects, had been frequently coming to see how we were getting on, and many a pleasant hour's prayer and singing we had enjoyed with them, accompanied by our little harmonium, which had been sent to us by kind friends in England; and every Sunday evening we had had a little service in the midst of the shavings and carpenters' benches.

"But on this grand opening day the men came down in hundreds, and a great surprise some of them got—especially the sceptical among them. The entrance was decorated with palms. At the further end of the reading-room the trophy of Union Jacks and the Royal Standard, which you see there now, was put up by a band of Jack-tars who had come to help us as well as to see the fun. Over the trophy was our text, 'In the name of the Lord will we set up our banners,' for we liked to feel that we had taken possession of this little spot in Egypt for God—and we believe that it will always be His.

"Everything was bright and hearty. There were about five hundred soldiers and sailors, and between two and three hundred officers and civilians of all nationalities. On the platform we had Osman Pasha—"

"Ha!" interrupted the sympathetic sergeant, "I only wish we could have had Osman Digna there too! It would do more to pacify the Soudan than killing his men does!"

"I daresay it would," responded the lady with a laugh, "but have patience, Hardy; we shall have him there yet, and perhaps the Mahdi too—or some future grand occasion. Well, as I was saying, we had Osman, the Governor of Alexandria, on our platform, and a lot of big-wigs that you know nothing about, but whose influence was of importance, and whose appearance went far to make the place look gay. Of course we had music, beginning with 'God save the Queen,' and speeches—brilliant as well as heavy; sententious and comic—like all other similar gatherings, and the enthusiasm was unbounded. How could it be otherwise with sailors to cheer and soldiers to back them up? And you may be sure that in such a meeting the enthusiasm about the undertaking did not fail to extend to the 'Soldiers' Friend' who had originated the whole. In short, it was a splendid success."

"Of course it was," said the sergeant, with emphasis; "first, because of God's blessing, an', second, because the Institoot was greatly needed. Why, madam, if it wasn't for this place the thousands of soldiers stationed here, not to mention the sailors, would have no place to go to spend their leave and leisure time but the drinkin' dens o' the town; an *you* know well, though p'r'aps not so well as I do, what terrible places these are, where men are tempted, fleeced, debauched, and sometimes murdered."

"Quite true, Hardy. Did you hear of the case that occurred just two days ago? A sergeant of one of the regiments, I forget which, after paying his fare to a donkey-boy, turned quietly to walk away, when the scoundrel felled him with a stick and robbed him of one pound 10 shillings. The case is before the law-court now, and no doubt the robber will receive a just reward.

"Well, as I was remarking, the opening day carried us to high tide, so to speak, and there has been no ebb from that day to this. One comical incident, however, occurred just at the beginning, which might have done us damage. The day after the opening all was prepared for the reception of our soldier and sailor friends. The tables were arranged with books and games, the writing-table with pens, ink, and blotting-paper, and the bar with all sorts of eatables, magnificent urns, coloured glass, etcetera. About one o'clock William, our barman, tasted the coffee. His usual expression of self-satisfaction gave place to one of horror. He tasted the coffee again. The look of horror deepened. He ran to the boiler, and the mystery was cleared up. The boiler had been filled with salt-water! Our Arab, Ibraim, who carries up seawater daily to fill our baths, had filled the boiler with the same. Luckily there was time to correct the mistake, and when our friends came trooping in at four o'clock they found the coffee quite to their taste.

"You know very well," continued the superintendent, "our rules never to force religion on any of our customers, our object being to *attract* by all the legitimate means in our power. We have our Bible-classes, prayer-meetings, temperance soirees, and the like, distinct—as at Portsmouth—from the other advantages of the Institute; and are quite content if some, who come at first from mere curiosity or for the enjoyment of temporal good things, should afterwards continue to come from higher and spiritual motives. But if our military friends prefer to read our papers and books, and play our games, and use our bar, they are at perfect liberty to do so, without what I may style religious interference. It's all fair and above-board, you see. We fully recognise the freedom of will that God has bestowed on man. If you don't care for our spiritual fare you may let it alone. If you relish it—there it is, and you are welcome. Yet we hold by our right to win men if we can. In point of fact, we have been very successful already in this way, for our motive power from beginning to end is Love.

"One of our most helpful soldier friends—a sergeant—has brought several men to the Saviour, who are now our steady supporters. One of these men, whom our sergeant was the means of bringing in, was a professed unbeliever of good standing and ability. The first time he was prevailed on to come to a prayer-meeting, he sat bolt upright while we knelt, being a straightforward sort of man who refused to pretend when he could not really pray. He is now a happy follower of Jesus.

"Our large rooms are constantly filled with soldiers, some chatting, some making up for past privations by having a good English meal, and others reading or playing games. Just now happens to be our quietest hour, but it won't be long before we have a bustling scene."

As if to verify the lady's words there came through the doorways at that moment a sound of shouting and cheering, which caused all the staff of the Institute to start into active life.

"There they come!" exclaimed the lady, with an intelligent smile, as she hurried from the room, leaving Hardy to follow at a pace that was more consistent with his dignity—and, we may add, his physical weakness.

The shouts proceeded from a party of sailors on leave from one of the ironclads lying in the harbour. These, being out for the day—on a spree as some of them styled it—had hired donkeys, and come in a body to the Institute, where they knew that food of the best, dressed in British fashion, and familiar games, were to be had, along with British cheer and sympathy.

When Hardy reached the door he found the place swarming with blue-jackets, trooping up at intervals on various animals, but none on foot, save those who had fallen off their mounts and were trying to get on again.

"They're all donkeyfied together," remarked a sarcastic old salt—not one of the party—who stood beside Hardy, looking complacently on, and smoking his pipe.

"They don't steer as well on land as on sea," replied Hardy.

"'Cause they ain't used to such craft, you see—that's w'ere it is, sarjint," said the old salt, removing his pipe for a moment. "Just look at 'em—some comin' along sidewise like crabs, others stern foremost. W'y, there's that grey craft wi' the broad little man holdin' on to its tail to prevent his slidin' over its head. I've watched that grey craft for some minutes, and its hind propellers have bin so often in the air that it do seem as if it was walkin' upon its front legs. Hallo! I was sure he'd go down by the head at last."

The donkey in question had indeed gone down by the head, and rolled over, pitching its rider on his broad shoulders, which, however, seemed none the worse for the fall.

"Ketch hold of his tail, Bill," cried another man, "and hold his stern down—see if that won't cure his plungin'. He's like a Dutchman in a cross sea."

"Keep clear o' this fellow's heels, Jack, he's agoin' to fire another broadside."

"If he does he'll unship you," cried Jack, who was himself at the same moment unshipped, while the owner of the donkey, and of the other donkeys, shouted advice, if nothing worse, in Arabic and broken English.

In a few minutes the sailors "boarded" the Institute, and drew the whole force of the establishment to the bar in order to supply the demand.

"Ah! thin, ye've got Irish whisky, haven't ye?" demanded a facetious seaman.

"Yes, plenty, but we call it coffee here!" answered the equally facetious barman, whose satellites were distributing hot and cold drinks with a degree of speed that could only be the fruit of much practice.

"You'll have to be jolly on mild swipes," said one; "no tostikatin' liquors allowed, Dick."

"H'm!" growled Dick.

"Got any wittles here?" demanded another man, wiping his lips with his sleeve.

"Yes, plenty. Sit down and order what you want."

"For nothin'?" asked the tar.

"For *next* to nothing!" was the prompt reply. Meanwhile, those whose appetites were not quite so urgent had distributed themselves about the place, and were already busy with draughts, billiards, etcetera, while those who were of more sedate and inquiring temperament were deep in the columns of the English papers and magazines.

"I say, Fred Thorley, ain't it bang up?" remarked a sturdy little man, through a huge slice of cake, with which he had just filled his mouth.

"Fuss-rate!" responded Fred, as he finished a cup of coffee at a draught and called for more. "Didn't I tell you, Sam, that you'd like it better than the native grog-shops?"

"If they'd on'y got bitter beer!" sighed Sam.

"They've got better beer," said his friend; "try some ginger-pop."

"No thankee. If I can't git it strong, let's at least have it hot. But, I say, what's come o' the lobsters? Don't seem to be many about. I thought this here Institoot was got up a-purpose for *them*.

"So it was, lad, includin' us; but you don't suppose that because *you* are out on the spree, everybody else is. They're on dooty just now. Wait a bit an' you'll see plenty of 'em afore long."

"Are all that come here Blue Lights?" asked Sam, with a somewhat doleful visage.

"By no manner o' means," returned his friend, with a laugh; "tho' for the matter o' that they wouldn't be worse men if they was, but many of 'em are no better than they should be, an' d'ee know, Sam, there are some of 'em actually as great blackguards a'most as yourself!"

"There's some comfort in that anyhow," returned Sam, with a pleasant smile, "for I hates to be pecooliar. By the way, Fred, p'r'aps they may be able to give you some noos here, if you ax 'em, about your friend Jack Molloy. *He* was a Blue Light, wasn't he?"

"Not w'en I know'd 'im, but he was a fuss-rate seaman an' a good friend, though he *was* fond of his glass, like yourself, Sam."

It chanced that at this point Sergeant Hardy, in moving about the place, taking profound interest in all that he saw, came within earshot of the two friends, to whom he at once went up and introduced himself as a friend of Jack Molloy.

"Indeed," said he, "Molloy and I fought pretty near to each other in that last affair under General McNeill, so I can give you the latest news of him."

"Can you, old man? Come, sit down here, an' let's have it then," said Thorley. "Jack was an old messmate o' mine. What'll you take to drink, mate?"

"Nothing, thankee. I'm allowanced by the doctor even in the matter o' tea and coffee," said the sergeant. "As to bein' an' old man—well, I ain't much older than yourself, I daresay, though wounds and sickness and physic are apt to age a man in looks."

Sitting down beside the sailors, Hardy told of the great fight at McNeill's zereba, and how Molloy and others of his friends had gone to rescue a comrade and been cut off. He relieved Fred's mind, however, by taking the most hopeful view of the matter, as he had previously relieved the feelings of Marion. And then the three fell to chatting on things in general and the war in particular.

"Now don't this feel homelike?" said Sam, looking round the room with great satisfaction. "If it wasn't for the heat I'd a'most think we was in a temperance coffee-house in old England."

"Or owld Ireland," chimed in a sailor at the neighbouring table.

"To say naething o' auld Scotland," added a rugged man in red hair, who sat beside him.

"Well, messmate," assented Fred, "it *do* feel homelike, an' no mistake. Why, what ever is *that*?"

The sailor paused, and held up a finger as if to impose silence while he listened, but there was no need to enforce silence, for at that moment the sweet strains of a harmonium were heard at the other end of the long room, and quietude profound descended on the company as a rich baritone voice sang, with wonderful pathos, the familiar notes and words of "Home, Sweet Home!"

Before that song was finished many a warrior there had to fight desperately with his own spirit to conceal the fact that his eyes were full of tears. Indeed, not a few of them refused to fight at all, but, ingloriously lowering their colours, allowed the tell-tale drops to course over their bronzed faces, as they thought of sweethearts and wives and friends and home circles and "the light of other days."

Chapter Twenty Two-Led into Captivity

We turn once more to the Nubian desert, where, it will be remembered, we left several of our friends, cut off from McNeill's zereba at a critical moment when they were all but overwhelmed by a host of foes.

The grand-looking Arab who had so opportunely appeared on the scene and arrested the spears which were about to finish the career of Jack Molloy was no other than the man who had been saved by Miles from the bullet of his comrade Rattling Bill. A kind act had in this case received its appropriate reward, for a brief though slight glance, and a gracious inclination of the Arab's head, convinced our hero that the whole party owed their lives to this man's gratitude.

They were not however exempt from indignity, for at the moment when Jack Molloy fell they were overwhelmed by numbers, their arms were wrenched from their grasp, and their hands were bound behind their backs. Thus they were led, the reverse of gently, into the thick bush by a strong party of natives, while the others, headed by the black-bearded chief, continued their attack on the zereba.

It soon became evident that the men who had charge of the prisoners did not share, or sympathise with, the feelings of the chief who had spared their lives, for they not only forced them to hurry forward as fast as they could go, but gave them occasional pricks with their spear-points when any of them chanced to trip or stumble. One of the warriors in particular—a fiery man—sometimes struck them with the shaft of his spear and otherwise maltreated them. It may be easily understood that men with unbroken spirits and high courage did not submit to this treatment with a good grace!

Miles was the first to be tested in this way. On reaching a piece of broken ground his foot caught in something and he stumbled forward. His hands being bound behind him he could not protect his head, and the result was that he plunged into a prickly shrub, out of which he arose with flushed and bleeding countenance. This was bad enough, but when the fiery Arab brought a lance down heavily on his shoulders his temper gave way, and he rushed at the man in a towering rage, striving at the same time, with intense violence, to burst his bonds. Of course he failed, and was rewarded by a blow on the head, which for a moment or two stunned him.

Seeing this, Armstrong's power of restraint gave way, and he sprang to the rescue of his friend, but only to meet the same fate at the hands of the fiery Arab.

Stunned and bleeding, though not subdued, they were compelled to move on again at the head of the party—spurred on now and then by a touch from the point of the fiery man's lance. Indeed it seemed as if this man's passionate nature would induce him ere long to risk his chief's wrath by disobeying orders and stabbing the prisoners!

Stevenson, the marine, was the next to suffer, for his foot slipped on a stone, and he fell with such violence as to be unable to rise for a few minutes. Impatient of the delay, the fiery man struck him so savagely with the spear-shaft that even his own comrades remonstrated.

"If I could only burst this cord!" growled Simkin between his teeth, "I'd—"

He stopped, for he felt that it was unmanly, as well as idle, to boast in the circumstances.

"We must have patience, comrade," said Stevenson, as he rose pale and bloodstained from the ground. "Our Great Captain sometimes gives us the order to submit and suffer and—"

A prick in the fleshy part of his thigh caused him to stop abruptly.

At this point the endurance of Jack Molloy failed him, and he also "went in" for violent action! But Jack was a genius as well as a sailor, and profited by the failures of his comrades. Instead of making futile efforts to break his bonds like them, he lowered his hairy head, and, with a howl and a tremendous rush, like a fish-torpedo, launched himself, or, as it were, took "a header," into the fiery man!

"No fellow," as Jack himself afterwards remarked, "could receive fifteen stone ten into his bread-basket and go on smiling!" On the contrary, he went down like a nine-pin, and remained where he fell, for his comrades—who evidently did not love him—merely laughed and went on their way, leaving him to revive at his leisure.

The prisoners advanced somewhat more cheerfully after this event, for, besides being freed from pricks of the spear-point, there was that feeling of elation which usually arises in every well-balanced mind from the sight of demerit meeting with its appropriate reward.

The region over which they were thus led, or driven, was rather more varied than the level country behind them, and towards evening it changed still further, becoming more decidedly hill-country. At night the party found themselves in the neighbourhood of one of the all-important wells of the land, beside which they encamped under a small tree.

Here the prisoners were allowed to sit down on the ground, with one man to guard them, while the others kindled a fire and otherwise arranged the encampment.

Supper—consisting of a small quantity of boiled corn and dried flesh—was given to the prisoners, whose hands were set free, though their elbows were loosely lashed together, and their feet tied to prevent their escape. No such idea, however, entered into the heads of any of them, for they were by that time in the heart of an unknown range of hills, in a country which swarmed with foes, besides which, they would not have known in what direction to fly had they been free to do so; they possessed neither arms, ammunition, nor provisions, and were at the time greatly exhausted by their forced march.

Perhaps Jack Molloy was the only man of the unfortunate party who at that moment retained either the wish or the power to make a dash for freedom. But then Jack was an eccentric and exceptional man in every respect. Nothing could quell his spirit, and it was all but impossible to subdue his body. He was what we may term a composite character. His frame was a mixture of gutta-percha, leather, and brass. His brain was a compound of vivid fancy and slow perception. His heart was a union of highly inflammable oil and deeply impressible butter, with something remarkably tough in the centre of it. Had he been a Red Indian he would have been a chief. If born a nigger he would have been a king. In the tenth century he might have been a Sea-king or something similar. Born as he was in the nineteenth century, he was only a Jack-tar and a hero!

It is safe to conclude that if Molloy had been set free that evening with a cutlass in his hand he would—after supper of course—have attacked single-handed the united band of forty Arabs, killed at least ten of them, and left the remaining thirty to mourn over their mangled bodies and the loss of numerous thumbs and noses, to say nothing of other wounds and bruises.

Luckily for his comrades he was *not* free that night.

"Boys," said he, after finishing his scanty meal, and resting on an elbow as he looked contemplatively up at the stars which were beginning to twinkle in the darkening sky, "it do seem to me, now that I've had time to think over it quietly, that our only chance o' gittin' out o' this here scrape is to keep quiet, an' pretend that we're uncommon fond of our *dear* Arab friends, till we throws 'em off their guard, an' then, some fine night, give 'em the slip an' make sail across the desert for Suakim."

"No doubt you're right," answered Miles, with a sigh, for, being tired and sleepy just then, he was not nearly as sanguine as the seaman, "but I have not much hope of gaining their confidence—especially after your acting the thunderbolt so effectively on one of them."

"Why, man alive! they won't mind that. It was all in the way of fair fight," said Molloy; "an' the rascal was no favourite, I could see that."

"It's a wonder to me you could see anything at all after such a ram!" remarked Moses Pyne, with a yawn, as he lay back and rested his head on a tuft of grass. "The shock seemed to me fit to sink an iron-clad."

"But why *pretend* to be fond of the Arabs?" asked Stevenson. "Don't you think it would be sufficient that we should obey orders quietly without any humbug or pretence at all about it, till a chance to escape shall come in our way?"

"Don't you think, Stevenson," said Miles, "that there's a certain amount of humbug and pretence even in quiet obedience to orders, when such obedience is not the result of submission, but of a desire to throw people off their guard?"

"But my obedience *is* the result of submission," returned the marine stoutly. "I do really submit—first, because it is God's will, for I cannot help it; second, because it is the only course that will enable me to escape bad treatment; third, because I wish to gain the good-will of the men who have me in their power whether I escape or not; and, fourth—"

"Hallo! old man, how many heads are you goin' to give us in that there sermon?" asked Moses.

"This is the last head, Moses, and you needn't be anxious, for I ain't going to enlarge on any of 'em. My fourth reason is, that by doing as common-sense bids me, our foes will be brought thereby to that state of mind which will be favourable to everything—our escape included—and I can't help that, you know. It ain't my fault if they become trustful, is it?"

"No, nor it ain't no part o' your dooty to spoil their trustfulness by failin' to take advantage of it," said Molloy, with a grin; "but it do seem to me, Stevenson, as if there wor a strong smack o' the Jesuit in what you say."

"I hope not," replied the marine. "Anyhow, no one would expect me, surely, to go an' say straight out to these fellows, 'I'm goin' to obey orders an' be as meek as a lamb, in order to throw you off your guard an' bolt when I get the chance!'"

"Cer'nly not. 'Cause why? Firstly, you couldn't say it at all till you'd learned Arabic," returned Molloy; "secondly—if I may be allowed for to follow suit an' sermonise—'cause you shouldn't say it if you could; an', thirdly, 'cause you'd be a most awful Jack-ass to say it if you did. Now, it's my advice, boys, that we go to sleep, for we won't have an easy day of it to-morrow, if I may judge from to-day."

Having delivered this piece of advice with much decision, the seaman extended himself at full length on the ground, and went to sleep with a pleased smile on his face, as if the desert sand had been his familiar couch from infancy.

Some of the other members of the unfortunate party were not, however, quite so ready for sleep. Miles and his friend Armstrong sat long talking over their fate—which they mutually agreed was a very sad one; but at last, overcome by exhaustion, if not anxiety, they sank into much-needed repose, and the only sound that broke the stillness of the night was the tread of the Arab sentinel as he paced slowly to and fro.

The country, as they advanced, became more and more rugged, until they found themselves at last in the midst of a hill region, in the valleys of which there grew a considerable amount of herbage and underwood. The journey here became very severe to the captives, for, although they did not suffer from thirst so much as on the plains, the difficulty of ascending steep and rugged paths with their hands bound was very great. It is true the position of the hands was changed, for after the second day they had been bound in front of them, but this did not render their toil easy, though it was thereby made a little less laborious.

By this time the captives had learned from experience that if they wished to avoid the spear-points they must walk in advance of their captors at a very smart pace. Fortunately, being all strong and healthy men, they were well able to do so.

Rattling Bill, perhaps, suffered most, although, after Molloy, he was physically one of the strongest of the party.

Observing that he lagged behind a little on one occasion while they were traversing a somewhat level valley, Stevenson offered him his arm.

"Don't be ashamed to take it, old boy," said the marine kindly, as his comrade hesitated. "You know, a fellow sometimes feels out o' sorts, and not up to much, however stout he may be when well, so just you lay hold, for somehow I happen to feel as strong as an elephant to-day."

"But I *ain't* ill," returned Simkin, still declining, "and I don't see why I shouldn't be as able as you are to carry my own weight."

"Of course you are better able to do it than I am, in a general way," returned his friend, "but I said that sometimes, you know, a fellow gives in, he don't well know why or how, an' then, of course, his comrades that are still strong are bound to help him. Here, hook on and pocket your pride. You'll have to do the same thing for me to-morrow, may-hap, when *I* give in. And if it does come to that I'll lean heavy, I promise you."

"You're a good fellow, Stevenson, even though you *are* a Blue Light," said Simkin, taking the proffered arm.

"Perhaps it's *because* I am a Blue Light," returned the marine, with a laugh. "At all events, it is certain that whatever good there may be about me at all is the result of that Light which is as free to you as to me."

For some minutes the couple walked along in silence. At last Rattling Bill spoke.

"I wonder," he said, "why it is that a young and healthy fellow like me should break down sooner than you, Stevenson, for I'm both bigger and stronger—and yet, look at us new. Ain't it strange! I wonder why it is."

"It is strange, indeed," returned the marine quietly. "P'r'aps the climate suits me better than you."

"I know what you're thinkin'," said Simkin, almost testily. "Why don't you say that *drink* is the cause of it—straight out, like a man?"

"Because I knew you were saying that to yourself, lad, so there was no need for me to say it," returned his friend, with a side-glance and a twinkle of the eyes.

"Well, whoever says it, it's a fact," continued Simkin, almost sternly, "an' I make no bones of admitting it. I have bin soakin' away, right and left, since I came to this country, in spite o' warnin's from you and other men like you, and now I feel as if all my boasted strength was goin' out at my heels."

Stevenson was silent.

"Why don't you say 'I told you so?'" asked Simkin, sharply.

"Because I *never* say that! It only riles people; besides," continued the marine, earnestly, "I was asking God at the moment to enable me to answer you wisely. You see, I think it only fair to reveal some of my private thoughts to *you*, since you are making a father-confessor of *me*. But as you admit that drink has done you damage, my dear fellow, there is no need for me to say anything more on that subject. What you want now is encouragement as to the future and advice as to the present. Shall I give you both just now, or shall I wait?"

"'Commence firing!'" replied Simkin, with a half-jesting smile.

"Well, then, as to encouragement," said Stevenson. "A point of vital importance with men who have gone in for drink as much as you have, is total-abstinence; and I regard it as an evidence of God's love to you that He has brought you here—"

"God's love that brought me *here*!" exclaimed the soldier in surprise. "Well, that *is* a view o' the case that don't seem quite plain."

"Plain enough if you open your eyes wide enough. See here: If you was in camp now, with your present notions, and was to determine to give up drink, you'd have to face and fight two most tremendous devils. One devil is called Craving, the other is called Temptation, and all the Arabs in the Soudan rolled into one are not so terrible or so strong as these two when a man is left to fight them by himself. Now, is it not a sign of our Father's love that he has, by bringing you here, removed the devil Temptation entirely out of your way, for you can't get strong drink here for love or money. So, you see, you have only got Craving to fight, and that's encouraging, ain't it?"

"D'ye know, I believe you are not far wrong," said Simkin, gravely; "and it *is* encouraging to know that Temptation's out o' the way, for I feel that the other devil has got me by the throat even now, and that it's him as has weakened me so much."

"That's it, friend. You've got the truth by the tail now, so hold on; but, at the same time, don't be too hard on Craving. It's not *his* fault that he's here. You have poured liquor down your throat to him daily, and cultivated his acquaintance, and helped him to increase his strength regularly, for many months—it may be for years. I don't want to be hard on you, lad, but it's of no use shiftin' the burden on to the wrong shoulders. It is not Craving but *you* who are the sinner. Now, as to advice: do you really want it?"

"Well," replied Simkin, with a "humph!" "it will be time enough for you to shut up when I sound the 'cease firing!'"

"My advice, then, is that you go down on your knees, plead *guilty* straight off, and ask for grace to help you in your time of need."

"What! go down on my knees here before all them Arabs? If I did, they'd not only laugh at me, but they'd soon rouse me up with their spears."

"I'm not so sure about that, Simkin. Arabs are accustomed to go on their own knees a good deal in public. It is chiefly Christians who, strange to say, are ashamed to be caught in that position at odd times. But I speak not of ceremonies, but of realities. A man may go on his knees, without bending a joint, any time and everywhere. Now, listen: there is this difference between the courts of men and the court of heaven, that in the former, when a man pleads guilty, his sentence is only modified and softened, but in the latter, the man who pleads guilty receives a free pardon and ultimate deliverance from *all* sin for the sake of Jesus Christ. Will you accept this deliverance, my friend?"

What the soldier replied in his heart we cannot tell, for his voice was silent. Before the conversation could be resumed a halt was called, to partake of the midday meal and rest.

That evening the party came upon a strange and animated scene. It was one of the mountain camps of Osman Digna, where men were assembling from all quarters to swell the hordes with which their chief hoped to drive the hated Europeans into the Red Sea. Camels and other beasts of burden were bringing in supplies for the vast army, and to this spot had been brought the poor fellows who had been wounded in recent battles.

Here the captives were thrust into a small dark hut and left to their meditations, while a couple of Arab sentries guarded the door.

Chapter Twenty Three-Shows that Suffering tends to draw out Sympathy

The word *captivity*, even when it refers to civilised lands and peoples, conveys, we suspect, but a feeble and incorrect idea to the minds of those who have never been in a state of personal bondage. Still less do we fully appreciate its dread significance when it refers to foreign lands and barbarous people.

It was not so much the indignities to which the captive Britons were subjected that told upon them ultimately, as the hard, grinding, restless toil, and the insufficient food and rest—sometimes accompanied with absolute corporeal pain.

"A merciful man is merciful to his beast." There is not much of mercy to his beast in an Arab. We have seen an Arab, in Algiers, who made use of a sore on his donkey's back as a sort of convenient spur! It is exhausting to belabour a thick-skinned and obstinate animal with a stick. It is much easier, and much more effective, to tickle up a sore, kept open for the purpose, with a little bit of stick, while comfortably seated on the creature's back. The fellow we refer to did that. We do not say or think that all Arabs are cruel; very far from it, but we hold that, as a race, they are so. Their great prophet taught them cruelty by example and precept, and the records of history, as well as of the African slave-trade, bear witness to the fact that their "tender mercies" are not and never have been conspicuous!

At first, as we have shown, indignities told pretty severely on the unfortunate Englishmen. But, as time went on, and they were taken further and further into the interior, and heavy burdens were daily bound on their shoulders, and the lash was frequently applied to urge them on, the keen sense of insult which had at first stirred them into wild anger became blunted, and at last they reached that condition of partial apathy which renders men almost indifferent to everything save rest and food. Even the submissive Stevenson was growing callous. In short, that process had begun which usually ends in making men either brutes or martyrs.

As before, we must remark that Jack Molloy was to some extent an exception. It did seem as if nothing but death itself could subdue that remarkable man. His huge frame was so powerful that he seemed to be capable of sustaining any weight his tyrants chose to put upon him. And the influence of hope was so strong within him that it raised him almost entirely above the region of despondency.

This was fortunate for his comrades in misfortune, for it served to keep up their less vigorous spirits.

There was one thing about the seaman, however, which they could not quite reconcile with his known character. This was a tendency to groan heavily when he was being loaded. To be sure, there was not much reason for wonder, seeing that the Arabs forced the Herculean man to carry nearly double the weight borne by any of his companions, but then, as Miles once confidentially remarked to Armstrong, "I thought that Jack Molloy would rather have died than have groaned on account of the weight of his burden; but, after all, it *is* a tremendously heavy one—poor fellow!"

One day the Arabs seemed to be filled with an unusual desire to torment their victims. A man had passed the band that day on a fast dromedary, and the prisoners conjectured that he might have brought news of some defeat of their friends, which would account for their increased cruelty. They were particularly hard on Molloy that day, as if they regarded him as typical of British strength, and, therefore, an appropriate object of revenge. After the midday rest, they not only put on him his ordinary burden, but added to the enormous weight considerably, so that the poor fellow staggered under it, and finally fell down beneath it, with a very dismal groan indeed!

Of course the lash was at once applied, and under its influence the sailor rose with great difficulty, and staggered forward a few paces, but only to fall again. This time, however, he did not wait for the lash, but made very determined efforts of his own accord to rise and advance, without showing the smallest sign of resentment. Even his captors seemed touched, for one of them removed a small portion of his burden, so that, thereafter, the poor fellow proceeded with less difficulty, though still with a little staggering and an occasional groan.

That night they reached a village near the banks of a broad river, where they put up for the night. After their usual not too heavy supper was over, the prisoners were thrust into a sort of hut or cattle-shed, and left to make themselves as comfortable as they could on the bare floor.

"I don't feel quite so much inclined for sleep to-night," said Miles to Molloy.

"No more do I," remarked the sailor, stretching himself like a wearied Goliath on the earthen floor, and placing his arms under his head for a pillow.

"I feel pretty well used up too," said Simkin, throwing himself down with a sigh that was more eloquent than his tongue. He was indeed anything but Rattling Bill by that time.

Moses Pyne being, like his great namesake, a meek man, sympathised with the others, but said nothing about himself, though his looks betrayed him. Armstrong and Stevenson were silent. They seemed too much exhausted to indulge in speech.

"Poor fellow!" said Moses to Molloy, "I don't wonder you are tired, for you not only carried twice as much as any of us, but you took part of *my* load. Indeed he did, comrades," added Moses, turning to his friends with an apologetic air. "I didn't want him to do it, but he jerked part o' my load suddenly out o' my hand an' wouldn't give it up again; an', you know, I didn't dare to make a row, for that would have brought the lash down on both of us. But I didn't want him to carry so much, an' him so tired."

"Tired!" exclaimed the sailor, with a loud laugh. "Why, I warn't tired a bit. An', you know, you'd have dropped down, Moses, if I hadn't helped ye at that time."

"Well, I confess I *was* ready to drop," returned Moses, with a humbled look; "but I would much rather have dropped than have added to your burden. How can you say you wasn't tired when you had fallen down only five minutes before, an' groaned heavily when you rose, and your legs trembled so? I could *see* it!"

To this the seaman's only reply was the expansion of his huge but handsome mouth, the display of magnificent teeth, the disappearance of both eyes, and a prolonged quiet chuckle.

"Why, what's the matter with you, Jack?" asked Stevenson.

"Nothin's the matter wi' me, old man—'cept—"

Here he indulged in another chuckle.

"Goin' mad, with over-fatigue," said Simkin, looking suspiciously at him.

"Ay, that's it, messmate, clean mad wi' over-fatigue."

He wiped his eyes with the hairy back of his hand, for the chuckling, being hearty, had produced a few tears.

"No, but really, Jack, what is it you're laughing at?" asked Armstrong. "If there *is* a joke you might as well let us have the benefit of laughing along wi' you, for we stand much in need of something to cheer us here."

"Well, Billy boy, I may as well make a clean breast of it," said Molloy, raising himself on one elbow and becoming grave. "I do confess to feelin' raither ashamed o' myself, but you mustn't be hard on me, lads, for circumstances alters cases, you know, as Solomon said—leastwise if it warn't him it was Job or somebody else. The fact is, I've bin shammin', mates!"

"Shamming!"

"Ay, shammin' *weak*. Purtendin' that I was shaky on the legs, an' so not quite up to the cargo they were puttin' aboard o' me."

"If what you've been doing means shamming *weak*, I'd like to see you coming out *strong*," observed Miles, with a short laugh.

"Well, p'r'aps you'll see that too some day," returned the sailor, with an amiable look.

"But do you really mean that all that groaning—which I confess to have been surprised at—was mere pretence?"

"All sham. Downright sneakin'!" said Molloy. "The short an' the long of it is, that I see'd from the first the on'y way to humbug them yellow-faced baboons was to circumwent 'em. So I set to work at the wery beginnin'."

"Ah, by takin' a header," said Simkin, "into one o' their bread-baskets!"

"No, no!" returned the seaman, "that, I confess, was a mistake. But you'll admit, I've made no more mistakes o' the same sort since then. You see, I perceived that, as my strength is considerable above the average, the baboons would be likely to overload me, so, arter profound excogitation wi' myself, I made up my mind what to do, an' when they had clapped on a little more than the rest o' you carried I began to groan, then I began to shake a bit in my timbers, an' look as if I was agoin' to founder. It didn't check 'em much, for they're awful cruel, so I went fairly down by the head. I had a pretty fair guess that this would bring the lash about my shoulders, an' I was right, but I got up wery slowly an' broken-down-like, so that the baboons was fairly humbugged, and stopped loadin' of me long afore I'd taken in a full cargo—so, you see, boys, I've bin sailin' raither light than otherwise."

"But do you mean to tell me that the load you've bin carryin' is not too heavy for you?" asked Moses.

"That's just what I does mean to tell you, lad. I could carry a good deal more, an' dance with it. You see, they ain't used to men o' my size, so I was able to humbug 'em into a miscalkilation. I on'y wish I could have helped you all to do the same, but they're too 'cute, as the Yankees say. Anyway, Moses, you don't need to trouble your head when I gives you a helpin' hand again."

"Ah, that expression, 'a helping hand,' sounds familiar in my ears," said Stevenson, in a sad tone.

"Yes, what do it recall, lad?" asked Molloy, extending himself again on his broad back.

"It recalls places and friends in Portsmouth, Jack, that we may never again set eyes on. You remember the Institoot? Well, they've got a new branch o' the work there for the surrounding civilian poor, called the *Helping Hand*. You see, Miss Robinson understands us soldiers out and out. She knew that those among us who gave up drink and sin, and put on the blue-ribbon, were not goin' to keep all the benefit to ourselves. She knew that we understood the meaning of the word 'enlist' That we'd think very little o' the poor-spirited fellow who'd take the Queen's shillin' and put on her uniform, and then shirk fightin' her battles and honouring her flag. So when some of us put on the Lord's uniform—which, like that of the Austrians, is white—and unfurled His flag, she knew we'd soon be wantin' to fight His battles against sin—especially against drink; so instead of lookin' after our welfare alone, she encouraged us to hold out a *helpin' hand* to the poorest and most miserable people in Portsmouth, an' she found us ready to answer to the call."

"Ah, they was grand times, these," continued the marine, with kindly enthusiasm, as he observed that his comrades in sorrow were becoming interested, and forgetting for the moment their own sorrows and sufferings. "The Blue-Ribbon move was strong in Portsmouth at the time, and many of the soldiers and sailors joined it. Some time after we had held out a helping hand to the poor civilians, we took it into our heads to invite some of 'em to a grand tea-fight in the big hall, so we asked a lot o' the poorest who had faithfully kept the pledge through their first teetotal Christmas; and it *was* a scrimmage, I can tell you. We got together more than forty of 'em, men and women, and there were about three hundred soldiers and sailors, and their wives to wait on 'em an' keep 'em company!"

"Capital!" exclaimed Miles, who had a sympathetic spirit—especially for the poor.

"Good—good!" said Molloy, nodding his head. "That was the right thing to do, an' I suppose they enjoyed theirselves?"

"Enjoyed themselves!" exclaimed the marine, with a laugh. "I should just think they did. Trust Miss Robinson for knowin' how to make poor folk enjoy themselves—and, for the matter of that, rich folk too! How they did stuff, to be sure! Many of 'em, poor things, hadn't got such a blow-out in all their lives before. You see, they was the very poorest of the poor. You may believe what I say, for I went round myself with one o' the Institoot ladies to invite 'em, and I do declare to you that I never saw even pigs or dogs in such a state of destitootion—nothin' whatever to lie on but the bare boards."

"You don't say so?" murmured Moses, with deep commiseration, and seemingly oblivious of the fact that he was himself pretty much in similar destitution at that moment.

"Indeed I do. Look here," continued the marine, becoming more earnest as he went on; "thousands of people don't know—can't understand—what misery and want and suffering is going on around 'em. City missionaries and the like tell 'em about it, and write about it, but telling and writin' *don't* make people *know* some things. They must *see*, ay, sometimes they must *feel*, before they can rightly understand.

"One of the rooms we visited," continued Stevenson, in pathetic tones, "belonged to a poor old couple who had been great drinkers, but had been induced to put on the blue-ribbon. It was a pigeon-hole of a room, narrow, up a dark stair. They had no means of support. The room was empty. Everything had been pawned. The last thing given up was the woman's shawl to pay the rent, and they were starving."

"Why didn't they go to the work'us?" asked Simkin.

"'Cause the workhouse separates man and wife, in defiance of the Divine law—'Whom God hath joined together let no man put asunder.' They was fond of each other, was that old man and woman, and had lived long together, an' didn't want to part till death. So they had managed to stick to the old home, ay, and they had stuck to their colours, for the bit o' blue was still pinned to the tattered coat o' the man and the thin gown o' the woman, (neither coat nor gown would fetch anything at the pawn-shop!) and there was no smell o' drink in the room. Well, that old couple went to the tea-fight. It was a bitter cold night, but they came all the same, with nothing to cover the woman's thin old arms.

"The moment they appeared, away went one o' Miss Robinson's workers to the room where they keep chests full of clothes sent by charitable folk to the Institoot, an' you should have seen that old woman's wrinkled face when the worker returned wi' the thickest worsted shawl she could lay hold of, an' put it on her shoulders as tenderly as if the old woman had been her own mother! At the same time they gave a big-coat to the old man."

"But, I say," interrupted Simkin, "that Christmas feed an' shawl an' coat wouldn't keep the couple for a twel'month, if they was sent home to starve as before, would it?"

"Of course not," returned the marine, "but they wasn't sent off to starve; they was looked after. Ay, an' the people o' the whole neighbourhood are now looked after, for Miss Robinson has bought up a grog-shop in Nobbs Lane—one o' the worst places in Portsmouth—an' converted it into a temperance coffee-house, wi' lots of beds to send people to when the

Institoot overflows, an' a soup-kitchen for the destitoot poor, an' a wash'us for them and the soldiers' wives, an', in short, it has changed the whole place; but if I go on like this I'll send Moses to sleep, for I've heard 'im smotherin' his yawns more than once a'ready!"

"It's not for want of interest in what you're sayin' though, old man," returned Moses, with a tremendous unsmothered yawn, which of course set all his comrades off, and confirmed them in the belief that it was time to seek repose.

Scarcely a single comment was made on the narrative, as each laid his weary head on his arm or on a folded garment, and stretched himself out on the hard ground, in nearly as destitute a condition as the poor folk about whom they had been hearing; for while their bed was as hard as theirs, and the covering as scant, the meal they had recently consumed was by no means what hungry men would call satisfying.

There is reason to believe, however, that their consideration of the sad lot of "the poor" at home did not render less profound or sweet that night's repose in the great African wilderness.

Chapter Twenty Four-Adventures among the Soudanese, and Strange Meeting with the Mahdi

Day after day, for many days, our captives were thus driven over the burning desert, suffering intensely from heat and thirst and hunger, as well as from fatigue, and treated with more or less cruelty according to the varying moods of their guards.

At last one afternoon they arrived at a city of considerable size, through the streets of which they were driven with unusual harshness by the Arab soldiers, who seemed to take pleasure in thus publicly heaping contempt on Christian captives in the sight of the Mohammedan population.

Their case seemed truly desperate to Miles, as he and his comrades passed through the narrow streets, for no pitying eye, but many a frown, was cast on them by the crowds who stopped to gaze and scoff.

What city they had reached they had no means of finding out, being ignorant of Arabic. Indeed, even though they had been able to converse with their guards, it is probable that these would have refused to hold communication with them.

Turning out of what appeared to be a sort of market-place, they were driven, rather than conducted, to a whitewashed building, into which they entered through a low strong door, studded with large iron-headed nails. As they entered a dark passage, the door was slammed and locked behind them. At first, owing to their sudden entrance out of intensely bright day, they seemed to be in profound darkness, but when they became accustomed to the dim light, they found that they were in the presence of several powerful men, who carried long Eastern-like pistols in their girdles, and curved naked swords in their hands. These stood like statues against the wall of the small room, silently awaiting the orders of one whose dress betokened him of superior rank, and who was engaged in writing with a reed in Persian characters. A tall, very black-skinned negro stood beside this officer.

After a few minutes the latter laid down the reed, rose up, and confronted the prisoners, at the same time addressing some remark to his attendant.

"Who is you, an' where you come fro?" asked the negro, addressing himself to Miles, whom he seemed intuitively to recognise as the chief of his party.

"We are British soldiers!" said Miles, drawing himself up with an air of dignity that would have done credit to the Emperor of China. You see, at that moment he felt himself to be the spokesman for, and, with his comrades, the representative of, the entire British army, and was put upon his mettle accordingly. "We come from Suakim—"

"Ay, black-face!" broke in Jack Molloy at that moment, "and you may tell him that if he has the pluck to go to Suakim, he'll see plenty more British soldiers—an' British seamen too—who'll give him an' his friends a hot and hearty welcome wi' bullet, bayonet, and cutlash whenever he feels inclined."

"Are you officer?" asked the negro of Miles, and not paying the smallest attention to Molloy's warlike invitation.

"No, I am not."

Turning to the armed men, the officer gave them an order which caused them to advance and stand close to the Englishmen—two beside each prisoner—with drawn swords. An extra man took up his position behind Molloy, evidently having regard to his superior size! Then two men, who looked like jailers, advanced to Stevenson, cut the cords that bound his arms, and proceeded to put iron fetters on his wrists.

"Comrades," said Molloy, in a low voice, when he perceived that his turn was coming, "shall we make a burst for it—kill them all, get out into street, cut and slash through the town, and make a grand run for it—or die like men?"

"Die like fools!" growled Simkin, as he suffered his hands to be manacled.

"No, no, Jack," said Armstrong; "don't be rash. Let's bide our time. There's no sayin' what'll turn up."

"Well, well," sighed Molloy, resigning himself to his fate, "there's only one thing now that's sartin sure to turn up, an' that is the sod that'll cover our graves."

"You're not sure even of that, man," said Moses Pyne, who was beginning to give way to despair, "for may-hap they'll only dig a hole in the sand, an' shove us in."

"More likely to leave the dogs an' vultures to clear us out o' the way," said Simkin, whose powers of hope were being tested almost beyond endurance.

While the prisoners indulged in these gloomy anticipations, the operation of fixing their irons was finished, after which they were taken across an inner court which was open to the sky. At the other side of this they came to another heavy iron-studded door, which, when opened, disclosed a flight of steps descending into profound darkness.

"Go in!" said the negro, who had accompanied them.

Molloy, who was first, hesitated, and the tremendous flush on his face, and frown on his shaggy brows, seemed to indicate that even yet he meditated attempting his favourite "burst"! But Stevenson, pushing past him, at once descended, saying, as he went, "Don't be foolish, Jack; we *must* learn to submit."

There were only three steps, and at the bottom a room about fifteen feet square, to enlighten which there was a small hole high up in one of the walls. It did little more, however, than render darkness visible.

"God help us!" exclaimed Miles, with a sensation of sinking at the heart which he had never felt before.

And little wonder, for, as their eyes became accustomed to the dim light, it was seen that the walls were blank, with nothing on them to relieve the eye save the little hole or window just mentioned; that the floor was of hard earth, and that there was not a scrap of furniture in the room — not even a stool, or a bundle of straw on which to lie down.

"'I will trust, and not be afraid,'" said Stevenson, in a low voice.

"Who will you trust?" asked Simkin, who was not aware that his comrade had quoted Scripture.

"I will trust God," answered the marine.

"I wouldn't give much for your trust, then," returned Simkin bitterly, as well as contemptuously, for he had given way to despair. "You Blue Lights and Christians think yourselves so much better than everybody else, because you make so much talk about prayin' an' singin', an' doin' your duty, an' servin' God, an' submitting. It's all hypocrisy."

"Don't you believe that Sergeant Hardy is a good soldier?" asked Stevenson.

"Of course I do," replied Simkin, in some surprise at the question.

"An' *he* doesn't think much of himself, does he?" continued the marine.

"Certainly not. He's one o' the kindest an' humblest men in the regiment, as I have good reason to know."

"Yet he frequently talks to us of attendin' to our duty, an' doin' credit to the British Flag, an' faithfully serving the Queen. If this is praiseworthy in the sergeant, why should the talk of duty an' service an' honour to God be hypocrisy in the Christian? Does it not seem strange that we Blue Lights—who have discovered ourselves to be much worse than we thought ourselves, an' gladly accept Jesus as our Saviour from sin—should be charged with thinkin' ourselves '*better* than other people'!"

"Come now," cried Jack Molloy, seating himself on the floor, and leaning his back against the wall; "it do seem to me, as you putt it, Stevenson, that the charge ought to be all the other way; for we, who make no purfession of religion at all, thinks ourselves so far righteous that we've got no need of a Saviour. Suppose, now, as we've got to as low a state o' the dumps as men can well come to, we all sits down in a row an' have a palaver about this matter—Parson Stevenson bein' the chief spokesman."

They all readily agreed to this proposal. Indeed, in the circumstances, any proposal that offered the faintest hope of diverting their minds from present trouble would have been welcome to them at that moment. The marine was nothing loath to fall in with the fancy of his irrepressible comrade, but we do not propose to follow them in the talk that ensued. We will rather turn at once to those events which affected more immediately the fortunes of the captives.

On the morning after their arrival in the city there was assembled in the principal square a considerable concourse of Soudan warriors. They stood chatting together in various groups in front of a public building, as if awaiting some chief or great man, whose richly caparisoned steed stood in front of the main entrance, with its out-runner standing before it.

This runner was a splendid specimen of physical manhood. He was as black as coal, as graceful as Apollo, and apparently as powerful as Hercules,—if one might judge from the great muscles which stood out prominently on all his limbs, he wore but little clothing—merely a pair of short Arab drawers of white cotton, a red fez on his head, and a small tippet on his shoulders. Unlike negroes in general, his features were cast in a mould which one is more accustomed to see in the Caucasian race of mankind—the nose being straight, the lips comparatively thin, and the face oval, while his bearing was that of a man accustomed to command.

The appearance of a few soldiers traversing the square drew the eyes of all in their direction, and caused a brief pause in the hum of conversation. Our friends, the captives, were in the midst of these soldiers, and beside them marched the negro interpreter whom they had first met with in the prison.

At the door of the public building the soldiers drew up and allowed the captives to pass in, guarded by two officers and the interpreter. Inside they found a number of military men and dignitaries grouped around, conversing with a stern man of strongly marked features. This man—towards whom all of them showed great deference—was engaged when the captives entered; they were therefore obliged to stand aside for a few minutes.

"Who is he?" asked Molloy of the negro interpreter.

"Our great leader," said the negro, "the Mahdi."

"What! the scoundrel that's bin the cause o' all this kick-up?" asked Jack Molloy, in surprise.

The interpreter did not quite understand the seaman's peculiar language, but he seemed to have some idea of the drift of it, for he turned up his up-turned nose in scorn and made no reply.

In a few minutes an officer led the captives before the Mahdi, who regarded them with a dark frown, directing his attention particularly to Jack Molloy, as being the most conspicuous member of the party, perhaps, also, because Molloy looked at him with an air and expression of stern defiance.

Selecting him as a spokesman for the others, the Mahdi, using the negro as an interpreter, put him through the following examination:—

"Where do you come from?" he asked, sternly.

"From Suakim," answered Molloy, quite as sternly.

"What brought you here?"

"Your dirty-faced baboons!"

It is probable that the negro used some discretion in translating this reply, for the chief did not seem at all offended, but with the same manner and tone continued—

"Do you know the number of men in Suakim?"

"Yes."

"Tell me—how many?"

To this Molloy answered slowly, "Quite enough—if you had only the pluck to come out into the open an' fight like men—to give you such a lickin' that there wouldn't be a baboon o' you left in the whole Soudan!"

Again it is probable that the interpreter did not give this speech verbatim, for while he was delivering it the Mahdi was scanning the features of the group of prisoners with a calm but keen eye.

Making a sign to one of his attendants to lead Molloy to one side, he said a few words to another, who thereupon placed Miles in front of his master.

"Are you an officer?" was the first question put.

"No," answered our hero, with quiet dignity, but without the slightest tinge of defiance either in tone or look.

"Will you tell me how many men you have in Suakim?"

"No."

"Dare you refuse?"

"Yes; it is against the principles of a British soldier to give information to an enemy."

"That's right, John Miles," said Molloy, in an encouraging tone; "give it 'im hot! They can only kill us once, an' —"

"Silence!" hissed the Mahdi between his teeth.

"Silence!" echoed the interpreter.

"All right, you nigger! Tell the baboon to go on. I won't run foul of him again; he ain't worth it."

This was said with free-and-easy contempt.

"Do you not know," resumed the Mahdi, turning again to Miles with a fierce expression, "that I have power to take your life?"

"You have no power at all beyond what God gives to you," said Miles quietly.

Even the angry Mahdi was impressed with the obvious truth of this statement, but his anger was not much allayed by it.

"Know you not," he continued, "that I have the power to torture you to death?"

Our hero did not at once reply. He felt that a grand crisis in his life had arrived, that he stood there before an assemblage of "unbelievers," and that, to some extent, the credit of his countrymen for courage, fidelity, and Christianity was placed in his hands.

"Mahdi," he said, impressively, as he drew himself up, "you have indeed the power to torture and kill me, but you have *not* the power to open my lips, or cause me to bring dishonour on my country!"

"Brayvo, Johnny! Pitch into him!" cried the delighted Molloy.

"Fool!" exclaimed the Mahdi, whose ire was rekindled as much by the seaman's uncomprehended comment as by our hero's fearless look and tone, "you cannot bring dishonour on a country which is already dishonoured.

What dishonour can exceed that of being leagued with the oppressor against the oppressed? Go! You shall be taught to sympathise with the oppressed by suffering oppression!"

He waved his hand, and, quickly leaving the court, walked towards his horse, where the fine-looking negro runner stood and held his stirrup, while he prepared to mount. Instead of mounting, however, he stood for a few seconds looking thoughtfully at the ground. Then he spoke a few words to the runner, who bowed his head slightly as his master mounted and rode away.

Grasping a small lance and flag, which seemed to be the emblems of his office, he ran off at full speed in front of the horse to clear the way for his master.

At the entrance to the building an official of some sort took hold of Miles's arm and led him away. He glanced back and observed that two armed men followed. At the same time he saw Molloy's head towering above the surrounding crowd, as he and his comrades were led away in another direction. That was the last he saw of some at least, of his friends for a considerable time.

Poor Miles was too much distressed at this sudden and unexpected separation to take much note of the things around him. He was brought back to a somewhat anxious consideration of his own affairs by being halted at the gate of a building which was more imposing, both in size and appearance, than the houses around it. Entering at the bidding of his conductors, he found himself in an open court, and heard the heavy door closed and bolted behind him.

Thereafter he was conducted to a small chamber, which, although extremely simple, and almost devoid of furniture, was both cleaner and lighter than that in which he and his comrades had been at first immured. He observed, however, with a feeling of despondency, that it was lighted only by small square holes in the roof, and that the door was very substantial!

Here his conductor left him without saying a word and bolted the door. As he listened to the retreating steps of his jailer echoing on the marble pavement of the court, a feeling of profound dejection fell upon our hero's spirit, and he experienced an almost irresistible tendency to give way to unmanly tears. Shame, however, came to his aid and enabled him to restrain them.

In one corner of the little room there was a piece of thick matting. Sitting down on it with his back against the wall, the poor youth laid his face in his hands and began to think and to pray. But the prayer was not audible; and who can describe the wide range of thought—the grief, the anxiety for comrades as well as for himself, the remorse, the intense longing to recall the past, the wish that he might awake and find that it was only a wild dream, and, above all, the bitter—almost vengeful—self-condemnation!

He was aroused from this condition by the entrance of a slave bearing a round wooden tray, on which were a bowl of food and a jug of water.

Placing these before him, the slave retired without speaking, though he bestowed a glance of curiosity on the "white infidel dog," before closing the door.

Appetite had ever been a staunch friend to Miles Milton. It did not fail him now. Soldier-life has usually the effect of making its devotees acutely careful to take advantage of all opportunities! He set to work on the bowlful of food with a will, and was not solicitous to ascertain what it consisted of until it was safely washed down with a draught from the jug. Being then too late to enter on an inquiry as to its nature, he contented himself with a pleasing recollection that the main body of the compost was rice, one of the constituents oil, and that the whole was by no means bad. He also wished that there had been more of it, and then resumed his previous—and only possible—amusement of meditation.

Thinking, like fighting, is better done on a full stomach! He had gradually thought himself into a more hopeful state of mind, when he was again interrupted by the entrance of visitors—two armed men, and the magnificent negro runner whom he had observed holding the Mahdi's horse. One of the armed men carried a small bundle, which he deposited on the ground, and then stood beside his companion. Both stood like sentinels with drawn swords, ready, apparently, to obey the commands of the runner.

Advancing to the captive, the latter, producing a key, unlocked and removed his manacles. These he handed to one of the men, and, turning again to Miles, said, to his great surprise, in English—

"Undress, and put on de t'ings in bundle."

We may here observe that up to this time Miles and his comrades in adversity had worn, day and night, the garments in which they had been captured. Our hero was not sorry, therefore, at the prospect of a change. Untying the bundle to see what substitute was given for his uniform, he found that it contained only a pair of loose cotton drawers and a red fez.

"Is this all?" he asked, in surprise.

"All," answered the negro.

"And what if I refuse to undress?" asked Miles.

"Your clo'es will be tore off your back and you be bastinado!"

This was said so calmly, and the three grave, powerful men seemed so thoroughly capable of performing the deed, that our hero wisely submitted to the inevitable and took off his uniform, which one of the guards gathered up piece by piece as it was removed. Then he pulled on the drawers, which covered him from the waist to a little below the knees. When he had put on the red fez he found himself clothed in exactly the same costume as the runner, with the exception of a small green tippet which barely covered the top of his shoulders, and seemed to be worn rather as an ornament than a piece of clothing, though perhaps it formed a slight protection from the sun.

In this cool costume they left him, carrying away his uniform, as if more thoroughly to impress on him what uncommonly cool things they were capable of doing in the hot regions of the Soudan!

Chapter Twenty Five-Miles is promoted—Molloy overthrows the Mahdi, and is elevated for so doing

Next day Miles Milton became painfully aware of the fact that his life in captivity was not to be one of ease or idleness.

Soon after daybreak the door of his prison creaked on its ponderous hinges, and he started up from the mat on which he had slept without covering of any kind. His visitor was the Mahdi's runner, who, after closing the door, came and sat down beside him, cross legged *à la* Turk and tailor.

For a brief space the handsome black stared steadily at Miles, who returned the compliment as steadily, not being sure whether curiosity or insolence lay at the foundation of the stare.

"Englishmin," said the runner at last, "you is unfortnit."

"I am indeed," returned Miles; "at the same time I am fortunate in so unexpectedly finding one who recognises the fact, and who can tell me so in my own tongue. May I venture to hope that you are friendly towards me?"

"Yes; I am your friend, but my friendness can do for you not'ing. Like youself, I am captive—slave. But in my own land I was a chief, and friend of the great and good Gordon, so I is friend to all Englishmin. Once I was 'terpreter to Gordon, but the Mahdi came. I fell into his hands, and now I do run befront his horse, an' hold de stirrup! I comes to you from the Mahdi wid bad news."

"Indeed! But I need not wonder. You could scarcely come from him with good news. What have you to tell?"

"The Mahdi has made you his runner," answered the negro.

"That is strange news rather than bad, is it not?"

"No; it is bad. He do dis 'cause he hate you. Somehow you has anger him. He say he will tame you. He try to tame *me*," said the negro, with sudden and tremendous ferocity, "an' him t'ink he do it! But I only waits my chance to kill him.

"Now he send me again to dirty work, an' put you in my place to humble you—to insult you before every one, who will say, 'Look! de bold Christin dog lick de dust now, an' hold de Mahdi's stirrup.'"

"This is indeed bad news. But how is it that you, who seem to be free, do not use your opportunity to escape? I saw you holding the Mahdi's horse. It seems to be a splendid one. Why did you not jump on its back and fly?"

The runner frowned, and then, changing his mood, smiled sadly.

"You is young," he said, "and knows not'ing. At night I am locked up like yourself. In de day-time de city is full of enemies, who all knows me. Do you t'ink dey will salute, and say, 'Go in peace,' to de runner of de Mahdi when he is running away with his best horse?"

"Perhaps not," said Miles, "but I would try if I were you."

"You will be me very soon," returned the runner, "and you can try. I did try—twice. I was caught both times and beat near to death. But I did not die! I learn wisdom; and now I submit and wait my chance to kill him. If you is wise you begin *at once* to submit and wait too."

"There is truth in what you say," rejoined Miles, after a few minutes' thought. "I will take your advice and submit and wait, but only till the opportunity to escape offers. I would not murder the man even if I had the chance."

"Your words remind me of de good Gordon. He was not vengeful. He loved God," said the runner, in a low and very different tone. "But," he added, "Gordon was a white man. He did not—could not—understand de feelings of de black chief."

As the last remark opened up ground which Miles was not prepared to traverse, he made no rejoinder but asked the runner what the Mahdi required of him in his new capacity.

"He require you to learn de city, so as you know how to run when you is told—an' I is to teach you, so you come wid me," said the runner, rising.

"But am I to go in this costume, or rather in this half-naked state?" asked Miles, rising and spreading out his hands as he looked down at his unclothed chest and lower limbs.

"You not cause for be ashamed," replied the runner, with a nod.

This was true, for the hard travelling which Miles had recently endured, and the heavy burdens which he had borne, had developed his muscles to such an extent that his frame was almost equal to that of the negro, and a fit subject for the sculptor's chisel.

"Your white skin will p'r'aps blister at first," continued the runner, "but your master will be glad for dat. Here is a t'ing, however, will save you shoulders. Now, you makes fuss-rate runner."

He took the little green tippet off his own shoulders and fastened it on those of his successor.

"Come now," he added, "let us see how you can run."

They passed out into the street together, and then poor Miles felt the full sense of his degradation, when he saw some of the passers-by stop to gaze with looks of hatred or contempt or amusement at the "Christian captive."

But he had not much leisure to think or feel, for the negro ran him down one street and up another at a pace which would soon have exhausted him if, besides being a naturally good runner, he had not recently been forced to undergo such severe training. During the run his guide pointed out and named most of the chief places, buildings, and mosques.

"You will do," said the negro, pausing at length and turning towards his companion with a look of approval, "You a'most so good as myself!"

With this compliment he proceeded to instruct the new runner in his duties, and at night Miles found himself again in his prison, ready to do full justice to his bowl of rice-compost, and to enjoy his blanket-less mat bed—if a man can be said to enjoy anything about which he is profoundly unconscious during the time of its enjoyment!

Next morning he awoke with a sensation that led him for a moment to fancy he must have gone supper-less to bed. While he was waiting impatiently for breakfast he revolved several ideas in his mind, one of which was that, come what might, he would not suffer any indignity, however gross, to get the better of him. He would take a leaf out of his friend Stevenson's book, and bear patiently whatever was sent to him, in the hope that by so doing he might gain the good-will of his captors, and thus, perhaps, be in a better position to take advantage of any opportunity to escape that might occur.

He was very confident of his power of self-restraint, and trusted a good deal to that determination of will which we have before referred to as being one of his characteristics. That same day his powers were severely tested.

All the morning he was left in his prison to fret in idleness, but towards the afternoon he was called by his friend the ex-runner to go out to his work.

"Do what you is told an' hold you tongue, an' keep your eyes on de ground. Dems my advice," said the negro, as he resigned the bridle of the Mahdi's steed to his successor, and placed the lance of office in his hand.

Just as he did so the Mahdi came out of a door-way and advanced towards them, while the negro retired and mingled with the crowd which had assembled to see the chief mount his horse.

Miles tried faithfully to attend to his friend's injunctions, but could not resist one glance at his new master, which showed him that a cynical smile rested on his swarthy countenance, a smile which he also observed was copied by those of the crowd who did not prefer to regard him with scowling looks—for the people of the Soudan were, naturally enough, filled with indignation against all Europeans, and especially against the British, at that time.

The glance did not improve Miles's state of mind, nevertheless he forced himself to look at the ground with an utterly expressionless face, as he held the Mahdi's stirrup. He received a slight push from his master's foot instead of thanks when he had mounted, but Miles resolutely kept his eyes on the ground and restrained his rising wrath, ignorant of the fact that the Mahdi wished to point out the direction in which he was to run.

A smart blow from the riding-switch on his naked back aroused him to his duty, and caused a slight laugh among the onlookers.

Never before, perhaps, was the Mahdi so near his end as at that moment, for, as our hero felt the sting, and heard the low laugh, all the blood in his body seemed to leap into his brow, and the lance of office quivered as his hand tightened on it. The fact that two guards with drawn swords stood at his side, and that their weapons would have been in his heart before he could have accomplished the deed, would probably have failed to restrain him had not his pride of purpose, as we may style it, come to his aid. He looked up, with a frown indeed, but without uttering a word. The Mahdi pointed along one of the streets, and Miles instantly bounded away—heartily glad to be able to let off his superfluous feeling in violent action.

For several hours his master kept him running—evidently on purpose to try his powers, as a jockey might test the qualities of a new horse, and, strong though he was, the poor youth began at last to feel greatly distressed, and to pant a good deal. Still his pride and a determination not to be beaten sustained him.

At one point of his course he was passing a band of slaves who were labouring to lift a large beam of wood, when the sound of a familiar voice caused him to look up, and then he saw his friend Jack Molloy, in costume like his own, *minus* the fez and tippet, with one of his great shoulders under the beam, and the sweat pouring down his face.

"Hallo, Miles!" exclaimed the seaman.

But our hero did not dare to pause, and could not speak. His glancing aside, however, had the effect of causing him to stumble, and, being too much exhausted at the time to recover himself, he fell heavily to the ground. As he slowly rose up, half-stunned, the Mahdi could scarcely avoid riding him down. As it was, he stooped, and, a second time laid his riding-switch smartly on the poor youth's naked shoulders.

Jack Molloy, who saw the cruel act, lost all control of himself, uttered one of his leonine roars, sprang into the middle of the road, and seized the reins of the Mahdi's horse. The startled animal reared and attempted to swerve. Molloy assisted the swerve by a violent side-pull at the reins. At the same time he caught one of the upraised forelegs, and, with an almost superhuman exertion of strength hurled both horse and rider to the ground!

A very howl of consternation and amazement burst from the populace as they beheld their Mahdi lying flat and motionless on his back as if dead!

Of course Jack Molloy was instantly seized by an overpowering number of soldiers, bound hand and foot, and carried back to his dungeon, while the Mahdi was tenderly raised and conveyed to the house which he inhabited at that time.

Miles had also been seized and dragged somewhat violently back to his prison. As for the other members of the captive band, none of them were there at the time. They were all separated at the time our hero was taken from them, and each remained for a considerable time in ignorance of the fate of his fellows. We may say at once here that they were all put to severe and menial labour. Each also had his uniform exchanged for a pair of Arabian drawers, and a felt cap or a fez, so that they were little better than naked. This would have mattered little — the weather being very warm — if their skins had been accustomed to the powerful rays of a tropical sun. But the effect on them was so severe that their taskmasters, in an unwonted gush of pity, at last gave them each a loose garment of sacking, which served as a partial protection.

After the incident which has just been related, Miles was permitted to remain during the rest of that day and night in his room. Not so Jack Molloy. The anger of the populace was so powerfully aroused against the impetuous sailor that they clamoured for his instant execution, and at last, unable or unwilling to resist the pressure of public opinion, the officers in charge of him gave in. They put a rope round his neck, and led him to a spot where criminals were wont to be executed.

As he went along and saw only scowling faces whenever he looked round in the hope of meeting some pitying eye, the poor man began to feel convinced that his last hour had in very truth arrived.

"Well, well, who'd ha' thowt it would ever come to this?" he sighed, shaking his head mournfully as he came in sight of the place of execution. "But, after all, ye richly desarve it, John Molloy, for you've bin a bad lot the greater part o' your life!"

Again he looked on either side of him, for hope was strongly enshrined in his broad bosom, but not a friendly or even pitiful face could he see among all the hundreds that surrounded him.

Arrived at the place, he glanced up at the beam over his head, and for one moment thought of trying, like Samson, to burst the bonds that held him; but it was only for a moment. The impossibility of freeing himself was too obvious. He meekly bowed his head. Another instant and the rope tightened round his neck, and he felt himself swinging in the air.

Before his senses had quite left him, however, he felt his feet again touch the ground. The choking sensation passed away, and he found himself supported by two men. A burst of mocking laughter then proved to the wretched man that his tormentors had practised on him the refined cruelty of half-hanging him. If he had had any doubt on this subject, the remark of the interpreter, as he afterwards left him in his cell to recover as best he might, would have dispelled it —

"We will 'ang you *dead* de nex' time!"

Chapter Twenty Six-Cruel Treatment—Despair Followed by Hope and a Joyful Discovery

After the rough treatment he had received, the Mahdi, as we may well believe, did not feel more amiably disposed towards his prisoners.

Of course he had no reason for blaming Miles for what had occurred, nevertheless he vented his wrath against white men in general on him, by keeping him constantly on the move, and enforcing prolonged and unusual speed while running, besides subjecting him publicly to many insults.

It was a strange school in which to learn self-restraint and humility. But our hero profited by the schooling. Necessity is a stern teacher, and she was the head-mistress of that school. Among other things she taught Miles to reason extensively—not very profoundly, perhaps, nor always correctly, but at all events in a way that he never reasoned before. The best way to convey to the reader the state of his mind will be to let him speak for himself. As he had a habit of thinking aloud—for sociability, as it were—in the dark cell to which he had been relegated, we have only to bend down our ear and listen.

One night, about a week after the overthrow of his tyrant master, Miles was seated on the hard floor of his cell, leaning against the wall, with his knees drawn up and his face in his hands—his usual attitude when engaged in meditation after a hard day's work.

"I wouldn't mind so much," he murmured, "if I only saw the faintest prospect of its coming to an end, but to go on thus from day to day, perhaps year to year, is terrible. No, that cannot be; if we cannot escape it won't be long till the end comes. (A pause.) The end!—the end of a rope with a noose on it is likely to be *my* end, unless I burst up and run a-muck. No, no, Miles Milton, don't you think of that! What good would it do to kill half-a-dozen Arabs to accompany you into the next world? The poor wretches are only defending their country after all. (Another pause.) Besides, you deserve what you've got for so meanly forsaking your poor mother; think o' that, Miles, when you feel tempted to stick your lance into the Mahdi's gizzard, as Molloy would have said. Ah! poor Molloy! I fear that I shall never see you again in this life. After giving the Mahdi and his steed such a tremendous heave they would be sure to kill you; perhaps they tortured you to—"

He stopped at this point with an involuntary shudder.

"I hope not," he resumed, after another pause. "I hope we may yet meet and devise some means of escape. God grant it! True, the desert is vast and scorching and almost waterless—I may as well say foodless too! And it swarms with foes, but what then? Have not most of the great deeds of earth been accomplished in the face of what seemed insurmountable difficulties? Besides—"

He paused again here, and for a longer time, because there came suddenly into his mind words that had been spoken to him long ago by his mother: "With God *all things* are possible."

"Yes, Miles," he continued, "you must make up your mind to restrain your anger and indignation, because it is useless to give vent to them. That's but a low motive after all. Is it worthy of an intelligent man? I get a slap in the face, and bear it patiently, because I can't help myself. I get the same slap in the face in circumstances where I *can* help myself, and I resent it fiercely. Humble when I *must* be so; fierce when I've got the power. Is not this unmanly—childish—humbug? There is no principle here. Principle! I do believe I never had any principle in me worthy of the name. I have been drifting, up to this time, before the winds of caprice and selfish inclination. (A long pause here.) Well, it just comes to this, that whatever happens I must submit with a good grace—at least, as good grace as I can—and hope that an opportunity to escape may occur before long. I have made up my mind to do it—and when I once make up my mind, I—"

He paused once more at this point, and the pause was so long that he turned it into a full stop by laying his head on the block of wood which formed his pillow and going to sleep.

It will be seen from the above candid remarks that our hero was not quite as confident of his power of will as he used to be,—also, that he was learning a few useful facts in the school of adversity.

One evening, after a harder day than usual, Miles was conducted to the prison in which he and his companions had been confined on the day of their arrival.

Looking round the cell, he observed, on becoming accustomed to the dim light, that only one other prisoner was there. He was lying on the bare ground in a corner, coiled up like a dog, and with his face to the wall. Relieved to find that he was not to be altogether alone, Miles sat down with his back against the opposite wall, and awaited the waking of his companion with some interest, for although his face was not visible, and his body was clothed in a sort of sacking, his neck and lower limbs showed that he was a white man. But the sleeper did not seem inclined to waken just then. On the contrary, he began, ere long, to snore heavily.

Miles gradually fell into a train of thought that seemed to bring back reminiscences of a vague, indefinable sort. Then he suddenly became aware that the snore of the snorer was not unfamiliar. He was on the point of rising to investigate this when the sleeper awoke with a start, sat bolt upright with a look of owlish gravity, and presented the features of Jack Molloy.

"Miles, my lad!" cried Jack, springing up to greet his friend warmly, "I thought you was dead."

"And, Jack, my dear friend," returned Miles, "I thought—at least I feared—that you must have been tortured to death."

"An' you wasn't far wrong, my boy. Stand close to me, and look me straight in the eyes. D'ee think I'm any taller?"

"Not much—at least, not to my perception. Why?"

"I wonder at that, now," said Molloy, "for I've bin hanged three times, an' should have bin pulled out a bit by this time, considering my weight."

His friend smiled incredulously.

"You may laugh, lad, but it's no laughin' matter," said Molloy, feeling his neck tenderly. "The last time, I really thought it was all up wi' me, for the knot somehow got agin my windpipe an' I was all but choked. If they had kep' me up half a minute longer it would have bin all over: I a'most wished they had, for though I never was much troubled wi' the narves, I'm beginnin' now to have a little fellow-feelin' for the sufferin's o' the narvish."

"Do you really mean, my dear fellow, that the monsters have been torturing you in this way?" asked Miles, with looks of sympathy.

"Ay, John Miles, that's just what I does mean," returned the seaman, with an anxious and startled look at the door, on the other side of which a slight noise was heard at the moment. "They've half-hanged me three times already. The last time was only yesterday, an' at any moment they may come to give me another turn. It's the uncertainty o' the thing that tries my narves. I used to boast that I hadn't got none once, but the Arabs know how to take the boastin' out of a fellow. If they'd only take me out to be hanged right off an' done with it, I wouldn't mind it so much, but it's the constant tenter-hooks of uncertainty that floors me. Hows'ever, I ain't quite floored yet. But let's hear about yourself, Miles. Come, sit down. I gets tired sooner than I used to do since they took to hangin' me. How have they bin sarvin' you out since I last saw ye?"

"Not near so badly as they have been serving you, old boy," said Miles, as he sat down and began to detail his own experiences.

"But tell me," he added, "have you heard anything of our unfortunate comrades since we parted?"

"Nothing—at least nothing that I can trust to. I did hear that poor Moses Pyne is dead; that they had treated him the same as me, and that his narves couldn't stand it; that he broke down under the strain an' died. But I don't believe it. Not that these Arabs wouldn't kill him that way, but the interpreter who told me has got falsehood so plainly writ in his ugly face that I would fain hope our kind-hearted friend is yet alive."

"God grant it may be so!" said Miles fervently. "And I scarcely think that even the cruellest of men would persevere in torturing such a gentle fellow as Moses."

"May-hap you're right," returned Molloy; "anyhow, we'll take what comfort we can out o' the hope. Talkin' o' comfort, what d'ee think has bin comfortin' me in a most wonderful way? You'll never guess."

"What is it, then?"

"One o' them little books as Miss Robinson writes, and gives to soldiers and sailors—'The Victory' it's called, havin' a good deal in it about Nelson's flagship and Nelson himself; but there's a deal more than that in it—words that has gone straight to my heart, and made me see God's love in Christ as I never saw it before. Our comrade Stevenson gave it to me before we was nabbed by the Arabs, an' I've kep' it in the linin' o' my straw hat ever since. You see it's a thin little thing—though there's oceans o' truth in it—an' it's easy stowed away.

"I forgot all about it till I was left alone in this place, and then I got it out, an' God in his marcy made it like a light in the dark to me.

"Stevenson came by it in a strange way. He told me he was goin' over a battle-field after a scrimmage near Suakim, lookin' out for the wounded, when he noticed somethin' clasped in a dead man's hand. The hand gripped it tight, as if unwillin' to part with it, an' when Stevenson got it he found that it was this little book, 'The Victory.' Here it is. I wouldn't change it for a golden sov, to every page."

As he spoke, footsteps were heard approaching the door. With a startled air Molloy thrust the book into its place and sprang up.

"See there, now!" he said remonstratively, "who'd ever ha' thowt that I'd come to jerk about like that?"

Before the door opened, however, the momentary weakness had passed away, and our seaman stood upright, with stern brow and compressed lips, presenting to those who entered as firm and self-possessed a man of courage as one could wish to see.

"I knowed it!" he said in a quiet voice to his friend, as two strong armed men advanced and seized him, while two with drawn swords stood behind him. At the same time, two others stood guard over Miles. "They're goin' to give me another turn. God grant that it may be the last!"

"Yes—de last. You be surely dead dis time," said the interpreter, with a malignant smile.

"If *you* hadn't said it, I would have had some hope that the end was come!" said Molloy, as they put a rope round his neck and led him away.

"Good-bye, Miles," he added, looking over his shoulder; "if I never come back, an' you ever gets home again, give my kind regards to Miss Robinson—God bless her!"

Next moment the door closed, and Miles was left alone.

It is impossible to describe the state of mind in which our hero paced his cell during the next hour. The intense pity, mingled with anxiety and fierce indignation, that burned in his bosom were almost unbearable. "Oh!" he thought, "if I were only once more free, for one moment, with a weapon in my hand, I'd—"

He wisely checked himself in the train of useless thought at this point. Then he sat down on the floor, covered his face with his hands, and tried to pray, but could not. Starting up, he again paced wildly about the cell like a caged tiger. After what seemed to him an age he heard footsteps in the outer court. The door opened, and the sailor was thrust in. Staggering forward a step or two, he was on the point of falling when Miles caught him in his arms, and let him sink gently on the ground, and, sitting down beside him, laid his head upon his knee. From the inflamed red mark which encircled the seaman's powerful neck, it was obvious enough that the cruel monsters had again put him to the tremendous mental agony of supposing that his last hour had come.

"Help me up, lad, and set my back agin the wall," he said, in a low voice.

As Miles complied, one or two tears that would not be repressed fell from his eyes on the sailor's cheek.

"You're a good fellow," said Molloy, looking up. "I thank the Lord for sendin' you to comfort me, and I *do* need comfort a bit just now, d'ee know. There—I'm better a'ready, an' I'll be upside wi' them next time, for I feels, somehow, that I couldn't stand another turn. Poor Moses! I do hope that the interpreter is the liar he looks, and that they haven't treated the poor fellow to this sort o' thing."

Even while he spoke, the door of the cell again opened and armed men entered.

"Ay, here you are," cried the sailor, rising quickly and attempting to draw himself up and show a bold front. "Come away an' welcome. I'm ready for 'ee."

But the men had not come for Molloy. They wanted Miles, over whom there came a sudden and dreadful feeling of horror, as he thought they were perhaps going to subject him to the same ordeal as his friend.

"Keep up heart, lad, and trust in the Lord," said the sailor, in an encouraging tone as they led our hero away.

The words were fitly spoken, and went far to restore to the poor youth the courage that for a moment had forsaken him. As he emerged into the bright light, which dazzled him after the darkness of his prison-house, he thought of the Sun of Righteousness, and of the dear mother who had sought so earnestly to lead him to God in his boyhood.

One thing that greatly encouraged him was the fact that no rope had been put round his neck, as had been done to Molloy, and he also observed that his guards did not treat him roughly. Moreover, they led him in quite a different direction from the open place where he well knew that criminals were executed. He glanced at the interpreter who marched beside him, and thought for a moment of asking him what might be his impending fate, but the man's look was so forbidding that he forbore to speak.

Presently they stopped before a door, which was opened by a negro slave, and the guards remained outside while Miles and the interpreter entered. The court into which they were ushered was open to the sky, and contained a fountain in the centre, with boxes of flowers and shrubs around it. At the inner end of it stood a tall powerful Arab, leaning on a curved sword.

Miles saw at a glance that he was the same man whose life he had saved, and who had come so opportunely to the rescue of his friend Molloy. But the Arab gave him no sign of recognition. On the contrary, the glance which he bestowed on him was one of calm, stern indifference.

"Ask him," he said at once to the interpreter, "where are the Christian dogs who were captured with him?"

"Tell him," replied Miles, when this was translated, "that I know nothing about the fate of any of them except one."

"Which one is that?"

"The sailor," answered Miles.

"Where is he?"

"In the prison I have just left."

"And you know nothing about the others?"

"Nothing whatever."

The Arab seemed to ponder these replies for a few minutes. Then, turning to the interpreter, he spoke in a tone that seemed to Miles to imply the giving of some strict orders, after which, with a wave of his hand, and a majestic inclination of the head, he dismissed them.

Although there was little in the interview to afford encouragement, Miles nevertheless was rendered much more hopeful by it, all the more that he observed a distinct difference in the bearing of the interpreter towards him as they went out.

"Who is that?" he ventured to ask as he walked back to the prison.

"That is Mohammed, the Mahdi's cousin," answered the interpreter.

Miles was about to put some more questions when he was brought to a sudden stand, and rendered for the moment speechless by the sight of Moses Pyne—not bearing heavy burdens, or labouring in chains, as might have been expected, but standing in a shallow recess or niche in the wall of a house, busily engaged over a small brazier, cooking beans in oil, and selling the same to the passers-by!

"What you see?" demanded the interpreter.

"I see an old friend and comrade. May I speak to him?" asked Miles, eagerly.

"You may," answered the interpreter.

The surprise and joy of Moses when his friend slapped him on the shoulder and saluted him by name is not easily described.

"I *am* so glad to see you, old fellow!" he said, with sparkling eyes. "I thought you must be dead, for I've tried so often to find out what had become of you. Have some beans and oil?"

He dipped a huge ladleful out of the pot, as if he were going to administer a dose on the spot.

"No, thank you, Moses, I'm a prisoner. These are my guards. I wonder they have allowed me even to exchange a word with you. Must be quick. They told us you had been half-hanged till you were frightened to death."

"They told you lies, then. I've been very well treated, but what troubles me is I can't find out where any of our comrades have gone to."

"I can tell only of one. Molloy is alive. I wish I could say he's well. Of the others I'm as ignorant as yourself. But I've seen a friend who—"

At this point he was interrupted by the interpreter and told to move on, which he was fain to do with a cheery good-bye to Moses and a wave of the hand.

Arrived at the prison, he found that Molloy had been removed to a more comfortable room, into which he was also ushered, and there they were left alone together.

"D'you feel better now, my poor fellow?" asked Miles, when the door was shut.

"Better, bless you, yes! I feels far too well. They've given me a rare blow-out of beans an' oil since you were taken off to be hanged, and I feels so strong that the next turn off won't finish me! I could never have eaten 'em, thinkin' of you, but, d'ee know, I was quite sure, from the way they treated you as you went out, that it warn't to be hangin' wi' you this time. An' when they putt me into this here room, an' produced the beans an' oil, I began to feel quite easy in my mind about you. It was the man that brought your marchin' orders that told 'em to putt me here. D'ee know, lad, I can't help feelin' that a friend o' some sort must have bin raised up to us."

"You're right, Jack, I have just seen the Arab whose life I saved and who saved yours! It's very strange, too, that beans and oil should have been your fare to-day, for I have also seen Moses Pyne in the street, not half-an-hour since, cooking and selling beans and oil!"

"You don't mean that?"

"Indeed I do. I've spoken to him."

Sitting down on a stool—for they were promoted to a furnished apartment—Miles entered into an elaborate account of all that had befallen him since the hour that he had been taken out, as they both thought, to be hanged!

Chapter Twenty Seven-In which
Hopes and Fears rise and fall

"There is a tide in the affairs of men," undoubtedly, and the tide in the affairs of Miles Milton and his comrades appeared to have reached low-water at this time, for, on the day mentioned in the last chapter, it began to turn, and continued for a considerable time to rise.

The first clear evidence of the change was the "blow-out" of beans and oil, coupled with the change of prison. The next was the sudden appearance of the beans-and-oil-man himself.

"Why, I do believe—it's—it's Moses," exclaimed Molloy, as his old comrade entered the prison. "Give us your flipper. Man alive! but I'm right glad to see you. We thought you was—let's have a look at your neck. No; nothing there. I knowed as that interpreter was a liar. But what brings you *here*, lad? What mischief have 'ee bin up to?"

"That's what puzzles myself, Jack," said Moses, shaking hands warmly with Miles. "I've done nothing that I know of except sell beans and oil. It's true I burned 'em sometimes a bit, but they'd hardly put a fellow in jail for that—would they? However, I'm glad they've done it, whatever the reason, seeing that it has brought us three together again. But, I say," continued Moses, while a look of anxiety came over his innocent face, "what can have become of our other comrades?"

"You may well ask that, lad. I've asked the same question of myself for many a day, but have never bin able to get from myself a satisfactory answer. I'm wery much afeared that we'll never see 'em again."

It seemed almost to be a spring-tide in the affairs of the trio at that time, for while the seaman was speaking—as if to rebuke his want of faith—the door opened and their comrade Armstrong walked in.

For a few moments they were all rendered speechless! Then Miles sprang up, seized his friend by both shoulders, and gazed into his face; it was a very thin and careworn face at that time, as if much of the bloom of youth had been wiped from it for ever.

"Willie! Am I dreaming?" exclaimed Miles.

"If you are, so must I be," replied his friend, "for when I saw you last you had not taken to half-nakedness as a costume!"

"Come now," retorted Miles, "you have not much to boast of in that way yourself."

"There you are wrong, Miles, for I have to boast that I made my garment myself. True, it's only a sack, but I cut the hole in the bottom of it for my head with my own hand, and stitched on the short sleeves with a packing-needle. But, I say, what's been the matter with Molloy? Have they been working you too hard, Jack?"

"No, Willum, no, I can't exactly say that, but they've bin hangin' me too hard. I'll tell 'ee all about it in coorse o' time. Man alive! but they *have* took the flesh off your bones somehow; let's see—no, your neck's all right. Must have bin some other way."

"The way was simple enough," returned the other. "When they separated us all at first, they set me to the hardest work they could find—to dig, draw water, carry burdens that a horse might object to, sweep, and clean up; in fact, everything and anything, and they've kep' us hard at it ever since. I say *us*, because Rattlin' Bill Simkin was set to help me after the first day, an' we've worked all along together. Poor Simkin, there ain't much rattle in him now, except his bones. I don't know why they sent me here and not him. And I can't well make out whether I'm sent here for extra punishment or as a favour!"

"Have you seen or heard anything of Stevenson?" asked Moses.

"I saw him once, about a week ago, staggering under a great log— whether in connection with house-builders or not I can't tell. It was only for a minute, and I got a tremendous cut across the back with a cane for merely trying to attract his attention."

The tide, it will be seen, had been rising pretty fast that afternoon. It may be said to have come in with a rush, when, towards evening, the door of their prison once more opened and Simkin with Stevenson were ushered in together, both clothed alike in an extemporised sack-garment and short drawers, with this difference, that the one wore a species of felt hat, the other a fez.

They were still in the midst of delighted surprise at the turn events seemed to be taking, when two men entered bearing trays, on which were six smoking bowls of beans and oil!

"Hallo! Moses, your business follows you even to prison," exclaimed Molloy.

"True, Jack, and I'll follow my business up!" returned Moses, sitting down on the ground, which formed their convenient table, and going to work.

We need scarcely say that his comrades were not slow to follow his example.

The tide may be said to have reached at least half-flood, if not more, when, on the following morning, the captives were brought out and told by the interpreter that they were to accompany a body of troops which were about to quit the place under the command of Mohammed, the Mahdi's cousin.

"Does the Mahdi accompany us?" Miles ventured to ask.

"No. The Mahdi has gone to Khartoum," returned the interpreter, who then walked away as if he objected to be further questioned.

The hopes which had been recently raised in the breasts of the captives to a rather high pitch were, however, somewhat reduced when they found that their supposed friend Mohammed treated them with cool indifference, did not even recognise them, and the disappointment was deepened still more when all of them, except Miles, were loaded with heavy burdens, and made to march among the baggage-animals as if they were mere beasts of burden. The savage warriors also treated them with great rudeness and contempt.

Miles soon found that he was destined to fill his old post of runner in front of Mohammed, his new master. This seemed to him unaccountable, for runners, he understood, were required only in towns and cities, not on a march. But the hardships attendant on the post, and the indignities to which he was subjected, at last convinced him that the Mahdi must have set the mind of his kinsman against him, and that he was now undergoing extra punishment as well as unique degradation.

The force that took the field on this occasion was a very considerable one—with what precise object in view was of course unknown to all except its chiefs, but the fact that it marched towards the frontiers of Egypt left no doubt in the mind of any one. It was a wild barbaric host, badly armed and worse drilled, but fired with a hatred of all Europeans and a burning sense of wrong.

"What think ye now, Miles?" asked Armstrong, as the captives sat grouped together in the midst of the host on the first night of their camping out in the desert.

"I think that everything seems to be going wrong," answered Miles, in a desponding tone. "At first I thought that Mohammed was our friend, but he has treated me so badly that I can think so no longer."

"Don't you think he may be doing that to blind his followers as to his friendship?" said Moses; "for myself, I can't help thinkin' he must be grateful for what you did, Miles."

"I only wish you had not touched my rifle that day," said Rattling Bill, fiercely—being fatigued and out of temper—"for the blackguard would have bin in 'Kingdom come' by this time. There's *no* gratitude in an Arab. I have no hope at all now."

"My hope is in God," said Stevenson.

"Well, mate, common-sense tells me that that *should* be our best ground of hope," observed Molloy; "but common experience tells me that the Almighty often lets His own people come to grief."

"God *never* lets 'em come to grief in the sense that you mean," returned the marine. "If He kills His people, He takes them away from the evil to come, and death is but a door-way into glory. If he sends grief and suffering, it is that they may at last reach a higher state of joy."

"Pooh! according to that view, *nothing* can go wrong with them that you call His people," said Simkin, with contempt.

"Right you are, comrade," rejoined Stevenson; "*nothing* can go wrong with us; *nothing* can separate us from the love of God which is in Christ Jesus our lord; and *you* may be one of '*us*' this minute if you will accept God's offer of free salvation in Christ."

Silence followed, for Simkin was too angry, as well as worn out, to give his mind seriously to anything at that time, and the others were more or less uncertain as to the truth of what was advanced.

Sleep, profound and dreamless, soon banished these and all other subjects from their minds. Blessed sleep! so aptly as well as beautifully styled, "Tired Nature's sweet restorer." That great host of dusky warriors—some unquestionably devout, many cruel and relentless, not a few, probably, indifferent to everything except self, and all bent on the extermination of their white-skinned foes,—lay down beside their weapons, and shared in that rest which is sent alike to the just and to the unjust, through the grand impartiality, forbearance, and love of a God whom many people apparently believe to be a "respecter of persons!"

A few days later the little army came to the edge of a range of hills, beyond which lay the plains of the vast Nubian desert. At night they encamped at the base of the hill-country, through which they had been travelling, and the captives were directed to take up their position in front of an old ruined hut, where masses of broken stones and rubbish made the ground unsuitable for camping on.

"Just like them!" growled Simkin, looking about for a fairly level spot. "There's not a place big enough for a dog to lie on!"

Supper made Rattling Bill a little more amiable, though not much more forgiving to his foes. A three-quarters moon soon afterwards shed a faint light on the host, which, except the sentries, was sound asleep.

Towards midnight a solitary figure moved slowly towards the place where the captives lay and awakened Miles, who sat up, stared, winked, and rubbed his eyes two or three times before he could bring himself to believe that his visitor was no other than the chief of the host — Mohammed!

"Rise. Com. I speak small Engleesh."

Miles rose at once and followed the chief into the ruined hut.

"Clear de ground," he said, pointing to the centre of the floor.

Our hero obeyed, and, when the loose rubbish was cleared away, the moonbeams, shining through the ruined roof, fell on a ring bolt. Being ordered to pull it, he raised a cover or trap-door, and discovered beneath what appeared to be a cellar.

"Now," said Mohammed, "listen: you an' friends go down — all. I shut door and cover up — rubsh. When we all go 'way, com out and go home. See, yonder is *home*."

He pointed to the north-eastward, where a glowing star seemed to hang over the margin of the great level desert.

"You are generous — you are kind!" exclaimed Miles, with a burst of enthusiasm.

"Me grateful," said Mohammed, extending his hand in European fashion, which Miles grasped warmly. "Go, wake you comerads. Tell what me say, and com quick!"

Miles was much too well-disciplined a soldier to hesitate, though he would have liked much to suggest that some of the troops might, before starting, take a fancy to explore the ruin, and to ask how long they should remain in the cellar before venturing out. Quietly awaking all his comrades, and drawing their surprised heads together, he whispered his tale in their wondering ears. After that they were quite prepared to act, and accompanied him noiselessly into the ruin.

"Is the cellar deep?" asked Miles, as he was about to descend.

"No; not deep."

"But what about grub — whittles, meat, an' water — you know," said Molloy, with difficulty accommodating his words to a foreigner. "We'll starve if we go adrift on the desert with nothin' to eat or drink."

"Here—food," said Mohammed, unslinging a well-filled haversack from his shoulders and transferring it to those of the sailor. "Stop there," he continued, pointing to the cellar, "till you hears guns—shoot—noise. I have make prep'rations! After that, silence. Then, com out, an' go *home*." Once again he pointed towards the glowing star in the north-east.

"Mohammed," exclaimed Molloy, becoming suddenly impressed with the generous nature of the Arab's action, "I don't know as you're a descendant o' the Prophet, but I do know that you're a brick. Give us your flipper before we part!"

With a grave expression of kindliness and humour the chief shook hands with the seaman. Then the captives all descended into the hole, which was not more than four feet deep, after which the Arab shut the trap, covered it as before with a little rubbish, and went away.

"Suppose he has bolted the door!" suggested Moses.

"Hold your tongue, man, and listen for the signal," said Miles.

"I forget what he said the signal was to be," observed Simkin.

"Guns—shoot—noise—after that silence!" said Armstrong. "It's a queer signal."

"But not difficult to recognise when we hear it," remarked Miles.

The time seemed tremendously long as they sat there listening—the cellar was too low for them to stand—and they began to fancy that all kinds of horrible shapes and faces appeared in the intense darkness around them. When they listened intensely, kept silent, and held their breath, their hearts took to beating the drums of their ears, and when a sudden breath or sigh escaped it seemed as if some African monster were approaching from the surrounding gloom.

"Is that you, Simkin, that's breathin' like a grampus?" asked Molloy, after a long pause.

"I was just goin' to ask you to stop snorin'," retorted the soldier.

"Hush! There's a shot!"

It was indeed a distant shot, followed immediately by several more. Then a rattle of musketry followed—nearer at hand.

Instantly, as if the earth had just given birth to them, the host of dusky warriors sprang up with yells of surprise and defiance, and, spear in hand, rushed in the direction of the firing. For a few minutes the listeners in the cellar heard as it had been a mighty torrent surging past the ruined hut. Gradually the force of the rush began to abate, while the yells and firing became more distant; at last all sounds ceased, and the listeners were again oppressed by the beating on the drums of their ears.

"They're all gone—every mother's son," said Molloy at last, breaking the oppressive silence.

"That's so," said Rattling Bill; "up wi' the trap, Miles. You're under it, ain't you? I'm suffocating in this hole."

"I'm not under it. Molloy came down last," said Miles.

"What if we can't find it?" suggested Stevenson.

"Horrible!" said Moses, in a hoarse whisper, "and this may be a huge cavern, with miles of space around us, instead of a small cellar!"

"Here it is!" cried the sailor, making a heave with his broad back. "I say—it won't move! Ah, I wasn't rightly under it. Yo! heave-o!" Up went the door with a crash, and the soft moonlight streamed in upon them.

A few seconds more and they stood outside the hut—apparently the only living beings in all that region, which had been so full of human life but a few minutes before.

"Now we must lose no time in getting away from this place, and covering as much of the desert as we can during the night," said Miles, "for it strikes me that we'll have to lie quiet during the day, for fear of being seen and chased."

They spoke together in whispers for a few minutes, deciding the course they meant to pursue. Then Molloy shouldered the provision bag, Miles grasped his official lance—the only weapon they had among them,—and off they set on their journey across the desert, like a ship entering on an unknown sea, without the smallest idea of how far they were from the frontier of Egypt, and but a vague notion of the direction in which they ought to go.

Chapter Twenty Eight-A Horrible Situation

All that night our fugitives walked steadily in the direction of their guiding-star, until the dawn of day began to absorb its light. Then they selected a couple of prominent bushes on the horizon, and, by keeping these always in their relative positions, were enabled to shape their course in what they believed to be the right direction. By repeating the process continuously they were enabled to advance in a fairly straight line.

Molloy, as we have said, carried the provision bag, and, although it was a very heavy one, he refused to let his comrades relieve him of it until breakfast-time. Then it was discovered that inside of the large bag there were rolled tight up four smaller bags with shoulder-straps to them.

"A knowin' feller that Mohammed is," said Jack Molloy, as he handed a bag to each; "he understands how to manage things. Let's see what sort o' grub he has. Corn-cakes, I do believe, an' dates, or some sort o' dried fruit, an' — water-bottles! well, that is a comfort. Now then, boys, go ahead. We can't afford to waste time over our meals."

The others so thoroughly agreed with their friend on this point that they began to eat forthwith, almost in silence. Then, the provisions having been distributed, they resumed their march, which was almost a forced one, so anxious were they to get as far away as possible from the Arab army.

Coming to a large mimosa bush in the course of the morning they halted and sat down to rest a little, and hold what the sailor called a "palaver."

"You see, boys," he said, "it'll be of no manner of use our scuddin' away before the wind under a press o' canvas like this, without some settled plan—"

"Ain't our plan to git away from the Arabs as fast as we can?" said Moses Pyne, who sat on a stone at the sailor's feet.

"Yes, Moses, but that's only part of it," returned Molloy. "We must keep away as well as get away—an' that won't be quite so easy, for the country is swarmin' wi' the dark-skinned rascals, as the many tracks we have already passed shows us. If we was to fall in wi' a band of 'em—even a small one—we would be took again for sartin', for we've got nothin' to fight wi' but our fists."

"These would offer but poor resistance to bullet and steel," said Armstrong, "and that lance you're so fond of, Miles, wouldn't be worth much."

"Not much," admitted Miles, surveying the badge of his late office, "but better than nothing."

"What if the Arabs should change their course and fall in with us again?" asked Moses.

"No fear o' that, seein' that Mohammed himself gave us our sailin' orders, an' laid our course for us; but it would never do to fall in wi' other bands, so I proposes that we cast anchor where we are, for there's pretty good holdin' ground among them bushes, keep quiet all day, an' travel only at night. I've got the krect bearin's just now, so w'en the stars come out we'll be able to fix on one layin' in the right direction, and clap on all sail, slow and aloft—stu'n s'ls, sky-scrapers, an' all the rest on it."

"A good plan, Jack," said Armstrong, "but what if it should come cloudy and blot out the stars?"

"Besides," added Miles, "you forget that men of the desert are skilled in observing signs and in following tracks. Should any of them pass near this little clump of bushes, and observe our footsteps going towards it, they will at once come to see if we are still here."

Molloy put his head on one side and looked perplexed for a moment.

"Never mind. Let 'em come," he said, with a sudden look of sagacity, "we'll circumwent 'em. There's nothin' like circumwention w'en you've got into a fix. See here. We'll dig a hole in a sandbank big enough to hold us all, an' we'll cut a big bush an' stick it in front of the hole so as they'll never see it. We can keep a bright look-out, you know, an' if anything heaves in sight on the horizon, down we go into the hole, stick up the bush, an there you are—all safe under hatches till the enemy clears off."

"But they will trace our footsteps up to the hole or the bush," said Miles, "and wonder why they can trace them no further. What then?"

Again the seaman fell into perplexed meditation, out of which he emerged with a beaming smile.

"Why, then, my lad, we'll bamboozle 'em. There's nothin' like bamboozlement w'en circumwention fails. Putt the two together an' they're like a hurricane in the tropics, carries all before it! We'll bamboozle 'em by runnin' for an hour or two all over the place, so as no mortal man seein' our footprints will be able to tell where we comed from, or what we've bin a-doin' of."

"You don't know the men of the desert, Jack," rejoined Miles, with a laugh. "They'd just walk in a circle round the place where you propose to run about and bamboozle them, till they found where our tracks *entered* this bit of bush. Then, as they'd see no tracks *leaving* it, of course they'd know that we were still there. D'you see?"

"That's a puzzler for you, Jack," remarked Moses, as he watched the perplexed expression looming up again like a cloud on the sailor's face.

"By no manner o' means," retorted Molloy, with sudden gravity. "I sees my way quite clear out o' that. You remember the broad track, not half a mile off from where we now sit?"

"Yes; made I suppose by a pretty big band o' some sort crossin' the desert," said Moses.

"Well, lad, arter runnin' about in the bush to bamboozle of 'em, as aforesaid, we'll march back to that track on the sou'-west'ard — as it may be — an' then do the same on the nor'-west'ard — so to speak — an' so lead 'em to suppose we was a small party as broke off, or was sent off, from the main body to reconnoitre the bit o' bush, an' had rejoined the main body further on. That's what I call circumwentin', d'ee see?"

While this palaver was going on, Stevenson and Bill Simkin were standing a short way off taking observation of something in the far distance. In a few minutes they ran towards their comrades with the information that a band of men were visible on the horizon, moving, they thought, in an opposite direction to their line of march.

"It may be so," said Miles, after a brief survey, "but we can't be sure. We must put part of your plan in force anyhow, Jack Molloy. Away into the scrub all of you, and stoop as you go."

In saying this, our hero, almost unintentionally, took command of the little party, which at once tacitly accorded him the position. Leading them — as every leader ought — he proceeded to the centre of the clump of bushes, where, finding a natural hollow or hole in the sand, at the root of a mimosa bush, three of them went down on hands and knees to scoop it out deeper, while the others cut branches with Molloy's clasp-knife.

Using flat stones, chips of wood, and hands as shovels, they managed to dig out a hole big enough to conceal them all, the opening to which was easily covered by a mass of branches.

It is doubtful whether this ingenious contrivance would have availed them, if "men of the desert" had passed that way, but fortune favoured them. The band, whether friends or foes, passed far off to the westward, leaving them to enjoy their place of fancied security.

To pass the first day there was not difficult. The novelty of the position was great; the interest of the thing immense. Indefinite hopes of the future were strong, and they had plenty to say and speculate about during the passing hours. When night came, preparation was made for departure. The provision bags were slung, a moderate sip of water indulged in, and they set forth, after a very brief prayer by Stevenson, that God would guide them safely on their way. There was no formality in that prayer. The marine did not ask his comrades to kneel or to agree with him. He offered it aloud, in a few seconds, in the name of Jesus, leaving his hearers to join him or not as they pleased.

"See that you lay your course fair now, Molloy," said Miles, as they sallied out upon the darkening plain.

"Trust me, lad, I've taken my bearin's."

It was very dark the first part of the night, as the moon did not rise till late, but there was quite enough light to enable them to proceed with caution, though not enough to prevent their taking an occasional bush or stump for an advancing foe. All went well, however, until dawn the following morning, when they began to look about for a suitable clump of bushes in which to conceal themselves. No such spot could they find.

"Never mind, lads," said the inexhaustible Molloy, "we'll just go on till we find a place. We're pretty tough just now, that's one comfort."

They were indeed so tough that they went the whole of that day, with only one or two brief halts to feed. Towards evening, however, they began to feel wearied, and, with one consent, determined to encamp on a slight eminence a short way in advance, the sides of which were covered with low scrub.

As they approached the spot an unpleasant odour reached them. It became worse as they advanced. At last, on arriving, they found to their surprise and horror that the spot had been a recent battle-field, and was strewn with corpses and broken weapons. Some days must have elapsed since the fight which strewed them there, for the bodies had been all stripped, and many of them were partially buried, while others had been hauled half out of their graves by those scavengers of the desert, hyenas and vultures.

"Impossible to halt here," said Armstrong. "I never witness a sight like this that it does not force on me the madness of warfare! What territorial gain can make up for these lost lives—the flower of the manhood of both parties?"

"But what are we to do?" objected Molloy. "Men must defend their rights!"

"Not necessarily so," said Stevenson. "Men have to learn to bear and forbear."

"I have learned to take advantage of what luck throws in my way," said Rattling Bill, picking up a rifle which must have escaped the observation of the plunderers who had followed the army.

The body of the poor fellow who had owned it was found concealed under a bush not far off. He was an English soldier, and a very brief inspection showed that the battle had been fought by a party of British and Egyptian troops against the Soudanese.

It seemed as if the plunderers had on this occasion been scared from their horrible work before completing it, for after a careful search they found rifles with bayonets, and pouches full of ammunition, more than sufficient to arm the whole party.

"There are uniforms enough, too, to fit us all out," said Simkin, as they were about to leave the scene of slaughter.

"No dead men's clo'es for me," said Moses Pyne, with a shrug of disgust.

Jack Molloy declared that he had become so used to loose cotton drawers, and an easy-fittin' sack, that for his part he had no desire to go back to civilised costume! and as the rest were of much the same opinion, no change was made in the habiliments of the party, except that each appropriated a pair of boots, and Miles exchanged his green tippet for a flannel shirt and a pith helmet. He also took a revolver, with some difficulty, from the dead hand of a soldier, and stuck it in his belt.

Thus improved in circumstances, they gladly quitted the ghastly scene, and made for a bushy hillock a few hundred yards in advance.

On the way they were arrested by the sound of distant firing.

"Mohammed must have met our countrymen!" exclaimed Molloy, with excited looks, as they halted to listen.

"It may be so, but there are other bands about besides his," said Miles. "What's that? a cheer?"

"Ay, a British cheer in the far distance, replied to by yells of defiance." Molloy echoed the cheer in spite of his better judgment.

"Let's run an' jine 'em!" he exclaimed.

"Come along, then!" cried Miles, with the ardour of inexperienced youth.

"Stop! are ye mad?" cried Stevenson. "Don't it stand to reason that the enemy must be between us an' Suakim? and that's the same as sayin' they're between us an' our friends. Moreover, the cheerin' proves that our side must be gettin' the best of it, an' are drivin' the enemy this way, so all we've got to do is to hide on that hillock an' bide our time."

"Right you are, comrade," cried Rattling Bill, examining his cartridges, and asserting with an oath that nothing would afford him greater pleasure than a good hand-to-hand fight with the black, (and something worse), scoundrels.

"Don't swear at your enemies, Simkin," said the marine quietly; "but when you get the chance fire low!"

Agreeing with Stevenson's advice to "bide their time," the little band was soon on the top of the hillock, and took up the best position for defending the place, also for observing the fight, which, they could now see, was drawing gradually nearer to them.

They were not kept waiting long, for the natives were in full flight, hotly pursued by the English and Indian cavalry. A slight breeze blowing from the north carried not only the noise, but soon the smoke of the combat towards them. As they drew nearer a large detachment of native spearmen was seen to make for the hillock, evidently intending to make a stand there.

"Now comes *our* turn," said Armstrong, examining the lock of his rifle to see that all was right.

"'England expec's every man,' etceterer," said Molloy, with a glance at Miles. "Capting, you may as well let us know your plans, so as we may work together."

Miles was not long in making up his mind.

"You'll fire at first by command," he said quickly, but decidedly; "then down on your faces flat, and load. After that wait for orders. When it comes to the push—as it's sure to do at last—we'll stand back to back and do our best. God help us to do it well! Don't hurry, boys—especially in square. Let every shot tell."

He had barely concluded this brief address when the yelling savages reached the hillock. Miles could even see the gleaming of their teeth and eyes, and the blood of the slightly wounded coursing down their black skins as they rushed panting towards the place where he and his little party were crouching. Then he gave the word: "Ready—present!"

The smoke, fire, and death to the leading men, which belched from the bushes, did not check the rush for more than a moment. And even that check was the result of surprise more than fear. A party of those Arabs who were armed with rifles instantly replied, but the bullets passed harmlessly over the prostrate men.

Again the voice of Miles was heard: "Ready—present!" and again the leading men of the enemy fell, but the rushing host only divided, and swept round the hillock, so as to take it on both sides at once.

"Now—form square! and pick each man," cried Miles, springing up and standing back to back with Armstrong. Molloy stood shoulder to shoulder with him and backed Bill Simkin, while Stevenson did the same for Moses Pyne. The bushes did not rise much above their waists, and as the dusky host suddenly beheld the knot of strange-looking men, whose bristling bayonets glistened in the setting sunshine, and whose active rifles were still dealing death among their ranks, they dashed at the hill-top with a yell of mingled rage and surprise. Another moment and spearmen were dancing round the little square like incarnate fiends, but the white men made no sound. Each confined himself to two acts—namely, load and fire— and at every shot a foremost savage fell, until the square became encircled with dead men.

Another moment and a party of Arab riflemen ran to the front and took aim. Just then a tremendous cheer was heard. The defenders of the hillock made a wild reply, which was drowned in a furious fusillade. The entire savage host seemed to rush over the spot, sweeping all before it, while smoke rolled after them as well as lead and fire. In the midst of the hideous turmoil, Miles received a blow which shattered his left wrist. Grasping his rifle with his right hand he laid about him as best he could. Next moment a blow on the head from behind stretched him senseless on the ground.

The return of our hero to consciousness revealed to him that he was still lying on the battle-field, that it was night, and that an intolerable weight oppressed his chest. This last was caused by a dead native having fallen across him. On trying to get rid of the corpse he made the further discovery that nearly all his strength was gone, and that he could scarcely move his right arm, although it was free, and, as far as he could make out, unwounded. Making a desperate effort, he partially relieved himself, and, raising his head, tried to look round. His ears had already told him that near to him wounded men were groaning away the little of life that remained to them; he now saw that he was surrounded by heaps of dead men. Excepting the groans referred to, the night was silent, and the moon shone down on hundreds of up-turned faces—the bloodless grey of the black men contrasting strangely with the deadly pallor of the white, all quiet and passionless enough now—here and there the head of a warrior resting peacefully on the bosom or shoulder of the foe who had killed him!

A slight noise on his right caused Miles to turn his head in that direction, where he saw a wounded comrade make feeble efforts to raise himself, and then fall back with a deep groan. In other circumstances our hero would have sprung to his assistance, but at that moment he felt as if absolutely helpless; indeed, he was nearly so from loss of blood. He made one or two efforts to rise, but the weight of the dead man held him down, and after a few brief attempts he fainted.

Recovering again, he looked round, attracted by the sound of a struggle on his right. One of those fiends in human form, the plunderers of a battlefield, had, in his ghoulish progress, come across the wounded man who lay close to Miles, and the man was resisting him. The other put a quick end to the strife by drawing a knife across the throat of the poor fellow. A horror of great darkness seemed to overwhelm Miles as he saw the blood gush in a deluge from the gaping wound. He tried to shout, but, as in a nightmare, he could neither speak nor move.

As the murderer went on rifling his victim, Miles partially recovered from his trance of horror, and anxiety for his own life nerved him to attempt action of some sort. He thought of the revolver for the first time at that moment, and the remembrance seemed to infuse new life into him. Putting his right hand to his belt, he found it there, but drew it with difficulty. Doubting his power to discharge it by means of the trigger alone, he made a desperate effort and cocked it.

The click made the murderer start. He raised himself and looked round. Our hero shut his eyes and lay perfectly still. Supposing probably that he must have been mistaken, the man resumed his work. Miles could have easily shot him where he kneeled if he had retained power to lift his arm and take an aim. As it was, he had strength only to retain the weapon in his grasp.

After a short time, that seemed an age to the helpless watcher, the murderer rose and turned his attention to another dead man, but passing him, came towards Miles, whose spirit turned for one moment to God in an agonising prayer for help. The help came in the form of revived courage. Calm, cool, firm self-possession seemed to overbear all other feelings. He half closed his eyes as the murderer approached, and gently turned the muzzle of the revolver upwards. He even let the man bend over him and look close into his face to see if he were dead, then he pulled the trigger.

Miles had aimed, he thought, at the man's breast, but the bullet entered under his chin and went crashing into his brain. A gush of warm blood spouted over Miles's face as the wretch plunged over him, head first, and fell close by his side. He did not die at once. The nature of the ground prevented Miles from seeing him, but he could hear him gradually gasp his life away.

A few minutes later and footsteps were heard ascending the hillock. Miles grasped his revolver with a hand that now trembled from increasing weakness, but he was by that time unable to put the weapon on full cock. Despair had well-nigh seized him, when a familiar voice was heard.

"This way, lads. I'm sure it was hereabouts that I saw the flash."

"Macleod!" gasped Miles, as the big Scotsman was about to pass.

"Losh me! John Miles, is that you? Are ye leevin?"

"Scarcely!" was all that the poor youth could utter ere he became again insensible.

A fatigue party tramped up with a stretcher at the moment. Macleod with a handkerchief checked the ebbing tide of life, and they bore away from the bloody field what seemed little more than the mortal remains of poor Miles Milton.

Chapter Twenty Nine-Describes a few Meetings and several Surprises

The fight described in the last chapter was only one of the numerous skirmishes that were taking place almost daily near Suakim at that time. But it turned out to be a serious occasion to our hero, for it cost him one of his hands, and put an end to his soldiering days for ever.

On being taken to the British lines the surgeons saw at once that amputation a little above the wrist was absolutely necessary. Of course Miles—although overwhelmed with dismay on hearing the fiat of the doctors—could offer no objection. With the informal celerity of surgical operations as practised in the field, the shattered limb was removed, and almost before he could realise the full significance of what was being done our poor hero was *minus* his left hand! Besides this, he was so cut and battered about, that most of his hair had to be cut off, and his head bandaged and plastered so that those of his old comrades who chanced to be with the troops at the time could recognise him only by his voice. Even that was scarcely audible when he was carried into Suakim.

At this time the hospitals at Suakim were overcrowded to such an extent that many of the wounded and invalids had to be sent on by sea to Suez and the hospitals at Ramleh. Miles was sent on along with these, and finally found rest at Alexandria.

And great was the poor fellow's need of rest, for, besides the terrible sufferings and hardships he had endured while in captivity, the wounds and bruises, the loss of blood and of his left hand, and the fatigue of the voyage, his mind was overwhelmed by the consideration that even if he should recover he was seriously maimed for life. In addition to all this suffering, Miles, while at Suakim, had received a blow which well-nigh killed him. A letter came informing him of the sudden death of his father, and bitter remorse was added to his misery as he lay helpless in his cot on the Red Sea.

The consequent depression, acting on his already exhausted powers after he reached Alexandria, brought him to the verge of the grave. Indeed, one of the nurses said one day to one of her fellows, with a shake of her head, "Ah! poor fellow, he won't last long!"

"Won't he!" thought Miles, with a feeling of strong indignation. "Much *you* know about it!"

You see Miles possessed a tendency to abstract reasoning, and could meditate upon his own case without, so to speak, much reference to himself! His indignation was roused by the fact that any one, calling herself a nurse, should be so stupid as to whisper beside a patient words that he should not hear. He did not know that the nurse in question was a new one—not thoroughly alive to her duties and responsibilities. Strange to say, her stupidity helped to render her own prophecy incorrect, for the indignation quickened the soldier's feeble pulse, and that gave him a fillip in the right direction.

The prostration, however, was very great, and for some time the life of our hero seemed to hang by a thread. During this dark period the value of a godly mother's teaching became deeply impressed on him, by the fact that texts from God's Word, which had been taught him in childhood, and which he seemed to have quite forgotten, came trooping into his mind, and went a long way to calm and comfort him. He dwelt with special pleasure on those that told of love and mercy in Jesus to the thankless and undeserving; for, now that strength, health, and the high hopes of a brilliant career were shattered at one blow, his eyes were cleared of life's glamour to see that in his existence hitherto he had been ungodly—not in the sense of his being much worse than ordinary people, but in the sense of his being quite indifferent to his Maker, and that his fancied condition of not-so-badness would not stand the test of a dying hour.

About this time, too, he became desperately anxious to write to his mother, not by dictation, but with his own hand. This being impossible in the circumstances, he began to fret, and his power to sleep at length failed him. Then a strange desire to possess a rose seized him—perhaps because he knew it to be his mother's favourite flower. Whatever the cause, the longing increased his insomnia, and as he did not say, perhaps did not know, that the want of a rose had anything to do with his complaint, no one at first thought of procuring one for him.

He was lying meditating, wakefully, about many things one day when one of the nurses approached his bed. He did not see her at first, because his head was so swathed in bandages that only one eye was permitted to do duty, and that, as Molloy might have said, was on the lee-side of his nose— supposing the side next the nurse to represent the wind'ard side!

"I have been laid up a long time," said a lady, who accompanied the nurse, "and have been longing to resume my visits here, as one or two patients whom I used to nurse are still in hospital."

The heart of Miles gave a bound such as it had not attempted since the night he witnessed the murder on the battle-field, for the voice was that of Mrs Drew.

"This is one of our latest arrivals," remarked the nurse, lowering her voice as they advanced. "A poor young soldier—lost a hand and badly wounded—can't sleep. He has taken a strange longing of late for a rose, and I have asked a friend to fetch one for him."

"How lucky that we happen to have one with us!" said Mrs Drew, looking back over her shoulder where her daughter stood, concealed from view by her ample person. "Marion, dear, will you part with your rose-bud to a wounded soldier?"

"Certainly, mother, I will give it him myself."

She stepped quickly forward, and looked sadly at the solitary, glowing eye which gazed at her, as she unfastened a rose-bud from her bosom. It was evident that she did not recognise Miles, and no wonder, for, besides the mass of bandages from out of which his one eye glowed, there was a strip of plaster across the bridge of his nose, a puffy swelling in one of the cheeks, and the handsome mouth and chin were somewhat veiled by a rapidly developing moustache and beard.

Miles did not speak—he could not speak; he scarcely dared to breathe as the girl placed a red rose-bud in his thin hand. His trembling fingers not only took the rose, but the hand that gave it, and pressed it feebly to his lips.

With a few words of comfort and good wishes the ladies passed on. Then Miles drew the rose down under the bed-clothes, put it to his lips, and, with a fervently thankful mind, fell into the first profound slumber that he had enjoyed for many days.

This was a turning-point. From that day Miles began to mend. He did not see Marion again for some time, for her visit had been quite incidental, but he was satisfied to learn that she was staying at the Institute with her mother, assisting the workers there. He wisely resolved to do and say nothing at that time, but patiently to wait and get well, for he had a shrewd suspicion that to present himself to Marion under existing circumstances would be, to say the least, injudicious.

Meanwhile, time, which "waits for no man," passed on. As Miles became stronger he began to go about the hospital, chatting with the convalescent patients and trying to make himself generally useful. On one of these occasions he met with a man who gave him the sorrowful news that Sergeant Hardy was dead, leaving Miles his executor and residuary legatee. He also learned, to his joy, that his five comrades, Armstrong, Molloy, Stevenson, Moses, and Simkin, had escaped with their lives from the fight on the hillock where he fell, and that, though all were more or less severely wounded, they were doing well at Suakim. "Moreover," continued his informant, "I expect to hear more about 'em to-night, for the mail is due, and I've got a brother in Suakim."

That night not only brought news of the five heroes, but also brought themselves, for, having all been wounded at the same time, all had been sent to Alexandria together. As they were informed at Suakim that their comrade Miles had been invalided home, they did not, of course, make further inquiry about him there.

While they stayed there, awaiting the troop-ship which was to take them home, they made Miss Robinson's Institute their constant rendezvous, for there they not only found all the comforts of English life, but the joy of meeting with many old comrades, not a few of whom were either drawn, or being drawn, to God by the influences of the place.

It chanced that at the time of their arrival Mrs Drew and her daughter had gone to visit an English family living in the city, and did not for several days return to the Institute; thus the invalids failed to meet their lady friends at first. But about this time there was announced a source of attraction in the large hall which brought them together. This attraction—which unites all creeds and classes and nationalities in one great bond of sympathy—we need hardly say was music! A concert was to take place in the great hall of the Institute for some local charity, we believe, but are not sure, at which the *élite* of Alexandria was expected, and the musical talent of Alexandria was to perform—among others the band of the somethingth Regiment. And let us impress on you, reader, that the band of the somethingth Regiment was something to be proud of!

This brought numerous friends to the "Officers' House," and great numbers of soldiers and Jack-tars to the various rooms of the Institute.

In one of these rooms, towards evening, our friend Stevenson was engaged, at the request of the Superintendent, in relating to a number of earnest-minded men a brief account of the wonderful experiences that he and his comrades had recently had in the Soudan, and Jack Molloy sat near him, emphasising with a nod of his shaggy head, or a "Right you are, messmate," or a slap on his thigh, all the marine's points, especially those in which his friend, passing over second causes, referred all their blessings and deliverances direct to his loving God and Father. In another room a Bible-reading was going on, accompanied by prayer and praise. In the larger rooms, tea, coffee, etcetera, were being consumed to an extent that "no fellow can understand," except those who did it! Games and newspapers and illustrated magazines, etcetera, were rife elsewhere, while a continuous roar, rather the conventional "buzz," of conversation was going on everywhere. But, apparently, not a single oath in the midst of it all! The moral atmosphere of the place was so pure that even bad men respected—perhaps approved—it.

Just before the hour of the concert our friends, the five invalids, sat grouped round a table near the door. They were drinking tea, and most of them talking with tremendous animation—for not one of them had been wounded in the tongue! Indeed it did not appear that any of them had been very seriously wounded anywhere.

While they were yet in the midst of their talk two lady-workers came down the long room, followed by two other ladies in deep mourning, the younger of whom suddenly sprang towards our quintet, and, clasping her hands, stood speechless before them, staring particularly at Jack Molloy, who returned the gaze with interest.

"Beg pard'n, Miss Drew," exclaimed the sailor, starting up in confusion, and pulling his forelock, "but you've hove me all aback!"

"Mr Molloy!" gasped Marion, grasping his hand and looking furtively round, "is it possible? Have you *all* escaped? Is—is—"

"Yes, Miss, we've all escaped, thank God, an' we're all here—'cept John Miles, in coorse, for he's bin invalided home—"

"He's no more invalided home than yourself, Jack," said a seaman, who was enjoying his coffee at a neighbouring table; "leastwise I seed John Miles myself yesterday in hospital wi' my own two eyes, as isn't apt to deceive me."

"Are ye sure o' that, mate?" cried Molloy, turning in excitement to the man, and totally forgetting Marion.

"Mother, let us go out!" whispered the latter, leaning heavily on Mrs Drew's arm.

They passed out to the verandah—scarcely observed, owing to the excitement of the quintet at the sailor's news—and there she would have fallen down if she had not been caught in the arms of a soldier who was advancing towards the door.

"Mr Miles!" exclaimed Mrs Drew, as she looked up in amazement at the scarred and worn face.

"Ay, Mrs Drew, through God's mercy I am here. But help me: I have not strength to carry her *now*."

Marion had nearly fainted, and was led with the assistance of her mother to a retired part of the garden, and placed in an easy-chair. Seeing that the girl was recovering, the other ladies judiciously left them, and Miles explained to the mother, while she applied smelling-salts to Marion, that he had come on purpose to meet them, hoping and expecting that they would be attracted to the concert, like all the rest of the world, though he had scarcely looked for so peculiar a meeting!

"But how did you know we were here at all?" asked Mrs Drew in surprise.

"I saw you in the hospital," replied Miles, with a peculiar look. "Your kind daughter gave me a rose!"

He pointed as he spoke to a withered bud which was fastened to his coat.

"But—but—that young man had lost his hand; the nurse told us so," exclaimed Mrs Drew, with a puzzled look.

Miles silently pointed to the handless arm which hung at his left side.

Marion had turned towards him with a half-frightened look. She now leaned back in her chair and covered her face with both hands.

"Mr Miles," said the wise old lady, with a sudden and violent change of subject, "your friends Armstrong and Molloy are in the Institute at this moment waiting for you!"

Our hero needed no second hint. Next minute he dashed into the entrance hall, with wonderful vigour for an invalid, for he heard the bass voice of Molloy exclaiming—

"I don't care a button, leave or no leave, I'll make my way to John Mi— Hallo!"

The "Hallo!" was caused by his being rushed into by the impetuous Miles with such force that they both staggered.

"Why, John, you're like the ram of an iron-clad! Is it really yourself? Give us your flipper, my boy!"

But the flipper was already in that of Willie Armstrong, while the others crowded round him with congratulations.

"Wot on airth's all the noise about in that there corner?" exclaimed a Jack-tar, who was trying hard to tell an interminable story to a quiet shipmate in spite of the din.

"It's only that we've diskivered our captin," cried Molloy, eager to get any one to sympathise.

"Wot captin's that?" growled the Jack-tar.

"Why, him as led us on the hillock, to be sure, at Suakim."

When acts of heroism and personal prowess are of frequent occurrence, deeds of daring are not apt to draw general attention, unless they rise above the average. The "affair of the hillock," however, as it got to be called, although unnoticed in despatches, or the public prints, was well-known among the rank and file who did the work in those hot regions. When, therefore, it became known that the six heroes, who had distinguished themselves on that hillock, were present, a great deal of interest was exhibited. This culminated when a little man rushed suddenly into the room, and, with a wild "hooroo!" seized Molloy round the waist—he wasn't tall enough to get him comfortably by the neck—and appeared to wrestle with him.

"It's Corporal Flynn—or his ghost!" exclaimed Molloy.

"Sure an' it's both him an' his ghost togither!" exclaimed the corporal, shaking hands violently all round.

"I thought ye was sent home," said Moses.

"Niver a bit, man; they tell awful lies where you've come from. I wouldn't take their consciences as a gift. I'm as well as iver, and better; but I'm goin' home for all that, to see me owld grandmother. Ye needn't laugh, you spalpeens. Come, three cheers, boys, for the 'heroes o' the hillock!'"

Most heartily did the men there assembled respond to this call, and then the entire assembly cleared off to the concert, with the exception of Miles Milton. "He," as Corporal Flynn knowingly observed, "had other fish to fry." He fried these fish in company with Mrs and Marion Drew; but as the details of this culinary proceeding were related to us in strict confidence, we refuse to divulge them, and now draw the curtain down on the ancient land of Egypt.

Chapter Thirty-Conclusion

Once more we return to the embarkation jetty at Portsmouth.

There, as of old, we find a huge, white-painted troop-ship warping slowly in, her bulwarks and ports crowded with white helmets, and eager faces gazing at the equally eager but anxious faces on shore.

Miss Robinson's coffee-shed shows signs of life! Our friend Brown is stimulating the boiler. The great solitary port-hole has been opened, and the never-failing lady-workers are there, preparing their ammunition and getting ready for action, for every troop-ship that comes to Portsmouth from foreign shores, laden with the bronzed warriors of Britain, has to face the certainty of going into action with that unconquerable little coffee-shed!

We do not, however, mean to draw the reader again through the old scene, further than to point out that, among the many faces that loom over these bulwarks, five are familiar, namely, those of our friends Miles Milton, William Armstrong, Moses Pyne, Stevenson, and Simkin. Jack Molloy is not with them, because he has preferred to remain in Egypt, believing himself to be capable of still further service to Queen and country.

A feeling of great disappointment oppresses Miles and his friend Armstrong, for they fail to recognise in the eager crowd those whom they had expected to see.

"My mother must be ill," muttered Miles.

"So must my Emmy," murmured his friend.

There was a very anxious little widow on the jetty who could *not* manage to distinguish individuals in the sea of brown faces and white helmets, because the tears in her eyes mixed them all up most perplexingly. It is not surprising that Miles had totally failed to recognise the mother of old in the unfamiliar widow's weeds—especially when it is considered that his was a shrinking, timid mother, who kept well in the background of the demonstrative crowd. Their eyes met at last, however, and those of the widow opened wide with surprise at the change in the son, while those of the son were suddenly blinded with tears at the change in the mother.

Then they met — and such a meeting! — in the midst of men and women, elbowing, crowding, embracing, exclaiming, rejoicing, chaffing, weeping! It was an awkward state of things, but as every one else was in the same predicament, and as all were more or less swallowed up in their own affairs, Miles and his mother were fain to make the best of it. They retired under the partial shelter of a bulkhead, where block-tackles and nautical débris interfered with their footing, and tarry odours regaled their noses, and there, in semi-publicity, they interchanged their first confidences.

Suddenly Mrs Milton observed a tall young fellow standing not far off, looking wistfully at the bewildering scene, apparently in deep dejection.

"Who is that, Miles?" she asked.

"Why, that's my comrade, chum, and friend, whom I have so often written about, Willie Armstrong. Come. I will introduce you."

"Oh! how selfish of me!" cried the widow, starting forward and not waiting for the introduction; "Mr Armstrong — I'm *so* sorry; forgive me! I promised to let you know that your wife waits to meet you at the Soldiers' Institute."

The difference between darkness and light seemed to pass over the soldier's face, then a slight shade of anxiety clouded it. "She is not ill, is she?"

"No, no, *quite* well," said Mrs Milton, with a peculiar smile; "but she thought it wiser not to risk a meeting on the jetty as the east wind is sharp. I'm so sorry I did not tell you at once, but I selfishly thought only — "

"Pray make no apology, madam," interrupted Armstrong. "I'm so thankful that all is well. I had begun to fear that something must be wrong, for my Emmy *never* disappoints me. If she thinks it wiser not to meet on the jetty, it *is* wiser!"

A crowd of men pushed between them at this moment. Immediately after, a female shout was heard, followed by the words, "There he is! Och, it's himsilf — the darlint!"

Mrs Flynn had discovered the little corporal, and her trooper son, Terence, who had come down with her, stood by to see fair-play while the two embraced.

Drifting with a rather rapid tide of mingled human beings, Miles and his mother soon found themselves stranded beside the coffee-shed. Retiring behind this they continued their conference there, disturbed only by wind and weather, while the distribution of hot coffee was going on in front.

Meanwhile, when leave was obtained, Armstrong made his way to the Institute, where the old scene of bustle and hilarity on the arrival of a troop-ship was going on. Here, in a private room, he discovered Emmy and the *cause* of her not appearing on the jetty.

"Look at him—Willie the second!" cried the little woman, holding up a bundle of some sort. The soldier was staggered for a moment—the only infantry that had ever staggered him!—for his wife had said nothing about this bundle in her letters. He recovered, however, and striding across the room embraced the wife and the bundle in one tremendous hug!

The wife did not object, but the bundle did, and instantly set up a howl that quite alarmed the father, and was sweetest music in the mother's ears!

"Now tell me," said the little woman, after calming the baby and putting it in a crib; "have you brought Miles Milton home all safe?"

"Yes, all right, Emmy."

"And is he married to that dear girl you wrote about?"

"No, not yet—of course."

"But are they engaged?"

"No. Miles told me that he would not presume to ask her while he had no home to offer her."

"Pooh! He's a goose! He ought to make sure of *her,* and let the home look after itself. He may lose her. Girls, you know, are changeable, giddy things!"

"I know nothing of the sort, Emmy."

The young wife laughed, and—well, there is no need to say what else she did.

About the same time, Mrs Milton and her son were seated in another private room of the Institute finishing off that interchange of confidences which had begun in such confusion. As it happened, they were conversing on the same subject that occupied Emmy and her husband.

"You have acted rightly, Miles," said the mother, "for it would have been unfair and selfish to have induced the poor girl to accept you until you had some prospect of a home to give her. God will bless you for doing *the right*, and trusting to Him. And now, dear boy, are you prepared for bad news?"

"Prepared for anything!" answered Miles, pressing his mother's hand, "but I hope the bad news does not affect you, mother."

"It does. Your dear father died a bankrupt. I shrank from telling you this when you were wounded and ill. So you have to begin again the battle of life with only one hand, my poor boy, for the annuity I have of twenty pounds a year will not go far to keep us both."

Mrs Milton tried to speak lightly on this point, by way of breaking it to her son, but she nearly broke down, for she had already begun to feel the pinch of extreme poverty, and knew it to be very, very different from what "well-off" people fancy. The grave manner in which her son received this news filled her with anxiety.

"Mother," he said, after pondering in silence for a few moments, and taking her hand in his while he slipped the handless arm round her waist, "the news is indeed serious, but our Father whom you have trusted so long will not fail us now. Happily it is my right hand that has been spared, and wonders, you know, may be wrought with a strong right hand, especially if assisted by a strong left stump, into which spoons, forks, hooks, and all manner of ingenious contrivances can be fitted. Now, cheer up, little mother, and I'll tell you what we will do. But first, is there *nothing* left? Do the creditors take everything?"

"All, I believe, except some of the furniture which has been kindly left for us to start afresh with. But we must quit the old home next month. At least, so I am told by my kind little lawyer, who looks after everything, for *I* understand nothing."

"Your mention of a lawyer reminds me, mother, that a poor sergeant, who died a short time ago in Egypt, made me his executor, and as I am painfully ignorant of the duties of an executor I'll go and see this 'kind little lawyer' if you will give me his address."

Leaving Miles to consult his lawyer, we will now turn to a meeting — a grand tea-fight — in the great hall of the Institute, that took place a few days after the return of the troop-ship which brought our hero and his friends to England. Some telling incidents occurred at this fight which render it worthy of notice.

First, Miss Robinson herself presided and gave a stirring address, which, if not of much interest to readers who did not hear it, was a point of immense attraction to the hundreds of soldiers, sailors, and civilians to whom it was delivered, for it was full of sympathy, and information, and humour, and encouragement, and, above all, of the Gospel.

Everybody worth mentioning was there — that is, everybody connected with our tale who was in England at the time. Miles and his mother of course were there, and Armstrong with Emmy — ay, and with Willie the second too — who was pronounced on all hands to be the born image of his father. Alas for his father, if that had been true! A round piece of dough with three holes punched in it and a little knot in the midst would have borne as strong a resemblance to Miles as that baby did. Nevertheless, it was a "magnificent" baby! and "*so* good," undeniably good, for it slept soundly in its little mother's lap the whole evening!

Stevenson was also there, you may be sure; and so were Moses and Sutherland, and Rattling Bill Simkin and Corporal Flynn, with his mother and Terence the Irish trooper, who fraternised with Johnson the English trooper, who was also home on the sick-list — though he seemed to have a marvellous colour and appetite for a sick man.

"Is that the 'Soldiers Friend?'" asked Simkin, in a whisper, of a man who stood near him, as a lady came on the platform and took the chair.

"Ay, that's her," answered the man — and the speaker was Thomas Tufnell, the ex-trooper of the Queen's Bays, and the present manager of the Institute — "Ay, that's the 'Soldier's Friend.'"

"Well, I might have guessed it," returned Simkin, "from the kindly way in which she shook hands with a lot of soldiers just now."

"Yes, she has shook hands with a good many red-coats in her day, has the 'Soldier's Friend,'" returned the manager. "Why, I remember on one occasion when she was giving a lecture to soldiers, and so many men came forward to shake hands with her that, as she told me herself, her hand was stiff and swelled all night after it!"

"But it's not so much for what she has done for ourselves that we're grateful to her," remarked a corporal, who sat on Simkin's right, "as for what she has done for our wives, widows, and children, through the *Soldiers' and Sailors' Wives' Aid Association*. Lookin' arter them when we're away fightin' our country's battles has endeared her to us more than anything else."

Thus favourably predisposed, Simkin was open to good impressions that night. But, indeed, there was an atmosphere—a spirit of good-will—in the hall that night which rendered many others besides Simkin open to good impressions. Among the civilians there was a man named Sloper, who had for some time past been carefully fished for by an enthusiastic young red-coat whom he had basely misled and swindled. He had been at last hooked by the young red-coat, played, and finally landed in the hall, with his captor beside him to keep him there—for Sloper was a slippery fish, with much of the eel in his nature.

Perhaps the most unexpected visitors to the hall were two ladies in mourning, who had just arrived from Egypt by way of Brindisi. Mrs and Miss Drew, having occasion to pass through Portsmouth on their way home, learned that there was to be a tea-fight at the Institute, and Marion immediately said, "I should like *so* much to see it!"

However much "*so* much" was, Mrs Drew said she would like to see it *as* much, so away they went, and were conducted to the front row. There Miles saw them! With his heart in his mouth, and his head in confusion, he quietly rose, bade his wondering mother get up; conducted her to the front seat, and, setting her down beside the Drews, introduced them. Then, sitting down beside Marion, he went in for a pleasant evening.

And it *was* a pleasant evening! Besides preliminary tea and buns, there were speeches, songs, recitations, etcetera,—all being received with immense satisfaction by a crowded house, which had not yet risen to the unenviable heights of classical taste and *blaséism*. As for Miles and Marion, nothing came amiss to them! If a singer had put B flat in the place of A natural they would have accepted it as quite natural. If a humourist had said the circle was a square, they would have believed it—in a sense—and tried to square their reason accordingly.

But nothing is without alloy in this life. To the surprise of Miles and his mother, their "kind little lawyer" also made his appearance in the hall. More than that, he insisted, by signs, that Miles should go out and speak with him. But Miles was obdurate. He was anchored, and nothing but cutting the cable could move him from his anchorage.

At last the "kind little man" pushed his way through the crowd.

"I *must* have a word with you, my dear sir. It is of importance," he said.

Thus adjured, Miles unwillingly cut the cable, and drifted into a passage.

"My dear sir," said the little man, seizing his hand, "I congratulate you."

"You're very kind, but pray, explain why."

"I find that you are heir to a considerable fortune."

Miles was somewhat interested in this, and asked, "How's that?"

"Well, you remember Hardy's will, which you put into my hands a few days ago?"

"Yes; what then? *That* can't be the fortune!"

"Indeed it is. Hardy, you remember, made you his residuary legatee. I find, on inquiry, that the old cousin you told me about, who meant to leave all his money to build a hospital, changed his mind at the last and made out a will in favour of Hardy, who was his only relative. So, you see, you, being Hardy's heir, have come into possession of something like two thousand a year."

To this Miles replied by a whistle of surprise, and then said, "Is that all?"

"Upon my word, sir," said the 'kind little lawyer,' in a blaze of astonishment, "you appear to take this communication in a peculiar manner!"

"You mistake me," returned Miles, with a laugh. "I don't mean 'is that all the fortune?' but 'is that all you have to say?'"

"It is, and to my mind I have said a good deal."

"You certainly have. And, believe me, I am not indifferent or unthankful, but—but—the fact is, that at present I am *particularly* engaged. Good-bye, and thank you."

So saying, Miles shook the puzzled old gentleman heartily by the hand, and hurried back to his anchorage in the hall.

"I've done it, mother!" whispered Miles, two days thereafter, in the privacy of the Institute reading-room.

"Miles!" said the startled lady, with a reproachful look, "I thought you said that nothing would induce you—"

"Circumstances have altered, mother. I have had a long consultation with your 'kind little lawyer,' and he has related some interesting facts to me."

Here followed a detailed account of the facts.

"So, you see, I went and proposed at once—not to the lawyer—to Marion."

"And was accepted?"

"Well—yes. I could hardly believe it at the time. I scarcely believe it now, so I'm going back this afternoon to make quite sure."

"I congratulate you, my darling boy, for a good wife is God's best gift to man."

"How do you know she is good, mother?"

"I know it, because—I know it! Anybody looking in her face can *see* it. And with two thousand a year, why—"

"One thousand, mother."

"I thought you said two, my son."

"So I did. That is the amount of the fortune left by the eccentric old hospital-for-incurables founder. When poor Hardy made out his will he made me residuary legatee because the trifle he had to leave—his kit, etcetera,—was not worth dividing between me and Armstrong. If it had been worth much he would have divided it. It is therefore my duty now to divide it with my friend."

But in our anxiety to tell you these interesting facts, dear reader, we have run ahead of the tea-fight! To detail all its incidents, all its bearings, all its grand issues and blessed influences, would require a whole volume. We return to it only to mention one or two gratifying facts.

It was essentially a temperance—that is, a total-abstinence, a blue-ribbon—meeting, and, at the end, the "Soldiers' Friend" earnestly invited all who felt so disposed to come forward and sign the pledge. At the same time, medals and prizes were presented to those among the civilians who had loyally kept their pledge intact for certain periods of time. On an average, over a thousand pledges a year are taken at the Institute, and we cannot help thinking that the year we are writing of must have exceeded the average—to judge from the numbers that pressed forward on this particular night.

There were soldiers, sailors, and civilians; men, women, and children. Amongst the first, Rattling Bill Simkin walked to the front—his moral courage restored to an equality with his physical heroism—and put down his name. So did Johnson and Sutherland—the former as timid before the audience as he had been plucky before the Soudanese, but walking erect, nevertheless, as men do when conscious that they are in the right; the latter "as bold as brass"—as if to defy the world in arms to make him ever again drink another drop of anything stronger than tea.

Moses Pyne also "put on the blue," although, to do him justice, he required no protection of that sort, and so did Corporal Flynn and Terence and their mother—which last, if truth must be told, stood more in need of the pledge than her stout sons.

Among the civilians several noted personages were influenced in the right direction. Chief among these was sodden, blear-eyed, disreputable Sloper, whose trembling hand scrawled a hieroglyphic, supposed to represent his name, which began indeed with an S, but ended in a mysterious prolongation, and was further rendered indecipherable by a penitent tear which fell upon it from the point of his red, red nose!

Some people laughed, and said that there was no use in getting Sloper to put on the blue-ribbon, that he was an utterly demoralised man, that he had no strength of character, that no power on earth could save *him*! They were right. No power on earth could save him—or them! These people forgot that it is not the righteous but sinners who are called to repentance.

Time passed away and wrought its wonted changes. Among other things, it brought back to Portsmouth big, burly Jack Molloy, as hearty and vigorous as he was when being half-hanged in the Soudan, but—*minus* a leg! Poor Jack! a spent cannon-ball—would that it had been spent in vain!—removed it, below the knee, much more promptly than it could have been taken off by the surgeon's knife. But what was loss to the Royal Navy was gain to Portsmouth, for Jack Molloy came home and devoted himself, heart and soul, to the lending of "a helping hand" to his fellow-creatures in distress—devoting his attentions chiefly to the region lying round Nobbs Lane, and causing himself to be adored principally by old women and children. And there and thus he probably works to this day—at least, some very like him do.

When not thus engaged he is prone to take a cruise to a certain rural district in the south of England, where he finds congenial company in two very tall, erect, moustached, dignified gentlemen, who have a tendency to keep step as they walk, one of whom has lost his left hand, and who dwell in two farm-houses close together.

These two gentlemen have remarkably pretty wives, and wonderfully boisterous children, and the uproar which these children make when Molloy comes to cast anchor among them, is stupendous! As for the appearance of the brood, and of Jack after a spree among the hay, the word has yet to be invented which will correctly describe it.

The two military-looking farmers are spoken of by the people around as philanthropists. Like true philanthropists, whose foundation-motive is love to God, they do not limit their attentions to their own little neighbourhood, but allow their sympathies and their benefactions to run riot round the world—wheresoever there is anything that is true, honourable, just, pure, lovely, or of good report to be thought of, or done, or assisted.

Only one of these acts of sympathy and benefaction we will mention. Every Christmas there is received by Miss Robinson at the Soldiers' Institute, Portsmouth, a huge hamper full of old and new garments of all kinds—shoes, boots, gowns, frocks, trousers, shawls, comforters, etcetera,—with the words written inside the lid—"Blessed are they that consider the poor." And on the same day come two cheques in a letter. We refuse, for the best of all reasons, to divulge the amount of those cheques, but we consider it no breach of confidence to reveal the fact that the letter containing them is signed by two old and grateful Blue Lights.